TRAIL OF EVIDENCE

A Novel by

Albert J. Harnois

Trail of Evidence
By Albert J. Harnois

Copyright - 2010 Albert J. Harnois

This novel is dedicated to my granddaughter

Erin,

a talented writer and promising author.

Chapter 1

Wednesday, August 13, 2008

He opened his eyes but couldn't see a thing in the darkness. He didn't know where he was, but wasn't too concerned; he was often disoriented when he first awoke. It was an unwelcomed side effect of spending too much time in hotel rooms. He listened carefully for any telltale sounds, but didn't hear any. Yet somehow, he knew he wasn't alone. He could feel a presence nearby.

He slowly moved his left hand away from his body, his fingers silently walking along the crisp sheets until they came to rest upon the warm skin of a body next to his. As his mind raced to try to assemble the pieces of the puzzle, something off to the right caught his attention, and from the corner of his eye he glimpsed the faint reflection of a red light coming from somewhere in the room. He turned his head slowly until he saw three red numbers starring back at him like demon eyes, and quickly recognized the demon as his own alarm clock, which was now telling him it was 4:50 a.m. He remembered he'd set it for 5:00, so he quickly reached over and flipped the alarm button to the off position before the sound of the screaming demon could pierce the tranquility of the night.

Although he'd only gotten a few hours sleep, he was now fully awake and ready to go. He eased himself out of bed and quietly made his way to the bathroom, glancing over his shoulder as he walked. He was glad she was still asleep because he didn't have the energy for another go-round this morning. They were having more and more of those lately, and always over the same issue – the number of hours he devoted to the company. She never seemed to understand the demands of his job, and in the current environment things were only going to get worse.

Ten minutes later he'd finished showering and was getting dressed inside the large walk-in closet, with the door closed behind him so as to not awaken her. He hadn't bothered to shave because he could do that in the car, where he always kept a battery powered shaver for times like this. By 5:20 a.m. Jake Hammond was behind the wheel of his roadster and heading for the highway. As far as he could tell, no one in the house had heard a thing.

The drive was uneventful and a half hour later he pulled into his reserved spot in the parking garage, locked his car, and then headed for the elevator. When he got to his office on the tenth floor, the report, which was the reason for an earlier than normal start today, was there on the corner of his desk, just as he'd known it would be. It didn't take him long to scan the statistics and realize it contained pretty much what he'd expected. He'd only been with the company for two years, but during that time he'd grown more and more concerned over its direction, and now his gut told him things were about the fall apart. He wondered if the other members of the Committee had similar misgivings, and wanted to give Fred a call to get his read on this, because Fred had been around long before Deb Cutter staged her coup and got rid of Hank Talbot. But it was still only 6:15. He was sure Fred was already at his desk, but decided to give him a few more minutes to settle in before calling.

On the twenty fifth-floor Fred Campbell was sitting behind his own desk reading the same report Jake had just reviewed. He'd been watching things closely for the past few weeks and made a mental note to speak with Jake as soon as possible so they could decide what additional steps, if any, Jake and his staff should take to monitor the situation.

When Fred's phone rang, he checked the caller ID and saw Jake's name and number come up. He quickly picked up the handset before the system could send the call to his voice mail.

"How are you, Jake? Can you believe it, I was just thinking of calling *you*?"

"I guess you've seen the latest report, then."

"Yeah, that's one of the things I want to discuss, but I have a few others as well. I think now would be a good time for us to stand back and take a look at what's going on in the company. What does your calendar look like for the rest of the week?"

"How much time do you think we'll need?"

"I'd say about an hour, maybe two. I can make it tomorrow morning at ten o'clock, if that works for you. I'll set aside two hours, from ten to twelve."

"That'll work. I'll rearrange a few things. Do you want to meet here or in your office?"

"I'll come down there so you can access any documents you might need for our discussion. I appreciate your willingness to see me on such short notice."

"Not a problem. See you tomorrow, Fred."

"Oh, and Jake, one more thing just came to mind. As you know, we're financing some dealerships in Florida, where Tropical Storm Fay is expected to cause some serious water damage. It might be a good idea if we discussed the inventory insurance program we've implemented to see if we're adequately covered.

"That sounds good to me."

"Thanks, Jake."

After they'd both hung up, Jake tried Joe Nash's number and wasn't surprised when Joe answered on the second ring. He was Jake's senior person and they'd worked together for many years, long before they ended up at New Commerce together, and Jake knew Joe was as much a workaholic as he was. A few minutes later Joe knocked on the door, walked in, and took a seat opposite the huge mahogany desk.

"What's up?" asked Joe.

"I'm meeting with Fred Campbell in the morning to discuss the new product lines. I'd like you put together a package of procedures and sample work papers from our last review in Marietta, and also give me an updated list showing every review we've completed in the past two years, with dates and locations. Can you have all of that ready by end of business today so I can bring it home with me and review it this evening?"

"No problem. I'll put it together myself and have it to you within the hour."

"Thanks, Joe. I appreciate it."

Jake had a feeling the new product lines were going to start requiring a lot more attention very soon.

***

At 7:13 a.m. he pulled the black Town Car into the driveway a little faster than he should've, and he winced at the sound of squealing tires. He hoped she hadn't heard the noise, because if she had, there'd be hell to pay. As soon as he'd brought the car to a full stop he jumped out and headed for the house. At 7:15 sharp he was ringing the doorbell, right on time, thank God. If there was one thing he'd learned in the four years he'd been driving for Deb Cutter, it was that she had no tolerance for people who didn't follow her instructions to the letter. And she'd made it very clear when he dropped her off yesterday that she wanted to be picked up at *exactly* 7:15 this morning.

Five seconds after he rang the bell, the door opened and a woman with a stunning figure dressed in a sharp business suit appeared. She handed him her briefcase as she brushed by him without the slightest acknowledgement and walked straight to the car. He had to rush to beat her there, and he got the door open just in time. She slid effortlessly into the back seat and held out her hand, an annoyed look on her face. He hurried to hand her the briefcase, then closed the door and got behind the wheel. Within minutes they were on Maine Highway 17 headed toward downtown Augusta and the headquarters building of the New Commerce Commercial Finance Company.

They always rode in silence while she read the Wall Street Journal, made phone calls, or otherwise kept occupied. There was never any conversation between the front seat and back, because Deb Cutter was not one to make small talk with the help. This morning she sat quietly starring out the window, enjoying the ride and thinking about what she'd accomplished over the past few years. It'd taken her a long time to get here, and she'd stepped on a lot of toes along the way, but it'd been worth it. The plans she'd implemented four years ago had paid off. They'd just had another record year, the second in a row. She'd known in her heart she was right, in spite of all the resistance she'd gotten from the other members of the Executive Committee. What the hell did they know anyway? Most of them had been hand-picked by her predecessor, and their typical response to her ideas was usually something along the lines of "That's not what Hank would do."

She owed a lot to Hank Talbot. He'd been her coach and mentor from the beginning and she probably wouldn't have gotten here without him, but frankly, she no longer gave a damn what he would do, or even what he thought. He'd been in charge way too long and just didn't understand that the world was changing and New Commerce had to change with it if it was going to survive, and so she'd finally decided he had to go. It'd been tough convincing the Board, but in the end, Hank had reluctantly agreed to *retire*. Once she'd taken over as CEO she expanded into new markets and began offering new product lines. She knew it was risky, but she was counting on higher volumes to at least partially offset those risks. That's why one of her first directives had been to change the incentive program for managers so that their bonuses were now tied to originations; the more loans they made, the bigger their bonuses.

She was still deep in thought as they pulled up in front of the New Commerce building at 7:40 a.m. As soon as the driver opened her door she sprang out, briefcase in hand, and headed for the main entrance. When the security guard spotted her he rushed to open the door. "Good morning, Miss Cutter" he said, as he did every morning. And as *she* did every morning, she ignored him and headed straight for the elevator. He was used to this, of course, but it seemed to him that this morning she was walking even faster than usual. She must have a busy day ahead of her, he thought, as he smiled and returned to his seat behind the desk.

The building had twenty five floors, and Deb's office, along with most other executive offices, was on the top floor. When the elevator finally came to a stop, she stepped out briskly and walked straight toward the large glass double doors. The door to the left had the company logo etched on it, and the one to the right, "New Commerce Commercial Finance." The receptionist wasn't in yet, so she swiped her security card in the card reader and waited for the click. As soon as she heard it, she pushed the heavy door open and went in. She passed the deserted receptionist's desk, took a sharp left, and headed down a long corridor toward her assistant's desk, which was just outside of her own office. Her assistant wasn't in yet, and she cursed herself for having forgotten to tell her to get here early today. She would've liked a cup of coffee, but wasn't about to get it herself, so she'd have to wait until her assistant decided to show up.

As soon as she settled in behind her huge desk, she picked up the report that was sitting on the corner and began reviewing the current results. She starred in disbelief as the figures for the inventory financing business jumped out at her. There was yet *another* increase in items that had been sold by the dealers but for which New Commerce had not yet received payment, items referred to in the industry as SAUs, (Sold And Unpaid). She could just imagine what those short-sighted clowns on the Executive Committee would be thinking when they read the report. They'd probably try to get her to drop the new product lines and go back to the core business lines they were familiar with. Yeah, like that was going to happen.

The new product lines had been providing great returns, and she felt sure that would continue, as long as they could keep increasing originations. She was determined to keep the momentum going and had already increased the number of underwriters at the divisions and support staff at the headquarters location, and she'd even approved a few new positions for the Security and Compliance Department, something Jake Hammond had been badgering her and the Board for since he'd joined the company a couple of years ago. Jake, the Chief Security and Compliance Officer, was *not* one of Deb's strongest supporters because he felt the new direction she was taking the company in was a bit too risky. He preferred to take a more conservative approach, and he made his opinion known to his fellow Executive Committee members at every possible opportunity. He was a real thorn in her side, but his relationship with the Board and the other members of the Committee made him difficult to ignore.

The remaining Executive Committee members were split in their views. Most of the division managers were in favor of Deb's approach, pretty much because their bonuses were tied to the number of new loans booked, and they were able to increase their incomes substantially with the new product offerings. Tom D'Angelo, the CFO, also supported her. But although Fred Campbell had originally given his tentative support to her plans, he was starting to have second thoughts.

Deb knew that delinquencies, as a percentage of total assets, would have to drop if she was going to have any hope of getting Fred and Jake off her back. The best way to do that, at least in the short term, was to increase originations and make even more new loans, especially in the new product lines, and she knew just how to do that. She picked up the phone and began dialing the number of the Atlanta area office of New Commerce, located in Marietta, GA.

Chapter 2

At Walters Marine in Tallahassee, things were slower than normal, even for a Wednesday morning in mid August. There were only three customers browsing the inventory of personal water craft and small boats on the showroom floor, and no one was in the yard outside where the larger boats were kept. They obviously didn't need him in the showroom, so Dan decided to stay in his office to catch up on some paperwork. They'd sold a nineteen foot Sea Ray yesterday and he needed to get the payment out to his finance company, New Commerce. And he wanted to keep a close eye on the weather forecast because Tropical Storm Fay was heading this way.

He signed the check, stuffed it into an envelope and dropped it into the "out" basket on the corner of his desk. Then he eased himself out of his chair and walked around the large metal desk he salvaged from a local thrift shop years ago. He headed for the far corner of the office where he kept a small color TV, which, like everything else in the room, was second hand. He didn't believe in spending a lot of money on his office, because it was out of the sight of customers and he preferred, instead, to put the money into the areas customers *did* see, the main showroom and the three smaller offices where they were brought to complete the paperwork once they decided on a particular boat or personal water craft, "PWCs" as they were referred to.

He reached the TV, turned it on, and sat in the old leather chair just to the right of the matching sofa, both of which were worn and obviously in need of a lot of work. He knew they looked pitiful, but somehow felt they had character, in spite of, or maybe because of, the cracked leather, badly scratched wood trim, and the sagging cushions. That's why he had declined Joyce's offer to make throw covers for them. Throw covers wouldn't do anything for the sagging cushions, but would hide the real "character" of the furniture.

When the old TV warmed up a bit the picture came into focus. It was already tuned to the local weather station, the only one Dan ever watched, and the meteorologist was giving an update on Fay, the sixth named storm of the 2008 hurricane season. It was still just a tropical storm but was becoming more and more unpredictable and could cause a lot of damage, especially from flooding. It had passed over Cuba, crossed over the Keys, headed east and then west again. By the time Fay left the east coast, Port St. Lucie was under water and Melbourne had gotten twenty five inches of rain. And now she was heading up the west coast toward Tallahassee.

Fay's bizarre behavior and heavy rains were starting to concern Dan so he decided to wrap things up. He shut off the TV and headed toward the showroom floor, but before he reached the office door his phone rang. He answered with his customary greeting, "Walters Marine, how can I help you?"

"Hi sweetheart, it's me," the voice at the other end said. "Have you been watching the forecast? I'm getting a little worried. When are you planning to come home?"

"As a matter of fact honey, I was just on my way out to the showroom to tell the crew to wrap it up. Once we get the customers out of here we can start putting up the storm shutters. It shouldn't take more than a couple of hours, but I don't want you to wait for me. Things could get pretty nasty out there, so you should head out to your mom's house as soon as you can. When I finish up here, I'll swing by the house to check on everything and then follow you there. With any luck I'll probably be just a few hours behind you."

They had talked about the evacuation plans yesterday, and Joyce had everything ready to go. They had plotted her route together, making sure she'd avoid the back roads that might be flooded. She and the kids were ready.

"By the way, has the crew I hired to shutter the house shown up yet?" asked Dan.

"Yes, they've been here for an hour and are working fast. They're just about finished. That new storm system you had installed is really great. It would've taken a lot longer the way we used to do it, with plywood. I'm glad you had the house done at the same time as the dealership."

"Yeah, me too. Now, I want you to head out as soon as the crew leaves. With any luck you'll be at your mom's house in time for dinner. With normal traffic it should be just under five hours."

"OK, but be sure to come as soon as you can."

"Don't worry, I will. I've got to go now. Love you."

"Love you too."

After hanging up, Dan went out to the showroom, looked around to see where everyone was, and spotted Randy standing by himself behind the counter. He went over to him and said "I think it's time to wrap things up. Let's lock up and get the rest of the staff together to start boarding up. The weather's getting pretty bad and I want you all out of here as soon as possible. They're saying we'll be getting three inches of rain an hour."

"Sure thing *boss*," replied Randy, grinning from ear to ear. He loved calling Dan *boss* which, of course, he was. But it wasn't as much *what* he said as *how* he said it. Not in a disrespectful way, but in kind of a joking way, as he always did, and always with a huge grin on his face. He was the only one in the dealership who could have gotten away with it.

As Randy headed toward the customers, Dan headed to the back storeroom where he kept the aluminum storm shutters. When the last customer was gone and the main doors locked, Randy and the others joined Dan in the storeroom to begin the task of moving the shutters outside in preparation for the boarding up process. None of them was enthusiastic about having to do it, but they knew the cost of hiring a crew would impact their bonuses, so within minutes, each of them was on his way out to the showroom with an aluminum shutter that was clearly labeled with black marker indicating which window or door it was made for. Before long, the entire building would be closed up tight, and better protected from the elements.

Unfortunately, though, there wasn't enough space inside the showroom for all the boats, so the bigger ones would have to stay outside. That bothered Dan a bit, but there wasn't anything he could do about it. At least the water damage would be minimized now that each boat had a custom cover on it. And the eight foot chain link fence around the yard was pretty effective in keeping out looters. Knowing his inventory was adequately insured now that he had switched to a new finance company helped him feel a little better too. Not only did New Commerce *require* insurance, they actually *arranged* for it, which made things easier for him. They paid the premiums and just passed along the cost to him, which saved him a lot of paperwork. So, any inventory losses should be covered.

A few hours later the rain was really coming down hard and the wind was picking up. Dan and Randy were alone because they'd sent everyone else home about an hour earlier. Dan had tried to convince Randy to leave too, but he'd insisted on staying, which didn't surprise Dan at all, considering they'd been best friends their whole lives and always did everything together. They were getting ready to lock the front door when they spotted the flashing lights. They watched John Forsyth get out of his squad car at curbside and start running toward the building. Dan opened the door just in time for the deputy to make it through without having to break his stride.

"Hey guys. Need any help?"

"Thanks, John, but we're just wrapping up. Everyone else is gone and Randy and I were getting ready to head out as well. What brings you out to this part of the city? Isn't your normal beat on the other side of town?"

"Yeah, but I wanted to personally check on your situation. I'd hate to have anything happen to my *mentor*, you know" he said, smiling.

Dan had been one of the first people to welcome John and his family into town a few years ago when they moved here from New England, and even helped him land the job in the Sheriff's Department. Actually it hadn't been all that difficult, in light of John's significant experience in law enforcement, but Dan's introductions to the right people hadn't hurt. Dan was an established businessman and well respected in the community, and his recommendation meant a lot.

"You know," said John, "the mayor has recommended that everyone evacuate the area as soon as possible. The rain is getting heavier and we're expecting significant flooding in this area. You need to get out now unless you plan to take your chances and wait it out here."

"Thanks. We're heading out now. Joyce and the kids have already gone ahead to her mother's in Decatur, and I'll be joining them there as soon as I close up here and check the house."

"None too soon either. It looks like it's going to be a bad one."

As they all left the dealership together Dan took a last look around to make sure everything was properly secured, and then closed and locked the front door. The wind was really picking up now, and the rain was so heavy that he had difficulty seeing the pickup truck that he knew was parked at curbside, directly in front of the dealership. As he dashed toward the spot where he had left it, he looked back just in time to see the lights in one of the "Walters Marine" neon signs go out, an early victim of tropical storm

Fay. It was probably a short circuit caused by the heavy rain.

He stared at the sign, and for a brief moment considered going back, but a firm look from John convinced him to pass on that idea. There wasn't much he could do about the sign now anyway. If it were the only thing he'd have to repair when all of this was over he'd be lucky. The weather bureau predictions had not given much reason for hope.

It was only about twenty yards to the truck and he had his heavy duty rain coat on, but he was soaked by the time he slid into the front seat. The wind was blowing the rain sideways, making a raincoat all but useless. Randy took off first, heading north toward his neighborhood. Dan started the truck, but waited for John to pull out before sliding the gear shift into drive. The deputy headed south toward the coastal areas with the lights of his cruiser flashing. He needed to make one last check of the shoreline to be certain everyone had gotten out. Dan pulled out behind him but headed in the opposite direction. Fifteen minutes later he pulled into the driveway of the sprawling white ranch house in an upscale neighborhood.

He killed the engine, raised the hood on his slicker and jumped out of the truck, slamming the door behind him. He ran up the walkway and a second later was inside the foyer, trying to drip off a bit so he wouldn't leave puddles everywhere. It didn't take him long to check out the inside of the house. First he went to the kitchen to make sure all appliances were turned off and unplugged. Then he opened the door just to the right of the fridge and went into the garage to check the water heater and make sure the main gas valve was shut off and the garage doors locked. Satisfied the garages were secure Dan made his way back into the house. He wanted to check every room to make sure all electronic equipment and other valuable items were elevated to avoid any possible water damage. It wasn't that he thought Joyce had forgotten to. She was very thorough, and he was sure she had taken care of this, as they had discussed. But it wouldn't hurt to double check. So he headed for the west end of the house.

First, he went through Danny's room, then Nancy's, and then the guest room. Everything in those rooms was fine, as expected. So he headed to the final room in this part of the house, the master bedroom that he and Joyce shared, and which took up the entire west end of the house. When he got there he went directly to one of the walk in closets and checked the small fireproof container on the floor that normally held their important documents to see if Joyce had remembered to remove the most important ones. The container itself was just too heavy to carry, so they'd agreed she would only take the most important papers with her. He opened the heavy lid and thumbed through the documents. He noted that she had, in fact, been thorough once again, and grinned as he thought about how she always was. You could always count on Joyce.

He did a quick run through of the other rooms, and since everything inside was in order, he checked all the other doors before going out the front door to check on things outside. A walk around the house told him that everything there was in order as well. The crew had done a great job of boarding up and Joyce had taken in the lawn furniture. He was satisfied that there was nothing further he could do, so he locked the front door and got back in his truck. The whole process had taken less than a half hour. It was still pouring and he was drenched when he got to the truck, but he figured he'd be able dry off during his ride to Decatur. He settled in his seat, started the truck and headed for the on ramp of I-10 East.

He normally would've headed north on state roads and picked up I-75 in Cordele. It was the most direct route to his in-laws. But he and Joyce had decided to avoid back roads on this trip, and instead head east toward Jacksonville to pick up I-75 in the Winfield area. He was sure that's what she had done earlier, and that's what he was going to do now. Even though he'd have to go out of his way, he felt it was the safest bet. The interstates were less likely to be flooded, and he didn't want to take any chances. Besides, it probably would take longer on the back roads anyway, because of the lower speed limits.

An hour later, he had made little progress. Just about everyone in Tallahassee wanted to be somewhere else, and it seemed to Dan that most of them were headed east on I-10, probably planning to head north at some point, likely at I-75. All travel lanes were jammed and the cars that were moving at all seldom reached the legal speed limit. In fact, the traffic had been stop and go for the last five miles. At this pace it would take hours longer than anticipated to reach Joyce and the kids. He probably should have thought about this, but he hadn't. He'd assumed that the highway would be better than the back roads. Now he wasn't so sure anymore.

He was thankful Joyce and the kids had gotten an earlier start. Hopefully they beat this traffic and would soon be safe at Joyce's parents' house. In hindsight, he probably should've insisted they go even earlier. He'd never forgive himself if anything happened to them.

They'd been stopped dead for some time now and his mind began to wander. He was thinking about Joyce and the kids when the traffic began to move again. His mind was occupied with plans for the party they'd be having in a couple of weeks to celebrate their twentieth anniversary and soon they were going a little faster than they had in some time. Dan was moving mechanically, breaking and accelerating with the traffic, but not really *seeing* the traffic. Now, as they accelerated, he was still totally engrossed in his thoughts of Joyce and didn't see the brake lights of the white Ford Explorer. Although he was probably going no more than fifty miles an hour when he finally slammed on his own brakes, by then he was too close to the Explorer. His truck rammed into its back end, sending it into the car in front of it, which in turn, spun around to face oncoming traffic.

Dan heard the loud crashing sounds, but they seemed far away. It was almost like he was asleep and dreaming of Joyce when his dream was interrupted by this *noise* that was coming from somewhere outside the house. But he knew he wasn't in his house, or in his cozy bed. He was in his truck, on the interstate, trying to get to his family.

Chapter 3

The first call came in shortly after 4 p.m. A motorist on I-10 called from his cell phone to report a multi car accident just east of Tallahassee. He didn't know how many cars were involved, but it looked pretty bad to him. From where he was he could see at least a dozen cars piled up ahead. He said they definitely needed to send some ambulances.

The highway patrol dispatcher immediately put out a call for all available patrol cars to lend assistance, called for ambulances and rescue units, and then notified local hospitals to expect accident victims. She didn't know how many victims they should expect, but knew the heavy traffic reported earlier made it likely the number of injuries would be high. She promised to get back to them with more details as soon as she had any.

Within minutes, a dozen highway patrol cruisers were headed toward the scene. The traffic backup made forward progress difficult, but luckily, the breakdown lanes were still pretty empty, except for a few idiots who thought they could cut the line by driving in them. They were quickly forced onto the grassy areas to the right so the cruisers could pass.

Deputy John Forsyth had just completed his rounds of the shore areas and was headed back to the office when his cruiser nearly collided with one of the highway patrol cruisers headed toward the I-10 on ramp. He knew from the speed of the other cruiser that something serious must have happened, but wasn't plugged into the highway patrol radio frequency. So he decided to follow along to see if there was anything he could do to help. He made a sharp right turn and headed onto the I-10 ramp right behind the highway patrol cruiser.

It wasn't long before he got to the heavy traffic where cars were backed up as far as he could see. It looked like miles of stopped cars and all the travel lanes were completely blocked. He couldn't see any accident, but was sure that that must be what was causing the backup. The highway patrol cruiser he was following swerved into the breakdown lane and sped past the stopped cars. John followed directly behind him. It took them almost fifteen minutes to travel less than two miles and by the time they arrived at what John now could see was an accident scene, camera crews in helicopters were already circling overhead. Never in his career had he seen anything quite like what his eyes took in at that moment. Dozens of police cruisers, fire trucks and ambulances dotted the landscape. Flames were shooting up everywhere and cars were piled high, one on top of the other, most of them looking like nothing more than twisted heaps of metal. He had no idea how many cars might be involved or how many people might be injured, but he thought this could be as big a disaster as any tropical storm could cause.

He grabbed his radio mic and called his office to let them know where he was and that it'd be a while before he could get back. Cleaning up this mess was going to take more than a few hours.

***

In Decatur, Nancy Walters was playing with her grandfather in the living room and her brother Danny was busy in the den working on a new model car he found waiting for him when they arrived. Both Nancy and Danny loved visiting their grandparents because there was always something special for them to do there. Today, Nancy and

Gramps had decided to play one of her favorite card games, Animal Rummy. And best of all, Gramps had agreed to play on the living room rug, her favorite spot. Usually Gramps tried to get her to move to the dining room table because, as he said, "The floor seems to be getting harder and harder as each year passes." But Nancy loved lying on the floor, and that's where they were today.

Joyce was in the kitchen starting to prepare dinner. As Mrs. Robertson approached the room she could hear the radio playing and figured Joyce was trying to get an update on the storm. "How's it going dear?" she asked as she entered the small kitchen? "Is there anything I can do to help?"

"Thanks mom, but it's under control. Dinner's coming along great. You've done enough for us already, so just go sit and relax while I finish getting dinner ready. It shouldn't be too much longer now."

"I can see you've got everything here under control. But how are *you* doing? You look tired."

"Well, it was a long drive and the kids were getting a little restless. But that's not what's bothering me. To be honest, I'm kind of worried that I haven't heard from Dan yet. I know he won't be able to get here until later but I had hoped that he'd be able to call me by now to let me know how he's doing."

"I wouldn't worry about it too much, dear. You know he had to finish closing up the dealership and then swing by the house to check on things there before he could get on the road. He was probably rushing to get on the road to beat the traffic. I'm sure just about everyone in Tallahassee is trying to get out right about now so he's probably in pretty heavy traffic and can't get to a phone."

"I know. I've been listening to the radio and they're saying traffic out of the city is really heavy and most of the highways are jammed. I just hope Dan got on the road early enough to stay ahead of it."

"Now, why don't you let me help you with dinner, dear? I don't feel right letting you do all the work. After all, you're our guests."

"I want to do it, mom. Just because you were nice enough to let us come for a visit, it doesn't mean you have to wait on us hand and foot. Besides, it helps keep my mind off things. Now, go into the living room with Dad and Nancy, and I'll call you all when dinner is ready. It'll just be a few more minutes."

About twenty minutes later they heard Joyce's announcement. "Alright, everyone, dinner is ready. Everything's on the table in the dining room, except for the roast, which I'm going to get right now. Come and sit down so we can eat before it gets cold."

Nancy and Danny happily took their grandparents by the hand to lead them into the dining room. The kids were starving after the long trip and mom had made one of their favorite meals. They couldn't wait to eat.

As Joyce crossed the narrow hallway separating the dining room and kitchen she heard the voice on the radio saying something about a special bulletin. She hurried to turn up the volume so she could hear what was being said. Surely it would be an update on the storm and she wanted to know what was happening. Hopefully it would be good news. Maybe the storm was weakening and hadn't caused as much damage as officials had expected.

"This just in from Tallahassee, Florida. At about four o'clock this afternoon there was an accident on interstate ten involving possibly as many as one hundred vehicles. Traffic is backed up for miles. It looks like thousands of people trying to escape the storm may now be stranded on the highway. Although there are no confirmed figures at this time, police estimate that scores of people have been injured, many of them seriously. Medical helicopters were called in to evacuate the more seriously hurt. We'll continue to provide updates as more information becomes available."

Joyce stood in the middle of the kitchen, frozen in place. Laughter from the dining room and shouts of "Hey mom, let's eat" startled her out of what seemed to be a trance. Just then, her mom walked into the kitchen. She had come in to help with the roast, and had overheard the radio announcer. She and Joyce looked at each other for a moment without saying a word, each knowing what the other was thinking, but neither wanted to say it out loud. Joyce was the first to break the silence.

"My God, mom, did you hear that? There's been a major accident on I-10 just outside of Tallahassee. That's the route Dan was going to take. What if he's involved in the accident? He could be seriously hurt. I need to call someone to get information. I have to find out if Dan is OK."

"I know how you feel, dear, but how will you be able to get any information about Dan? Even if the telephone lines aren't tied up and you get through to Tallahassee, there are thousands of people on the highway. How will anyone be able to tell you if Dan is one of them?"

"I don't know, but I've got to find out. Maybe I can get a hold of John Forsyth. He's a friend of ours in the Sheriff's Department. He might be able to tell me something. At least he might know what time Dan left and whether or not he'd be passed the accident location by now. Mom, you take the roast into the dining room and let the kids start. I'll be there in a minute."

As Joyce's mom headed for the dining room, Joyce began dialing 1-850-555-1212 for information on the Tallahassee areas. She needed the home number for John Forsyth and the number of the Sheriff's Office in Tallahassee.

"Hello, information? I'd like to get the number for John Forsyth in Tallahassee, Florida please. Yes, that's F O R S Y T H. The address is Amber Lane. And also, please give me the number for the Leon County Sheriff's Office on Municipal Way, in Tallahassee."

A few seconds later the operator came back with the requested numbers, which Joyce jotted down on the pad near the phone. She hung up and immediately dialed the first number. She let the phone ring ten times, but no one answered. It shouldn't have surprised her that there was no one home at the Forsyth's. John's family, like everyone else, would probably be either on their way out of the city or already at some safe location. She hung up and dialed the second number.

After a few rings a voice at the other end answered "Leon County Sheriff's Department. How can I help you?"

"Yes hello. I'm trying to reach Deputy Forsyth. Is he there, please?"

"I'm sorry, but Deputy Forsyth is on patrol at the moment. Is there someone else who might be able to help you?"

"This is Joyce Walters, calling from Decatur. My husband, Dan, was planning to meet me here as soon as he closed up the dealership, but I haven't heard from him, and he's overdue. I thought maybe John might know something about where Dan is. Is there any way you could patch me through to John?"

"Well, Mrs. Walters, Deputy Forsyth is currently at the scene of a major traffic accident on I-10. I can try to get a message to him, but I don't think he'll be able to take the call right now. If you give me a number where you can be reached I'll make sure he gets the message as soon as possible. I'm sure he'll call you the first chance he gets."

Joyce gave her the number at her mom's house and hung up the phone. Then she thought of Randy and decided to try his number next. Since the families spent so much time together, she didn't need to call information. She knew the number by heart, and dialed it. But after a dozen rings, she gave up and replaced the receiver in its cradle. There wasn't anyone left in Tallahassee she could call. They had all left ahead of Fay. All she could do now was wait, and hope. Hope that Dan would show up soon. Hope that John would return her call and be able to shed some light on Dan's location. Hope that her worst fears would not be realized.

She tried to compose herself as she made her way to the dining room, but apparently wasn't too successful. Both kids noticed the worried look on her face and, at the same time, as though in one voice, asked "Mom, what's the matter? What's wrong?"

"Oh, it's nothing, really" she replied. I'm just a bit worried that we haven't heard from your dad yet. I'm sure there's really nothing to worry about, but you know me, I always have to worry about something."

She didn't say anything about the news from the radio, and neither did Mrs. Robertson. But they both said a silent prayer that everything would be alright.

It was an unusually quiet dinner, and the kids sensed there was more to it than they were being told but didn't want to upset their mom more by pursuing the matter. They'd just have to wait until she was ready to talk about it.

Chapter 4

Doug Armstrong stood by the window of his fifteenth floor office looking out onto the street below, and the light midday traffic. The rain had been falling in steady streams all morning and there was no sign of a let up. He knew this weather system wasn't part of the one hitting the southeastern part of the country, because Milwaukee was too far away to be affected by that system, or the one hitting the east coast, for that matter, but he found little consolation in that thought. The worst of the hurricane season was still weeks away, claims were already heavier than usual, and forecasters were warning of a more active season than normal.

Insurance claims always skyrocketed during hurricane season and even in a normal year the company would take a pretty big hit to earnings. Those were anticipated and budgeted for, but it was looking more and more like this might be the worst season in a long time, and the past few days weren't encouraging, especially with the news of Tropical Storm Fay. Doug's shoulders drooped slightly as he thought of the prospect of a bigger than normal hit to the bottom line. The new owners would not be happy, and right now that was giving him a headache.

It had been two years since the takeover and Doug still wasn't comfortable with the new arrangements. He'd known it would be difficult taking orders from someone else because he'd been the boss for a long time and liked calling the shots. But the company hadn't been doing all that well in recent years, primarily because the economy was continuing to worsen under the Bush Administration, and the future was becoming more uncertain, not just for Great Waters, but for everyone. The large infusion of new capital and the backing of a multi-national conglomerate seemed like the best thing for both the company and the community at the time, even if the new owners were from a foreign county

He didn't like the new owners *or* their management style, but he'd hoped the money and stock options he received as part of the buyout would ease the pain of losing some control over the operations of Great Waters Insurance Group. Now he knew he'd been wrong, because he hadn't lost *some* control, he'd lost it *all*. He was CEO in title only, and no longer had any real say in any of the major business decisions. Great Waters was now a wholly owned subsidiary of Ping Industries, headquartered in Tokyo, Japan. Ping had a presence in all major cities throughout the world and insurance was but a small part of their world-wide operations. They owned or controlled companies in a dozen different countries, across numerous industries including insurance, auto, mining, steel, shipping, and commercial and consumer finance.

The new owners were very aggressive and demanding, and no quarterly results ever satisfied them. Nothing mattered except the current earnings and the price of the stock. Keeping the stockholders happy in the short run was more important than keeping the company viable in the long run, because if the stockholders were kept happy then the Ping management folks would keep their jobs and continue to make lots of money. If not, no one was safe. That's just how big business operated these days.

Thinking about the future had given Doug a lot of headaches lately, but this one was by far the worst. He hadn't ever had a migraine before, but guessed that this was what they felt like. Every flash of lightning was like being stabbed between the eyes with a sharp knife and the thunder made his whole body hurt. He felt as though his head would explode at any minute, and almost wished it would happen so he could be rid of the pain. He longed to be able to lie down in a dark room, forget everything, and just sleep it off. But he just couldn't stop worrying about Fay and those other hurricanes and tropical storms that would surely follow close behind her. And then he remembered Ping Industries again, and a feeling of nausea swept over him. He barely made it to his private bathroom before he threw up.

When he made it back to his desk, he opened the top right drawer and took out the bottle of aspirin that he kept there. He popped three into his mouth, poured himself some water from the pitcher on the corner of his desk, and washed down the aspirin with a big gulp. The sounds of the wind and rain in the background seemed to grow louder and the flashes of lightning were coming more frequently. He buried his head in the palms of his hands once again, trying to relax.

The knock on his door jolted him back to reality. The door swung open and Jennifer, his secretary, came in with the latest weather reports. "Excuse me for interrupting, Mr. Armstrong. I thought you'd want to get the latest weather update as soon as possible. Tropical Storm Fay passed over Cuba, crossed over the southern parts of Florida, and is now headed up towards Tallahassee. Forecasters say it has the potential to turn into a major hurricane and heavy rains and serious flooding are expected." Of course, Doug knew all about Fay. He, himself, had been watching her progress for some time now, and the pounding in his temples suddenly got worst.

On the fifth floor, in the Claims Department, Jane Donahue and Peter Wild were busy getting ready for the onslaught of claims they knew would be coming in soon. They canceled all upcoming vacations for claims processors and were recalling those already out on vacation. They were even considering the possibility of bringing in some temporary workers. They knew if the rainfall from Fay was anywhere near as bad as some meteorologists were forecasting, the water damage would be serious.

Jane was about to call the Personnel Dept. to alert them to the possibility she'd need some extra help in the next few days when she heard the commentator's voice. She'd been monitoring Fay's progress on the small TV in her office and now the normal broadcasting was interrupted for a special bulletin. She assumed it would be just another update on Fay, but decided to hold off on her call anyway so she could listen to the bulletin, just in case. What she heard wasn't what she expected. As she listened to the commentator's voice a chill ran down her spine.

"Just in from Tallahassee, Florida, a major multi car accident on I-10 just east of the city, involving perhaps as many as one hundred cars. Although details are sketchy, initial reports from the scene indicate that numerous people may have died. As a result of the accident thousands of others are stranded on the interstate."

Chapter 5

Jake was up late going over the package Joe Nash had prepared for him earlier in the day. He knew Amie was aggravated, as she always was when he brought work home with him, which was quite often, he had to admit. She felt he put in enough hours at the office, and didn't see why he needed to do even more work when he came home. But when there was work that needed doing, he did it. It wasn't unusual for him to work sixty hours each week between Monday and Friday, then put in another ten or more hours over the weekend. And even though Amie didn't like it, it was what he got paid for, and rather handsomely, at that. It was the price he had to pay for the lifestyle they enjoyed.

At eleven o'clock, Amie decided to go to bed. She had no idea how much longer Jake would be working and was pretty bushed after her own day at the office. The kids were already in bed because it was Wednesday, and their bedtime on weekdays was 9 p.m. for Susan and 10 p.m. for the boys, no exceptions. The boys always made a fuss and felt they should be allowed to stay up later, but Amie never fell for that one. Even though Tommy was thirteen and Teddy was eleven, they still needed their sleep. Susan, who was eight, didn't even try to make a case for staying up later and always seemed to get at least ten hours of sleep a night.

"I'm going to head upstairs to bed, honey" she said as she poked her head into his office. "Try not to be too late."

"I won't, sweetheart. I should be finished in just a bit and then I'll be right up. But don't wait for me, just in case."

She knew that story well. It was what Jake always said, but it was seldom "just a bit." More often than not she was fast asleep long before he came up and had no idea what time he really *did* make it to bed. When she'd ask him the next day what time he had come to bed, he'd always say something like "I was right behind you. You must've fallen asleep the minute your head hit the pillow." But she knew better, because sometimes she waited hours for him before finally dozing off.

She gently closed the door to his office and checked the front door to make sure it was locked before turning out the porch lights and heading up the stairway to the second floor where the bedrooms were located. She had already performed her nightly routine of checking the garage, the back door, and all the first floor windows. When she got to the second floor she checked each of the kid's bedrooms, as she always did, just to make sure they were asleep, and then went to their bedroom at the far end of the hall.

She undressed quietly, and decided to freshen up before getting into her nightgown, just in case. She never knew when Jake might actually come to bed at a reasonable hour, and she wanted to be ready. It hadn't happened in a very long time, but you never could tell. As she slipped under the covers, she wondered, once again, if the life-style they'd grown accustomed to was worth the sacrifices and the toll Jake's job was taking on their marriage. They could live in a smaller house, drive less expensive cars, and send the kids to public schools. They'd lived that way for many years when they were younger. As she lay awake, starring at the ceiling, she thought about the early years they'd spent together. Even though they'd had many difficult times, they were always happy times.

When she'd first met Jake, she quickly realized what a real "go-getter" he was. Although he hadn't been able to go to college after high school because of family issues, he'd managed to scrape up enough money to enroll in a data processing course at a local business school, which allowed him to land an entry level job with a bank. It was during his first year there that they'd met, through a friend of the family. They started dating, and were married less than a year later, when they were both still only nineteen.

After they'd been married for just eight months Jake was drafted into the Army. It was during the Vietnam conflict, and it was a tough time. But even though they were apart, it was still a relatively happy time because Jake was stationed stateside and managed to come home every few months. After he received his discharge he came back to Maine, he got his job back at the bank and used his benefits from the GI bill to help pay for college tuition. It took him seven years, but he finally graduated with a BS in Business Administration, and he did it with honors. Those were long years, and a bit tough on the family because Jake was working full time and attending classes three nights a week, but even then they still had been able to make sure they had quality time together.

While still working at the bank, Jake continued his education and received an MBA with a major in Accounting. Over the next few years he moved from his position at the bank to a management position with a large national retail organization, and then to a senior consulting position with a national public accounting firm, and all the while his work schedule continued to increase. It was while he was with one of the "big eight" firms, as they were called at the time, that he met Fred Campbell. New Commerce was one of his clients, and he often conducted both IT and financial audits there.

Two years ago Jake was asked to join New Commerce. He negotiated a deal which included a position on the Executive Committee and the title of Chief Security and Compliance Officer, with a salary, bonus and stock options that he could never even have dreamed of just a few years earlier.   But once on board, it didn't take him long to realize that some major changes were needed in the way reviews were conducted at New Commerce, and ever since, he'd found himself putting more and more hours on the job, and spending even fewer hours with his wife and kids.

The more she thought about it, the angrier she got, and the less likely it was that she'd get to sleep any time soon. Now it felt like Jake was hardly ever home at all, and when he was, he was busy working in his office.   The children were growing up fast, and they needed their father, but it seemed that he felt his company needed him more than his family did.   She finally fell asleep at around 1 a.m., wondering, again, if it was all worth it.

Shortly after 1:30 a.m. Jake finally made it to bed. He'd gone through the entire package Joe gave him, reading and re-reading all the documents to make sure he was comfortable with the coverage his department was providing. Even though he had been intricately involved in the development of all the programs and procedures, he wanted to make sure nothing had been inadvertently changed, and wanted to be especially sure that the schedule he developed using a complex risk assessment methodology was still being adhered to and the review cycles were still meaningful, particularly for the divisions offering the new product lines.

He set his alarm for five o'clock because once again he wanted to be at his desk a bit earlier than usual so he could get a head start on the day. His meeting with Fred would put him behind schedule and, once behind, it was tough to catch up again. It was after 2 a.m. when he finally drifted off to sleep.

Chapter 6

Thursday, August 14, 2008

It was now 4 a.m. The first call had come in twelve hours earlier and John Forsyth had arrived at the scene shortly after that. He and the other rescue personnel had been working almost non-stop ever since. The Red Cross had set up tents and provided coffee and food for the workers, but few of them took a break. There was too much to do, too many people who needed help. They were all exhausted, but, somehow, still managed to go on.

John and the highway patrol troopers had helped the paramedics with the initial check of the accident victims. Those who were still alive were moved to the "triage" area that was set up just inside the perimeter line. There, the doctors examined each victim to determine the seriousness of their injuries. Those most seriously hurt were loaded onto the EVAC helicopters for immediate transport to a designated hospital. Those who could survive a longer commute were loaded into waiting ambulances. Most victims were sent to Tallahassee Memorial. The most badly burned victims were sent, via EVAC helicopters, to the Shriners Hospital in Tampa.

By now all the fires were extinguished, but the firemen were still busy dousing the ashes, and smoke filled the air like a thick cloud of dust. It was getting difficult to see beyond a few feet, and John's eyes were burning and he found it hard to see. But what he *could* see horrified him. What remained at the scene were the bodies of those who hadn't survived, and the burned and mangled vehicles they'd been in. It reminded him of a scene from a science fiction movie that depicted the world after a nuclear war.

It would take a long time, perhaps days, before the area could be cleared, and it would be weeks, if not months, before all the bodies could be identified. But the heartbreak the victim's families would suffer would go on for much longer than that. Getting the news of the tragedy would be just the beginning of their nightmare. What would follow would be almost as unbearable as the initial shock. First, they'd have to identify the remains, which in many cases would be difficult to do because some bodies were burned beyond recognition. Then they'd need to make funeral arrangements. After the funerals, estates would need to be settled. And, finally, insurance claims would have to be filed. From his past experiences, John knew that this last challenge could be the most difficult of all. He'd seen cases drag on for years when insurance companies denied claims and families were forced to file lawsuits.

He was heading toward one of the mangled vehicles to help a paramedic pull out a body when he heard someone calling his name.

"Is there a Deputy Forsyth here?"

"Over here" he yelled, waving his hands in the air so he could be seen. "I'm John Forsyth."

The trooper saw his hands and headed toward him. "Your office has been trying to reach you. They'd like you to check in with them as soon as you have a chance."

"Thanks. I'll do that."

All of the injured were now safely out of the area so John decided to finally take a break and contact his office. He hadn't been in touch since yesterday when he reached the accident scene. Things had been so hectic he hadn't even thought about the office. Now it occurred to him that he hadn't seen any other deputies at the scene, and wondered why not.

It took him a few minutes to reach his cruiser, which was parked on the grass median a few hundred yards away.

He climbed into the driver's seat, grabbed his mic and clicked the button with his thumb. The radio was always tuned into the correct frequency for the Leon County Sheriff's office in Tallahassee. "This is Deputy Forsyth. I'm still at the accident scene on I-10. Someone's been trying to reach me?"

The dispatcher responded immediately. "John, this is Becky. We've been trying to reach you since yesterday. We finally asked the highway patrol to see if they could track you down. They said things were hectic there but they'd try to get the message to you as soon as they could."

"They just got to me a few minutes ago. We finally got all of the injured out of here, and are beginning to get to those who didn't make it. I haven't seen anyone else from the department. Did any of them come out?"

"After you called in, we sent other deputies to help, but by the time they arrived, the highway patrol, fire department, paramedics and doctors were all already on the scene. So our guys took on the task of traffic control. They've been working through the night to help the motorists who weren't involved in the accident get off the highway."

"How are they doing? Do they need me to help out?"

"No, they're all set. After blocking off the on ramps and clearing traffic from the west bound lanes, they were able to get east bound traffic that was stuck behind the accident scene turned around. By now things are pretty much under control. They're hoping to be able to open the east bound lanes as soon as some of the smoke clears."

"OK, good. Sorry I didn't call in sooner, but things were kind of hectic here. Was there anything specific you needed?"

"I just wanted to let you know you've gotten several messages from Joyce Walters. She's been calling since yesterday afternoon and sounds pretty upset. As of her last call, at about midnight, she hadn't heard from her husband, who was supposed to meet her at her mom's house in Decatur shortly after dinner. She was wondering if you might know his whereabouts. I told her I'd get a message to you as soon as I could."

John felt a chill go up his spine. He'd been so busy he hadn't thought about Dan, and he certainly hadn't been looking for him among the injured. He knew Dan was planning to head out this way after checking on his house. Surely, if he'd been ahead of the accident, he'd be in Decatur by now. He wondered if he had made it, and Joyce hadn't called back to leave a follow up message, but he knew that wasn't likely. Joyce was very thorough and thoughtful. She would definitely have called again if Dan were there.

"Did she leave a number where I can reach her?"

"Yes, I can patch you through if you'd like."

"That'd be great, Becky. There's no way I'm going to find a phone out here. Put her through as soon as you can."

***

Joyce sat at the kitchen table sipping her coffee and trying to stay calm. It wasn't working. It was now 4:45 a.m. and she hadn't slept a wink. How could she? She never heard back from John Forsyth and hadn't been able to make contact with anyone else she knew in Tallahassee. She had tried calling the Sheriff's Department several times, and even called the highway patrol headquarters. But no one could give her any specific information on Dan's whereabouts. It was obvious now that he had somehow been involved in the accident on I-10, either in an actual crash or by being tied up in the traffic behind the crash. But surely, if he had just been tied up in the traffic, he would have been able to call her by now. Something very bad must have happened.

"Have you been up all night, dear?" she heard her mother say. It startled her because she hadn't heard any footsteps. Donna Robertson was a short woman, barely five feet tall, and she weighed a mere one hundred and ten pounds, so she made hardly any sound at all when she walked, especially with slippers on.

"I couldn't sleep not knowing where Dan is. I just *know* something awful happened to him. Otherwise he would've found a way to contact me. I called the Sheriff's Department several times last night trying to reach John Forsyth to see if he knew anything, but he's been at the scene of the accident since yesterday afternoon and they haven't been able to reach him. They promised they'd get a message to him as soon as they could, asking him to call me."

"I know it's difficult, dear, but we've got to keep our hopes up. If Dan's been stuck in traffic behind the accident he wouldn't be able to get to a phone.   Maybe we should turn on the TV to see if there's any more news."

They went into the living room and turned on the TV. Joyce switched the channel to WSB-TV Action News 2, in Atlanta. If any station in the area were going to cover the I-10 accident it would be that one, and it was the only locally available station that broadcasted twenty four hours a day. They both sat and patiently listened as the news caster ran down a few local events. "There was another murder in downtown Atlanta last night, bringing this year's total to one hundred and twenty one. The body of an unidentified female was discovered shortly after midnight in an alley off of South Street. Officials are asking anyone with information about the crime to contact Atlanta police." There were five or six more news items discussed. It was fifteen minutes before there was any mention of the accident.

"A multi vehicle accident yesterday left more than fifty people injured and at least ten dead. The accident occurred in the east bound lanes of I-10, just outside of Tallahassee. West bound lanes were closed for several hours due to the heavy smoke from car fires, but have just been re-opened. East bound lanes are still closed, and will be for some time. Rescue workers have evacuated all of the injured parties, but the Highway Patrol estimates it could be at least another day before the damaged and burned vehicles and related debris are totally cleared away. Most of the injured were brought to Tallahassee Memorial Hospital, but a few of those who suffered more serious burns were taken to the Shriners Hospital in Tampa. The Florida Highway Patrol will be setting up an information telephone line shortly to provide information on accident victims. We'll provide that number as soon as we have it."

Joyce was on the verge of losing control. Her eyes filled with tears, just a few at first, and then soon more and more. Suddenly her whole body shook and she began to sob loudly. Her mom wrapped her arms around her to try to console her, but there wasn't much she could say at a time like this that would be of any help.

Bob Robertson hadn't slept any better than his daughter or his wife. And when he heard the television set, he decided to go downstairs and see what was happening. He was just coming into the living room when the phone rang. He picked it up and answered "Robertson residence."

"Could I speak with Joyce Walters, please? I'm calling from the Leon County Sheriff's office in Tallahassee. Deputy Forsyth is returning her call."

Joyce was still sobbing and taking heavy breaths, but had turned to look at her father when he answered the phone. He was signaling to her that the call was for her, and started walking toward her with the cordless handset. She jumped out of her chair and met him halfway. When he told her it was the Leon County Sheriff's Department she grabbed the handset and, wiping tears from her eyes and breathing heavily, spoke into the phone.

"This is Joyce Walters. Who is this?"

"Mrs. Walters, I'm the dispatcher with the Sheriff's Department. We've located John Forsyth, and I'm ready to patch him through if you can take his call now."

"Of course I can. Please put him through right away."

After a click, she heard John's voice at the other end.

"Hello, Joyce? This is John Forsyth. I called as soon as I got your message. "

"John, thank God it's you! I've been trying to reach you since yesterday afternoon. I haven't been able to get a hold of anybody in Tallahassee and I have no idea what's going on, except for what I hear on the news. Dan never made it to mom's house and I haven't heard from him. I'm really worried. Is there anything you can do to help me find him?"

"Of course I'll do everything I can, Joyce. I had no idea he hadn't gotten there yet. When I saw him yesterday he was on his way to check out your house and was planning to head out right after that. I haven't heard from him or seen him since then. It hadn't occurred to me that he might've gotten caught up in the traffic. I've spent the last thirteen hours at the accident scene, and didn't see him there. I'll check at your home and at the dealership, and if he's not there, I'll start checking the hospitals. Don't worry, I'll find him and get back to you as soon as I do. Will you still be at this number?"

"Yes, unless you think it would be safe for me to head back to Tallahassee."

"No, I don't think you should do that. There's been a lot of flooding throughout the city, and the highways are still a mess. And I don't know what shape your neighborhood is in. You best stay put until I get back to you. If you haven't heard from me in two hours, check back with the Sheriff's office. Now that I'm away from the accident scene they should be able to get in touch with me."

"OK, whatever you think is best, John. But please get back to me as soon as you can."

"I will. I promise."

She hit the "end call" button on the handset and gave it back to her father. All she could do now was to sit and wait. She felt the tears returning, but when she heard the kids coming down the stairs she pulled herself together. For their sake, she had to be strong.

"Mom, what's happening? Where's Dad?" Danny asked as he entered the living room. Nancy was right behind him and seconded that question. "Yeah mom, what's going on? Where's Dad?"

Bob and Donna Robertson collected the kids and led them to the sofa. "Sit down children and we'll try to explain everything to you" Donna said. She looked at Joyce and asked "Would you like me to try to explain?"

"No" said Joyce. "I'll do it." She joined the kids on the sofa and began. "Your dad hasn't made it home yet. There was an accident on the interstate and traffic's been backed up all night. We don't know exactly where he is right now, but I just spoke with John Forsyth, and he's going to be looking for your dad. He'll call us as soon as he finds him."

"Was he in the accident?" asked Danny. "Is he hurt?"

"We don't know. But I'm confident that he's OK and just hasn't been able to get to a phone yet. According to the news reports, the highway's been closed all night, and the west bound lanes were just opened. The east bound lanes aren't open yet so it's possible he's still stuck on the highway. I'm sure Deputy Forsyth will be able to find out what's happening and get back to us."

"There's nothing more we can do right now" said Donna. "Why don't I make us some breakfast?

"That's a good idea" said Joyce. Anything that would help to keep the kids' minds and her own off of the current situation was a good idea. She and Donna headed toward the kitchen, while Grandpa stayed behind, trying to find a way to keep the kids occupied.

Meanwhile, in Tallahassee, Deputy Forsyth was on his way to Walters Marine.

Chapter 7

John Forsyth arrived at Walters Marine just after 6 a.m. It'd been an hour since he spoke with Joyce Walters and then had let Becky know where he was going. The roads were in tough shape, many of them under water, so he had to make a lot of detours. What should've been a fifteen minute drive turned into an hour's journey, but he felt lucky to have made it at all. He stopped his cruiser at curbside, or what he guessed was curbside, because he couldn't actually *see* the curb. As best he could figure the water was about six inches above the curb. He glanced over the building and, after a quick scan of the area, decided it looked like the dealership was mostly undamaged, except for maybe some water inside, which of course he couldn't see. And even though it looked deserted, he decided to check it out, just in case. It was possible that Dan was inside checking on his inventory.

He opened the door to get out and saw that the water was almost level with the bottom of the door. An inch more and it would've gotten inside the cruiser. He stepped out carefully, got a solid footing, and began to make his way toward the building. It was slow going, and pretty miserable. It was still raining, and he had to take small, steady steps to avoid falling. But even with the slow movements, the moving water soaked him to just below the belt.

When he got to the main entrance he rang the bell, and after a few seconds he rang it again, and then again and again. It soon became clear no one was going to answer. He tried the door, but it was locked. He couldn't see inside because of the storm shutters on the door and all the windows so he made his way to the side yard where the larger boats were kept. The gate was locked. It definitely looked like no one had been here since he, Dan and Randy had left yesterday. Satisfied that Dan wasn't here, he made his way back to the cruiser.

At seven o'clock he finally arrived at the Walters residence. He went through the same drill here as he had at the dealership. First he checked the front door and rang the bell several times. When there was no answer, he went around the house seeing if there were any other doors unlocked. None were. Not seeing any indication of activity, he decided that Dan hadn't come back here either. Now he started to get really worried. If Dan wasn't at the dealership, wasn't here, and wasn't in Decatur with Joyce, then there weren't too many options left. He might have been in the traffic that had been backed up on the highway, but that didn't seem likely. If he had, he surely was out of that traffic now, and would've called Joyce, who, in turn, would've contacted John through the Sheriff's office. Neither of the two remaining options was good. Dan could be in a local hospital, or, heaven forbid, he could still be on the highway, one of the many casualties of the accident. Given a choice between those two options, John hoped the hospital was where he was. So he decided to start checking with them.

As soon as he got back into the car he radioed the office. "This is Deputy Forsyth checking in from the Walters residence. Are you there, Becky?"

"John, this is Becky. Go ahead."

"I didn't find Dan at either the dealership or his residence. It doesn't look like he's been back to either location since he left yesterday. Have you heard back from Joyce yet?"

"She just called a minute ago. I told her I hadn't heard from you, but would check in with you right away. I tried to reach you on the radio but you must have been outside. Do you want me to try to get her now and patch you through?"

"No. I'm heading back to the office, and I'll call her from there. In the meantime, would you start contacting the local hospitals? They should have a list of patients who were brought in from the accident scene. I'd like to know something more specific before I call Joyce back. Hopefully, by the time I get there you'll have the lists and we'll know if Dan's on them."

"I'll get right on it. If Mrs. Walters should call back, what do you want me tell her?"

"Just say that I'm on my way in and I'll call her back shortly."

"OK. I got it."

"Thanks, Becky."

He started the engine and slid the gearshift into drive. At this point he was thankful that the car even started. The water level was rising steadily and he wasn't sure if he'd make it back to the office without stalling out. He'd take it slow and easy and try to not to get much water up into the engine compartment. The last thing he needed right now was a long walk back to the office in the pouring rain, with water levels rising by the minute.

It was a slow process, but a half hour later he finally made it back to the office, and hadn't needed to walk, for which he was very thankful. He was also thankful that the office was built on a slight hill, or something that came as close to being a hill as you could expect in Florida. Since it was one of the emergency facilities, the property had been built up a bit before construction was started. Now, along with the sand bags that surrounded the building, it proved to be just enough. The water hadn't made it inside, yet.

The rain was still coming down hard as John made his way to the front door of the Sheriff's office. He had to maneuver through the obstacle course of sandbags, which made his trip from the parking lot a bit longer, but at this point, it didn't really matter since he couldn't get any wetter if he jumped into a pool. He was soaked to the skin.

He pulled open the front door with some difficulty. The pelting rain was beating against it, adding to the normal resistance of the heavy metal structure. But the inner glass doors easily gave in to his push. Once inside, he took off his shoes, socks and rain gear, and dropped them onto the rubber mat to the left of the door before walking barefooted to his desk, leaving a trail of water the whole way.

It was now almost eight o'clock and he knew Joyce was probably frantic. He wanted to pick up the phone and call her right away, but the pool of water that was forming at his feet made him decide to get into some dry clothes first. He always kept dry clothes at the office for just such occasions. And he wanted to check the hospital lists too.

By quarter past eight, John was dry and ready to make the call. He had gotten the patient lists from Becky. Dan's name wasn't on any of them.

***

She answered the phone on the first ring. It wasn't difficult, since she had it in her lap, where it had been for the past hour.

"Yes, hello, this is Joyce Walters."

"Hi, Joyce."

"Yes. Is that you, John? Have you located Dan? How is he? Please tell me he's alright. I'm going out of my mind, here."

"You've got to stay calm, Joyce. I checked the dealership and the house, and didn't find him at either location. But that doesn't necessarily mean anything. He could be stuck in traffic, still. I'm going to head back out shortly. I'll go back to the accident area and take a look around. If he's still stuck in traffic, I'll be able to find him. In the meantime, we're checking with all local hospitals, just in case. If he's been hurt, he'll be on one of their lists. Don't worry, if he's anywhere in the area, we'll find him."

He didn't want to tell her that Dan's name wasn't on any of the hospital patient lists. That would just make matters worse. And it was still possible that he was at a local hospital and still hadn't been checked in, so his name wouldn't be on their list yet. But John knew Dan wasn't stuck in traffic. The backup had been cleared, and everyone who had been on the highway was now on their way to someplace else, unless they were hospitalized or dead. But he wasn't about to tell Joyce that. She was worried enough already. He wanted to find out exactly where Dan was before getting back to her.

"I'll call you back as soon as I have any information. Meanwhile, just stay put. There isn't anything you can do here, and the roads are still a mess. I promise I'll call you back."

"Thanks, John. I really appreciate it. Please find him."

"We will. Try to stay calm. I'll call you. Bye for now."

"Goodbye John."

***

At 10 a.m. sharp, Fred was knocking on Jake's door. "Come in and have a seat, Fred."

"Thanks for seeing me on such short notice, Jake. I really appreciate it."

"No problem. Do you want some coffee before we begin?"

"No thanks. We've both got tight schedules, so why don't we just get started, if that's OK with you."

"Of course. Why don't you start by telling me what's on your mind. If you don't cover the issues I want to discuss, we can go over them when you're done."

"We'll, as you know, the current delinquency report shows a jump across the board, both in our core product lines and our inventory finance businesses. I don't think anyone would consider it a major problem just yet, but I've been noticing a trend lately, and I want to make sure we're on top of things before they get out of control. We've reported great results and lower than average delinquencies in the past year, and the analysts have reacted favorably, which in turn has helped us to raise more capital. But all that can change in a heartbeat if they think the quality of our portfolio is declining, and we'd be in serious trouble if we couldn't raise the necessary capital to keep funding new loans."

"I know. I have concerns too, and I'd be surprised if Tom D'Angelo doesn't."

"To be honest, Jake, our core products don't really concern me that much. I know each of the customers and deals in those lines, and they're all basically sound. It's our newer businesses that I'm worried about. I think those deals deserve more scrutiny, especially in light of the more relaxed underwriting guidelines Deb initiated when she took over. So, naturally, my first thought was that you and your staff could help me out here."

"Well be glad to do whatever we can, Fred."

"Thanks. Maybe you can start by helping me to understand what you're covering during your reviews. Can you give me a quick rundown of your procedures, especially relative to the inventory finance portfolio?"

"Sure, I'd be glad to. I was going to prepare an update for the next Audit Committee meeting on Tuesday anyway, so after you called I decided to get a head start. I went over our schedules and review procedures last night and prepared a synopsis for you. Here, take a look at this." Jake motioned to Fred to follow him to the conference table, where he'd spread some documents out on the table.

They discussed the risk assessment methodology used to rate each major business process to determine the frequency of reviews, and then went over the schedules for the current and past two years. They also discussed the specific steps performed during all standard division reviews.

"OK. I think I understand your procedures" said Fred. "I'm a little worried, though, that there aren't any reviews of our inventory divisions scheduled for this year. Even though you just reviewed them last year, a lot can change in a short period of time in that business."

"I agree with you, and fortunately, our schedule isn't cast in concrete, so maybe there's something we can do to help you out."

"But the members of the Audit Committee already approved your schedule, didn't they?"

"Yes, but you may recall that when we first went with the new risk assessment approach, we wanted to make sure to have the flexibility to conduct any special reviews that might be needed, so we got them to agree that we could change the schedule at senior management's request, as long as we brought them up to speed as soon as possible."

"Yes, that's right, I recall that."

"That was built into the process for situations such as this so we can address management concerns on a timely basis. If you'd like, we can discuss this at Tuesday's Audit Committee meeting and I can schedule a review of one or more of the inventory finance divisions ASAP."

"That sounds good to me, Jake. In the meantime you should probably start planning for the reviews because I'd like to get started soon. Why don't we start with our Atlanta area location, since they have the largest portfolio?"

"OK. I'll put this on the agenda for Tuesday's meeting, and I'll have Joe start planning for the review. Is there anything else you wanted to cover this morning Fred?"

"No, I think that covers it. Oh, wait a second, I almost forgot. We haven't discussed our inventory insurance coverage yet. What's going on with that? In light of the damages expected from Tropical Storm Fay, I want to make sure we're covered."

"That's a good question, Fred. In the past, we've looked to see if there's evidence in the files that our dealers have adequate inventory insurance. But, it's been the divisions' responsibility to periodically verify the existence of that coverage and make a notation in the file. Now that Deb's let me add a couple of people to my staff, we'll be able to start verifying the coverage ourselves, but only on a sample basis. It's a pretty time consuming thing to do, because we'll need to contact the insurance carrier for each customer selected, and preferably, do it by sending a written verification request. I was planning to begin that process during our next review, so we can do that as part of an upcoming special review, which we could begin as soon as the week after next. Unfortunately, that will be *after* Fay has gone through the area."

"Thanks, Jake. I think I'll give Jeff Anderson, in Marietta, a call. I'm going to ask him to try to verify that we have insurance coverage in place, at least on new deals and on those where policies are up for renewal. It's probably too late to do anything now if we aren't adequately covered, but I'd like to know anyway so I can be more comfortable during the next storm."

"Good idea! And I'll get Joe started on the planning for the review, and we'll include a test of insurance coverage while we're there."

"I'll let you know what I find out from Jeff as soon as I get a hold of him. Was there something more that you wanted to discuss?"

"Well, it's just that I'm worried about the effect the economic downturn will have on our new business lines. I was thinking, maybe it's time for us to discuss this at Executive Committee to see if we need to make some changes to our product lines."

"My thoughts exactly, Jake, but it won't be pleasant, I'm sure. You know how Deb feels about those product lines."

"Yeah, but we need to do what's best for the company and the stockholders. We can talk to a few other members of the Committee before the meeting to see if we can line up some support."

"Sounds like a plan."

They both stood, signaling the end of the meeting. Fred left and headed to his office on twenty-five. Jake gave Joe a call and asked him to step in for a minute.

Chapter 8

He'd been up at his usual time of 5:30 a.m. on Wednesday, and it was now just after 10 a.m. on Thursday. He hadn't slept in almost thirty hours, and he was tired. Every muscle in his body ached, but he had to keep going. He promised Joyce he'd keep looking until he found Dan, or until he got the call saying Dan had finally made it to Decatur. He owed Dan a lot and he wasn't quitting until Dan was found.

He'd left the office as soon as he finished talking to Joyce, which was almost two hours ago. It was slow going because some of the roads were impassable. Although it had stopped raining, it would be some time before the water would recede. After a number of detours, he arrived at the I-10 on ramp. It was blocked by a highway patrol cruiser, and for a moment John thought he might not be able to get back to the accident scene. But as he approached the cruiser, he recognized the trooper on duty. They had worked together throughout most of the night helping to evacuate the injured. He pulled his cruiser close to where the trooper was standing and rolled down his window.

The trooper recognized John as well, and walked up to his car.

"John. What are you doing back here? I thought you'd left for the day."

"Don't I wish? I'm beat, and I'm sure you are too, but there's still more to do. As a matter of fact, the reason I'm back here is to follow up on the issue that took me away in the first place. Is it possible for me to get back to the scene?"

"No problem. Let me move my cruiser so you can get by."

The Highway Patrol had done a great job of clearing out all the vehicles that hadn't been involved in the accident and less than a minute after driving up the ramp John arrived at the accident scene. Yesterday, it had taken him fifteen minutes to travel the same distance.

Even though he had left the area only a few hours earlier, he was still shocked by what he saw. It wasn't something you could get use to. The area was still littered with burned vehicles and he could see bodies everywhere he looked. Rescue workers had removed most of them from the vehicles and laid them on the ground so others could retrieve them for delivery to the morgue. In some cases the cars were so badly mangled and burned that the fire department had had to use power saws and the "jaws of life" to remove doors and frames to get to the victims. Even though he had seen his share of accidents and other tragedies, John felt overwhelmed. And the pungent smell of burned flesh didn't help either. He felt sick to his stomach, but had to go on.

He began the gruesome task of looking at each of the bodies to see if any of them was Dan. Some were burned so badly he wasn't sure he'd recognize Dan if he were one of them, but he had to give it a try. He started at the back of the rubble, near where he was now standing, and moved slowly toward the bodies, stopping briefly at each to examine it. His plan was to check all the bodies that had been removed from the vehicles and then, if he hadn't yet found Dan, to work his way to the front of the column of charred vehicles, looking into each one until he had checked every body and vehicle at the scene. He knew that some bodies had already been removed and delivered to the morgue, and would check there next, if he didn't find Dan here.

It was hard for him to keep ahead of the rescue workers who were removing the bodies. They were now working very quickly, and he had to move just as quickly to stay ahead of them. He rushed from one body to the next.

None appeared to be Dan. When he had examined all of the bodies that were lying on the ground, he began looking into each charred pile of metal. Most were empty, but he knew from speaking with some of the firemen on the scene that they hadn't yet gotten to the cars at the front of the pile. There would be some bodies there, for sure.

As he approached the last few vehicles, he stopped dead in his tracks. The blackened remains of a pickup truck caught his eye. It was only two or three vehicles from the very front of the pile up, which meant it had to have been one of the first vehicles involved in the accident. And although it was badly burned and he couldn't make out the model or year, there was something familiar about it. He could see that a customized tail gate had been added to the truck, and knew that Dan had one just like it. Of course, that didn't mean it was Dan's truck. But if definitely could be. He bypassed the remaining vehicles and went straight for the truck. He knew that every vehicle had been checked and any survivors removed, so if there was anyone left in the truck, he'd be beyond help. His stomach sank at the thought of what he might find, and he took a deep breath as he slowly approached the truck. He made his way to the driver's side and, as he got closer, noticed that the door had been forced open. A good sign, he thought, because they wouldn't have gone to the trouble if the driver were dead. Would they?

He reached the truck and hesitated before leaning into the opening. What he saw as he peered into the cab was shocking but not unexpected. There was nothing left but burned and twisted metal. No cloth on the seat. No material on the dashboard or doors. Everything had gone up in smoke. It looked like a skeleton, just the empty shell of its former self. But to his relief, there were no human remains. Whoever had been driving this truck must have survived and been evacuated with the other victims. He was relieved to not have found a body, but still didn't know if it was Dan's truck. The only way he could determine that now was to see if there was anything left of the license plate. If it were

Dan's truck, and if the plate were recognizable, he'd know one way or the other. Dan, he knew, had one of those "Save Our Seas" specialty plates. It read "Walters."

He headed for the rear of the truck to check it out. The plate was there, but badly charred. Most of the paint was gone, and he couldn't tell if it was a "Save Our Seas" specialty plate or not, but the raised letters of the tag number were still noticeable. He brushed away as much of the charred materials as he could and ran his fingers along the embossed letters. He silently read each letter with his fingers and spelled out "W A L T E R S."

                              ***

It was almost 11:30 by the time John got back to his office, and Becky had just gotten an updated patient list from Tallahassee Memorial. There were seventy six names of accident victims on the list, but Dan Walters wasn't one of them. So next, she contacted the Shriners Hospital in Tampa again. When she had contacted them previously, they didn't yet have a list and weren't able to help her. Now, they said they could fax a list to her within a few minutes, but if she was looking for someone in particular, it'd be faster if she gave them the name. There were only ten seriously burned victims that had been flown there. She told them "Dan Walters."

After a short pause, the person at the other end of the line came back on. "There's no Dan Walters on our list. However, we do have one patient whom we haven't been able to ID. He's a male, approximately forty years old. His clothes and personal possessions were totally destroyed in the fire and he hasn't regained consciousness yet, so he hasn't been able to give us his name. If there's someone who could come down here to try and identify him, we'd appreciate it. Any medical history we can get on him would be helpful."

As soon as Becky had hung up she filled John in on her conversation with the people at Shriners. His first reaction was to jump into his cruiser and drive to Tampa, but that was about two hundred and seventy five miles away, a drive of more than four hours on a good day. Who knows how long it would take today. The entire state had been hit hard by Fay.

He tried to force himself to calm down and think clearly. A drive to Tampa was out of the question. But, if he could get a ride on a helicopter, he'd be there in two hours, even under the current weather conditions. But where would he get a helicopter? All the EVAC helicopters had left the scene, because they'd completed their work and weren't needed any more. The Sheriff's Department had a helicopter it used for traffic enforcement and emergencies, but they probably wouldn't release it to him to be used on a personal mission. And that's what this was, a personal mission. But he decided to speak with the Sheriff anyway. Maybe he'd have some ideas. And he'd have to give Joyce a call to give her an update. He wasn't looking forward to that because he still didn't have anything definite to tell, except that he hadn't found Dan yet.

The Sheriff was sympathetic, but there wasn't anything he could do just then. His one and only chopper had been in the air non-stop since the accident. They only had one pilot, and he was exhausted. The pilot and chopper wouldn't be back in the air until tomorrow

There wasn't anything else John could do right now, except call Joyce

Chapter 9

Jeff Anderson's phone rang at 11:35. His caller ID told him that Fred Campbell was calling. He picked up immediately, knowing that it must be something important for Fred to call him personally, since normal business issues were generally communicated by Fred's staff.

"This is Jeff Anderson speaking. How can I help you?"

"Jeff, Fred Campbell here. How are you today?"

"Great, Fred. And you?"

"I'm fine, Jeff, but I have some things I'd like to discuss with you, if you have a few minutes. It shouldn't take much longer than that."

"Of course, Fred." - Jeff knew better than to say *no, I'm busy* when the Chief Credit Officer wanted to talk with him.

"Jake Hammond and I just met to discuss a couple of concerns relative to our new inventory portfolio. Although there's been an increase in the number of SAUs, right now my immediate concern is with the adequacy of inventory insurance coverage at the dealerships. With Fay battering Florida, we should take a close look at each dealer we have in that state to see if we're OK. You seemed to be in good shape when Jake's folks did their review last year, but they only looked for *evidence* of coverage, and didn't actually verify coverage with the insurance companies. Can you do me a favor and take a quick look at this? I know you're comfortable with the quality of your staff's work, but humor me. Run a check on a sample of dealers and verify their inventory insurance directly with the insurance carriers. I'll be able to sleep better tonight knowing we're covered."

"Not a problem. I'll get right on it, and should be able to get back to you before end of business today."

"Thanks, Jeff. I really appreciate it."

As he hung up the phone, Jeff cursed under his breath. He was already inundated with work and didn't need another stupid wild goose chase. He couldn't imagine why Fred wanted him to personally handle this request. As the division manager, he had a lot more important things to do. But he wasn't ready to cross the CCO. So he sucked it up and headed out to the operations area to begin his task.

***

It was just before noon when the phone rang, and again, Joyce picked it up on the first ring. She'd been holding the phone for hours waiting for the call.

"Hello. This is Joyce Walters."

"Joyce, this is John Forsyth."

"John, I've been waiting for your call. Have you found Dan?"

"Not yet. I went back to the accident scene to look for him and didn't find him there. However, I'm sorry to say that I *did* find his truck. He was definitely involved in the accident. His name hasn't shown up on any hospital lists, but there's one patient at the Shriners Hospital in Tampa who hasn't been identified yet. He's alive, but not conscious."

"Oh my God, NO!" she cried. "I've got to go there."

"Please, Joyce. I know this is difficult, but you must calm down. We have to think this thing through. Tampa is too far away for a drive right now. I'm working on the possibility of getting a lift on a helicopter, but have no idea how long it'll be before that can happen. If I can get down there, I'll be able to see whether or not it's Dan."

"I'm not going to sit here and wait any longer, John. I need to be there to help. If Dan is in the hospital, I want to be there with him. If it's not Dan, I want to help find him. I'm going to head out now. If the highway is passable, I'll be there this evening. The kids can stay here with my parents."

"OK, Joyce, I can't say I blame you. But I'd rather you didn't make this trip alone. Can anyone else come with you?"

"I could ask my dad to come with me, and my mom could stay with the kids. Let me talk with them and I'll call you right back. Where can I reach you?"

"I'm in the office, call me here."

"Thanks, I'll get back to you shortly."

As soon as she hung up the phone, Joyce began to sob loudly. Her mother was at her side and wrapped her arms around her to try to comfort her. "It's OK. It's OK. I'm sure everything will work out. I've been praying for Dan since yesterday."

Joyce's dad had been keeping the kids busy in the den, but they had heard the phone ring and were now in the living room too. The kids began to cry, not because they knew what was going on, but simply because Joyce was crying. There had to be something very wrong, so their emotions took over.

When she saw the kids, Joyce knew she had to be strong for them, and somehow regained her composure. She wrapped her arms around the two of them and hugged them tight. After a few minutes, the crying subsided and she led them to the sofa to explain what she had learned and what she was planning.

"Deputy Forsyth just called. He hasn't found your dad, but he *did* find his truck. There's no question that your dad was involved in the accident on I-10. But we don't know yet if he's been hurt, or if so, how badly. His name hasn't shown up on any hospital lists, but there is one burn victim at the Shriners Hospital who hasn't been identified.

Deputy Forsyth is trying to get down there, but can't get transportation right now. I've decided to head back to Tallahassee. I'm going to leave right away, and with any luck, I'll be there this evening. If John can get to Tampa tonight or tomorrow, I'll try to go along with him."

She turned to face her father. "Dad, I was wondering if you'd mind coming with me to Tallahassee. Mom could stay here with the kids." She turned to face her mother. "Would you mind, mom? I'd really appreciate it. We should be able to make it by nightfall. I don't know exactly where we'll stay tonight, but we'll find something. We'll try my house first. Hopefully we can stay there."

"Of course I don't mind staying with the kids, if that's what you want. But are you sure it's safe to drive back to Tallahassee tonight?"

"I don't know, but I've got to try. I'll be careful and I'll have my cell phone with me so I can keep in touch."

"I'll put a few things together and maybe your mom can pack us a lunch in case we can't find any place to eat later" said her dad. "We can fill up the gas tank on the way out."

Chapter 10

It was unusual for the claims manager to handle such calls, but Customer Service was stumped. Everyone knew that Jane was one of the most knowledgeable people in the company when it came to the new computer systems, and they assumed that this had to be a computer glitch. What else could it be? So they had asked the customer if they could call him back once they "looked into it." That's when they called Jane. It was 4 p.m.

"Jane Donahue," she answered.

"Hi, Jane. This is Frank in Customer Service. Sorry to bother you, but we have a *situation* here, and thought you'd be able to help us out. "

"What is it, Frank?"

"We just got a call from Jeff Anderson at New Commerce Commercial Finance. He asked about coverage that we supposedly provided on some of his customers' inventories. But the thing is, Jane, we haven't been able to find any records of the policies he asked about. We don't know where else to look and thought that maybe you'd have some ideas. Could it be a computer glitch? Maybe a problem from the recent conversion to the new systems that Ping had us put in?"

"I doubt that seriously, Frank. I was involved with the conversion, and everything from the old system was reconciled to the new system. It might be a data entry problem, but that wouldn't be considered a computer glitch. And the reconciliation controls we have surrounding data entry are designed to ensure that everything that's suppose to get entered actually does. Furthermore, any premiums received would've had to have been applied *somewhere,* otherwise we'd have a discrepancy in receipts. So if they're not on the system, we probably haven't received any premiums for them, which likely means we didn't provide coverage. Did you document the information you got from Jeff, like policy numbers, date of issue, etc.? "

"Yeah, we did."

"OK. Why don't you drop off that information and I'll try to look into it as soon as I can. Things are heating up around here, with the first damage reports and claims calls starting to come in. Do you have a phone number for Jeff?"

After jotting down the phone number of Jeff Anderson, Jane hung up the phone, only to have it ring again immediately. It was going to be a long night.

***

In Marietta, Jeff Anderson was getting nervous. All the files he had reviewed looked to be in order, with indications of insurance coverage for customer inventories noted, as required. But when he selected a few for further verification and called the insurance carrier, he wasn't able to get the confirmation of coverage he'd hoped for. Instead, after a few minutes of being on hold, he was asked if they could call him back. Although they hadn't exactly said there was a problem, he sensed something wasn't right. It should've been a routine call that they could respond to immediately. He didn't know if it was just that they were overloaded with claims calls right now, or if it was something more. In any event, not being able to get a quick answer made him nervous.

While waiting for a return call from Great Waters, he decided to have his account managers personally check on their Florida customers. This wasn't something they normally did, but in light of the weather situation and his phone call to Great Waters, he thought it'd be a good idea to get a feel for what was going on. He'd been listening to the news, and it wasn't good. It looked like many areas of Florida were under water. He needed to know just exactly where the dealerships were and what the situation was at each location.

By close of business on Thursday, Jeff Anderson hadn't gotten a return call from Great Waters, and none of his account managers had made contact with any of the Florida customers. He decided to call Fred Campbell to give him an update. Although it was now almost 5:30, he knew Fred would still be in his office. He dialed Fred's number, and the phone was picked up on the first ring.

"Fred Campbell" the voice at the other end said.

"Fred, this is Jeff Anderson. Do you have a few minutes?"

"Sure thing, Jeff, what is it?"

"After we spoke this morning I reviewed our procedures and looked at some files to see if they contained evidence of insurance. They all did. But when I tried to verify coverage on some of the Florida dealerships, I wasn't able to get information from the insurance carrier, Great Waters Insurance Group in Milwaukee. They didn't say there was a problem, but they also didn't verify coverage. They said they'd get back to me later today, but I haven't heard from them yet. I don't know if it's something worth worrying about or not. I know they must be swamped with calls right now because of Fay, but it should've been a simple task to check a few policies, and I got the distinct impression that they *did* check, because I was on hold for a while before they said they'd have to call me back."

"I agree with you, Jeff, it does sound a bit strange. Let's give them till mid-morning tomorrow. If you haven't heard back from them by then, let me know. I know their CEO, Doug Armstrong. I'm sure if I give him a call he can help us out."

"OK. Thanks Fred. I'll call you back by 10 a.m. tomorrow, one way or the other."

After hanging up the phone Fred dialed Jake's number. He knew Jake would still be in his office because he never left before 6:30.

Jake was in his office with Joe Nash, discussing the review that he assumed would be taking place in a couple of weeks. Joe had reviewed the procedures that were used last year, and also had taken a look at the work papers to refresh his memory. Then he customized the procedures to ensure that the upcoming review would concentrate on the areas Jake and Fred were most concerned with. When the phone rang Jake saw that Fred was at the other end of the line and picked up immediately.

"Hi Fred, what can I do for you?"

"I just spoke with Jeff Anderson and we're both a little concerned over something. Do you have a couple of minutes to discuss it?"

"Sure. I'm here with Joe Nash going over our procedures for the review we discussed. Do you want me to come up there?"

"No. I'll come down there. Joe should probably hear this too. I'll be there in a couple of minutes."

"OK. See you then."

Jake hung up the receiver and filled Joe in on the short discussion. It seemed clear that something new must have come up. Why else would Fred want to come down to the tenth floor at this time of the afternoon? They didn't have to wait long to find out. Within ten minutes Fred was knocking at Jake's door.

"Come on in, Fred. Have a seat. You know Joe Nash?"

"Sure, hello Joe."

"Hello Fred, nice to see you again."

"So, Fred, what brings you down here at this time of day?"

"My discussion with Jeff Anderson left me a bit concerned. Now, I'm not sure we should wait until the Audit Committee meeting on Tuesday to get approval for a special review in Marietta. After I left you this morning I asked Jeff to take a look at some of our inventory finance files and, on a sample basis, verify insurance coverage on the inventories. He called me just a while ago to say that all the files looked good, and all had evidence of insurance. However, when he selected a sample of files and tried to verify insurance coverage with the carrier, he wasn't able to get any information right away. Instead, they said they'd get back to him by end of day, but haven't yet."

"Do you think that's unusual considering the number of claims they must be getting right now?"

"At first I thought maybe that was it, but Jeff said they kept him on hold while they checked their records, and then came back and asked if they could get back to him. It sounds to me like they looked in their files and didn't find anything. If they were just too busy to look, they would've said that right up front, don't you think?"

"I would think so, but who knows. What do you want to do?"

"At this point, I think we shouldn't wait until the Audit Committee meeting on Tuesday to get approval for a special review. If you agree, I'll contact Deb Cutter and Tom D'Angelo as soon as I can to discuss this situation and get them to sign off on the review. Hopefully I can get to them tonight, but if not, I'll be sure to touch base with them first thing in the morning. How soon could you be ready to begin the review?"

"We've got everything ready now. All I have to do is pull a few staff members off of other projects and have them make travel arrangements. If we can get flights out, we can probably be there on Sunday evening and begin our review on Monday morning."

"That sounds good to me. I told Jeff that if he hasn't heard from Great Waters by mid morning tomorrow, I'll give their CEO a call. I've known Doug for a while and I'm sure he'll do everything he can to help us out. In the meantime, I think you should go ahead and make your travel arrangements. I'm sure Deb and Tom will agree to the review, and in the event they don't, you can always cancel the flights and use the credits some other time."

"I'll do that, Fred. Let me know as soon as you've talked with Deb and Tom."

As soon as Fred left, Jake and Joe began reviewing current projects and staff availability. Joe would probably head up the field work, but he'd need at least three staff people to help him. Everyone was in the process of doing their own reviews, and many were already out of town. The selected staff members would need to be contacted as soon as possible so they could adjust their travel arrangements. Some would probably go directly from their current assignments to Atlanta, which would be easier for them than coming back to Maine and then going down to Atlanta.

After a short discussion about each staff member's strengths, they settled on Sue Richards, Chuck Lewis and Jason French. They were the most senior staff members and had all been involved in last year's review in Marietta. They were familiar with the portfolio, and would be best able to hit the ground running. Joe left Jake's office and began the process of contacting each of the selected staff members. Contacting them would be the easy part, of course. The real challenge was going to be coordinating travel arrangements. But New Commerce had a contract with an outside travel agency and it would be their job to get everyone to Atlanta from wherever they currently were, and within a reasonable time of each other. Joe would call the agency to tell them to expect the calls from the other three team members.

As soon as Fred got back to the twenty-fifth floor he went directly to Tom D'Angelo's office. Tom had a couple of people in his office with him, but Fred told Tom's assistant he needed to speak with Tom as soon as possible so she buzzed him and relayed the message. Within minutes Tom and Fred were in a private conference room discussing the situation in Marietta.

"Tom, sorry I interrupted your meeting, but I think you and I need to talk with Deb about a rather pressing issue."

"No problem, Fred. I was just going over some last minute details with the staff in preparation for my meeting with the financial analysts in New York on Monday. I've got plenty of time to finish that up. Tell me what's on your mind."

Fred spent the next ten minutes giving Tom an update on what had transpired in the past two days. When he finished, Tom agreed that they should speak with Deb to get her buy-in on the review and together they walked the few steps down the hall to Deb's office.

Although it was just a few steps away from Tom's office, there was little resemblance between Deb Cutter's office and his own. Tom's was much like Fred's and Jake's. But Deb's was almost twice the size of those, and furnished much more lavishly. When she took over as CEO she had all the existing furniture and drapes removed. Her office was now much more feminine. Light colored floral prints adorned the windows. French provincial style furniture with light fabrics was scattered around the room. All of the wood, including her desk, was now a light cream with speckles. Many of the items were antiques, and very pricy. She had spared no expense in redoing her office, and had made certain no one would mistake it for a *man's* office.

Deb's assistant asked them to wait a moment while she checked to see if "Miss Cutter" could see them now. It didn't matter to her that Tom and Fred were members of the Executive Committee and had indicated they needed to see her boss right away. It was her job to run interference for the boss, and she did her job quite well. She knocked on the large door behind her desk and opened it just enough to slide through, but not enough for anyone to see inside. She disappeared inside, and less than a minute later returned to say "Miss Cutter will be with you in just a moment. Please take a seat."

Tom and Fred were pretty certain there was no one in Deb's office with her, and knew this was her way of saying "I'm the boss. My time is more valuable than yours. I'll get to you when I'm ready." She always took every opportunity to send that message, and this time was no different. They gave each other a knowing look and took a seat, as they'd been told to. About five minutes later Deb Cutter came out of her office to greet them.

"Tom, Fred. Hello. Please come in. I'm sorry to have kept you waiting. I was in the middle of something I needed to finish up." She motioned to a couple of seats in front of her desk, clearly suggesting they use them. She, herself, sat behind her desk. She had never mastered the art of putting her company at ease as others did, by either sitting around a small table, or taking a seat facing them, in front of her desk. She preferred to have a "barrier" between herself and her subordinates. It wasn't something that went unnoticed.

Tom took the lead. "The reason we're here, Deb, is because we believe we have a situation that requires immediate attention by Jake Hammond and his staff. We'd planned to discuss it at Tuesday's Audit Committee meeting, but now feel it can't wait that long. We're concerned with the inventory portfolio in Marietta. As you may recall, Jake completed a review there last year and isn't scheduled to do one this year, based on the results of the risk assessment process. However, with tropical storm Fay hitting the entire state of Florida, Fred wanted to make sure our dealer inventories there were adequately covered by insurance."

Now Fred took over the discussion. "The short version is that we've been unable to verify insurance coverage for some dealers. I'm not saying it doesn't exist, but the insurance company hasn't been able to give us any assurances yet. They're still looking into it. Because I have other concerns, especially with SAU's, I'd like to have Jake's folks go down there as soon as possible to begin a special review. Tom, Jake and I are in agreement on this, and if you agree, we can have a review started on Monday."

Deb stood up and stared out her window for a moment, contemplating the request she had just received. When she turned toward Tom and Fred, they recognized the look on her face. It was the same one she always had when she was about to argue *against* something. So they braced themselves for what was coming.

"I don't get it," she said in a rather harsh tone. "You come in here with this request for a "special review" making it sound like there's an emergency. Yet, you have nothing specific to tell me about what, exactly, the problem is. An increase in items sold and unpaid isn't anything to get overly excited about, at least not until there's a clear trend of significant increases. And just because you haven't been able to get *immediate* verification that our dealers' inventories are adequately insured doesn't mean they aren't. Why couldn't this wait until Tuesday?"

Although Deb Cutter had been Chief Operating Officer before becoming CEO, her rise to the top had been quick. She was politically astute, and had clawed her way up, in spite of her limited field experience. She had no real financial background, and had never been a credit officer. She *did* have a fairly good understanding of how the divisions operated, having spent a few years at one, but for the most part, what she knew about commercial finance came from books. Many people at New Commerce wondered how she rose so quickly. Tom was not one of them. He knew Deb's political strengths and also knew about her relationship with the recently retired CEO. And while he didn't have a great deal of respect for her knowledge of the industry, he had to respect her cunning and political genius. And so far, her new approach had been working, - or so it seemed.

Fred responded to her question. "Because of my concerns, I feel strongly that we need to do this review. And while we could wait until Tuesday, I don't think we need to.

Other than the three of us, there's only one other member that the Committee would look to for advice, and that's Dave Banner, our CIO. And we know Dave isn't going to have any objections. He always goes along with anything that doesn't negatively impact Information Systems. So, the three of us are really the ones to decide, and I'd like Jake to get started as soon as possible.

"My preference would be to wait and see what you hear from the insurance company. We may be spending a lot of money sending a team to Marietta unnecessarily. But if you feel that strongly about it, go ahead. However, I still want to discuss this at Audit Committee. And what I'd like from Jake at that time is a rundown of how this special review will impact his annual schedule, specifically, what reviews, if any, will have to be postponed until next year. And I'd also like an estimate of what this special review is going to cost us."

"No problem" said Fred. "We'll make sure to have that ready on Tuesday. Thanks for your support. We'll get Jake and his folks on this right away."

They returned to Tom's office to recap, and agreed that Fred would inform Jake, both of the go-ahead, and Deb's request for more information on Tuesday. Fred made the call to Jake a little after seven.

* * *

The information Frank had dropped off regarding the New Commerce customers was still on the corner of Jane's desk. She glanced at it several times during the day, but hadn't had a chance to actually pick it up and look at it. New Commerce was a good customer, and she knew she should look into the issue as soon as she could so she decided this was as good a time as any. She picked up the documents and began her research. The first thing she noticed was the sequence of some of the policy numbers on the paper. Strangely, the higher ones were consecutively numbered, with no breaks. That was highly suspicious, since that meant they had all been opened at the same time, or close together, without interruption, and before any policies could be written for other customers. The other thing she noticed was the policy numbers themselves. At Great Waters, numbers were assigned by type of coverage, i.e., life, property, casualty, etc. And although the numbers on the page before her had a correct prefix, she knew that some of the numbers themselves were beyond the range of currently assigned numbers. It was no wonder Customer Service couldn't find those in the system. They hadn't been issued yet.

Before doing anything else, Jane decided to check a few things. She wanted to make sure the policy numbers she had before her hadn't been transposed, or the incorrect prefix used. She logged onto the system, accessed the current data base, and began to work on each possibility. She checked coverage types, looking to see if the numbers before her existed in one of the other coverage types. Then she tried various numerical combinations to see if someone had transposed the numbers. Nothing she tried showed the numbers in question. Finally, she did a search on customer name, but again found nothing. As a last resort, she decided to access the closed accounts data base. Although all accounts, both active and closed, were previously kept on one data base, the new system that Ping had installed was designed to save time and space. Now, expired or closed policies were removed from the active data base, and could only be accessed by logging onto a different data base.

It took her a couple of seconds to get in, but she quickly found a few of the policy numbers there. The ones she found had all elapsed. For some reason, the customer had not renewed them. The higher numbered policies, of course, weren't there. She'd have to call Jeff Anderson, at New Commerce, first thing in the morning.

Chapter 11

Within an hour of speaking with John Forsyth, Joyce was on the road heading to Tallahassee, her dad in the passenger seat beside her. They'd been traveling for about six hours now, and might have been in Tallahassee an hour ago if she'd taken routes 84 and 61, as she often did. But today, she took I-75 right down to I-10, the same route she'd taken the previous day, but in reverse. She and Dan had agreed when planning their evacuation, that it'd be better to add the extra miles to the trip than to risk the back roads. She saw no reason to do anything differently on the way back.

They were heading west on I-10 and were now just a few miles east of the city. It was still raining here and traffic was moving slowly, but at least it was moving. They hadn't seen any cars in the east bound lanes since the last exit, so she assumed that section of the highway must still be closed. Tears came to her eyes as she pictured the burned remains of Dan's truck, and wondered again what had become of him. She wiped her eyes with the sleeve of her blouse and tried to concentrate on the traffic. Her exit would be coming up soon and she didn't want to miss it. They didn't have much time to spare. It was almost seven and she wanted to get home and check out the house to see if they'd be able to stay there tonight and then touch base again with John Forsyth.

***

Sue Richards was in Seattle, Chuck Lewis was in Detroit, and Jason French was at the company headquarters in Augusta, but they all got the news within a few minutes of each other. They were expected to be in Atlanta by late afternoon or early evening on Sunday. Joe had given them the name of a specific agent at the travel agency who was expecting their call. Sue and Chuck were told to fly out from their current locations rather than return to Maine, so they'd have time to start winding down, and possibly even wrap up, their current assignments. The travel agent would arrange flights for everyone so that they'd all get to Atlanta within a reasonable time of each other. They'd meet at the airport, Joe would pick up the rental car, and they'd proceed to the hotel. Rooms had already been reserved for each of them. They'd meet for dinner and then spend the evening going over the audit plans.

By seven thirty, all travel arrangements were finalized. Existing flights for Sue and Chuck had been canceled and new flights booked for everyone. Calls had been made to friends and family members to alert them to the new plans.

***

In Milwaukee, everyone in Claims was answering phones, including management. Second and third shift workers had been called-in early and first shift workers were staying late. Extra phone lines had been set up and calls were coming in fast and furious. Initial verification of coverage was done on the spot, through the new systems and real-time databases which allowed searches by policy numbers, customer names, or customer addresses. If customer records were found, operators would key in the required code and the claim would be sent to the appropriate adjuster's queue in the system. Those were the easy calls because operators could assure the customer that the claim had been assigned to an adjuster who'd be in touch with them soon. But, if records couldn't be found, the caller was told he'd have to either provide additional information or some form of evidence of coverage. Those calls seldom ended on a friendly note, and workers often were verbally abused by the callers. Fortunately, there hadn't been many of those calls today - at least not yet.

At around six o'clock, Jane had begun letting the staff take short dinner breaks, in small groups. Breaks were limited to thirty minutes to ensure everyone could get something to eat while minimizing disruptions to customer service. By 6:30 Jane decided to take a break herself, but not for dinner. She wanted to run some statistical analyses on calls received so far.

One of the nice features of the new system was that most everything was available in real-time, and if you knew how, you could get statistics on just about anything. She went back to her office and sat at her computer. She keyed in a few commands, and within minutes had a printout that showed her the number of claims calls received in the past twenty four hours, broken down by type of claim and geographic location. The report also showed how many calls resulted in verification of policies. In ninety five percent of them, the existence of policies had been verified and the claim sent to the adjusters. The next step on these was the site visit to determine if the specific damage or claim was covered by the policy. Just having a policy didn't automatically ensure payment. Damage could easily be something not covered by the specific policy.

Adjusters had also been held over the end of their shifts and were now beginning to review the records forwarded to them. Each adjuster was sent only the type of claims he specialized in. But their territories were large, and each was busy breaking out the claims by geographic location so they could begin to make travel plans. None of the current claims were from the local area, so reservations were needed for flights, hotels and car rentals. Although there were some adjusters in the field, they'd need reinforcements for this one.

Jane was still crunching numbers when her phone rang. It wasn't a number that customers had access to, but her friends and family knew it and often called her at the office. This time though, the one long ring told her it was an internal call rather than an outside call, which would have caused two short rings. She checked the caller ID and saw Al Goff's name and number. Al was the director of claims, to whom both Jane and Peter reported, along with Harry Strong, Supervising Claims Adjuster.

"Hi Jane. It's Al. I wanted to check in to see how things are going down there. Doug would like an update on volumes. Is that something you can give me quickly? I'd like to get back to him ASAP."

"As a matter of fact, Al, I can. The new system is great and I just sat down a few minutes ago to retrieve that information. Would you like me to bring up some reports?"

"That'd be great. Can you come up right now?"

"No problem, I'll be right there."

She hung up the phone, gathered her print-outs, and headed for the seventh floor. As she waited for the elevator she thought again how strange it seemed that Al's office was on the seventh floor when all his direct reports were on five. Just as well, she figured. If he were on five he'd surely be in their faces more often. As it was, they seldom saw him down there. When he *did* need to see them, they were called to his office.

She got off the elevator and turned right toward Al's office, just a few doors down. The door was open when she got there, but she knocked anyway before going in. She'd been there often, and found it to be quite comfortable. It was larger than either her office or Peter's, which was to be expected of course. But the furniture was a lot nicer too. Being a director has its perks. She hoped an office like this was in *her* future. She had earned it, both because of her years of dedicated service and the significant contribution she had made to the success of the recent system conversion.

She knew that without her efforts, the conversion could have been a disaster.

"Come on in and take a seat, Jane. What do you have for me?"

She looked at the diminutive man behind the large desk and had to hold back a laugh. It was the way she always felt when she saw him. Al was barely 5'5" and probably didn't weigh more than 125 pounds. He was in his early fifties, but not aging gracefully. He used the type of "comb-over" that so many men use to try to hide the fact they're going bald, but he wasn't any more successful than the others. Except for the "comb-over" and the wrinkled skin, he might have been mistaken for a fourteen year old.

She took a seat and began. "In the past twenty four hours, we've received almost three thousand calls. We have twenty phone lines manned, and we're averaging one hundred twenty calls per hour. The average call length is ten minutes. Of those calls received, ninety-five percent were found to have valid policies in effect and the claims were forwarded to the adjusters for follow up. If calls continue to come in at this rate, and if claims are found to be covered under policies, this could be one of our biggest hits in a while.

"That's what we were afraid of. Hurricane season has barely begun, but it looks like it could be a bad one. Our new owners will not be happy if payouts exceed plan."

"I know, but there's not much we can do about it."

"Thanks, Jane. Leave the reports here with me. I'll call you if I need anything further. In the meantime, be sure that nothing gets through to the adjusters unless you're absolutely positive valid policies exist."

He dismissed her with a nod, and she left barely a few minutes after having arrived. As soon as she was out the door, he picked up the phone and dialed "3638."

"This is Harry Strong. How can I help you?" the voice at the other end said.

"Harry, this is Al Goff. Can you come to my office for a minute?"

"No problem. I'll be right there." A few minutes later Harry was sitting across the desk from Al.

"I want to talk to you about the claims that have come in over the past twenty four hours. Jane tells me her crew has answered almost three thousand calls, about ninety-five percent of which had valid polices and were forwarded to your adjusters. Does that sound about right to you?"

"Sure does. My folks are splitting them up by geographic location and should be able to start their field work in the morning, or on Saturday at the latest, depending upon how travel arrangements go."

"That's good, Harry. Nice work. But the thing is, if claims keep coming in at the current pace, payouts resulting from Fay could create the single largest financial hit we've had in a while. And senior management and the new owners are concerned. We've got less money budgeted this year than normal, so we could miss our plan."

"I know, Al. I was concerned with the new budget right from the beginning. You know that. I stood right here in your office making a fuss over it."

"Yeah, I know. I know. But it was beyond my ability to change. Ping Industries set the figure."

"What the hell do they know, Al? We're the first U.S. insurance company they've owned."

"You're preaching to the choir, Harry. There's nothing we can do about the budget now. But what we *have* to do is make sure we make plan. You know as well as I do that missing plan isn't an option. If we don't make it, Ping will eliminate bonuses and probably chop off a few heads, just to make a point. And who do you think will be the first ones to go?"

"You mean *after* Doug Armstrong?"

"Yeah, after Doug."

"Well I guess maybe those who were responsible for missing the plan."

"That's right. And that would be the people who paid out the claims, wouldn't it? In other words, you and me."

"I hadn't thought of it that way. We never had this kind of an issue before."

"That's right, but things are different now. And we need to play by the new rules or get out. Do you understand what I'm saying here, Harry?"

"I'm not sure. What are the new rules?"

"The new rules are, you do whatever it takes to make plan."

"I'm not sure what you and I can do to ensure the company makes plan."

"Really? Think about it for a minute. What is it that's within your power to control?"

"Are you implying that we shouldn't pay the claims?"

"I never said that, did I?"

"No, but that seems to be the message. If payouts are too high, those who paid the claims may be held responsible."

"That's true enough. But I didn't give you any specific instructions related to your work as a claims adjuster. I was just having a friendly discussion about the forecast and how it was going to be a tough year. We all need to keep our eyes and ears open for ways to make plan, that's all I'm saying."

"OK, right. I understand."

"Well then, thanks for stopping by, Harry. You'll keep me posted on how your adjusters are doing, won't you?"

"Oh yeah. You can count on it."

The meeting between Al Goff and Harry Strong which took place on the evening of Thursday, August 14, 2008, lasted only a few minutes, but would have a lasting impact on how business was conducted at Great Waters

Insurance Group, a wholly owned subsidiary of Ping Industries.

***

It was still raining lightly, but the water was beginning to recede and many of the roads in Tallahassee were now passable. Joyce and her dad pulled up in front of the large white house at about 7:30 p.m. They had come directly here, with no stops except for gas and to use the rest rooms. They had eaten on the go, with each taking a turn at driving while the other downed a sandwich and soft drink. It was a long ride, but Joyce wasn't about to sit around in Decatur waiting for news of Dan. She had to be here to do whatever she could to find him. She pulled into the driveway and turned off the engine. Before getting out of the car she took out her cell phone and called her mom to let her know they had arrived.

"Hi mom, it's me. We're here at my house, but haven't gone in yet. I just pulled into the driveway. We're going to check out the inside to see if there's any damage and decide whether or not we can stay here tonight. I'll call you again in a little while to let you know where we'll be spending the night. How are the kids?"

"The kids are just fine dear. Don't worry about them. They send their love. Please let us know as soon as you have any news on Dan."

"We will, mom."

"Tell your dad I love him."

"I will. Talk to you later."

"Bye."

She pressed the call end key and turned to her dad. "Mom says to tell you she loves you, dad."

"Thanks, hon."

The water on the street was below curb level now, but the street itself still had about an inch or so on it. Thankfully, the driveway was slightly sloped and no longer under water. They couldn't go in by the garage, because she knew the door opener was unplugged and the door was locked. The front door was the only entrance they could use, unless they wanted to go around back to the kitchen door. They opted for the front door, which was a lot closer, and the logical choice.

They had to make their way up the walk in the rain. Luckily, Joyce had the key out and ready by the time they got to the door, so she didn't have to fumble for it. She inserted it into the first lock and turned it. That released the dead bolt. Next, she repeated the process on the keyhole of the door handle itself and pushed the door open. She didn't know what she'd see when she got inside, but said a silent prayer that everything would be undamaged. She stepped into the foyer, with her father right behind her. Although it was still light out, the clouds and rain made everything seem dark and dreary outside, and the shutters made everything dark inside. The first thing she did was flip the light switch on the left side of the doorway. But nothing happened. Either the electricity was out in the neighborhood or the circuit breakers had been tripped. Whichever it was, it wasn't a good sign. She gave her dad a questioning look, as if to say "What do we do now?"

"Let's not panic. It's probably the circuit breakers. Let's go to the garage and I'll check it out."

Joyce led her dad along the right side of the foyer, past the living room and den, and into the kitchen. They'd need a flashlight, so she felt her way to the "junk" drawer where they kept the flashlight, and just about everything else they didn't have a specific place for. She pulled out the flashlight and handed it to her father. Then she opened the door that led from the kitchen to the garage and they both went in. As they did, she flipped the light switch, but nothing happened. That light was out too.

Bob scanned the garage with the beam of the flashlight and found the electrical box, which was on the rear wall of the first stall. This part of the garage was empty so it was easy to get to. He opened the cover and saw that almost all of the circuits had, indeed, been tripped, just as he suspected. He reset each of them, and one by one, the lights came back on. There must have been a considerable amount of water in the house to trip those breakers, but at least the lights worked now. That was good, because he knew that any service that might have been needed from the utility company would have been very slow in coming.

With the garage lights on, they made their way back into the kitchen and flipped the light switch there. Those lights went on as well. And now, for the first time since arriving, they had a chance to take a look around. The first thing they noticed was the smell. Although they didn't need the lights to smell the dampness, and should've noticed it earlier, they'd probably been too pre-occupied with getting the lights on. They both looked down at the same time, expecting to see the floor covered with water. But it wasn't. The ceramic tile was damp, but looked more like it was drying after having been washed, rather than the survivor of a flood. As they headed back to the foyer they noticed that the ceramic tiles there were also "damp." Then they turned into the living room, which was carpeted.

As soon as she walked into the room Joyce knew there was still a fair amount of water under the carpet. It wasn't noticeable to the eye, but the "squishing" noise that each step caused was unmistakable. There was a great deal of water left on the floor, and there was probably as much in each of the other rooms. She knew it would have to be taken care of very soon to avoid the need to replace the carpeting throughout the entire house. They checked out each of the other rooms, one at a time, and except for the water, there didn't seem to be any other damage. From the water marks on the furniture it appeared that the water level inside the house had reached about eight or ten inches, but the furniture was in-tact. Nothing that had been raised off the floor was damaged. It looked like they had missed the bullet on this one. Even if they had to eventually replace the carpeting, it would be a relatively small price to pay. She knew it could have been much worse.

She tried the house phone and was glad to hear a dial tone. She dialed her mother's number to let her know they'd be spending the night here. It was better than trying to find a hotel room. The beds were dry. That was the important thing. They could put up with the soggy carpets, which were the least of her worries right now.

After she hung up, Joyce dialed the number of the Leon County Sheriff's office.

"Leon County Sheriff's Office, how may I help you?"

"Hello. This is Joyce Walters calling. Can you tell me if John Forsyth is there, please?"

"Hello Mrs. Walters. This is Becky. I'm sorry, but John isn't in the office right now. He went to his house to check on things there and try to get a little rest. Would you like me to try to reach him for you?"

"No thanks, Becky. I have his number and I'll call him there. But in case I miss him and he returns to the office before I get to talk to him, would you tell him I'm here in Tallahassee, and my dad and I are staying at my house tonight. He can reach me here or on my cell phone. Let me give you both numbers."

She read off the numbers slowly so Becky could get them, and then asked her to read them back. Of course, Becky got them right. Her job required that kind of attention to details. Joyce knew that, but didn't want to take any chances. She needed to speak with John as soon as possible. After hanging up, she dialed John's home number.

The phone rang a few times, and she was about to hang up when she heard his voice at the other end.

"Hello."

"Hello, is this John?"

"Yes, who's this?"

"It's Joyce Walters. I'm sorry to bother you, but I'm glad I was able to reach you tonight."

"Where are you, Joyce?"

"My dad and I just arrive at my house. The damage doesn't seem too bad so we're going to spend the night here. I just wanted to touch base with you to see if you have anything new to tell me."

"Sorry, Joyce, I don't. There wasn't anything more I could do at the office so I decided to come check things out here at my house and try to get a little sleep. It's been a while since I've had any. Luckily, my house is in pretty good shape too. I left word at the office that they should call me here if anything new develops. If I hear from them, I'll give you a call right away."

"Thanks, John. That would be great. What's on for tomorrow? Have you been able to figure out a way to get down to Tampa?"

"Not yet. I won't know anything until the morning. There's no way to get there tonight, but I may be able to arrange something for tomorrow. I'm still working on it."

"I need to get down there, John. I have to know if it's Dan. If there's any way I can hitch a ride with you, I'd appreciate it. Otherwise, I'm going to head out by car in the morning.

John knew that a car trip wasn't a good idea. The roads south of Tallahassee could still be a problem and the trip could take several hours. And although he didn't want to tell her, the odds that Dan was the unnamed accident victim at the Shriners Hospital were slim.

"Listen, Joyce. The best thing we can do tonight is to try to get some sleep. I'll check back with you first thing in the morning and we can discuss our next step. There really isn't anything else we can do right now. We're both too tired to try to make it to Tampa tonight, even if the roads are passable. After getting some sleep we'll be able to make a logical decision and we'll go from there. What do you say?"

"I guess you're right, John. But I don't think I'll be able to get any sleep, not knowing what's happened to Dan. You promise to call me first thing in the morning?"

"I promise."

They hung up, and Joyce filled her dad in on the conversation. He agreed with John's assessment. They unpacked the few things they'd brought with them, and tried to settle in for the night, but they both knew they wouldn't be getting much sleep.

Chapter 12

Friday, August 15, 2008

Jane Donahue was back at her desk at 6 a.m. Things had slowed down a bit last night after nine and she had let the day shift go home to get some rest. She left shortly after midnight, and got a few hours sleep before getting up at 4:30 to shower and grab a bite to eat. She always liked to get in early, and today she wanted to get an earlier start than normal. She had a lot to do before the day shift came back at 8:30 a.m.

She keyed the commands into the system and reviewed the data on-line while the report was printing. So far they had taken in almost five thousand calls, and policies were verified for about ninety five percent of them. When the reports were finished printing she put them in an interoffice envelope addressed to Al Goff. She knew the morning pickup was at about eight, so there wasn't any need to hand deliver the reports. Al probably wouldn't be in before eight anyway. Then she reviewed the phone messages and emails from the previous day and stacked them in order of importance. She'd try to get to at least the most important ones at some point during the day. On top of the stack, she placed a reminder to herself to call Jeff Anderson at New Commerce. She'd wait until about eight thirty to do that one because she wanted to give him a chance to settle in before hitting him with the news.

A couple of hours later she was still working through her emails when the first members of the day shift began to trickle in. It wasn't yet eight thirty, but most of them came in at around eight or eight fifteen so they could get a coffee and settle in before manning the phones. She hadn't realized it was so late. She finished the message she was typing and decided to start concentrating on the upcoming call to Jeff. She knew it would have to be handled diplomatically, and it wasn't going to be easy. She picked up the phone and dialed the number Frank had given her the previous day and after a couple of rings someone picked up at the other end of the line.

"Good morning. This is Jeff Anderson. How can I help you?"

"Good morning Jeff. This is Jane Donahue, from Great Waters Insurance Group. How are you today?"

"To be honest Jane, I'm a bit concerned. I started getting nervous when I couldn't get a verification of policies for some of my customers yesterday. I hope you have good news for me."

"When Frank took your call, he couldn't find some of the policy numbers on our system. He thought maybe it was a computer glitch as a result of our recent conversion to a new system, and that's why he asked if he could call you back. Since I was involved in the conversion, he asked me to look into it. I'm sorry I wasn't able to get back to you yesterday, but we're being hit hard with damage claims from Fay. We've been getting about 120 calls per hour and I've been lending a hand answering them."

"That's OK. I appreciate your call this morning. As you might imagine, though, things are getting a little tense at this end. Do you have the verifications I was looking for?"

"Let me go over that with you right now, if you have a few minutes. Is this a good time?"

"Absolutely! I really need to put this to bed as soon as I can."

"OK. First, let me verify the data you gave Frank yesterday. I want to make sure he took it all down correctly."

They spent the next few minutes double checking the policy numbers Frank had recorded. They were all correctly written down, as she knew they would be. But it was always best to check such things before getting people needlessly excited. Now she'd have to proceed with the bad news.

"I did some research on this myself last night. What I found was that some of the numbers you've given us are for policies which expired within the past year or two. I don't have any data which indicates the policies were renewed, and no premiums have been received on those. The other numbers were in a range that hasn't yet been issued. In other words, no policies were ever written with those account numbers."

"Wait a minute" interrupted Jeff. "What are you saying here? Are you telling me our customers aren't covered?"

"What I'm saying is that, right now, the policy numbers you gave us aren't currently active. Is there any way that you might have transposed the numbers or gotten the wrong information from your own files?"

"I thought about that after Frank said he'd have to get back to me. I went back into our files and double checked and found that the information I gave you is what we have on file. Are you positive the records couldn't have been lost during your system conversion?"

"Jeff, I was personally involved in every aspect of that conversion. We reconciled every file from the old system to the new; not only records counts, but number of customers, dollar values of coverage, and monthly premium payments. Everything was in balance at conversion."

"Well, Jane, my records show that we have coverage and that we've been sending premium payments to you. So, where do we go from here?"

"Unfortunately, Jeff, there isn't much I can do from this end without additional data. We don't have any unapplied premiums at this time. You'd need to provide proof of coverage and of premium payments before I can do anything else. You should be able to track that stuff from your end."

"As a matter of fact, we have our Security and Compliance Group coming in on Monday. I'll spend some time with them explaining our problem and see what they can do for me."

"That's a good idea, Jeff. Let me know if you come up with any additional data that I can use to help you out."

They agreed to touch base again on Monday, and ended the call. Jane went back to answering emails in the hope of catching up before the having to go out and help with the phones again. Jeff decided to give Fred Campbell another call.

***

She was happy it was Friday. Deb's week had been unbelievable. First, Tom D'Angelo and Fred Campbell asked if they could have Jake Hammond do a special review of the new inventory finance portfolios. Then the stock market took a dive, and New Commerce stock dropped along with most everyone else's. Some analysts were starting to call it the "economic crisis of 2008." Individually, either of the issues could be bad news for her, but together, they were like converging storms, and it was starting to look like she was going to get caught right in the middle of them. Although some stocks had taken a few hits in the spring when the sub-prime mortgage fiasco first came to light, companies like New Commerce that weren't involved with those mortgages had, at first, remained relatively unscathed. Deb had felt certain that the crisis wouldn't affect New Commerce, but it was starting to look like she'd been wrong.

As interest rates on adjustable mortgages began to move upward, more and more homeowners were unable to make their monthly payments and banks began to reposes houses, which in many cases had lost value. Financial institutions and investors who had previously been buying the mortgages from the banks stopped doing so. Large banks began to talk about going under. Losses were starting to pile up, with the largest institutions losing billions. Fannie Mae and Freddie Mac, the government backed agencies which were the two primary institutions buying mortgage backed securities, showed signs of instability, and the government was beginning to talk about bailouts.

Credit was becoming increasingly more difficult to obtain, not just for consumers, but for businesses too. The resulting slowdown in the economy was starting to have a two-fold impact on New Commerce. First, it was getting more difficult to raise capital to fund loans. Unlike banks, New Commerce did not take in deposits that could be used for that purpose. They had to raise the capital in the market at the best rates possible, and then use the funds to originate loans at higher rates. The difference in the rates, called the spread, was how they made a profit. And second, their customers were beginning to lose sales, resulting in their inability to make loan payments to New Commerce, hence, the increase in delinquencies, non performing assets, and items sold and unpaid.

Since Deb took the reins a few years ago, earnings had steadily improved. The last two years were record breakers, the best in the company's history. But it was beginning to look like 2008 would be a tough one. That's why she'd put so much pressure on the division managers to increase originations. The new product lines should help bring up volumes, but she needed more loans across the board, in all portfolios. She'd worry about selling them in the secondary market later. Maybe by the fourth quarter investors would be willing to buy commercial loans again.

A few minutes after the market opened, New Commerce stock dropped another two points.

***

Fred Campbell hung up the receiver. His conversation with Jeff Anderson hadn't been encouraging. They spent the last fifteen minutes discussing the insurance situation, and he was more concerned than ever. He decided to go down to the tenth floor to see Jake and give him the latest news. Joe Nash and Jason French were in Jake's office discussing the upcoming review in Marietta when Fred arrived. The door was open so he stuck his head in and waited for Jake to see him, which happened immediately. Jake's desk faced the doorway, and it was impossible to miss anyone standing there. He motioned to Fred to come in.

"Hi Fred, come on it. You've met Joe Nash, and this is Jason French. We were just discussing the review we'll be starting on Monday. What can we do for you today?"

"I just got off the phone with Jeff Anderson, in Marietta. I thought I'd fill you in on the latest developments, if you have a couple of minutes."

"Sure. Do you mind if Joe and Jason sit in on this? They'll be doing much of the field work, and could probably benefit from hearing this.

"No problem. Here's the situation. At my request, Jeff was doing some initial leg work to determine if our Florida dealers have adequate inventory insurance. He looked at a significant number of files and found evidence of coverage in each and every one. But, when he tried to verify coverage with Great Waters, he ran into a problem. Their customer service people couldn't seem to find the policies on their data base. They asked if they could get back to him after checking something out. They didn't call him back yesterday, which made us both a little nervous. Finally, someone named Jane Donahue called him back this morning. It appears she's a claims manager there at Great Waters, and a very knowledgeable person. She knows their systems as well as anyone."

"Yes, I think I've heard of her. What'd she have to say?"

"She told Jeff that some of the policies he asked about had expired within the last two years or so, while others simply didn't exist. Their numbers were in a range that hasn't been used yet. As far as Great Waters is concerned, the customers in question don't have any coverage with Great Waters."

"That doesn't sound good. How comfortable is Jeff that the information he gave her is what's really in our files? Any chance of transposition errors or anything like that?"

"Jeff got the original information from our files and then double checked it himself. After talking with Jane, he had Kathy Brown, his operations supervisor, checked the information again. He's certain that what he gave Jane is what's in our files. Jane told him there wasn't anything more she could do at her end. They have no unapplied premiums, which seems to indicate they haven't received any payments on the policies in questions. Now it's up to us to figure out what's going on. I think you'll agree we may have a serious problem on our hands. If some policies have expired and others never existed, and Great Waters hasn't been receiving premiums, where's the money going? "

"Good question, Fred. We need to make some changes to our plan so we can zero in on this particular issue before completing our normal procedures. I'll work with Joe this afternoon to make sure we've got it covered."

"Thanks, Jake. Now it's not just a matter of determining if our dealers have adequate inventory coverage, now we need to find out what's going on in our own house."

After a little more discussion they all agreed that it wouldn't make much sense to try to ship everyone out to Atlanta today rather than Sunday. Even if they could get flights and hotel rooms, there wasn't much they could accomplish before Monday morning anyway. But they'd alert Jeff to expect them early on Monday.

***

Joyce and her dad hadn't gotten much sleep and were both up and about before dawn. He checked out the rest of the house and yard in more detail, and came in through the back door just as she was getting ready to pour a cup of coffee.

"Good timing," she said. "Have a seat and enjoy some coffee before we head out."

"Thanks, dear. Everything looks OK outside. Your biggest problem with the house is going to be the carpets, but it could've been worse. We can get someone in here to pick up the rest of the water and see if they can be saved."

"First thing I want to do is check in with John Forsyth to see if there's any chance of getting a chopper to take us to Tampa. If not, I'm going to head down there in my car. I have to know whether Dan is there or not."

"I understand, sweetheart, but before heading down there, you and John should probably follow up with the local hospitals. They may have new patient lists. You'd hate to go all the way down to Tampa just to find out Dan's at Tallahassee Memorial."

"Yeah, I planned on doing that. It shouldn't take too long. Once I find out what's going on and whether or not John's available to help me today, I'll be able to let you know if I need you to come with me. If not, it would be a great help to me if you could go down to the dealership to check it out. If there's been any damage to the inventory, we'll need to file a claim. I'll give you Randy's phone number too. If he's available, he could probably go down with you."

"That sounds like a plan to me."

The phone rang at quarter past nine. "Hello" she answered.

"Hi, Joyce. It's John. Can you get down to the Sheriff's Office by ten? I think we can hop a ride on a chopper that's heading down to Tampa. In the meantime,

I'll get updated patient lists from the local hospitals to see if Dan shows up on any of them."

"That's great, John. It's just what I was hoping for. I'll be there in a half hour."

She hung up and turned toward her father. "That was John, Dad. I need to get to his office before ten. There's a good chance we can get a ride on a chopper that's heading to Tampa. In the meantime he's going to get some updated patient lists from local hospitals. Let's hurry up and finish here. I want to head out right away."

By quarter to ten they were at the Leon County Sheriff's Office. John had checked with all the local hospitals and Dan wasn't at any of them. Their next step was to head down to Tampa. The chopper was fueled and the pilot was sipping coffee and waiting for his passengers. The sheriff had been worn down by John's repeated pleas. After checking the local situation, he felt he could spare the chopper for most of the day. They'd be able use it to get to Tampa, but he'd need it to come right back. If the unnamed patient wasn't Dan, they could fly back with the pilot. If it was Dan and they decided to stay, they'd have to find their own way back at a later time.

That was fine with Joyce. Before climbing aboard, she handed her dad a piece of paper with Randy's phone number on it.

"Thanks for doing this, Dad. If you want, you can give Randy a call to see if he can meet you there. If not, you have the keys. The alarm code is on the paper also. Once you open the front door you'll have one minute to enter the code. The key pad is on the wall to the right of the door. You can call my cell phone if you have any problems."

"I'll take care of it, hon. Don't worry. You just take care of yourself. And good luck."

"Thanks, Dad."

Two minutes later the chopper lifted off and headed south, as Bob Robertson climbed back into his daughter's car and headed for Walters Marine. He figured he wouldn't bother Randy unless he really needed him. Everyone had lots of their own problems right now.

Chapter 13

The chopper touched down on the helipad at Shriners Hospital at just before noon. Joyce and John jumped out and headed for the building entrance even before the pilot had cut the engine. They were in the elevator on their way down to the main floor while the rotors were still turning. They'd agreed the pilot would wait until they determined whether or not the burn victim was Dan before heading back to Tallahassee. If it wasn't Dan, Joyce and John would return with him. If it was Dan, then one or both of them would stay behind.

On the main floor, Joyce identified herself to the receptionist who directed them to the third floor unit that housed the most severe burn victims, and where the unidentified accident victim was. Minutes later they were in sterile robes and masks, ready to be led into the patient's room, but before going in, the doctor wanted to have a few words with them. He had been called by the nurse, and was there almost immediately. He spoke in a low voice.

"The patient was brought in on Wednesday evening from the accident scene on I-10 East of Tallahassee. I must tell you before you go in that he's in critical condition, with third degree burns over more than sixty percent of his body. The prognosis isn't good. The most we can do at this stage is to try to keep his burns clean to prevent infection, and make him as comfortable as we can. The next forty eight hours will be critical. If he makes it through the weekend, there may be more hope of survival. But if he *does* make it, it'll be a long recovery process with the need for many skin grafts. Even so, he will likely remain badly scarred. "

Joyce felt faint and almost collapsed. John wrapped his arm around her just in time to keep her from falling to the floor. "Oh my God, I've got to go in there. I need to see him" she said. She rushed into the room but stopped short just inside the door. She saw what appeared to be the body of a man lying on the bed, totally wrapped in white cloth. She didn't think she'd be able to tell if it was Dan or not, because there was so little of him showing. She approached the bed slowly, and tears began to fill her eyes. She could hardly see where she was going, but John put his arm around her and guided her to the bedside. They both looked down at the patient in shock. He was heavily sedated and not aware of their presence. They could see little more than his eyes, nose and mouth, and a few fingers protruding from the bandages on his arms and hands.

On the small table by his bedside were the remains of a charred watch and wedding band the doctors had taken from the burned body. Both had been badly damaged by the heat of the fire and were not easily recognizable. As she picked them up to examine them, the doctor came in to talk with her. "Mrs. Walters, can you identify the patient or his jewelry? Do you know if this is your husband?"

"I don't know. I just don't know. It could be his watch and ring, but I'm not sure. They're so badly damaged." She began to cry and when John put his arm around her, she buried her head in his chest and sobbed louder.

"Mrs. Walters, I know this is difficult. But there may be a way to determine if this is your husband. After we treated him for his burns, we took a full set of X-Rays to see if there were any internal injuries that needed to be taken care off. Can you tell me if your husband had any broken bones at any time in his life?"

"Yes," she replied between sobs. "Several years ago he broke his right wrist and ankle in an accident. We were on vacation in Bermuda and had rented mopeds for the day. We weren't used to driving on the left side of the road, and neither of us had ever ridden a moped before. He took a bad fall at the first round-about. He was in the hospital for a few days and had casts on his ankle and wrist for weeks. Even after the wrist healed he had to use crutches for a long time. The ankle took a great deal longer to heal."

"Our X-Rays showed those exact injuries. This patient, at one time, has had a broken right wrist and ankle. I think the odds of him being anyone other than your husband are very small indeed. We may not know for sure until he regains consciousness and is able to speak."

She raised her hand to her mouth to stop a cry from escaping. "Oh my God, Oh my God" was all she could say.

"Mrs. Walters" she heard the doctor say, as though from a distant place. Her head was spinning and she couldn't concentrate. Everything was moving in slow motion. "Mrs. Walters" she heard again. This time she sensed that the voice was coming from somewhere to her left, so she turned in that direction. "Mrs. Walters, I can arrange for you to stay here with your husband as long as you'd like to. I think it would be helpful for him to have you by his side when he regains consciousness. Shall I make those arrangements?"

"Yes, please" she replied in a weak voice. She couldn't even imagine leaving his side at this point. She'd stay here as long as she could. Of course, she'd have to think about the children too. They'd want to see their father but she wasn't sure it was a good idea for them to see him like this. And she had to see about the house and dealership, and there was her dad back in Tallahassee to think about. It was all too overwhelming, and she began to sob again.

"Joyce" she heard John say. "Don't worry about anything else. I'll help and so will all your other friends. Right now, just concentrate on Dan. I'm going to head back to Tallahassee as soon as I know you're set up here. I'll check on your dad, and the dealership. We'll take care of everything at that end. You just stay here with Dan. Like the Doc said, it'll help if he sees you here when he wakes up."

"Mrs. Walters, I'll have a bed brought in to the room so you can sleep here next to your husband. You can have your meals in our cafeteria, or bring your food back here if you prefer. All we ask is that you not touch your husband right now. We need to be sure to avoid infections, which is one of our biggest concerns at the moment."

"I understand" she responded. "And I appreciate this. I couldn't imagine leaving him right now."

"Then I'm going to head back on the chopper" John said. "I'll go let the pilot know that I'll be going back with him as soon as you get settled in. Be back in a minute." John went to find the pilot to give him an update and ask him to contact the Leon County Sheriff's office to let them know what the plan was. He was back in Dan's room a few minutes later, and saw that a bed had already been wheeled in for Joyce. She was sitting on the chair next to Dan's bed, staring at him. She wanted to hold him and soothe his pain. But she was following the doctor's request, and not touching him. She knew that any touch would be much too painful for him now, anyway.

"Joyce. Is there anything else I can do before I head back?"

"No thank you, John. You've been wonderful. I couldn't have made it down here without you. I'll be fine. Could you please just let my dad know what's going on, and ask him to call my mom? Have him tell her I'll try to call her and speak with the children a little later. My dad should be at the dealership, but if not, you can try our house."

"I'll be glad to, Joyce. And if you need anything more, please call me at home or at the Sheriff's office. They always know how to reach me. I'll check back with you later tonight. I have your cell phone number, but I'll call the hospital number first so as not to disturb Dan. "

"Thanks John. I'll be fine. Please go on, now. You need to get back to Tallahassee."

A few minutes later the chopper was lifting off and heading north. John had already spoken with Bob Robertson and given him an update. There wasn't anything else he could do right now except sit back for the next hour and a half or so in the chopper.

***

Bob Robertson had gotten to the Walters Marine building at 10:20 a.m. He knew the building well, having been there often, and quickly made his way through each room checking for damage. There was still a couple of inches of water on the floor inside, but it was obvious there had been much, much more, and much of it had come through the roof. Everything was soaked; the walls, the furniture, and the inventory. He didn't know much about the inventory so he couldn't tell how badly the boats and PWCs were damaged, but it wasn't a pretty sight. Someone would have to start cleaning up in hear and think about filing an insurance claim so he decided to give Randy a call.

Fortunately, Randy's house hadn't received much damage and his family had been able to move back in. He still had a lot of cleanup to do, and the storm shutters were still on the house, but when Bob called he knew he had to come down to take a look at the dealership. After sizing up the situation Randy realized he'd need to get in touch with the insurance company as soon as possible. Bob had been right in his initial assessment; the merchandise could not be sold as new. They'd have to file an insurance claim and then, depending upon how much they could collect and what the insurance company wanted to do, they'd have to determine what to do with the boats and PWCs.

He'd worked with Dan for a long time and knew where most of the records were, so it didn't take him long to find the information he needed in Dan's office, including the policy number and phone number. He dialed the number for Great Waters Insurance Group and an operator quickly answered the phone. "Great Waters Insurance Group, how may I direct your call?"

"I'd like to speak with someone in the claims department please" said Randy.

"Certainly, sir, I'll put you right through."

After only two rings someone picked up. "Claims Department, how may I help you?"

"I'm calling from Walters Marine in Tallahassee, Florida. We've had some water damage to our inventory from tropical storm Fay. We have insurance coverage with Great Waters, and I'd like to know how to go about filing a claim."

"I can help you with that, sir. I just need to get some basic information from you before I can assign your claim to an adjuster. Can you give me your name, please?"

"I'm Randy Jones. I'm the sales manager here at Walters Marine. Mr. Walters isn't available at the moment, but I'm authorized to act on his behalf."

"Thank you, sir. Now, I believe you said you were calling from Walters Marine in Tallahassee. Is that correct?"

"Yes."

"Can you please give me the address, and if you have it, the number of your policy?"

"Sure. We're at 1555 East Gaines Street. And our policy number is C145843. It's coverage for our inventory of water craft."

"Thank you, one moment please while I bring up your records."

A few seconds later the operator was back on the line. "Excuse me, sir. I apologize for this inconvenience, but may I have that policy number again? I think I may have entered an incorrect number into our system."

"Sure. It's C as in cat, 145843."

"Thank you. Could you please hold while I bring up that information? I'll only be a moment."

At first Randy thought nothing of it. He was use to being put on hold. Hell, he considered himself lucky to have spoken to a real human being at all. It was a rare thing these days. Everyone had an automated answering service which made it almost impossible to get through to a living, breathing person. He had expected the same thing from the insurance company, especially following a tropical storm. He could only imagine how many calls they were getting. But after a couple of minutes he started to get pissed. She'd better come back on the line soon, or he'd give her a real piece of his mind when she *did* come back on.

"Thank you for holding, sir. I'm sorry to have kept you waiting so long. I've checked our records, and also asked my supervisor to double check. We have no policy issued under the number you gave me. Also, we checked our files for your company name and address and, again, were not able to find anything on file. "

"What are you talking about?" Randy said, a little too loudly perhaps. "I have the policy in my hand. It was obtained through our finance company, New Commerce Commercial Finance Corporation. They insisted on the coverage and arranged the whole thing. They pay the premiums and bill us directly. We've been paying them for the cost of the premiums for years."

"I'm sorry sir. We have nothing in our files. Perhaps you should contact your finance company to get clarification. It's possible there could be a mix up at their end. There isn't anything more I can do from here. If you can get any additional information from New Commerce, please call us back. We'd be glad to assist you in any way we can. Thank you for calling Great Waters Insurance Group." The line went dead. She had hung up on him.

Randy was standing there looking at the receiver in his hand.

"What is it?" asked Bob Robertson. He could see something was wrong.

"I don't know what to say. The insurance company says they have no record of our policy. They said we should contact our finance company, New Commerce, to see what the situation is."

"What does the finance company have to do with it?" asked Bob.

"They're the ones who arranged for the insurance coverage, and they pay the premiums directly, and then bill us for the amount later. It was the arrangement they had insisted on when we first gave them our account. Even though our other finance company didn't do it that way, it sounded logical to us that they'd want to make sure we had coverage. We've been paying them back for the premiums for the last couple of years."

"So, what do we have to do now?"

"I guess I'll contact our account manager at the New Commerce to get this straightened out as soon as possible. We'll need to get an adjuster down here fast so we can finalize our claim, and reopen for business as soon as possible. Every day we stay closed we're losing money and possibly some future business as well."

Randy was about to pick up the phone to dial New Commerce when it rang. He picked up the receiver and answered "Walters Marine, this is Randy Jones, how can I help you?"

"Randy, I'm glad you're there. It's John Forsyth. Is Joyce's dad there with you?"

"Yes, he's right here, just a second." Randy handed the received to Bob.

"Hello, this is Bob Robertson."

"Mr. Robertson, this is Deputy John Forsyth. We've found Dan. He's the burn patient they hadn't yet identified. Joyce is going to stay there by his side, but I need to head back to Tallahassee. She asked me to call you with an update, and also ask you to call your wife to fill her in."

"How's Dan?"

"Not good, I'm afraid. The doctor says he has third degree burns over more than sixty percent of his body. The next forty eight hours are crucial and will determine if he makes it or not. And even if he makes it, it'll be a very long recovery period and he's likely to remain badly scarred from the burns."

"Oh my God! How's Joyce taking it?"

"Not too good. It's very hard on her, but she refuses to leave his side. They've brought in a bed so she can sleep in his room."

"She shouldn't be alone there. I'm going to head down as soon as I can. Is there a way I can speak with her?"

"She'd prefer that you not call her cell phone. The hospital will be glad to put you through to her if you call the main number and ask for the third floor critical care unit. But in the meantime, could you please let your wife know what's going on?"

"I will."

"I'm not sure how much you should tell the children. I'll leave that to you and your wife."

"We'll handle it. Thanks."

"I'm on my way back and should be in the office in a couple of hours. Please feel free to call the office if you need anything. If I'm not there they'll know where to reach me."

"Thank you. I will."

Bob hung up the phone and turned to Randy, who had gotten the gist of the conversation. They both had tears forming in their eyes, and hugged one another in an effort to find consolation.

Randy was first to break the silence. "I think I got most of it from listening to your side of the conversation. How is he, exactly?"

"Not good, Randy. There's a chance he won't make it. The next forty eight hours are critical. I need to call Donna and we need to decide how to tell the children. Then I'm going to try to reach Joyce. I want to head down there right away."

"I understand, Bob. I can handle everything at this end. Make your call from Dan's office if you'd like. It's more private there. I'll call New Commerce from out here and try to see what's going on with the insurance policy."

A few minutes later they were both on the phone, Bob was breaking the news to Donna and Randy was trying to get through to his account manager at New Commerce.

The news hit Donna hard. She had worried that something like this had happened, but prayed she was wrong. The kids were watching her and saw her eyes fill up. They knew it wasn't good news. "What is it, Grandma?" they both cried out. "Is it mom? What's happened to dad? Can we talk to her?"

She fought to control her voice. "It's not your mother. It's your grandfather. Just let me finish talking to him and then I'll tell you everything he said."

A few moments later she hung up the receiver and turned to the kids. This was going to be one of the hardest discussions she would ever have in her life. But she was probably the best person to talk with them about this. Her gentle mannerism and soothing voice was what they would need right now, in addition to a shoulder to cry on.

"Let's go have a seat on the sofa so I can fill you in on what's happening" she told them. They followed her in silence, almost afraid of what they were about to hear. She started slowly and softly. "They've found your dad. He was involved in the big accident on interstate ten that we heard about Wednesday night. He's been burned rather badly and is in the Shriner's Hospital in Tampa. Your mom is with him right now."

Danny was the first to interrupt. "We want to go see him right away."

"I know" said Donna. "We'll get you there as soon as possible. But we need to take things one step at a time. Right now your mom is at the hospital, and your grandfather will try to head down there as soon as he can. He's at your dad's dealership right now checking on the damage. He'll have to drive, and it could take four or five hours or more for him to get there."

"We need to leave right away" cried Nancy. "I want to see my dad."

"We will. We'll leave shortly. We need to close up the house and pack a few things first. We'll go to Tallahassee and spend the night at your house. That will break up the trip and give us time to get more information about your dad before we go on to Tampa in the morning. We'll need to find someplace to stay in Tampa and we can work on that from your house, if Grandpa hasn't already taken care of it."

Danny and Nancy were understandably very upset. He was trying to act like a man, and was holding back the tears, but Nancy didn't feel she had anything to prove. She sobbed openly while they went about the business of packing and closing up the house. Before long they were ready to head out.

**

Ron Hayward couldn't wait to get out of there. It was 4:45 p.m., and he had another fifteen minutes to go before he was scheduled to leave, but wasn't sure he could make it that long. It'd been a grueling day. Everything was happening too fast and things were starting to fall apart. He needed the weekend to get his head together before the auditors showed up on Monday.

The calls from his Florida dealers had been coming in all day and he didn't know how much longer he'd be able to hold on. The stress was beginning to show, both on his face and in his attire. The top button on his shirt had been untied for several hours, his tie was loosened, and his sleeves rolled up. A far cry from the picture perfect appearance he always displayed. In spite of his height, which at 5' 5" gave him the dubious honor of being the shortest person in the office, he had a reputation for being one of the best dressed people there. But anyone seeing him this afternoon would surely believe that reputation might be in jeopardy.

He was starting to pack up when his phone rang again. He considered not answering it, but someone was sure to take notice if he didn't. "New Commerce Commercial Finance, Ron Hayward speaking" he said into the receiver.

"Ron, this is Randy Jones from Walters Marine in Tallahassee. I need to talk to you about insurance coverage."

His temples began to throb again but he held it together. "What can I do for you Mr. Jones?"

"We've had some serious water damage to our inventory as a result of Fay. I called Great Waters Insurance but they said they have no record of coverage for us. They suggested I call you guys. What's going on, Ron? We have our policy numbers and we've been paying you for the premiums."

"I know. I know, Randy. Calm down. I've had calls from other dealers about the same issue. I'm looking into it now, but I'm pretty sure it's a systems problem there at Great Waters. They recently converted to a new computer system and I suspect they've lost some records. It may take a little while, but it's all going to work out, I assure you. I'm on top of it."

"You'd better be, Ron. In the meantime, what do I do?"

"Just hold on till Monday. Once I speak to someone higher up at Great Waters I'm sure they'll come up with a plan to get you back in business. I guarantee everything will be OK. In the meantime, if you need to have someone come in to remove the water and get things cleaned up go ahead and do that."

"OK, I will. But I'd better hear from you on Monday, Ron."

"I'll try to get back to you before lunchtime, but no later than end of business, for sure."

They both hung up, and Ron finished packing his briefcase and immediately headed for the door, hoping to make it out before any more calls came in. He knew he'd have to come back to the office sometime over the weekend to try to figure out what to do next, but he couldn't think about that now.

Chapter 14

Monday, August 18, 2008

The travel agent had done the best she could, considering the short notice. They all arrived yesterday, with Chuck and Sue landing within twenty minutes of each other, but about four hours after Joe and Jason. They met in the main terminal, headed straight for the rental car which Joe had picked up earlier, and drove to the hotel. They were in their rooms by 5 p.m., which gave them plenty of time to check emails and freshen up before dinner. They met in the lobby at 6:15, headed out to dinner and afterwards spent a few hours going over the details of the review. They wrapped up just before midnight and headed to their rooms to get a few hours sleep.

This morning, at 7:15 sharp they all met in the lobby and headed to the dining room for the free continental breakfast the hotel provided. It took them all of a half hour to finish breakfast, and then they headed out for the division. They pulled up to the Marietta office of New Commerce Commercial Finance in their rental car just after eight o'clock. It was an upscale building in one of the newest office parks in the area. New Commerce had only been in this particular location for the past two years, having moved from their downtown location because of a rent increase. When they got to the lobby, they flashed their company IDs to the security guard and took the elevator to the third floor. They used the phone at the reception desk to dial Jeff Anderson's number and in less than a minute he was leading them into the main conference room, which they'd be using as their base of operations during the review.

It didn't take them long to settle in. Each had a notebook computer with a wireless modem, and the entire office had wireless network access, so it didn't matter where they sat. They spread out enough so they'd have adequate work space and began to unload their briefcases. Joe asked Jeff to have a seat so they could fill him in on their plans. A half hour later the briefing was finished, and Jeff had a general idea of what they'd be doing. They didn't give him too many details because, at this point, they didn't know who might be involved in the insurance issue, and everything was on a "need to know basis." Jeff didn't have a need to know everything just yet. They could fill him in at the appropriate time.

As soon as Jeff left the room they got started. Using the computer printout he'd gotten before leaving Augusta, Joe assigned each staff member specific accounts to review and each of them went to work pulling the paper files from the cabinets in the operations area of the division. Their first task would be to bring the files to the conference room where they could be controlled throughout the review. Nobody would have access to them without one of Jake's staff present. No documents would be removed or added until the review was complete. At no time would the files be left unguarded. Joe had had a special fireproof, locking cabinet delivered to the division on Friday afternoon, and he alone had the key. The files would be locked in the cabinet each night before they left, and be removed by them each morning. As an added precaution, to ensure the integrity of the data each drawer of the cabinet would be sealed every evening and each morning the seals would be examined for evidence of tampering.

By 9 a.m. they were all back in the conference room with the assigned files and they began the long and arduous task of examining documents and comparing the information to the computer printouts so they could immediately highlight any discrepancies. Next, they'd methodically verify everything in the file. Supporting documentation would be reviewed, insurance companies would be contacted, and all discrepancies followed up on.

Each of them had access to the company data files via a wireless connection once they logged onto the network. Their approach would be to first compare the documents in the paper files to the computer printout Joe brought along, and then go on-line to verify the current information on the system. All three sources had to be in agreement. It was a laborious task and they worked quietly and quickly for an hour or so with no unusual results. But then things began to take a turn.

Jason was the first to find a discrepancy. One of the paper files he was examining had no evidence of insurance coverage on the dealer's inventory, and that information agreed with the information he was looking at on-line. But the computer printout Joe had gotten on Friday didn't agree with the first two sources. According to that report, the dealer *was* covered by inventory insurance. Before long Sue and Chuck had come across similar situations as well. Within a couple of hours a clear pattern was developing. There were now fifteen dealers in the Florida and Georgia areas with potential issues. In each case, Friday's printout indicated that inventory insurance was in effect. However, none of the division's files indicated that, and the current computer system also had no evidence of coverage. Most peculiar of all, every file in question was assigned to one specific account manager: Ron Hayward. It looked very suspicious, but Joe knew better than to jump to conclusions. There was still a lot of leg work to be done.

He told the staff to keep working and he slipped out of the conference room to find an empty office for his call. Amazingly, the only empty one had a nameplate on the door which read "Ron Hayward." He asked one of the other account managers if it'd be OK to use the office and was told he was sure it'd be fine. Ron had stepped out a few minutes ago and said he'd be back in fifteen or twenty minutes. So Joe slipped into the office, closed the door and dialed Jake's number in Maine. It was time to give Jake an update and plan the next move.

When his phone rang Jake could tell from the area code showing on his display that the incoming call had originated in the Atlanta area. He picked up the phone and answered "Jake Hammond, how can I help you?"

"Jake. It's Joe. I know it's still early in our review, but we've already found something I think you should know about, and I think we'll need some help from our IT Audit Staff on this one. Do you have a couple of minutes?"

"Of course. Fill me in."

"At mid day on Friday I got a computer printout of all accounts in the Marietta portfolio in preparation for our review. As part of our field work, we're comparing the information in the division's files to that report, and also to the current system information which we're getting real-time. So far we've found fifteen accounts with discrepancies."

"Go on."

"In all fifteen cases, the division's files agree with the current system information, indicating that none of them have insurance coverage arranged by us. But the computer printout I got on Friday indicates that every one of them *does* have that coverage. There may be another explanation, but what I'm thinking right now is that someone has tampered with both the division files and the system files since I created the printout on Friday. I'm thinking we should try to figure out if the data on the system was changed, and if so, by whom. What do you think?"

"That's very interesting. Of course, there is another possibility. It's possible that the printout you got is wrong. Have you thought about that? We don't want to go off the deep end without checking that out first."

"Yeah, I thought about that. I've rechecked the parameters and they all look good. The extract was done perfectly, as far as I can see. So the data we printed appears to be what was on the file at the time. Of course, one of our IT folks should take a look at the parameters, just to make sure."

"OK. Send them up to me and I'll have someone take a look at them. Also, I'll check into whether or not there's a possibility that you were given access to the wrong data file, although I can't imagine how any incorrect version could give you the results you have. The records of fifteen accounts couldn't show one thing on a given day and then mysteriously show something else the next, but we have to make certain of everything at this point."

"I agree, Jake. In the meantime we'll continue our review at this end. You'll have my parameters in a couple of minutes. I'll email them to you as soon as I get back to the conference room."

Joe hung up the phone, opened the door to leave and almost tripped over Ron Hayward who was just coming back from a break. Ron turned pale upon seeing Joe come out of his office. He looked like, and felt like, he was about to pass out. Somehow he found his voice and meekly asked "Can I help you?"

"Oh, no thanks" replied Joe. "I just needed to use a phone for a private conversation and your office was empty. I'm sorry for the inconvenience. Your co-worker over there said it'd be OK."

"Sure, no problem. Anything I can help you with?" Ron offered.

"No. Nothing right *now*" Joe replied, with special emphasis on the *now*, and then rejoined his staff in the conference room.

***

As soon as he hung up from his call with Joe, Jake called Norm Cassidy, his top IT specialist and asked him to come into his office. He got there less than a minute later, knocked on the door and let himself in.

"Hi Norm, could you please close the door? I need to discuss something sensitive with you."

"Sure thing." Norm eased the door shut and took a seat.

"Norm, we've got a *situation* which will require your skills to resolve."

Over the next half hour Jake and Norm discussed the current special review in Marietta, and what Joe and the staff had uncovered so far. Norm reviewed the parameters that Joe had sent up and found them to be correct. And he agreed with Jake that it was unlikely that Joe had accessed a wrong version of the files on Friday. The most likely explanation was that the file had been changed subsequent to the time Joe created the report. Norm would be able to quickly determine if the data had been tampered with, but if so, it'd take a little longer to figure out the who, when and how of it.

"I need for you to drop what you're working on and get on this as soon as possible" Jake told him.

"OK. No problem. I can do most of this research on my own, but if I need any help from the technical staff, they might want to know what I'm looking for."

"Don't worry about it. If it comes to that, let me know before you contact them. I'll give Dave Banner a call and clear the way." If Dave tells them to cooperate and not ask questions, that's what they'll do. I can't imagine them arguing with the Chief Information Officer."

"Great! I'll get right on it and get back to you as soon as I can."

Norm got up from his chair and headed to the door. "Do you want the door open or closed" he asked as he was leaving.

"Would you close it please? I have a few confidential calls I need to make."

***

Some adjusters had headed out on Saturday and had been able to complete a few appraisals then, but most traveled on Sunday and were meeting their first customers this morning. They all had received their marching orders from their boss, Harry Strong, who had been very clear about one thing. They'd better not let anything slip through the cracks because he'd be checking each file before any payments were made. Great Waters was not in a position to pay false or improperly documented claims and any adjuster who wasn't doing his part for the company would have to answer to him. They had never received such a "warning" before. They all knew their jobs well and were very much aware of the company's position. They weren't exactly sure why Harry felt a need to give those marching orders this time around, but his tone told them he meant it, and they took him seriously. They'd do their best to make sure they didn't approve any claims unless it was crystal clear the loss was covered. Hopefully, that would keep Harry happy and off their backs.

Chapter 15

Joyce sat quietly, starring at the bandaged body in the bed. The room was mostly dark even though it was 10 a.m. and the sun was shining outside. Only a small beam of light penetrated the closed blinds, but it was all the light she could handle right now. Her eyes hurt and her head was pounding; she hadn't had a full night's sleep in five days, and she could hardly function anymore. The hospital staff had been great and did everything they could to try to make her comfortable, even bringing food to her in the room so she wouldn't have to leave his side. But nothing helped. She wouldn't be able to rest or eat until she knew Dan was out of danger.

It was Monday, and Dan hadn't regained consciousness yet. But that was by design. The doctors told Joyce if he were awake the pain would be unbearable, so they were providing the medication that kept him comfortable, and unconscious. He was still in serious danger, and they had to be sure his system wouldn't receive any additional shocks or stress. It was the best way to try to help him make it through this ordeal. She didn't like it. She wanted him to know she was there for him, and she wanted to tell him how much she loved him. But all she could do now was wait and see what would happen next. The doctors were all burn specialists and knew what they were doing. She had to trust them.

Her mom had driven to Tallahassee with the kids when she got the news about Dan, and she and dad were on their way here with the kids now. They'd left this morning and would probably get in before dinner time. She was looking forward to seeing the kids, but at first hadn't wanted them to come because she didn't think they should see him this way. But even under the best of conditions it'd be a very long time before he'd look much better. The doctors were brutally honest about that. She couldn't make the kids wait that long. And, if things took a turn for the worst, she'd never forgive herself if they didn't have a chance to see him before the end. She cried again at the thought that anything like that might happen.

A nurse came in quietly and tapped her on the shoulder. She whispered in her ear "Mrs. Walters, there's a call for you at the desk."

"Thank you. I'll be right there." She took a moment to compose herself and went out to take the call.

"Hello, this is Joyce Walters."

"Joyce. It's Randy. Sorry to bother you. I just wanted to check on Dan. How's he doing?"

"Not much change. He's still not awake. The doctors have him medicated so he'll sleep because they think the pain would be unbearable if he were awake."

"I'm so sorry, Joyce. Is there anything I can do for you down there?"

"Thanks, Randy, but the best thing you can do for us is to take care of the dealership for a while. I don't know how long it'll be before I get back to Tallahassee, and it'll be a long time before Dan's on his feet again. How are things going up there?"

"Don't worry, Joyce. I'll handle everything at this end. We've had a little water damage from a leak in the roof, but I've already been in contact with the insurance company, and I'll have a crew come in to clean up. I'll keep an eye on your house, too."

"You're a true friend. I don't know what we'd do without you right now."

"We're all praying for Dan. Don't forget to take care of *yourself*."

"I will."

She hung up the phone and turned to go back to Dan's room. Before she got to the door she heard the announcement over the loud speaker. - Code blue! Code Blue!

Doctors and nurses seemed to appear from nowhere and they all headed toward Dan's room. Someone was rolling in a cart of some kind. It all happened so fast it was hard to take it all in. She rushed into the room, but couldn't see Dan anymore. He was surrounded by people in white coats and someone was holding paddles over his chest, yelling *clear*.

***

Calls were still pouring in, but the regular staff could handle the volume so Jane was able to get back to her other responsibilities. She was at her computer terminal checking statistics on claims calls. This time, she had additional information to look at, because initial results from the adjusters' reviews were being entered into the system.

It seemed unusual to her, but it looked like about forty five percent of the claims the adjusters had worked on so far were denied. Based on her past experience at Great Waters, she knew that figure was high. She'd seldom seen more than ten percent of claims for any individual disaster denied. She examined the codes to see if there was any kind of pattern. She found that most were denied because the policy didn't cover the type of damage that had occurred. That was odd. The damage had to be from tropical storm Fay, and their policies always covered damage from hurricanes and tropical storms. She wondered what kind of damage these folks had.

Then she looked at the claims that *were* approved. The average amount was under a thousand dollars. If anyone relied on those approvals to gauge how bad the storm was, they'd have to conclude it wasn't much of a storm at all. But Jane knew differently. Anyone watching the news knew. The only explanation was that the badly damaged properties were all covered by other insurance companies. And that wasn't likely. Something wasn't right. She'd have to run the reports again. Maybe her parameters were wrong.

***

Joe and the staff had taken their lunch breaks in shifts so they wouldn't have to lock up all the files that now totally covered the twelve foot conference table. There were more than a hundred, and locking them all up and then having to take them out again would've been a waste of valuable time. By 2 p.m. they had each taken a twenty minute lunch break and were all back on the job. It'd been the only break they'd had since just after eight this morning, and they'd probably be there until at least ten tonight.

Each of them regularly gave Joe a status update on what they were finding, and he in turn updated a spreadsheet he was using to track all issues. This way he'd be able to periodically keep Jake up to date. The number of exceptions was rising by the hour. Although most had to do with insurance coverage, there were other areas of concern as well. The division was significantly behind on their dealer inventory checks, and much of the documentation in the files was disorganized. Some credit limits had been exceeded and some loans didn't have evidence of credit approvals. Except for the insurance issues, most of the exceptions weren't unusual, at least not the *type* of exceptions. The numbers were a bit higher than expected, though.

Joe checked Jake's calendar through Outlook but saw no opening until 6 p.m. He'd need to begin interviewing the account managers soon, and he wanted an update on what information Norm Cassidy might have on the system side. He didn't want to wait until six, so he decided to give Jake a call on the hope that he'd be able to squeeze in a few minutes for him. He dialed Jake's number, and was glad to hear his voice at the other end.

"Jake Hammond. How can I help you?"

"Hi Jake, it's Joe. Can you spare a couple of minutes?"

"Hold on just a second."

Joe was on "hold" for about twenty seconds or so, and then Jake came back on the line.

"Sorry about that, Joe. I was on a conference call, and I had to get someone from the staff to sit in on it while I talk with you."

"Thanks for taking my call Jake. I needed to speak with you before our next step down here. And I was hoping you'd have something for me from Norm."

"I do. But first, bring me up to speed on what's happening at your end."

"We've gone through most of the files I'd marked for review and we've found more exceptions than we'd normally expect. Many are the typical things, like past due dealer inventory checks, missing credit approvals, etc. But as we discussed earlier, most of the exceptions are related to insurance. We'll be finished our file reviews soon, and we'll need to begin the interviews. Before we do that, I was hoping to get an update from you on the changes made to the computer files."

"Norm and I have been working on that. We checked the account numbers you sent me earlier and determined that some of the data in those records was definitely changed over the weekend, but not as part of a normal file update process. We reviewed the system access logs and found that someone made those changes on Saturday, and the logon ID of the person making the changes belongs to none other than Ron Hayward. From what we can determine at this time, it looks like the only thing he changed was the insurance indicator that tells us whether or not a customer's inventory is covered. But we've still got a lot of work to do. For example, we need to figure out if premium payments were made by the customers, and if so, whether or not that information was also changed in the files."

"That's pretty much what I expected. I think it's time to discuss our findings with Jeff and then interview Ron and the other account managers. Do you agree?"

"Yes, I do. I know you've done this before and I trust you completely, but just a couple of reminders before you begin. First, be sure there are always at least two auditors in the room during interviews. Second, don't make any accusations; just ask questions. Be careful not to imply guilt. You're only on a fact finding mission right now. Finally, be sure *all* account managers and other appropriate employees are interviewed so no one will feel singled out."

"I got it covered, Jake. Don't worry. I'll begin the interviews right away, and give you a call this evening to bring you up to speed."

"Thanks, Joe."

"No problem. Talk to you later."

***

Ron Hayward had hoped to be in the office first thing on Saturday morning, but he'd forgotten about the promise he'd made to his nephew. They had plans to go to the lake, and he couldn't disappoint him. So he spent most of Saturday on the lake, and got to the office late in the evening. He returned on Sunday morning, and by the time he finished up later that afternoon he'd checked every account he managed and he still couldn't understand what was going on.

He'd received a number of calls on Friday from customers complaining about insurance issues and checked every file, and each of them seemed to have valid policies in effect. Yet, Great Waters had told the customers there was no record of them having current policies. At first he assumed it was a problem at Great Waters, because of their recent conversion to a new computer system. He'd assured every customer that he'd look into it and get back to them. Then over the weekend he noticed something very unusual. When he'd checked the files on Friday, each and every one had evidence of insurance coverage, but then on the weekend, he couldn't find any of the documentation in the files. So he checked the system, and there was no evidence there either. Something was very wrong, but he couldn't figure out what it was. Now that the auditors had the files, there wasn't any way he could continue his research without having to explain why he wanted to use the files.

His customers were expecting a return call from him, but he didn't know what to tell them. And besides, he didn't know all their names and phone numbers by heart. He'd need to get to the files for that information.

The knock on the door startled him, and his hands jerked over the keyboard. He looked up to see two of the auditors at his door. "Excuse me, Ron. I'm Joe Nash and this is Sue Richards. We're with the Security and Compliance Department. We'd like to speak with you for a few minutes. Can we come in?"

"Well, I'm really busy right now. Can this wait until tomorrow?"

"We won't take too much of your time, Ron" said Joe, as he and Sue eased themselves into the chairs in front of Ron's desk. It was obvious to Ron that he wasn't being given a choice.

"OK. As long as it doesn't take too long, I'm really swamped today."

"Thanks" said Sue.

"As you know" Joe began, "we're here doing an internal audit. I think you've been through a few of these before, right?"

"Yes" replied Ron. "I've been here a few years and I've seen the auditors a couple of times. But they've never interviewed me before."

"Sometimes procedures change slightly from one review to the next. And although we often interview employees as part of our reviews, we can't speak with everyone. It's not surprising that you haven't had that experience yet" replied Joe. "This time around, we'll be speaking with all of the account managers."

Knowing that they'd also be speaking with his fellow account managers seemed to put Ron's mind at ease a bit. Maybe this was just routine, he thought. He might still have a chance to resolve the problem on his own.

"Oh, OK. What is it you'd like to know?"

Chapter 16

They began by asking him about inventory checks at his customer locations. The system and division files indicated that they were in decent shape, but they knew the files were wrong in other areas, so they had to follow up on everything.

"Ron, tell us about the inventory checks at your dealers. How current are they?" asked Joe.

They could see him visibly relax. He knew his inventory checks were current and was happy to be able to talk about that topic. *Maybe things won't be so bad after all.*

"As you probably know, my dealers are on a forty five day cycle. As of right now, they're all current. None are due for review for another couple of weeks."

"How many accounts are you responsible for?" asked Sue.

"I have fifteen dealerships that I manage, which is a pretty typical number for account managers at this division."

"And how many field personnel do you have available to complete your inventory checks?"

They went on like this for some time. Joe and Sue asked questions for which they already knew the answers, - the approach they always took. You ask the safe questions first; the ones that'll be easy to answer and won't be threatening, and then when the person being interviewed is more at ease, you get into the areas that really interest you.

"Ron, can you tell us how many of your customers have opted to have New Commerce arrange for inventory insurance for them?"

He should've been expecting this one, but was still caught a little off guard. His face clearly showed discomfort and he hesitated before answering, as if he were trying to think of the ramifications of any answer he'd give. Joe and Sue both noticed the change in his appearance.

"We'll, I'm not exactly sure. I'd have to check the system, but I'd say about eighty five percent of them. Some insist on taking care of insurance themselves, but most like the idea of having us do it for them. Why do you ask?"

"It's just a normal part of our review. Can you get us a report that shows which customers arrange for their own insurance and which have coverage we've arranged for? Oh, and also, can you show us which customers have no insurance at all? I don't think there will be any of those, since we *require* the coverage, but let's check anyway, just in case."

"Sure, I guess so." Beads of sweat began to form on Ron's brow, even though it wasn't at all warm in his office. "How soon do you need it?"

"We'd like it as soon as possible. How soon can you get it to us?"

"It'll take a few minutes to enter the inquiry into the system, and then a bit longer to print the report, - probably a half hour in total, once I start on it."

"That'll be fine. If you could do that as soon as we wrap up here we'd appreciate it. We just have a few more questions and then we'll let you get back to work. If you could bring the report to us in the main conference room as soon as it's printed, that'd be great."

Joe continued with the questioning. "Do you periodically verify insurance coverage for your dealers?"

"Yes, of course."

"How often do you do that?"

"Well, I don't have a set schedule. I use that as a filler task whenever I have some time, and I methodically go through the files."

"And how, exactly, do you do the verifications?"

"I contact the insurance carriers."

"And when was the last time you did that?"

Now he was getting nervous again. They had to be on to something. Why else would they be asking these specific questions?

"I don't remember, exactly. I know I verified some coverage within the past few weeks."

"How do you keep track of which accounts you verified, and when you did it?"

"I … I don't have any formal records. I just sort of know which ones I've done."

Joe sometimes found that asking a follow up question and misquoting the speaker could lead to some additional and very interesting information being divulged, so he decided to use that approach now to see how Ron would react. "I may have misunderstood, but I thought I heard you say a little while ago that you weren't exactly sure how many of your customers had inventory insurance. If that's the case, how is it possible for you to keep track of which ones you've verified without a written record of some kind? Isn't it possible for you to miss some?"

"Well, um, I think what I said was that I wasn't sure how many of my customers opted to let us obtain insurance for them. But as you know, *all* of them are required to have inventory insurance, whether we arrange it or not. I assure you, however, that I know who my customers are. And the informal system I use is alphabetical. I review them in order, the A's, the B's, the C's, etc. It isn't that hard to keep track of."

"Where are you up to at the present time?"

"Excuse me?"

"What was the last letter you checked? D, E, G?"

"I'm into the K's right now."

"OK. When did you last complete the entire alphabet? In other words, when did you finish the Z's and start over again with the A's?"

"I don't know exactly."

"Can you give me an estimate?"

"Probably a few weeks ago."

"I see" said Joe. "And, have you ever had a situation where you found discrepancies during your verification process?"

"What do you mean?"

"I mean, when your files indicated coverage but the insurance company couldn't confirm coverage."

The sweating became visibly worse now and his breathing became heavier. Ron Hayward looked like he was about to pass out. Sue almost felt bad for him, but if he didn't do anything wrong, he had no reason to be worried. It was looking more and more like he had something to hide.

"I haven't actually ever found *that* kind of discrepancy" Ron answered.

"What kind of discrepancy *have* you found?" asked Joe.

"What I meant was that I've never found any discrepancies regarding insurance coverage" Ron replied.

"Oh, I see. I gathered from your response that you'd found something other than what we discussed."

"No. Nothing. I've never found any discrepancies." Now he was really sweating.

"So, all your customers currently have inventory insurance, is that correct?"

He had dug himself into a deep hole, and didn't exactly know how to get out. He had no choice but to keep the lie going. "Yes, that's right" he replied.

"OK. Thank you for your time, Ron. We'll let you get back to your work now. If we need anything further, we'll let you know. And please, bring that report in as soon as it's ready."

Joe and Sue stood up, shook Ron's hand and left. As soon as they had cleared the door, he fell back into his chair and started to shake. He didn't know what to do next. He knew it looked bad for him, but couldn't explain what was going on. He'd spent hours over the weekend trying to figure it out, and all he knew was that, somehow, his inventory financing accounts had been tampered with, and he had no idea how it could've happened. *Oh God, I'm in trouble. I don't know how this happened, but I'm going to get fired.*

When they got back to the conference room Joe and Sue filled the others in on what had transpired during the interview and they all agreed they'd use the same approach when interviewing the remaining account managers. While they had no cause, at the moment, to suspect any of *them* of having done anything wrong, you never knew.

They decided to complete the interviews before going on to the verification phase of their fieldwork. It'd be better to get them out of the way, and putting them off would only create unnecessary stress for those who expected to be interviewed. In the meantime, Joe decided to call Jake again, and had a suspicion Jake would be on the next plane to Atlanta.

***

Norm Cassidy had just filled Jake in on the new developments. They already knew Ron Hayward had accessed the system on Saturday and changed the insurance indicators on the file. They'd wondered what had happened to the premium payments the customers were making to New Commerce, and now Norm had a lead on that as well.

The phone rang and he answered "Jake Hammond."

Jake, it's Joe. Can you talk right now?"

"Yes. I have Norm here in my office and we were just going over some new information he discovered about the premium payments being made to us by the customers. Shall I put you on speaker?"

"That's fine, as long as you're OK with Norm hearing all the details from this end."

"Not a problem." Jake pushed the speaker button on his phone and continued "Go ahead, Joe, I have you on speaker now."

"OK. Well, let me cut to the chase. Sue and I interviewed Ron Hayward just a little while ago and he was very uncomfortable through the whole thing. As we got into it, he began sweating heavily. We asked specific questions about insurance coverage, and he indicated that he reviews insurance coverage on his accounts on a regular basis and he's never found an exception. He insisted that every account has the required coverage. While nothing he said is an obvious lie, at least not one I can prove right now, in my opinion, he was clearly hiding something."

"In light of what we've found regarding system access on Saturday, I'd say he has a reason to be uncomfortable. Norm, why don't you fill us in on the new information you've discovered."

"After we realized that Ron had accessed the files and changed the insurance codes on some accounts, we began to wonder what's been happening to the premium payments customers have been sending in. So I worked with our technical folks in IT, and we started looking at other fields on our data base. For the accounts in question, there's no indication we've received any premium payments. However, when we checked the date and time stamps for the fields in question, we found that they, too, were changed on Saturday. And guess whose access code was used?"

"Let me take a wild guess" said Joe. "Could it be Ron Hayward's?"

"Bingo" replied Norm.

"So let me summarize" said Jake. "On Saturday, Ron Hayward accessed the data files and changed a number of fields in several records, including the insurance indicators and the premium payment information."

"That's about it" replied Norm.

"So now, we need to figure out what happened to the money."

"Yes" added Norm. "But the interesting thing about all of this is that there's a system of controls in place which ensures adequate segregation of duties. What we need to figure out is how he got his hands on the money. Since all payments are processed by the Cash Management Department, Ron couldn't have gotten the money, unless, [. . .] unless the dealers were sending their payments directly to him."

"That's right" said Jake. "So one of the things you need to do, Joe, is contact some of the dealers to find out if that's what they've been doing. I trust you'll be as diplomatic as always, right? We don't want to let on that we have an internal issue."

"You got it, boss."

"OK. Norm, you need to take a look at some of the cash reconciliations to see if there's evidence that premium payments were received and applied. Joe, you can finish your interviews with the account managers, and then contact some of the dealers. I think it's time for me to take a little trip to Atlanta."

"I figured you'd say that" added Joe.

"I'll have someone work on the arrangements right away, and let you know when to expect me. Hopefully I'll be in the office first thing in the morning, but no later than mid-day, in any event."

They hung up the phone. In Marietta, Joe filled the staff in on the plans. In Augusta, Norm headed out to continue his research and begin reviewing the cash reconciliations. Jake called the travel agency.

Chapter 17

At 4:45 p.m. Randy still hadn't gotten a call from Ron Hayward so he decided it was time to bring this issue to the next level. To hell with Ron, he'd go to Ron's boss and try to find out what was going on. He dialed the main number for New Commerce Commercial Finance Corporation.

"New Commerce Commercial Finance, how may I direct your call?" the voice at the other end said.

"I'd like to speak with the person in charge of account managers, please."

"I'd be pleased to direct your call to your assigned account manager, if you have that name" she replied.

"No, I don't want to speak with my account manager. I've done that a number of times, with no results. I want to speak with his boss, and I'd like to speak with him *right now.*"

"Could you please hold while I connect you?"

Although all account managers in Alpharetta reported to Ben Newhouse, Ben had been out of the office for several days, so the operator dialed the number of *his* boss, Jeff Anderson.

"Jeff Anderson."

"Mr. Anderson, this is Ann at the front desk. Sorry to bother you, but I have a customer on the line who is very irate. He insists on speaking with the person who oversees the account managers, but Ben is out of the office. Should I connect you?"

"Yes, please do."

As soon as he hung up, Ann put the call through. "Hello, this is Jeff Anderson" he answered. "I'm the general manager of the Atlanta area office of New Commerce Commercial Finance. How can I help you?"

"Mr. Anderson, this is Randy Jones. I'm calling from Walters Marine in Tallahassee, Florida. I think you have a problem there at New Commerce, and someone needs to get on top of this quickly. I've been trying to get an answer since last week, and, frankly, I'm tired of getting the run around."

"I'm sorry you're having difficulties, Mr. Jones. I'm sure I can help you. Please, go on."

"When we gave you guys our account, we were told you'd take care of getting insurance on our inventory. We have a policy, and have been paying you monthly premiums which, we were told, you were forwarding to the insurance company, Great Waters Insurance Group in Milwaukee. The problem is they don't have any records of a policy on our inventory." There was a pause, as Randy tried to contain himself. He was on the verge of losing control and screaming at the idiots there at New Commerce. "You see, Mr. Anderson, we've had a lot of damage here at Walters Marine, as a result of Tropical Storm Fay. I called Great Waters and asked about filing a claim. That's when they told me we don't have any insurance. Well, let me tell you something, Mr. Anderson. I have proof we've been paying premiums to your company, and have an insurance policy in my hand. Now somebody had better straighten this thing out real fast before we get an attorney and sue the hell out of you guys."

"I assure you, Mr. Jones, I will look into this immediately. I promise you I'll get back to you tomorrow, at the latest."

"Yeah, yeah. I've gotten those promises before. Ron Hayward gave me the same song and dance. But believe me, this is the last one. If I don't hear from you tomorrow, you'll be speaking to our lawyer. You got that?"

"Yes sir, Mr. Jones. I assure you, you *will* hear from me tomorrow."

Before they hung up, Jeff got all the necessary information from Randy; company name and address, New Commerce loan number, insurance policy number, etc. and headed out to the conference room to speak with Joe Nash.

***

Bob and Donna Robertson and the kids arrived in Tampa just after 7 p.m. They went straight to the third floor, as Joyce had said they should, and stopped at the nurse's desk.

"Excuse me" Bob said to the nurse on duty. "Can you tell us where Dan Walters' room is?"

"Of Course. Are you Mr. Robertson?"

"Yes. And this is my wife Donna, and my grandchildren, Danny and Nancy."

"Mrs. Walters has been expecting you. Mr. Walter's room is right over here. Please follow me."

Joyce saw them as soon as they approached the room. She stood up and raced to the door to greet them. She hugged her mom and dad, and then each of the kids. "It's so good to see you all" she said, with tears in her eyes. It was obvious she'd been crying a lot. Her eyes were puffy and red. "Come in, please."

They filed into the room slowly and approached the bedside. Dan was still covered in bandages, and was still hooked up to an IV and the heart monitor. Danny and Nancy started crying and their mother tried to console them. Nancy was the first to speak. "Mom, is dad going to be alright?"

"Well honey, the doctors' aren't sure yet. Your dad has been very badly burned. They're hoping that they'll be able to give us a better idea tomorrow. If he's doing better by then, he should have a good chance. But even so, it'll be a very long time before he gets totally better."

Danny chimed in. "What if he hasn't gotten any better by tomorrow?"

"All we can do is wait and pray" she answered.

The kids went closer to their dad. They both had tears in their eyes as they stared down at him. Joyce wrapped her arms around the two of them and drew them closer to her. All three were crying softly now. Donna and Bob Robertson were standing a few feet back, trying to give Joyce and the kids some privacy. They, too, had tears in their eyes.

Danny was the first to speak to their dad. "Dad. Dad, it's Danny. Nancy and I just got here. I want you to know I love you. Please, you've got to get better, for us."

"Dad, I love you too" added Nancy. "Please get better. We're going to stay here until you do."

Joyce thought she saw a movement in Dan's eyes. It was ever so slight, but she was sure she'd seen it. Maybe he was able to hear them. Maybe he would regain consciousness soon. There was a flicker of hope in her mind, but she was torn. Although she didn't want him to feel the pain that she knew he would if he regained consciousness, it would be nice to know that he was aware of their presence. Knowing his family was with him would surely help him and give him hope.

As they were standing over him, the kids each holding one of his hands, the monitor, which had been beeping, began to sound a loud shrill. Within a few seconds the nurse was there, followed by a doctor. Joyce and the kids were asked to back away so they could get to Dan. Once again Joyce heard the "code blue" announcement, and again a cart was wheeled in. Donna, Bob, Joyce and kids were asked to step into the hall while someone was yelling "clear" next to the bed.

It only took a couple of minutes. The doctors worked furiously, and tried everything they could. But, in the end, nothing had worked. His heart could no longer take the stress. One of the doctors turned to Joyce and said "I'm sorry, Mrs. Walters. There's nothing more we can do. He's gone."

"No. Please God, no," she screamed. She ran into the room and threw herself on the bed crying and calling his name. "Dan. Dan. It's Joyce. I love you, please don't leave me."

The kids were crying uncontrollably. Donna and Bob tried to be strong for them, but found it difficult. With tears in her eyes, Donna hugged the children as Bob tried to console Joyce and help her off of the bed. She wouldn't move or let go of Dan. She hugged him and pleaded with him to wake up. Finally, a doctor was able to pull her away from the body. He offered to give her something to help her calm down, but she wouldn't have any of it.

The nurse disconnected the wires and tubes, and then left the room. The family needed some time alone with their husband, father, and son-in-law. It'd be awhile before they'd be able to let go. In the meantime, the hospital would notify the coroner. Time of death was 7:30 p.m., on Monday, August 18, 2008.

***

Jeff had filled Joe in on his conversation with Randy Jones. It was another nail in Ron's coffin and it was starting to look like there was little doubt about what had happened. All they had to do was prove it, and figure out how he got his hands on the money. Joe would call Randy and some of the other customers first thing in the morning to ask about the payment methods they used. If they hadn't paid Ron directly, then there'd be a whole other aspect to this investigation. That might mean collusion. Someone else might be in on the scheme.

Since they couldn't conduct interviews or call customers at this hour of the evening they decided to call it a night. They packed up their laptops and briefcases and placed all the division files in the fireproof cabinet Joe had

had delivered there on Friday. Then Joe locked the cabinet and placed a seal on each edge of each drawer; top, bottom, left and right. The seals were specifically made for such purposes, and could not be removed. If anyone opened a drawer, the seals would have to be broken, and there would be evidence of tampering. By eight o'clock they were at a local restaurant having dinner, and planning the next day's activities.

***

Ron had stayed late to try to figure out what was going on, but still had no luck. It just didn't make sense. Everything was fine up until last week. Then Fay hit Florida, customers started filing damage claims, and strange things began to happen. Documents from the files disappeared, and the computer records changed with no apparent explanation. He was positive all his customers had insurance coverage because he did regular reviews and never found any exceptions. Unfortunately for him, though, he didn't have any proof. Now it looked like they didn't have any insurance coverage and he was sure he'd be blamed. He was going to have to talk to the auditors in the morning. Maybe they could figure out what was going on. .

It was 8:30 p.m. when he finally packed up and locked his office door. He planned to grab a quick bite on his way home and then try to get a good night's sleep. Maybe things will look better in the morning, he thought. He took the elevator down to the main lobby and said good night to the guard on the way out. He was crossing the travel lane in front of the building when he heard the screech of tires. He turned toward the sound to see what it was. A black SUV was racing toward him, and it seemed to be picking up speed as it got closer and closer. He thought how stupid the driver was to be racing in the parking lot and figured it must be a teenager. He'd have to get his license plate and report him to the security guard who, in turn, could call the police.

When he realized the SUV wasn't going to slow down, Ron tried to move faster to get out of the way, but his legs didn't want to cooperate. He stood frozen in place, his mouth open, about to shout something at the driver when the SUV hit him. The driver never slowed down, and didn't stop after he ran him down. He just sped away and disappeared into the traffic, leaving nothing behind but silence, and the twisted and bloody body of Ron Hayward.

***

It was another late night for Jane Donahue. After her discussion with Jeff Anderson at New Commerce, she'd decided to take a closer look at some of the calls that had been rejected because of the lack of any evidence of coverage. The new system made that easy to do. All she had to do was key-in a few commands, and within minutes she had a report showing details of those calls. Everything the operators had entered, including the policy numbers that weren't valid, was listed on the report. She began her analysis to see if she could spot any kind of trend.

As a general rule, it was the customer's responsibility to prove they had coverage when the insurer had no record of it. It was a long and drawn out process, seldom ending well for the customer. They were considered to be wrong until they could prove otherwise, and often needed to hire an attorney, even when they had policies in their hands and proof of premium payments. It was company policy, and that's just the way things were. But this time, Jane decided she needed to be more pro-active. She didn't like the statistics she'd been tracking and her curiosity was peaked. It wouldn't hurt to spend just a little bit of time on this, especially at night, when she was "off the clock."

By eleven o'clock she'd found an interesting trend. The new system allowed operators to enter comments in a "memo" section. They could put in anything they felt would help explain what the caller was trying to convey. It often helped to have that information during later research. In fact, that was proving to be the case right now. Several of the callers had claimed that their premium payments were being made by their finance company, New Commerce Commercial Finance.

Things were getting more interesting by the hour. Maybe she'd give Jeff Anderson a call in the morning.

Chapter 18

Tuesday, August 19, 2008

Jake's flight landed at Hartsfield International Airport at 10:30 a.m. It wasn't a scheduled commercial flight because he hadn't been able to get a seat on any flight into Atlanta last night or today. But being an executive had its privileges and a quick phone call to Tom D'Angelo had netted him a ride on a private business jet. New Commerce had a time share contract, and when a jet was available and the trip warranted it, executives could make use of those jets. This was such a time.

A car was waiting for him at the business terminal. The driver loaded his luggage into the trunk, and within minutes they were out of the airport and on their way to Marietta. He pulled out his cell phone and dialed Joe's number. "I just landed at Hartsfield. I'm on my way in now, and should be there within an hour, traffic permitting."

"There are some new developments on this end, Jake. We'll fill you in on all the details when you get here, but I wanted you to know one thing. Last night, at about 8:30, Ron Hayward was killed in a hit and run accident, right here in front of the office. The police are investigating."

"My God, Joe, do you think this is a coincidence?"

"It's too soon to tell."

"OK. We'll talk more when I get there." Jake hung up and called Fred Campbell to fill him in on the latest development and ask him to postpone the Audit Committee meeting. Then he called Norm Cassidy to see if there was anything new at that end.

When they arrived at the office at 11:15 a.m. the area immediately in front of the building was still roped off with the yellow police tape, so he had the driver pull into the parking area just beyond the accident scene. He retrieved his carry-on luggage, signed the receipt for the driver and headed into the building. The security guard recognized him and waved him right in. He grabbed the elevator to the third floor, greeted the receptionist and headed straight for the conference room. Joe was there alone going over some documents and looked up when he heard Jake come in.

"Hey boss. How was your flight?" he asked with a grin. He already knew that Jake had come in on a private jet and was just busting him up.

Jake smiled and answered. "Well, there weren't any commercial flights available, so I had to suffer through a flight on a business jet. It was tough to take, but I didn't have much choice."

"Oh, make me suffer like that sometime, would you?" replied Joe.

"I'll see what I can do. So, where is everyone?"

"They're finishing up the interviews with the account managers. They should be back shortly."

"OK. While we wait for them to get back, fill me in on the new developments and then I can give you the latest on what Norm found."

"Well, there was another interesting development this morning. Jeff got a call from a claims manager at Great Waters. She's been reviewing statistics regarding claims that have come in since last week, and noticed something peculiar. Many of the callers who had their claims rejected because they didn't have valid policies in effect indicated their premiums were being paid by New Commerce, and that they, in turn, reimbursed the company when billed. It's not looking too good right now."

"Have you been able to contact some of the customers to figure out how they made their payments?"

"We're still working on that. We've contacted a few of them, but have a lot more to go. So far, they've all said their payments were sent to our Cash Management Department in Augusta. The mailing address they gave me is the one we use for all loan and premium payments."

"That's what I was afraid of. This adds a whole new dimension to our problem. If Ron wasn't getting the cash, then either someone else was working with him, or maybe he wasn't involved at all."

"But Jake, it's clear from what we've found so far that Ron Hayward *was* the person who changed the computer files."

"Not necessarily, Joe. It's true the system access logs show his ID was used, but that alone doesn't convince me. We have to figure out what happened to the money. If Ron was involved in some kind of fraud or embezzlement, what was his motive? There had to be something in it for him. And unless payments were sent to him directly, how'd he get his hands on the money?"

"As you said, Jake, maybe someone else was working with him. It'd have to be someone in the Cash Management area, don't you think?"

"Maybe. That's why I asked Norm to take a look at the cash reconciliations and bank deposits. He's also looking into any changes made to other fields on the files, including premium payment codes. It's possible that whoever changed the coverage codes might have forgotten to change the premium payment codes as well. I'm expecting him to call me shortly with the results of that research."

"At this end, we'll be starting the verification process shortly. We'll finish checking on insurance coverage and then go on to the reports of inventory checks. We'll also perform a few checks ourselves just to get an additional level of comfort in that area."

"That sounds good, Joe. Have you spoken with Jeff Anderson today?"

"Just briefly. He's been pretty busy with the police. They wanted to know everything they could about Ron Hayward."

"I trust you told Jeff that information about the insurance issue was confidential for the time being?"

"Yep, I did. He knows that you'll handle that at the appropriate time. If he gets any pressure from the cops he'll direct them to you."

"Good."

Just then Jake's cell phone rang.

"Jake Hammond."

"Jake. It's Norm. Can you talk right now?"

"Yes. As a matter of fact Joe and I are the only ones in the conference room. What do you have for me?"

"I checked the reconciliations of cash receipts for the past month and everything seems to be in order. I also reviewed the bank deposits and found them to be in agreement. Additionally, I examined the input reports that show postings to the customer accounts. As you know, payments received by Cash Management, bank deposit slips, and payment updates must all reconcile each day. Any exceptions are documented and researched. Every one of the days I checked was in perfect order. All payments received were posted to customer records and all money was deposited timely. However, [. . .] and this is the part that I find most interesting, the detail customer records no longer show the premium payments, which means someone has changed those fields as well as the coverage indicator fields on the customer files."

"So tell me, Norm, what's the bottom line? How many accounts are we talking about, and how much money's been diverted?"

"Right now I'd say approximately a hundred or so accounts are affected. But I have no way of knowing what the dollars are because I don't know how long someone's been diverting the money, assuming it *was* being diverted.

And let's keep in mind that we don't know if there are other things going on, I mean, besides the insurance thing."

"You're right. But we need to take one thing at a time. Once we figure out what's going on with the insurance premiums, we can take a look at other areas."

Joe jumped in. "We know that the dual control we have over receipts works, because we've tested that many times. And the folks who get the receipts are different from those who make the bank deposits, and the data entry people who post the payments are different than any of the others. So our systems of controls in those areas seem to be tight. We have three separate groups, all of which have to balance their work to the other two. Which means the money gets diverted *after* the deposits are made. Do you guys agree?"

"That would have to be someone with access to our bank accounts" added Norm. "There isn't any way Ron Hayward could have gotten that access."

"If not" added Jake, "whoever got the cash was either working with Ron, or had access to Ron's logon ID. Norm, I know you said that the fields were altered on Saturday by someone using Ron's ID. Can you also tell me *where* the access came from?"

"Yes. I hadn't looked at that earlier because it seemed clear who had gotten access. I'll check on that right now and get back to you."

After he hung up Jake decided to speak with Jeff Anderson. He tracked him down in the operations area. "Jeff, can you spare a few minutes?"

"Of course, Jake. Let's go to my office."

They got settled in around a small conference table in Jeff's office and went over some of the details of what Jake's staff had found so far. Then Jeff filled Jake in on his conversations with the police. "The detective in charge wants to speak with you as soon as you have a moment" he said. "His name's Tim Nagle. Here's his cell phone number. He'd like you to call him."

"OK, thanks, Jeff. I'll do that." He headed back to the conference room, and dialed Detective Nagle's number.

"This is Tim Nagle" the voice at the other end answered.

"Hello, Detective Nagle. This is Jake Hammond at New Commerce Finance. Jeff Anderson told me you wanted to speak with me."

"Yes. Thanks for calling. Would you have a few minutes for me right now? I'm actually just outside your building, still working at the accident scene."

"Sure. Come on up to the third floor. I'll meet you in the reception area."

Jeff offered them the use of his office and Jake and detective Nagle spent the next hour discussing Ron Hayward.

"Mr. Hammond, I'd like to get as much information as I can about Ron Hayward, but first, I was wondering if you could help me put things into perspective. Can you tell me a bit about your responsibilities at New Commerce?"

"Well, my title is Chief Security and Compliance Officer. I'm responsible for computer security, and for making sure the systems of internal controls within the organization are adequately protecting the company's assets. I also oversee the organization's compliance with regulatory requirements. I report directly to our Board of Directors, but administratively to the CFO."

"I understand that you and your staff are currently conducting a special review at this location."

"That's correct."

"Was this a regularly scheduled review?"

"No. We're doing a special review at the request of our Chief Credit Officer. He's been concerned with the rise in delinquencies at some locations, including this one."

"Listen, Mr. Hammond. Let's not beat around the bush. I understand that you're doing a special review because you've noted some irregularities in the accounts managed by Ron Hayward. Isn't that correct?"

"We *have* noted some irregularities, but only regarding insurance coverage on customers' inventories, and so far, yes, all of the accounts involved have been managed by Ron Hayward. But that isn't why we initiated this review. Why is this of interest to you? Do you suspect foul play in the accident?"

"We don't know yet, but I need to gather as much information as possible so I can determine the direction I should go in. Clearly, whoever hit Mr. Hayward didn't slow down, or even stop to see how badly he was injured. An eye witness said that the car sped up and disappeared into traffic."

"So, are you saying you think it wasn't an accident?"

"That's not what I'm saying at all. It's still too soon to reach any conclusions. I'll need to get more information on Ron Hayward, and speak to our forensic folds before making that determination."

"I understand."

"Is there anything else I should know right now, Mr. Hammond?"

"Not at this time, Detective. We're still reviewing the activity on the accounts that are the target of our internal review. We've got quite a bit of work left to do before we can draw any reasonable conclusions, but I promise to keep you in the loop."

"Please do that Mr. Hammond. Thanks for your time. We'll be in touch."

Just then Jake's cell phone rang. "Jake Hammond" he answered.

"Jake. It's Norm. After we spoke a while ago, I went back and checked the access records to see *where* the changes originated. We already knew the changes were made by Ron Hayward, or someone who was logged on as Ron. Now, we know that the changes originated there, at the Marietta office."

"Interesting" said Jake. "So now we've got to figure out how he got his hands on the money. Take a look at all the wire transfers that were made from our main bank account over the past few months. We need supporting documentation for each, and an explanation as to who processed it and why it was required. If Ron had inside help, there had to be an unauthorized transfer to an outside bank account."

"I'll get right on it."

***

By the time they'd left the hospital last night it was almost 10 p.m., and much too late to try to make it back to Tallahassee, so Joyce, the kids, and her parents spent the night at the local Holiday Inn Express, but even though they were all exhausted, no one got much sleep. They were still trying to cope with the reality of their loss.

They'd made arrangements to have Dan's body shipped back to Tallahassee as soon as the coroner released it. There wouldn't be a need for an autopsy, as the cause of death was evident, and there was no indication of foul play, but the coroner still had to release the body, which would probably happen first thing in the morning. The Barrett funeral parlor in Tallahassee had been notified to expect the body.

Since none of them had gotten much sleep, they were on the road by 6 a.m. They pulled into the driveway of Joyce's house just after noon time and were surprised to see the trucks parked in front of the garage. One of them was Randy's and the other, they saw from the writing on its side, belonged to a cleaning crew. When Randy spotted them in the driveway, he ran out to greet them.

"Joyce, how are you doing? I'm so sorry. Dan was a good friend. I'm going to miss him."

"I know. Thanks Randy."

He hugged each of the kids and then Bob and Donna. He'd been such a close friend of Dan's and the family that he was like a brother to Joyce and an uncle to the kids.

"What's going on, Randy? Joyce asked as she motioned toward the truck parked next to Randy's.

"Your dad gave me the key before he left and I called in this cleaning company. They've been sucking up the remainder of the water, and cleaning everything up. It looks like there's been minimal damage. They should be finished shortly, and you all can come right in."

"I don't know how I can ever thank you, Randy. I wasn't looking forward to coming home to the mess I saw on Thursday."

"Please, Joyce, don't mention it. It's the least I could do."

They got settled into the house and then Randy filled her in on the latest developments at the dealership. They still hadn't been able to open for business because of the problem with the insurance coverage. He'd had a crew clean up the water inside, but he couldn't move the merchandise until he could get a claims adjuster there, and that couldn't happen until they determined if Walters Marine had a valid policy in effect. He told her how Jeff Anderson had promised to get back to him by close of business today.

Chapter 19

Jeff had told Jake about the call from Randy Jones at Walters Marine, and about his promise to get back to him by end of business today. It was now 4 p.m. and he needed to make the call, but he wanted to know what he should say. Jake was with him now in his office, and they were discussing it.

"Should I try to put him off again? He's been put off a lot, and he threatened to have his attorney contact us."

"He'll probably end up with an attorney at some point anyway. It seems clear that he doesn't have any inventory insurance. But seeing as how we're the ones who paid for the equipment, Walter's Marine shouldn't have too much to worry about. His biggest problem is going to be from the lack of sales until he can get some replacement inventory. He'll probably want us to cover that."

"So what do you want me to tell him?"

"Why don't you tell him we can't confirm his coverage, but that we'll make good on any claims. In the meantime, see if you can get in touch with the manufacturers so we can figure out what they want to do with the inventory."

"OK. I'll get on it right now."

Jake went back to the conference room and a few minutes later Jeff was on the phone with Randy Jones. He explained that they couldn't confirm insurance coverage yet, but told him New Commerce would cover any losses on the equipment, and said he'd get in touch with the equipment manufacturers to see what they wanted to do with the merchandise and ask how soon they could get replacement items delivered. He thought the discussion had gone well and was about to close, when he got yet another surprise.

"One more thing, Mr. Anderson" Randy said. "The owner of Walters Marine has just died. He was involved in a major highway accident on interstate ten last week. You might've heard about it."

"Yes, I did. I'm sorry to hear that."

"Well, Mr. Anderson, the reason I'm telling you this is that your company was also supposed to provide life insurance for Mr. Walters. I haven't checked with the insurance company yet, but I wanted to advise you that I'll be doing that. You should probably follow up on your end to make sure that wasn't screwed up too."

"I certainly will do that, Mr. Jones, thank you for the information. And please, will you extend my deepest sympathy to the family?"

"I will."

"Thank you Mr. Jones. I will look into the life insurance issue and try to get back to you tomorrow." They hung up and Jeff set out to find Jake Hammond. It was starting to look like the missing inventory coverage might just be the tip of the iceberg. Randy decided to follow up with Great Waters on the life insurance issue.

"Great Waters Insurance Group, how may I help you?" the voice at the other end said.

"This is Randy Jones from Walters Marine in Tallahassee. Sorry to bother you again. I called earlier about our inventory insurance coverage, and now I have another question."

"Good afternoon Mr. Jones. I'll put you right through to Jane Donahue our claims manager. I'm sure she'll be able to help you." The operators had been alerted to the situation with New Commerce customers, and told to forward the calls to Jane.

A few seconds later he heard another voice on the line.

"This is Jane Donahue speaking. How may I help you?"

"Jane, this is Randy Jones from Walters Marine in Tallahassee, Florida."

"Yes, good afternoon Mr. Jones. I understand you had some questions about your inventory insurance coverage."

"Well, I'm actually calling on another issue, but before we get into that, let me fill you in on the inventory insurance issue. New Commerce is looking into it on their end. At first they insisted that it had to be a system conversion problem at your end, but now they seem to be backing off on that. I don't know what's going on, but they've promised to cover any losses on inventory, so that makes me feel a little better. However, another issue has come up."

"What's that?"

"They were also supposed to have arranged for life insurance on the owner of Walters Marine, Dan Walters. He recently died in that big traffic accident on I-10 just east of Tallahassee. Can you tell me if Great Waters has a life insurance policy on him?"

"Sure. If you can hold on for a second, I'll look it up right now. Do you have a policy number, by any chance?"

"Yes. Are you ready?"

"Go ahead."

"Our records indicate that the policy number is L179344-5211."

"OK, I have it. Hold on while I check the system."

A few seconds later Jane was back on the line.

"Mr. Jones?"

"Yes."

"I've checked our systems. They indicate there was a policy by that number in effect for Mr. Daniel Walters. However, that policy expired some time ago and was not renewed."

"I suspected as much. I'm afraid this is going to get pretty ugly. I don't know what's going on, but someone is going to have some serious explaining to do."

"I agree with you, Mr. Jones. I'm going to begin a review at this end, and I'll work with the folks at New Commerce to try to figure out what's going on there."

"Thanks, Jane. My contact at New Commerce is Jeff Anderson."

"I've been in contact with Jeff myself. I'll give him a call and see what we can do to work on this thing together."

They hung up, and Jane dialed Jeff's number. A woman answered.

"Mr. Anderson's office, Marie Costa speaking."

"Hello, this is Jane Donahue from Great Waters Insurance Group in Milwaukee. May I speak with Mr. Anderson please?"

"Mr. Anderson isn't in his office at the moment. Can I have him call you as soon as he returns?"

"Yes, please. Do you know how long that might be?"

"I can probably track him down in a few minutes. I'll give him your message right away. It shouldn't be long before he can call you."

"Thank you. Please tell him this is important."

She found him in the conference room with Jake Hammond. "Mr. Anderson. Sorry to bother you, but you received a call from a Jane Donahue of Great Waters Insurance Group. She said it was important." She handed him a paper with Jane's number on it.

"Thanks, Marie. I'll give her a call in a moment."

Jake and Jeff looked at each other, as if to say "now what?"

"Jake, could you join me in my office while I return this call? Maybe I can put her on speaker phone, if that's OK with you."

"Yeah, I think that would be a good idea."

They walked back to Jeff's office, and then he dialed Jane's number.

"Jane Donahue. How may I help you?"

"Jane, this is Jeff Anderson returning your call. I have Jake Hammond here in my office with me. Jake is our Chief Security and Compliance Officer. Would you mind if I put you on speaker?"

"No, go right ahead."

Jeff punched the speaker button on the phone. "OK, you're on speaker now. What can I do for you?"

"Well, Jeff, as you know from our previous discussions, a high percentage of the calls we got after Fay hit were from dealers who didn't have inventory insurance in effect. So far, all of those were customers of New Commerce and that's a concern, and I think we should work together to resolve that issue. But just a while ago I got a call from Randy Jones at Walters Marine about life insurance on the owner, Dan Walters."

"Yeah, I spoke with Randy earlier and didn't have a chance to follow up yet. What did you find?"

"I found that he did have a policy in effect at one time, but it's expired so he's no longer covered. I promised him that we'd work together to figure this thing out. I imagine he's not the only one who may have some concerns."

"Jane, this is Jake Hammond. We're looking into some irregularities at this end, but have a ways to go yet before we figure out what's going on. I agree with you that our two companies should work together on this. I was wondering if maybe I could discuss our situation with your Internal Auditor. Could you give me his or her name and phone number?"

"Sure. His name is Jim Seversen, spelled "Seversen" not Severson." She gave him the number, and said she'd tell Jim to expect his call. "If I can be of any further assistance, please let me know."

"Thanks, Jane. We will."

After they hung up, Jake was the first to speak.

"I think it's time to fill Fred, Tom and Deb in on what's going on. Now that we'll be working with people from Great Waters, we'll need to be very careful what we share and how we approach this investigation. I'll do that right now, and then contact Jim Seversen over at Great Waters. If we can't find a money trail at this end, it's possible it could be at their end."

Jeff noted how Jake used the word "investigation" rather than review.

***

It was six o'clock, and even though he didn't usually leave this early, Jeff was looking forward to going home. It'd been another stressful day. As he was locking his desk he heard the knock at the office door. "Detective Nagle is here to see you, Mr. Anderson" said Marie. "He says he has a few follow up questions."

"Thanks, Marie. Send him in, please."

The last thing he wanted right now was to be interrogated by Detective Tim Nagle, but Jeff knew he really didn't have a choice. Detective Nagle was very persistent.

"Thanks for seeing me so late Mr. Anderson. I know you were probably looking forward to heading out, so I won't keep you very long, I promise. Just a few follow up questions."

"Not a problem, Detective. Please, have a seat."

"I was wondering if Mr. Hammond was available to meet with us. I think maybe he could shed some light on the issues I'd like to discuss."

"I think he's still here. Hold on while I ask my assistant to track him down. Marie, could you come in here please?"

"Yes, Mr. Anderson. What can I do for you?"

"Could you try to locate Jake Hammond and ask him to join us here in my office? You'll probably find him in the main conference room."

"Yes, sir, right away."

Within minutes Jake was knocking at Jeff's door. Marie had warned him that Detective Nagle was there, and it didn't really surprise him at all. In fact, he was expecting him sooner. He knew that the accident investigation would require a lot more information about Ron Hayward then they'd given out so far.

"Come on in and have a seat, Jake. I believe you've already met Detective Nagle?"

"Yes, we've met. Good afternoon, Detective."

"Good afternoon to you, sir. I'm sorry to have to bother you again, but there are a few questions I need to ask."

"Not at all, Detective" replied Jake. "We'll be glad to do anything we can to help you. Please go ahead and ask your questions."

"Well, I'd like to know a little more about Ron Hayward. For example, what were his responsibilities here at New Commerce? And what do you know about his personal life?"

Jeff fielded this question. "Ron was an Account Manager, which means he had responsibility for overseeing the servicing of a number of our customers. I believe he had fifteen accounts assigned to him."

"Can you give me some more specifics? What, exactly, did he do to oversee the servicing of the accounts?"

"For one thing, he was the primary contact for the customers. They called him first with any questions on their account. He also made sure they were in complete compliance with their loan agreement, arranged for inventory checks, collected any past due payments, and if asked, arranged for inventory insurance for the customer."

"I see" said Detective Nagle. "And can you tell me how long he's been employed by New Commerce?"

This line of questioning went on for some time. Finally, after about fifteen minutes, Nagle asked the open ended question that hit them like a bullet.

"Is there anything you can think of relative to his work that might in any way be related to the accident"?

"I'm not sure I understand the question, detective."

"I'll get right to the point Mr. Hammond. Right now I'm not at all sure it *was* an accident, so I need to know if anything might be going on here at work that could have led to someone wanting Ron out of the way."

"I thought there was a witness. What makes you think now it wasn't an accident?"

"You understand that I can't get into all the details, but let me just say that the way the SUV sped up when Mr. Hayward stepped out of the building makes it look like an intentional hit and run. At first the witness thought it might be teenagers racing, but there weren't any other cars in the parking lot. The SUV was alone. Also, if it were an accident, it's likely the driver would've hesitated after the impact, trying to decide what to do next. But our driver never hesitated. He just kept speeding up and then disappeared into traffic. If this was intentional, I need to figure out why. "

"Oh my God" whispered Jeff. I can't believe something like that would happen to one of our employees."

"There have been some *irregularities* relative to some of Ron's accounts that we've just begun looking into. I can't say for sure yet what's going on, though" added Jake.

"Now listen, Mr. Hammond. This could turn into a homicide investigation real quick. I need to know everything that's been going on here."

"I understand that, detective. I'll give you as much information as I can, but I must insist that it remain confidential. We haven't completed our internal investigation yet, and we don't have proof of exactly what has transpired."

"I promise to handle any information you give me as confidential. But you've got to understand that our investigation, especially if it looks like a homicide, has to take priority over yours. Hopefully we can work together and share whatever we find. Agreed?"

"Agreed."

They spent the next hour discussing everything Jake and his staff had put together so far. Jake stressed over and over again that even though things were pointing to Ron, they still hadn't finalized their review and nothing was considered to be hard evidence. He talked about what steps remained for them to accomplish and mentioned how they'd be working with the people at Great Waters Insurance Group.

"You need to wrap up your review as quickly as possible" said Tim. "Do you need any technical assistance with the system review?"

"Thanks, but I think we have it covered" replied Jake.

"Just the same, whatever you uncover could end up being important evidence in a criminal case. I really need to have one of my people working with you on this. Ensuring an unbroken chain of evidence could be critical to our case."

"OK. I understand. As long as we all agree that this is our review for the time being, and my folks will take the lead."

"Agreed" replied Nagle. "I'll have someone check in with you first thing in the morning."

After the meeting broke up, Jake called Augusta to fill Fred in on the latest developments. They agreed that the two of them would bring Tom D'Angelo into the loop first thing in the morning, and then they'd figure out how and when to approach Deb Cutter.

Chapter 20

Wednesday, August 20, 2008

It'd been a week since she'd left for her parent's house to avoid the storm. Fay had run its course and it was a bright and sunny day in Tallahassee. There was lots of property damage from the rain, but the water was receding and things were starting to get back to normal for most folks. The Walters residence had been cleaned and the building was back to normal, but the family wasn't. They were exhausted from the events of the last few days, and now the task of making the funeral arrangements lay ahead.

They'd arranged for Dan's body to be shipped to Barrett's Funeral Home on North Monroe Street and it was supposed to arrive last night, so they'd made an appointment for 10:30 this morning. Finalizing the funeral arrangements was just one of many things on their "to do" list for today. Joyce hadn't gotten any real sleep in almost a week, and it was catching up with her. She sat at the kitchen counter staring out the window into the back yard. She wasn't looking at anything in particular, just staring blankly into the sky. She heard her mother's voice, as if in a dream.

"Honey, you've got to have something to eat. I've made breakfast and fed the kids, now you need to sit down and have something. You'll need your strength. Please, come and sit down." It wasn't until she felt her mother's hand on her arm that she realized she wasn't dreaming. This was really happening to her. She looked up and saw her mother with a pleading look on her face and tears in the corners of her eyes. She let herself be led to the table, and she sat down. She saw the food on a plate in front of her, but didn't seem to be able to figure out what to do with it.

With her mother's help Joyce ate a few bites of her breakfast and then got dressed. By ten o'clock she was on her way to Barrett's, with her dad driving the car, and her mom at home with the children. She didn't want to put the kids through the ordeal of selecting a casket and finalizing the arrangements. If all went as planned, she thought the funeral could be held on Saturday, which would give all their friends and relatives enough time to get here. They pulled into the parking lot at Barrett's at 10:15, a few minutes ahead of their appointed time. They were greeted at the door by Mr. Barrett himself, a very dignified gentleman of about fifty years, dressed in the black suit, white shirt and black tie that seem to be the mandatory attire for all funeral directors.

"Mrs. Walters. I'm Anthony Barrett. I'm so sorry for your loss. Please do come in." He led them into a private, well appointed office just to the left of the main entrance, and far from any of the viewing parlors. He found it was too unnerving for grieving relatives to actually see the parlors before being able to settle in. Once they'd gone over some of the preliminary details, they'd be more prepared to view the parlor and to select a casket.

Mr. Barrett informed her that her husband's remains had arrived, as scheduled, the night before and that he'd be able to have calling hours anytime she'd like, beginning tomorrow, Thursday the 21st of August. What were her wishes, he asked. They agreed on calling hours for Friday afternoon and evening, and assuming the church was available the funeral could be on Saturday. Mr. Barrett would make all the arrangements with the priest, and confirm the time with the family as soon as he'd done so. Then they discussed some of the financial arrangements. Of course, the final price would depend upon which casket they would choose, so Mr. Barrett took them into the back room to make a selection. Joyce selected a solid oak casket, because Dan always loved the look and feel of wood. That's what he'd want, she was certain of it. It was one of the most expensive models, but she didn't care. The insurance would take care of it.

By eleven o'clock all arrangements had been made and Bob and Joyce were on their way to Walters Marine. She planned to meet Randy there so they could discuss what was going on with the dealership. She knew there was some water damage, and wanted to make sure they could reopen as soon as possible because every day they stayed closed they lost money and jeopardized the future of the dealership.

Randy was waiting for them when they got there. He'd had a cleaning crew come in to take care of the water and clean up the furniture, and another crew had done some temporary patching on the roof to avoid additional damage in the event of more rain. The aluminum shutters were off the windows and doors and, from the outside at least, everything looked like it was back to normal. But the inventory was pretty much as he'd found it, clearly damaged and not able to be sold. He greeted them at curbside, and tried to prepare Joyce for what she was about to see.

"I've had a crew come in and clean up a bit, but the inventory hasn't been touched yet. It looks kind of bad, but the finance company has promised to make good on anything not covered by insurance. They're contacting the manufacturer to see about getting replacement inventory."

"Thanks, Randy. I can't tell you how much we appreciate everything you've done."

They made their way to the main entrance and Randy held the door open as Joyce and Bob went inside. Although she'd tried to prepare herself for what she was about to see, she still wasn't ready. The showroom looked more like a second hand store with used merchandise than a dealership stocked with brand new PWCs and boats. She thought of how hard Dan had worked to build this dealership and how disappointed he'd be if he saw this.

"My God, Randy, can anything be saved?"

"Unfortunately everything in here is damaged to some degree and cannot be saved. Many of the boats outside are also damaged, but a few made it OK. All in all, I'd say we lost about ninety five percent of our inventory."

"How long do you think it'll be before we can get replacements and open up for business again?"

"I don't know. The finance company was supposed to take care of that, but I think I'll call the manufacturer myself to see what the story is. As soon as I have any information I'll give you a call."

Since Randy obviously had everything under control at the dealership, Joyce decided to go back home and spend some time with the kids before continuing with her "to do" list. Randy went back to Dan's office to look for a contact name at the manufacturer. Dan always took care of the paperwork and Randy wasn't quite sure where everything was, but he'd poke around until he found the information.

***

Deb Cutter, Tom D'Angelo, Fred Campbell and Dave Banner were in Deb's office waiting for Jake's call. Fred had arranged the meeting after he and Jake spoke on the phone the previous afternoon. They'd agreed it was time to bring the other key members of the Executive Committee up to date. At 10:00 sharp, the phone rang. As usual, Deb's assistant answered, and buzzed Deb.

"Yes, what is it?" Deb answered. She never bothered to use her assistant's name, or for that matter, to use any civilities at all when dealing with anyone she felt was not her equal.

"It's Mr. Hammond on line one."

Without a thank you, Deb picked up the phone.

"Jake. I have Tom D'Angelo, Fred Campbell and Dave Banner here in my office with me. I'm going to put you on speaker phone. Hold on a second." She pressed the speaker button and replaced the handset in the cradle.

"OK Jake. You're on speaker. Go ahead."

"Thanks, Deb. I don't know how much Fred's told you so far, but we've uncovered enough issues down here already for me to tell you we've got a pretty serious problem. We've got a long way to go on our investigation, but I wanted the senior management team to be aware of what's going on."

"Jake, this is Fred. Everyone here knows what led to our decision to conduct a special review there in Marietta. I was able to fill Dave in on the background this morning. Why don't you start with why you decided to personally head up this investigation, and then go on from there?"

Over the next twenty minutes or so Jake recounted everything that'd transpired, including the hit and run "accident" that killed Ron Hayward, and he explained his plans for continuing the investigation. He'd work with Jim Seversen over at Great Waters to try to find out what happened to the premium payments. He'd perform a 100% verification of all customer files from the Atlanta office. And most importantly, he'd continue to follow the trail of evidence in the computer systems of New Commerce. This, he explained, was the most promising avenue of all.

Dave Banner immediately offered whatever technical assistance Jake needed. As Chief Information Officer, Dave could easily muster up an army of technical gurus. All Jake had to do was give the word.

"Thanks, Dave. I really appreciate the offer, and I'll probably take you up on it soon. So far, I've had Norm Cassidy doing most of my leg work."

"I know Norm" added Dave. "He's a good guy and very capable. But he'll probably need help at some point."

"I agree." "We'll be in touch as soon as we reach that point. Who should be our contact?"

"Steve O'Brien, in tech support, is the person you'll need. I'll talk to him as soon as we leave here so he'll be expecting your call. He'll be able to do whatever you need in strict confidence. He's my most trusted person."

"Thanks, Dave."

"Jake," said Deb, "I don't have to tell you how sensitive this issue is. When you're dealing with people outside of New Commerce, don't give out any information that will make us look bad."

"I understand your concern, Deb. We won't divulge more than we have to. But the issue with the police is touchy. They've made it perfectly clear their investigation has to take priority over ours."

"I know. I know, Jake. I trust you to handle everything well. I'm just concerned that this is a particularly bad time for any negative publicity. Our stock price is still going down, like everyone else's in this economy. We just don't need any kind of headlines that'll scare our investors. Do you agree, Tom?"

"Yes, of course. Hopefully, any information that gets to the public will be general in nature, and not reflect badly on us. Right now, the hit and run is just that. A hit and run accident. Even if investors hear of it, they're not likely to get excited. However, if the news of our investigation gets out, that'd be a whole different story."

Jake stepped back into the conversation. "I agree, too, and I've made it clear to Detective Nagle that we need to keep everything confidential for the time being, and of course, he agrees because he doesn't need newspaper reporters going wild on this. It wouldn't help his investigation either. And I'll be sure that Jim Seversen is on board too."

"OK. Thanks, everyone. Unless there's anything else anyone wants to add, I think we can adjourn for now."

"Thanks, Deb. And thanks to the rest of you too" added Jake. "I'll keep everyone posted."

By 10:30 Jake was back in the conference room. Joe and the staff were out completing the interviews with the remaining account managers. He took out the paper with the phone number on it and dialed it. After two rings, a voice answered. "Great Waters Insurance Group, this is Jim Seversen."

"Jim, this is Jake Hammond from New Commerce Commercial Finance."

"Hello Jake. Jane told me to expect your call. How can I help you?"

"I don't know how much Jane's told you, Jim, but we have an interesting situation here, and I think we'll need your help to get it resolved. We're conducting an investigation into some missing insurance premiums and policies. We have a number of customers who had inventory insurance with Great Waters, and a few who *thought* they had coverage. In all cases, we at New Commerce had arranged for the insurance and we were paying the premiums, and then billing our customers. As of last Friday our records confirmed that each of the accounts in question had coverage. However, something's happened over the weekend, and now our division paper files and our computer files no longer have evidence of that coverage."

"I see" responded Jim.

Jake continued. "Furthermore, Jane Donahue found that some of the policies were in effect, but expired, while others never existed. The thing is, though, even though we know our files have been tampered with, there's no evidence that any money's been taken. We've done a review of our cash management procedures, and all cash receipts have been processed. We're still reviewing the computer access logs to try to pinpoint exactly who did what, and when. We're also checking our banking systems to see if there've been any unauthorized cash transfers."

"Good idea. What can I do to help?"

"I'm wondering if you and your people could do some checking at your end to see if you've ever received premium payments on the accounts in question. We don't know how long this situation has been going on, so I'm not sure how far back you'd need to go, but if we can find any evidence that premiums were ever paid, that would help narrow our investigation."

"I'd be glad to help out, Jake. Can you send me some specific details?'

"I'll have the policy numbers in question emailed to you right away. I'm not sure how your systems work, but I thought maybe you'd be able to review your reconciliation procedures for cash receipts and premium postings for any outstanding issues. In the meantime, we'll continue the review at this end to see exactly how premium payments were handled, how they were transmitted, etc. Can we agree to touch base at the end of each day to share progress reports?"

"Sure Jake, not a problem."

"Thanks, Jim. I'll give you a call tomorrow afternoon, then."

As Jake was hanging up the phone Joe Nash came into the conference room.

"We've interviewed all the account managers and nothing out of the ordinary has surfaced. I think we should talk to a few other people at this point."

"Who did you have in mind?"

"I'd like to speak with Kathy Brown, the Operations Supervisor, and maybe a few of her people too."

"What are you thinking of?"

"Well, the way things work here in Marietta, account managers are the primary customer contacts. However, they don't really have anything to do with the processing of the day to day stuff. Even though account managers have access to most data fields in the customer records, the accounts are set up on the system and maintained by the operations folks. And they're the ones who arrange for insurance coverage. I think we need to follow that lead before we go in any other direction. There might be a reason why all cash reconciliations in Augusta are in order."

"That's interesting, Joe. I just finished speaking with Jim Seversen, the Internal Auditor over at Great Waters and I asked him to take a look at their cash receipts and premium application procedures just to see if he can track any premium payments for the accounts that have expired. If there were ever any premiums paid on those, he should be able to figure that out."

"So, you're thinking the same thing I am, then?"

"We know we've got a problem here at our end. That's clear from the exceptions we've already uncovered. But, I'm thinking we now need to figure out if and how premiums were remitted to Great Waters. If we can show we sent them, then there's a problem at their end as well. Maybe that's how the money was diverted."

"I was thinking of something along the same lines, Jake. Because our operations folks deal with the people at Great Waters on a regular basis, it's possible that there could be something going on there."

"I think it's time we speak with Kathy Brown, and I think I'd like to conduct this interview myself."

Jake checked the time. It was just before noontime and Kathy would probably be out to lunch. He decided to wait until early afternoon to conduct the interview. In the meantime, he'd call Norm Cassidy to get an update on what was happening at that end and grab a bite to eat.

Chapter 21

Jake and Joe had just come back from getting a bite to eat and were alone in the conference room preparing for the upcoming interview of Kathy Brown when Jake said "I don't think Ron Hayward did it."

It wasn't the first time Joe had experienced one of Jake's sudden revelations. Often, without notice, he'd spew some tidbit he'd been contemplating, and this seemed to be just such a time. "What are you thinking, Jake?"

"We still need to hear from Norm Cassidy to see if he uncovered any unauthorized wire transfers from our bank accounts. But we know controls in our Treasury area are solid, so I can't imagine Ron could've gotten wire transfer authority. And without it, there isn't any way he could've made transfers. Although collusion is possible, it's unlikely."

"I agree with that assessment" added Joe.

"Additionally" continued Jake, "there's no way Ron could've diverted the premium payments, as they were sent directly to the Cash Management area, and all cash receipts have been reconciled and reviewed. Norm's already taken a look at those."

"But the system changes were made by Ron."

"Not necessarily. There are a number of ways that someone else could've made those changes and made it look like it was Ron."

"So where do we go from here?" asked Joe.

"I'm having Norm work with Steve O'Brien in tech support to take a closer look at the files to see if they can come up with anything else. In the meantime, we need to review the building access logs and I think we should speak with Detective Nagle to see if he's talked to any of Ron's family and friends. I'd be interested in knowing if we can determine for sure whether Ron was in the building Saturday when the file changes were made, or if he has an alibi. I'd also like to get more background information on the staff here in Marietta to see if any of them have the technical background to be able to spoof someone's address and ID on our network. I have a feeling that might be what we're dealing with here" added Jake.

"OK. Why don't I give Norm a call to get an update from him, and then talk with Jeff and someone in HR to see if we can get access to the personnel files of the Marietta employees? In the meantime, you can speak with Detective Nagle, and also do the interview with Kathy Brown. I'm sure you can get one of the staff folks to sit in on it with you."

"Agreed" responded Jake.

Joe set out to find Jeff Anderson, while Jake tracked down the members of his staff so he could decide which one of them he'd ask to sit in on his interview with Kathy Brown. He found Sue and Chuck in the operations area still working on insurance verifications. Jason was in the office of one of the account managers, helping him get information from a file in response to a customer inquiry. He approached Jason and whispered that he'd like to see him as soon as he was finished with the customer call, and then he returned to the conference room to wait for him. Within a few minutes, Jason showed up, carrying the file he'd used in assisting the account manager.

"What's up, Jake?"

"I'm going to interview Kathy Brown, the Operations Supervisor, and I need to have someone present with me. Joe is working on something else for me, so I thought you could sit in on that meeting, if you don't mind."

"I don't mind at all. I'd be glad to. When's the meeting?"

"I'd like to do it now. I know she's back from lunch, because I saw her at her desk when Joe and I came back. Let me go out there now to ask her to come in to speak with us."

While Jason waited in the conference room, Jake headed out to the operations area. He could've sent Jason, of course, but he always found that people were more likely to cooperate with him than with a staff member. When the Chief Security and Compliance Officer asked to speak with someone, they generally didn't say no. And so it was with Kathy Brown. Within minutes Jake was back in the conference room with Kathy right behind him.

"Please take a seat, Ms. Brown" Jake said as he motioned to one of the chairs around the conference table. He had already cleared off an area around the spot he pointed to, moving the mound of files to the end of the table.

"How can I help you, Mr. Hammond? And, please, call me Kathy."

"Well, Kathy, I'm sure you know by now that we're conducting an audit of this division. As part of our review, we're interviewing a number of people to get a better understanding of their roles and responsibilities, and we'd like to ask you a few questions about yours. This shouldn't take very long."

"OK. Is there anything special you're looking for? I mean, I've seen this division audited before, but no one's ever interviewed me as part of those reviews. Is there something unusual going on?"

"It's not unusual for us to conduct interviews during our reviews, Kathy. We do it all the time, but obviously, we can't speak with everyone during each review. We decide on which interviews to conduct based upon a number of factors, including the scope of the review, our understanding of the functions being reviewed, and whether or not we've interviewed the affected parties previously. Since we haven't spoken with you previously, we need to make sure we have a good understanding of what you do and how you do it."

"I see" responded Kathy. "That sounds logical. Please, go ahead and ask your questions. I'll try to answer them to the best of my knowledge."

For the next hour Jake and Jason spoke with Kathy Brown about her role and responsibilities. They asked about how she and her staff process file maintenance changes, paying particular attention to who can edit which fields on the files, and which documentation was maintained to show evidence of the authorizations for such changes. She explained how assignments were made and stressed that no one was responsible for specific accounts, but processed changes on a "next available" basis. When a change is required, it's requested in writing by the account managers. The form is sent to Operations, and the next available analyst processes the change. The request form is then filed in the customer file to show evidence of the authorization.

"Thank you, Kathy. You've been very helpful. I think we're about done here for now. Oh, I just thought of one last question, if you don't mind. I just want to make sure my understanding is correct."

"Not at all, Mr. Hammond. Please go ahead."

"Based upon what you've told us, am I correct to assume that ALL changes are assigned randomly? No *one* person in Operations has the ability to process all changes to any one customer account?"

"That's correct, Mr. Hammond."

"How about changes across the board?"

"I'm sorry, I'm not sure I understand the question."

"I mean, would it be possible for one person to process a particular type of change for multiple customers? For example, would any one person handle insurance additions, changes and updates for all customers, or are those processed the same way others are, on a "next available" basis?"

"Typically, setting up, removing, or changing insurance indicators is done in the same manner as all other changes, on a "next available" basis. The only difference between these transactions and others is that account managers don't need to submit a request form for those changes. I'm the one who puts through the request form, which is later filed as all others are. I believe this is the standard operating procedure for all divisions."

"Thank you for that information, Ms. Brown. I think that'll be all for now, unless you have something more to ask, Jason."

"No, I'm all set too. Thanks so much for your time, Ms. Brown."

After Kathy Brown left the conference room, Jake and Jason reviewed the information they'd gotten from her. Most of it was pretty much as expected. "Thanks for your help in this, Jason" said Jake. "You can go back to what you were previously doing."

"Actually, I'm ready to go back and help Sue and Chuck with the verification process." He headed out to the Operations area, and Jake decided to give Detective Nagle a call before setting out to find Joe and Jeff. He found the card with Nagle's number in his wallet and dialed it.

"Nagle here" the voice at the other end said.

"Detective Nagle, this is Jake Hammond at New Commerce Finance. Do you have a moment to speak with me?"

"Jake, how are you? I was just thinking about you. How can I help you?"

"I was wondering if you've had an opportunity to trace Ron Hayward's activities over the past weekend. I'm interested in knowing where he was on Saturday morning."

"Actually, I do have that information. On Saturday morning and for most of the early afternoon, Ron was with his nephew, fishing. Several people saw him on the lake and can confirm the timing. He didn't get back from the fishing trip until late in the afternoon. We don't know exactly what he did next, but we do know that he went to his office later that day. The sign in log indicates he got there a little after 9 p.m.

"So what you're telling me is that there's no way that Ron Hayward was in his office, or even anywhere in our building, on Saturday morning?"

"That's right. Why do you ask?"

"Because the suspicious activities we traced to him took place on Saturday morning, from his terminal here in the building."

"That's interesting. So, where do you go from here?"

"We've got our technical people working on all angles. In my opinion, Ron's ID and IP address may have been spoofed by someone who wanted everything to point to Ron. I'm beginning to wonder myself, whether his death was really an accident."

"I couldn't agree more. I think we need to get together to compare notes. I'd like to meet with you first thing in the morning, if you can make it. I'll bring my technical guy with me, if you don't mind. He may need to interpret some technical jargon for me, if you know what I mean."

"I don't mind at all. How's first thing, say 8:30 a.m.?" asked Jake.

"That's great. I'll see you there at your office."

Jake hung up the phone and went in search of Joe and Jeff Anderson. There were a few questions he wanted to ask Jeff before meeting with Detective Nagle in the morning.

***

After speaking with Jake, Jim Seversen was ready to open up a special review of his own. He'd gotten the specific account numbers in question from Joe Nash and, as promised, was going to determine if anything had gone wrong at their end. The last thing Great Waters needed right now was a scandal, or even a hint of one. They were being battered with claims, the new owners were screaming about the lower profit projections, morale was pretty much at an all time low and the economy was tanking. Everyone was on edge.

The first thing on his agenda was a discussion with Jane Donahue. Not only was she the initial contact with New Commerce, she was also the project leader on the recently completed system conversion. Few at Great Waters knew more about its systems and operations than Jane. He picked up his receiver and dialed her number.

She answered almost immediately. "Jane Donahue."

"Jane. It's Jim Seversen. I spoke with Jake Hammond at New Commerce Commercial Finance this morning, and I'd like to discuss the situation with you. Do you have a few minutes?"

"Sure. Why don't I come to your office? The staff always gets a little uncomfortable when they see the Internal Auditor roaming around" she added, a little teasingly. "I'll be there in a few minutes."

"Thanks, Jane."

A few minutes later she was in Jim's office on the fifteenth floor. They spent the next hour discussing what Jane had found during her initial interactions with Jeff Anderson, what approach she recommended for reviewing premium payments, and how she might be able to assist Jim's staff in their review. By the time the meeting broke up, they had developed a detailed plan for the project. Jim would fill his staff in on the plans, and they'd start the field work in the morning.

Chapter 22

Thursday, August 21, 2008

Never one to be late, Tim Nagle arrived at the New Commerce offices in Marietta at 8:25 a.m., accompanied by one of his tech support people. The security guard on duty had been told to expect them, and gave them each a visitor's pass and sent them up to the third floor where they were greeted by the receptionist who led them into the conference room where Jake Hammond was waiting.

"Good morning, Jake."

"Hi Tim, how's it going?"

"Not bad, thanks."

"Come in. Please have a seat."

"Thanks, Jake. Let me introduce someone to you. This is Nick Hurley, from our Tech Support Group. I'm hoping you'll let him work with your folks. I think he'll be able to provide some valuable assistance." Tim then explained how Nick's responsibilities included assisting with investigations requiring technical computer expertise, as well as setting up and maintaining all computer systems and networks used by the department. "So, Jake, what do you have for me this morning?"

"I'll tell you, things are starting to take a turn and I now have reason to believe Ron Hayward may not have been involved with our situation after all. And that suspicion seems to be supported by the information you gave me yesterday when you told me Ron was on a lake for the entire morning and most of the afternoon on Saturday, because the unauthorized system changes were made on Saturday morning from right here in our office building. They were made using Ron's logon ID, and IP address but there are a number of other things that don't add up, so I've been having second thoughts about whether or not Ron is our man."

"If you're sure of the time and source location of the changes, I don't see how Ron could've made them" offered Tim. What's your take on this, Nick?"

"It looks to me like someone has spoofed Ron's ID and IP address to make it look like he processed the changes."

"I agree with you, Nick. Our IT specialists and tech support folks in Augusta are working on tracing the activity and in the meantime, we've expanded our review at this end. First of all, we looked at the sign in log at the front desk for Saturday, the 16th. Generally, only guests are required to sign the log. But outside of the normal business hours, for example on evenings and weekends, anyone entering the building, including employees, has to sign the log. There were a few employees who came in on that morning, but Ron Hayward was not one of them, unless, of course, the guard wasn't at his post when Ron entered the building."

"So, what you're saying is, although possible, it's highly unlikely anyone could get into the building without signing in?" asked Tim.

"That's right. But there's more. Our office area on the third floor is always locked during off hours, so, once in the building, employees have to swipe their magnetic ID cards in the card reader near the main entrance to gain access. That reader is electronically connected to our computer system which records all activity. We've reviewed the files for the 16th and found that Ron Hayward entered the building for the first time at 9:05 p.m. He was not in the building in the morning, which supports what your witnesses told you about his being on the lake."

"Is there any way someone could've gotten in without swiping his card?"

"Well, if he somehow managed to avoid the security guard on the first floor, and then, by chance, met a colleague on the third floor and walked in after that person had swiped his card, I guess it's possible. However, it's highly unlikely. I'd say we need to look at everyone who shows up on the access logs for Saturday morning."

"I agree with you" responded Tim. Have you checked on the backgrounds of the employees who *did* come into the office on the 16th?"

"We're working on that right now and I expect to hear more about that shortly."

"What can we do to help" asked Tim.

"We're trying to figure out which of them might have the technical expertise to do something like this. What might be helpful to us is if you could track down the type of vehicle that each of our targeted employees drives. If one of them owns a black SUV, and if that person has a technical background, it might be worth our while to take a closer look at him. What do you think?"

"Great idea. We've been looking at black SUVs but, frankly, without some kind of lead, it could take us days to narrow down the field. We didn't get a plate number, or even a partial number, from the witness. This'll be a good starting point. If any of the people on your list own a black SUV, we can take a look at it to see if there's any damage. From the condition of Ron's body, I'd say the vehicle had to sustain some damage."

"Do you have anything else that might help us in our internal investigation?"

"We've looked into Ron Hayward's bank accounts, and can't see anything suspicious. There's been no unusual activity, and the only deposits are the direct deposits of his payroll. If he had anything to do with the missing money, he certainly didn't run it through any of his bank accounts."

"It's looking more and more like Ron was set up" said Jake. "We're going to keep looking into the system access issues here, and in the meantime, I've asked Jim

Seversen over at Great Waters to look into their cash management procedures, and also try to figure out what might have happened to the premium payments we think were sent to them. If the cash didn't disappear at this end, then something may be going on at their end. If so, then there definitely was some collusion between someone here and someone there."

"That sounds like a plan" added Tim. No doubt we'll get to the bottom of this thing. If you can get me that list of employees, I'll get going on that while you move forward with your internal review. Let's meet or talk at least once a day so we can coordinate our activities. How about I give you a call tomorrow morning?"

"Agreed" replied Jake.

Jake produced a list of Marietta employees and handed it over to Detective Nagle. He then gave Nick Hurley the name and number of Norm Cassidy, and told him to feel free to give Norm a call. He'd already spoken with Norm, and he and Steve O'Brien were more than happy to have another body to work on the problem with them.

The meeting ended less than twenty minutes after it began, and everyone headed out to work on their various tasks just as Joe came into the conference room. He'd completed all of his interviews, and was looking for an update from Norm Cassidy. He'd spoken with the Director of HR in Augusta, and Norm Cassidy had been given access to the personnel records of all Atlanta employees, so Jake decided to give him a call to check on his progress while Joe was in the conference room. He dialed the phone and it was answered on the second ring.

"Norm. It's Jake. Do you have anything for us?"

"As a matter of fact, I do. It turns out we have five employees in the Marietta office who have various levels of experience in technical areas."

"Any evidence yet indicating who might've spoofed Ron's logon ID and IP address?" asked Joe.

"Not yet, but since we don't use IP address authentication for security purposes in our company, whoever spoofed Ron's IP address didn't need to do it to gain access. They did it to make our jobs harder when trying to track him or her."

"And it's working, isn't it" added Jake, smiling.

"Yeah, to some degree. But it was just a stalling tactic, not a road block."

At this point Joe spoke up again. "So whoever did this has quite an extensive technical background?"

"Definitely more than your ordinary PC user, that's for sure. We're probably looking for somebody who worked as a tech support person, with specific assignments in operating systems and/or network trouble shooting and security. It shouldn't take much longer to narrow it down."

"How are you going to figure it out?" asked Joe.

"The basic protocol for sending data over our network is the Internet Protocol (IP). The data is sent in packets, and the header of each packet contains the numerical source and destination address of the packet. In other words, it tells us where it came from and where it's going. If someone forges the header of a packet so it contains a different address, he can make it appear as though the packet was sent by a different machine than the one that actually sent it."

"It sounds pretty complicated to me" said Joe.

"It can be, depending on what you're trying to accomplish."

"So, there's no trail of evidence?"

"Actually, there is. Everything that's done on or to the system leaves a trail, but you have to know where to look. Under normal conditions, we rely on the IP address to identify the sender, and we stop there. But in a case like this one, where we suspect the IP address has been spoofed, there are other places to look. We can find when the packet header was changed, and by whom. But our real problem is figuring out when they gained access with Ron's ID. If they signed on as Ron before spoofing the IP address, then the trail will show that Ron did it, and that won't be of much help to us."

"So how did they get Ron's ID, I wonder" said Joe.

"Unfortunately," replied Jake, "our current system security leaves something to be desired. I've been after our Executive Committee to approve the use of a secure token system which would require every employee to use a two level identification process to gain access (e.g. a piece of hardware that generates a unique authentication code at fixed intervals combined with a PIN). But the cost of implementation has been a road block for us."

"So you're saying we don't have a very secure system?" asked Joe.

"No, that's not what I'm saying. It's just that it could be better. Our current authentication process only involves the use of a password, one level of authentication. Anyone with good social networking skills can obtain a password. That could be what happened here. But we do have firewalls that provide some additional security."

"So, we may never find out for sure who signed on as Ron?"

"That's right. Unless he or she was stupid enough to get system access with their own logon ID when spoofing the IP address."

"Do you think that's possible?"

"Anything's possible, but anyone who has enough knowledge and experience to spoof an address isn't likely to be stupid enough to use their logon ID to do it. So, it's not likely that we'll have much luck there."

"So where does that leave us?" asked Joe.

"What we'll need to do is tie all of the evidence together. Even if we can't figure out who spoofed Ron's IP address, we know approximately when they did it. We might get lucky and find it was done when only one of our "technically qualified" employees was in the building. Norm, give Joe the names of those five employees, and he'll cross check them to the sign in and computer logs to see if any of them were in on the morning of the 16th."

***

At the Milwaukee headquarters of Great Waters Insurance Group, Jim Seversen was meeting with three members of his staff to go over the planned review. He assigned one person the task of reviewing procedures in the Cash Management Department, he assigned another to look at the premium payment application procedures, and finally, he gave the last staff member the job of tracking payment history on the specific accounts Jake Hammond had sent over. He wanted a quick turnaround on this, and gave them the remainder of the day to complete their assigned tasks. He intended to get to the bottom of this mess so he could get New Commerce off his back. He felt confident they'd find no control issues or irregularities at Great Waters, but had to make certain before telling Jake Hammond where to get off.

Chapter 23

Friday, August 22, 2008

He needed to do a few things before meeting with his staff at 8:30, so Jim Seversen was at his desk at 8 a.m. He settled in and began reviewing the latest flurry of emails that'd come in yesterday. It'd been a hectic day, and he'd fallen behind on his correspondence, which was highly unusual for him. This New Commerce thing had gotten him a bit off tack, but he was hoping he'd be able to get back to Jake Hammond this morning to put this thing to bed once and for all.

When the knock on his door came at 8:30 sharp, he looked up from his keyboard to see the three staff members he'd spoken with yesterday waiting to be invited in. He motioned them to come. "What have you got for me?" he asked. Sharon Jones was the first to speak up. She'd been assigned the task of reviewing the procedures in the Cash Management Department.

"As you know, Jim, we review procedures in Cash Management every three years. The last time we looked at it was two years ago, and we were scheduled to look at it later this year. What I did was review the work papers for the last two audits, and then perform a quick review of my own to see if anything changed. I interviewed the key personnel and observed the actual reconciliation process. I then reviewed the supporting documentation for all daily reconciliations for the past month. All receipts received were properly posted, everything balances, and there are no outstanding reconciling items. I'm confident the controls we have in place would prevent any cash receipts that come through normal channels from being diverted without being detected, unless there was some collusion among multiple employees."

"Thanks, Sharon. Pete, what did you find?"

"I looked into our procedures for posting premium payments to customer accounts. All receipts processed through Cash Management are segregated by type; initial binders on new policies, premium payments, commissions, and misc. fees. Each type is totaled and balanced to the next processing function, so the amount of money received in Cash Management for premium payments is compared to the total amount of premium payments applied to individual customer accounts. Any discrepancy is researched and corrected immediately to ensure that all payments are properly recorded. This process, coupled with the balancing procedures in the Cash Management area which Sharon just described makes it virtually impossible for premium payments received by Cash Management to not be posted to customer accounts. However, just because all premium payments are posted somewhere, it doesn't guarantee that they're posted to the correct accounts."

"That's true," added Jim. "So, how would we know if the payments were posted to the wrong accounts?"

"Actually, we wouldn't, until a customer complained. I looked into that as well, and we haven't had any problems in recent months."

"OK. What do you have for me, Hank?"

Hank had been assigned the task of researching the premium payment history on some specific accounts Jim had given him. These were some of the problem policies that New Commerce claimed were still valid, but that Great Waters records showed as closed.

"Strangely enough" Hank said, "all of the policies in question were canceled because premium payments weren't received. Most have been closed for more than a year. Prior to that time payments were being applied regularly on all of them, and in all cases, payments were made by New Commerce on behalf of their customers."

"So it seems clear then, that New Commerce stopped making the premium payments, for whatever reason?"

"I'd say that's a fair statement" replied Hank.

"OK. Thanks guys. I appreciate your hard work and timely results on this. I'll get back to Jake Hammond right away and let him know that everything's in order at our end."

***

At 9 a.m. Joe Nash was in the conference room with Jake Hammond discussing his latest findings. After reviewing the building entry logs and comparing them to the list of employees Norm Cassidy gave them showing which ones had technical backgrounds, he identified two names that appeared on both lists. One of them was Sylvie Anderson. She'd entered the building at 7:30 on the morning of Saturday, August 16, 2008, and left just before noon.

"That's interesting," said Jake. Is there any relationship between Sylvie Anderson and our division manager, Jeff Anderson?"

"As a matter of fact, there is. Sylvie is Jeff's daughter. They're relationship doesn't show up on any official records, but I was able to get that information from speaking with some of the other analysts."

"Yet another twist for us to deal with. Funny that Jeff never mentioned anything about this during our conversations. You think it was just an oversight?"

"Could be, but I can't imagine him forgetting to mention this, in light of the investigation that's going on."

"I'm going to have to talk with him about this, but first, I'd like to see what Nagle has for us today. It'd be interesting if we find Sylvie drives a black SUV, wouldn't it?"

Jake was about to pick up the phone to call detective Nagle when it rang. His caller ID told him the call was from Jim Seversen. He picked it up on the second ring.

"Jake Hammond here," he said into the receiver.

"Jake, good morning, it's Jim Seversen from Great Waters. How are you today?"

"I'm fine, Jim, and you?"

"I'm good, thanks for asking. I wanted to let you know what we've found as a result of our special review. Do you have a couple of minutes?"

"Sure, go ahead."

"I had my staff review all of our procedures relative to cash management and the application of premium payments to customer accounts. Additionally, we researched activity on the specific policy numbers you gave me. Our controls look solid, and we didn't uncover any discrepancies. All cash receipts are accounted for and all premium payments were applied to customer accounts. On those specific accounts you gave me, premium payments stopped some time ago, and the accounts were canceled. I'm afraid we haven't uncovered anything unusual at our end, so it looks like the problem is at your end."

"Interesting" replied Jake. The thing is, Jim, we found pretty much the same thing at this end. All controls look good, and all cash receipts and payments are accounted for. The only thing we haven't gotten to, just yet, is to prove that the premium payments actually went out. We'll be doing that next, and should be able to say when and to whom they went. I'll get back to you as soon as we have that information, and then we can decide where we go next. How does that sound?"

"That's fine with me, Jake. I hope you can get to the bottom of this. In the meantime, I'll wait to hear back from you."

"Thanks, Jim. I'll get back to you shortly."

Jake hung up the phone and gave Joe a short recap of the discussion. It was looking more and more like there had to be some collusion between someone at New Commerce and someone at Great Waters. Somehow, premium payments were being sent from this end, and not being applied properly at the other end. Neither Joe nor Jake could think of another plausible explanation right now. The next thing they needed to pin down was how premium payments were being made. Joe was given that task to perform while Jake contacted Detective Nagle to see if there were any new developments on his end. Joe left the conference room as Jake was dialing Tim's number.

"Good morning, this is Detective Nagle."

"Hi Tim, it's Jake Hammond, do you have a few minutes to talk right now?"

"Sure thing, Jake. What's up?"

Jake filled Tim in on his conversation with Jim Seversen, and with all the other new developments, including the fact that two of the Marietta employees who were in the building on the morning of the 16th had technical backgrounds. Then he asked Tim whether or not he'd made any progress on finding if any of the employees drove black SUVs.

"As a matter of fact, Jake, two of your employees have them, but only one of the people you just named does. Sylvie Anderson. We're going to try to locate both vehicles this morning to see if either of them have damage that could've resulted from our hit and run accident."

"This gets better by the minute, doesn't it?" added Jake. "Oh, and did I mention that Sylvie Anderson is the daughter or our division manager, Jeff Anderson?"

"No, you didn't mention that."

"It seems a lot of people are forgetting to mention that, including Jeff Anderson. We've been interacting with him a great deal on this review, and he knows all about the hit and run, and yet, he never mentioned that his daughter works in the Marietta office, or that she's an operations analyst with a technical background who could have processed the changes to our files, or that she just happens to drive a black SUV. Do you think that's just a coincidence?"

"Could be, but I doubt it. Let me check out the vehicles before we do anything else. Then, depending on what I find, we can decide what our next step should be. Agreed?"

"I agree with that, as far as it goes, but we need to continue with other aspects of our internal review, it that's OK with you. We're still looking at the system access issues to see if we can determine who spoofed Ron's ID and IP address. I think we can do that without raising too much suspicion here in the Marietta office. This might just give us the final piece of information we need to wrap this up."

"OK, go ahead and do that. But if you can, try to stay away from Sylvie Anderson for the time being. I don't want her to get spooked and disappear."

***

Calling hours had started at 4:00, and by 4:15 Barrett's funeral home was overflowing with people, and crowds were already out the door and to the side walk. It was a closed casket because of the condition of the body, but Dan's picture was on a small table near the casket. Dan Walters had been a popular man and people from all over the city wanted to pay their respects to Joyce and the family. Although a number of others had died in the fiery crash on I-10, most of those funerals had already taken place, because those victims had died instantly at the crash site. Dan had been badly burned, but had hung on for four days. Now the whole city focused its attention on this funeral.

Calling hours were scheduled to conclude at 7 p.m., but at 6:45 the line of people waiting to pay their respects was still out the door. Joyce didn't want to turn anyone away but the children were exhausted so she asked her mom and dad if they could take them home while she stayed behind to greet the remaining people who had been waiting in line for so long. She wanted the kids to get some rest before the funeral tomorrow. It was sure to be the hardest day of their lives.

At nine o'clock the last person in line had paid his respects and Joyce was finally able to sit down to rest a bit before heading home. It had been a grueling experience and she was exhausted, but she was also overwhelmed and thankful for the large turnout of people who wanted her to know how sorry they were for her loss. Although some may have come out of curiosity, most knew Dan, either personally or because of their business dealings with him. In a way, it was heart-warming to know how many people cared for him.

They had all arrived together in one car, and Bob and Donna Robertson had taken it home when they left with the kids, so Joyce called to ask her dad to come back and pick her up. He was there in less than fifteen minutes, and they headed home together to try to get some sleep before the funeral.

Chapter 24

Saturday, August 23, 2008

Donna Robertson had been up for more than two hours, was already dressed, and was now busy helping Nancy and Danny get ready. Joyce was in her bedroom, trying to get dressed, but things just weren't going well. She was tired and wasn't sure she had the energy or even the will to keep going. She sat in front of her dresser, staring blankly at the mirror, and thinking about the events that led to this day.

It'd been a difficult ten days since she'd left Tallahassee to avoid the effects of tropical storm Fay. Joyce couldn't have imagined then how her life would be turned upside down in such a short period of time. She'd worried about water damage to the house and the dealership, but they had insurance, and she knew any damage could be repaired. She figured that, at worst, they'd have to deal with some inconveniences while waiting for the insurance settlements to come in. But now Dan was gone, the inventory at the dealership was damaged and couldn't be sold, and it looked like the insurance coverage she was counting on didn't exist. It was all too overwhelming, and she broke down once more and began to sob loudly.

Bob Robertson was passing by her bedroom when he heard her sobs. He knocked gently on the door and let himself in. When she saw her dad, really the only man left in her life, Joyce got up and flung herself into his arms. She hugged him tightly and cried on his shoulder.

"Oh Dad, what am I going to do? I don't know if I can go on. I miss Dan so much."

"I know dear, but you've got to go on. The kids need you now more than ever. It'll be difficult for them too. You can do it. I know it doesn't seem possible now, but with time, the pain will diminish and you'll be able to go on. And your mom and I will help."

"I don't know what I would do without you and Mom. You've been wonderful. You've always been there for me, and I want you to know how much I appreciate it."

"We know, dear. Now, try to get dressed. It's getting late. The car will be picking us up soon."

The funeral was scheduled for ten o'clock at St. John's church. Friends and relatives would meet at Barrett's funeral home at 9 a.m. for a final farewell, and the funeral procession would depart for the church at about 9:45. Joyce, the kids and her parents were picked up at 8:30 and driven the short distance to Barrett's, and less than fifteen minutes later they were ready to greet the people who were already waiting to pay their respects. The rest of the morning was a blur, with Joyce going through the motions with little knowledge of what was actually happening. Her mom, dad, or someone from Barrett's was always at her side gently directing her every move. She would later remember very little of that morning, and maybe that was just as well because it was better to remember Dan as he was before this awful time.

After the funeral, friends and family members had returned to the Walters residence for a luncheon, but were all gone by 1 p.m. Joyce asked Randy if he could stay behind for a little while to give her an update on what was happening at the dealership.

"Thanks so much for everything you've done, Randy. I hope you know how much I appreciate it."

"Please, Joyce, don't mention it. I owed Dan at least that much. He was my best friend in the whole world, and you and the kids are like family to me. I'll give you whatever help you need, for as long as you need. Is there anything you need right now?"

"I was just wondering if you could bring me up to date on the inventory issue. Have you had a chance to speak with the manufacturers yet?"

"Yes, I called them yesterday. They were very sympathetic and asked me to offer their condolences to you. There shouldn't be any problem getting new inventory to us, but they haven't yet heard anything from New Commerce about coverage on the old inventory. They pointed out how it's our responsibility to make sure we have adequate insurance, and how they can't be held responsible for the damage. They agreed to contact New Commerce first thing on Monday to see what the holdup is at their end. I'll follow up with them and with New Commerce on Monday to make sure someone is taking action on this so we can re-open as soon as possible."

"Thanks so much for stepping up on this thing, Randy. I don't know much about the business, and wouldn't have had a clue where to start."

"No problem. I'm sure we'll get to the bottom of this sooner or later. I just hope that New Commerce doesn't try to hang us out to dry on this. We'll give them a few more days, but if they can't get their act together, we may have to get some legal advice. Don't worry, though, I'll take care of it."

***

Even though it was a Saturday, Jake Hammond and his staff were in the office. They were updating their work papers with copies of all pertinent documents from the division files, completing the narratives describing the work they performed and the findings they noted, and documenting their conclusions. If things went as planned, most of the review could be wrapped up by Monday, and then Sue, Chuck and Jason could head back to Augusta, and to their next assignment. Jake would be staying behind with Joe to continue the investigation into the fraudulent file changes and assist the police in any way they could with the investigation into the death of Ron Hayward.

They now knew exactly how many customers had paid for insurance coverage they didn't have, and they'd calculated the approximate dollar exposure to New Commerce based upon the inventory values at those customer locations. Although they couldn't yet know the exact loss they might suffer as a result of the damage from Fay, their potential exposure was approximately $10 million, give or take a few thousand. It could be quite a hit to the bottom line if a great deal of the inventory at their dealers was damaged, and the third quarter financial results would be a disaster, which, in turn, would drive their stock price down even further. Deb Cutter would not be happy.

Tim Nagle was working through the weekend too, and called right after lunch.

"Jake, glad I was able to reach you. I've got some news for you. If you're going to be in the office for a while I'll swing by to give you an update."

"Sure, we'll be here for a few more hours, at least. I'll let the security guard know you're coming."

A half hour later Tim Nagle was in the third floor conference room of New Commerce, giving Jake an update. He'd found both of the black SUVs they were interested in. As it turned out, Sylvie's was the one with damage to the front bumper. They didn't know yet if the damage was related to the hit and run that killed Ron Hayward, but they impounded it and the forensic folks were going over it now, looking for any evidence that would implicate it in the accident. The other SUV didn't show any evidence it'd been involved in an accident, but they'd be taking a closer look at it anyway.

"What about an alibi for the time of the hit and run?"

"Sylvie Anderson claims she was in the office here until nine, and then went directly home to her parents' house, where she stayed for the remainder of the evening. As you know, the accident happened at about 8:15."

"How does she explain the damage to her SUV?"

"She says she noticed the damage Tuesday morning and immediately filed a claim with her insurance company. She claims someone must have backed into her car while it was in the parking lot, but doesn't know when it might have happened. I checked, and she *did* file a police report on Tuesday morning. I'll get a copy of that to see exactly what she said in it."

"I'll tell you, Tim, from my perspective I find it interesting that Jeff Anderson never mentioned to us that his daughter worked at New Commerce, even after he knew a black SUV was involved in the hit and run accident. You'd think he'd want to be as up-front as possible in a situation like this to make sure to clear the air as soon as possible."

"You're right. Except, of course, if he knew she was involved. Then he'd probably need some time to figure out what to do."

"So I've really got two problems on my hands. First, I probably have an employee who stole money from my customers and may have killed Ron Hayward, and second, I have a division manager who, at the very least, withheld information from both of us during our investigations. From the company's perspective, he will probably be terminated, and I assume, you may eventually want to charge him with obstruction."

"That's a possibility, but it's too soon to say."

"From our side, we know that Sylvie has the technical expertise to have altered our files and spoofed Ron's logon ID and IP address. My folks in Augusta are working on trying to prove who did it, and I should be getting that information soon. I'll let you know as soon as I do. In the meantime, keep me posted on any new developments. I need to know how to proceed on Monday morning."

"I'll do that."

"Thanks."

Nagle left the New Commerce offices and headed back to police headquarters and Jake and his staff continued to clean up their work papers in preparation of the staff's departure.   At this point it was looking like that might happen tomorrow, or Monday at the latest, depending on how quickly travel arrangements could be made.

Chapter 25

Monday, August 25, 2008

They worked all weekend, and their persistence paid off. Norm Cassidy and Steve O'Brien had spent hours following every lead, and with some input from Nick Hurley, they finally figured out what was going on, both with the system access issues and the insurance premium payments.

Ron Hayward's laptop had been taken as evidence by the Marietta Police Department, and Nick Hurley was able to analyze its contents. He found a program sitting in the background that recorded and analyzed all key strokes and transmitted that information to another computer. It was the type of program that's often inadvertently downloaded when a user visits an unsecure website, however, in Ron's case, the originating IP address of the downloaded program was within the New Commerce network itself. It was becoming obvious that another New Commerce employee was responsible, and they were now fairly certain they knew who it was. Even though someone else could've used her IP address, supporting evidence was mounting and they were pretty sure they'd be able to put this part of their review behind them soon.

Late on Friday afternoon Norm Cassidy had discovered that all the insurance premium payments on the canceled and bogus policies had, in fact, been paid to Great Waters Insurance. Interestingly, though, each and every payment in question was made by check rather than by an ACH bank transfer, as is normal for these types of payments.

And more interestingly, the individual who authorized the use of checks for the premium payments in question was the same individual whose IP address was used to spoof Ron's ID and password to process the unauthorized changes to the data files. Norm couldn't wait to share this new information with Jake Hammond.

***

In Marietta, Sue, Chuck and Jason were all sitting around the conference table enjoying their morning coffee, the first time they'd been able to relax since arriving a week ago. Their portion of the review was now complete and they were getting ready to do their final walkthroughs before heading out. They were all booked on the same flight back to Augusta and they'd be leaving for the airport in another half hour or so.

When the conference room phone rang, Sue picked it up. "This is Sue Richards" she said.

"Hi Sue. It's Norm Cassidy. How are you?"

"Hey Norm, I'm good, and you?"

"I'm good too. Tell me Sue, is Jake hanging around there someplace?"

"As a matter of fact, he's right here. Hold on." She put her hand over the mouth piece and told Jake it was Norm Cassidy. He grabbed the receiver immediately, anxious to hear about the latest developments.

"Norm, what do you have for me?"

"I think we've pretty much cracked the case for you, boss."

"OK, give it to me."

"We know that someone downloaded a program to Ron Hayward's PC which recorded all his key strokes and sent the data to an IP address located on our own network. That's how the perpetrator was able to figure out his ID and password and make it look like Ron was the one who processed the file changes. We also know for sure the premium payments for all policies in question were sent to Great Waters by check rather than ACH, and we know who authorized that payment method. But best of all, it just so happens that the person who authorized the check payments works at the IP address which originated the program download to Ron's PC."

"Good work! You guys have been pretty busy. So, are you going to tell me who the employee is?"

"I thought you'd never ask, boss."

"Well, I'm asking. Talk to me."

"It's Sylvie Anderson."

"Well, it all seems to fit. I'll give Detective Nagle a call to see if they've made any progress with her SUV. I also need to call Jim Seversen over at Great Waters to let him know what we've found regarding the premium payments. By the way, can you email me copies of some of the endorsed checks so we can work on finding out how and where they were cashed?"

"No problem. I'll get right on it."

"Thanks, Norm. Good work. And thank Steve for me too."

"Will do. Talk to you later."

Jake knew he'd have to call Fred Campbell and the other members of the senior management team soon to give them an update, but first he wanted to call Tim Nagle to fill him in on the latest developments and then speak with Jim Seversen. He could probably get both calls out of the way before lunch time, and then call Fred first thing this afternoon.

He dialed Tim Nagle's number first. As usual, Tim picked up before the second ring.

"Tim. It's Jake Hammond. Do you have a few minutes?"

"Sure Jake. What's up?"

"I think, with some help from your guy Nick, my folks may have come up with a major break in the case. " Over the next few minutes Jake proceeded to fill Tim in on what he'd learned from Norm, and then asked about the progress on the forensic review of Sylvie Anderson's black SUV.

"I haven't heard back from the forensic folks yet, but I'm going to head down there as soon as we hang up to see what I can find out. It's definitely looking like Sylvie Anderson's our person. She knows she's a suspect, because we've impounded her vehicle. What have you done from your end? Is she still working there?"

"Until now we haven't had anything specific on her, so she's still employed. But now I think we can put her on a leave of absence. I'm going to speak with the head of our HR Department as soon as we hang up. I certainly don't want her able to make any additional changes."

"That's a good idea. I'll try to call you later today to let you know how forensics is doing. If anything else comes up in the meantime, let me know."

After they'd hung up, Jake called Norm Cassidy and instructed him to have Sylvie's security access suspended immediately. He then called the head of HR and got approval for putting Sylvie on a paid leave of absence. He'd also have to speak with her father, Jeff Anderson, about what he knew, and when he knew it. Quite possibly, Jeff would have to be suspended as well. HR approved that in advance, but Jake would only make that decision after speaking with Jeff. His wanted to speak with Sylvie first, but when he attempted to contact her, he was told by one of her co-workers that she'd called in sick today, so he decided to have his discussion with her father first. He asked Joe to find Jeff and escort him to the conference room. At quarter past nine there was a knock on the conference room door, and Jeff Anderson entered, followed immediately by Joe Nash.

"You wanted to speak with me, Jake?" Jeff looked a bit uneasy as he spoke and seemed to have some difficulty making eye contact.

"Yes, Jeff. Please come in and take a seat."

"What can I help you guys with?"

"I understand that your daughter, Sylvie isn't at work today. I hope it isn't anything serious."

Jeff began to fidget. He'd known that sooner or later they'd figure out Sylvie was his daughter. But even though he'd expected it, hearing it out loud was like being hit in the gut with a hammer. It would all come out in the open now and he began to sweat.

"Actually, Jake, I'm not sure how Sylvie's doing. I haven't spoken to her today. Thank you for asking, though. Was there anything else you needed?"

"*Actually*, Jeff, yes there is. I do have a few questions I need to ask. This may take a while so please get comfortable. Can we get you anything? Coffee? A soft drink?"

"No, I'm all set, thanks. I just had coffee a little while ago. I've got a pretty busy schedule today, so if we can get right to it, I'd appreciate it."

"That's fine by me. Let me begin by saying I'm a little surprised you hadn't told us your daughter was working in the operations area at this division."

"I didn't think it was pertinent. We haven't broken any company rules, and I cleared it with HR before we hired Sylvie."

"Yes, I understand that. But when we began this review, you and I talked about some of the things I'd need to look at, and who I'd need to speak with, including account managers and operations personnel. It didn't occur to you at that point to mention it?"

"No, it didn't."

"And what about when you heard that Ron Hayward had been the victim of a hit and run, and the vehicle was a black SUV, like the one your daughter drives?"

"That's just a coincidence. There are a lot of black SUVs in the Atlanta area. Why should I feel a need to mention that my daughter drives one?" Jake didn't answer that rhetorical question, but went on with his own questions.

"Did you know that your daughter has quite an impressive technical background? I assume you're somewhat familiar with her work history, both as her father and as her boss. Can you tell us why she's working as an operations analyst here at New Commerce when she could be earning twice as much doing what she used to do as a highly skilled tech support person familiar with networks and operating systems?"

"Sylvie wanted a change. She said the stress of her work wasn't worth the money they were paying her and she asked me if there was anything she could do here at New Commerce. I had an opening, which I told her about, and she said she was interested. But I didn't hire her right away. I wanted to make sure everything was done on the up and up, so I contacted HR for some guidance and direction. They assured me it would be OK to hire Sylvie because she wouldn't be reporting directly to me. Only then did I have her come in for an interview, and I made sure that the hiring decision was made by Kathy Brown. I did not influence her decision in any way."

"Of course not" said Jake. "I'm sure that you being the division manager had no impact whatsoever on Kathy's decision." Jeff looked like he was about to say something, but before he could get the words out, Jake was asking his next question.

"So what you're saying, then, is that throughout our review, and in light of what's transpired, you never thought it would be pertinent to mention that Sylvie was your daughter?"

"Yes, that's true."

"And what about when the police impounded her SUV? Did you think at that time that someone should know that she's your daughter?"

"No."

"I see" said Jake. "Now, let's discuss something else for a moment. Can you tell me what the procedures are for forwarding insurance premium payments to the insurance carriers?"

"Like all divisions, we collect the premium amounts from our customers and send them to the appropriate insurance companies. Of course, we only do this for customers for whom we've arranged insurance. Others make their own payments directly to the insurance company."

"And how do you actually send those payments?"

"It's all done through the banking system, using the automated clearing house process. We create a file each day with any payments going out and transmit it electronically to the Federal Reserve's clearing house, which in turn makes sure that the receiving banks get credit. Those banks then credit their customers' accounts with the appropriate amounts."

"Yes, I understand that this is the standard procedure. Are there any exceptions to this procedure? In other words, do all premium payments get transmitted this way?"

"Yes, of course."

"Would you be surprised to hear that all the premium payments for the expired and non-existing policies we've found during our review were made by check rather than ACH?"

"I don't understand. Who would have authorized that?"

"Your daughter did."

Jeff clearly was stunned. He looked from Jake to Joe and back to Jake again, as though he was hoping that one of them would say it wasn't so. While he may have been less than forthcoming with the fact that his daughter worked at New Commerce and also owned a black SUV, the expression on his face indicated that he hadn't suspected her of any wrong doing. He looked directly at Jake and said, "If that's true, there has to be a good reason for it. Maybe that's how the insurance company wanted to receive the payments."

"We're working with the Internal Auditors at Great Waters and we'll definitely get to the bottom of this. However, in light of the overwhelming evidence against Sylvie, I have no choice but to temporarily suspend her pending the results of the joint investigation being conducted by us and the Marietta Police Department. I suspect they'll want to speak with Sylvie soon. As far as you're concerned, Jeff, I consider your actions to be intentional interference with our investigation. Although you may not have violated any formal policy by hiring your daughter to work in this division, your lack of cooperation and transparency in that matter has delayed our investigation and sheds serious doubt on your loyalty to the company and our ability to continue to trust you. Consequently, you also are being suspended, effective immediately. Joe will escort you out of the building. Please give him your magnetic ID card."

"But, you can't do this. I have rights. I want to speak with someone from HR."

"Of course, that's your right. However, HR has already approved your suspension. You must leave the building immediately. You may feel free to contact HR once you are off of the premises."

Joe collected Jeff's ID card and escorted him down to the first floor and out of the building. He told the security guard that Jeff was not to be let back into the building for any reason, without permission from Jake Hammond or himself. While Joe was escorting Jeff out, Jake called Norm Cassidy and told him to have Jeff's logon ID suspended, and then he put in a call to Jim Seversen over at Great Waters Insurance Group. He brought Jim up to speed on the latest developments, and promised to send him copies of the cashed checks that showed premium payments were made to Great Waters. Jim Seversen was taken aback by this new information, but promised to look into it further at his end. They agreed that it was beginning to look like there was some collusion between Sylvie Anderson and someone at Great Waters.

Jake's next step was to send Fred Campbell an email asking him to set up a conference call for late morning, with all members of the senior management team who were available. The staff had left for the airport, and he and Joe were about to grab a coffee when the conference room phone rang. It was Tim Nagle with an update.

"Jake Hammond."

"Jake. It's Tim Nagle. I thought you'd like to know that our forensic folks found some hair and skin samples on the front bumper of Sylvie Anderson's SUV. They've been able to match the DNA from the samples to Ron Hayward's DNA, proving that Anderson's SUV was the vehicle involved in the hit and run. We're going to bring her in for further questioning."

"She isn't at work today, but we've suspended her employment and her father's as well. He was escorted out of the building just a short while ago" said Jake. "While I don't think he was involved in the plot to divert funds, his lack of cooperation during our investigation was grounds enough to suspend him."

"Eventually we may also be talking with him as well" added Tim. "But for the time being, we're going to concentrate on his daughter. Did you want to sit in on our interview?"

"Yes I would, thanks. We suspect she's working with an accomplice at Great Waters Insurance Group, but don't know yet who that is. We might be able to get that information out of her during your interview."

"OK. I'll give you a call when we have her in custody. You can meet us at the station."

Chapter 26

At 11:15 the Marietta conference room phone rang, right on schedule. Fred Campbell had assembled the other members of the management team to get Jake's update, and they were calling in right now. Jake picked up with his customary "Jake Hammond here, how may I assist you?"

"Jake. It's Fred. I have Deb Cutter, Tom D'Angelo and Dave Banner with me. Are you ready to give us an update?"

"Absolutely. However, we may be interrupted by Detective Nagle of the Marietta Police Department. He's agreed to let me sit in on an interrogation. I'll give you the details in a second."

"OK, let's get started. I'll put you on speaker phone."

Over the next forty five minutes or so Jake filled them in on the developments to date and told them the interrogation he wanted to sit in on was of Sylvie Anderson, Jeff's daughter, which caught everyone at the other end off guard. Apparently none of them knew that Jeff had hired his daughter to work at his division. Jake then mentioned a possible law suit by Walters Marine and the fact that it probably wouldn't be the last. Tom D'Angelo agreed to meet with the folks in the Legal Department to figure out what their next step should be. Fred agreed to take responsibility for contacting the manufacturers, beginning with the supplier for Walters Marine, in the hope of getting things back on track *before* any legal action was taken.

At noon, as they were just about to wrap up, Joe Nash came into the conference room to tell Jake that Tim

Nagle was on the other line and wanted to know if Jake could come down to the station ASAP to sit in on the interrogation of Sylvie Anderson. Jake told the people on the other end of the conference call he needed to go and they agreed to end the call, with the understanding that Jake would get back to Fred and Tom as soon as the interrogation was over.

About twenty minutes later he was at the Marietta Police Department outside an interrogation room, where Detective Nagle was sitting across a table from Sylvie Anderson. Jake had hoped to be in the room with them, but was told that he'd have to observe the session through the one way glass because, as a civilian, he couldn't be allowed inside the room. However, Nagle had agreed that he'd ask any particular questions Jake wanted asked, once he'd completed his questioning. Jake didn't like it, but had no choice. It was better than being excluded completely, so he selected a spot between two men he assumed were detectives, and an attractive, well dressed, woman of about thirty, all of whom were apparently also there to observe the interrogation. The woman, he found out later, was an assistant district attorney.

Over the next half hour Nagle grilled Anderson relentlessly, and she never once asked for an attorney.

"Miss Anderson" he began, "tell me how your SUV was damaged."

"I already told you, I don't know. It must've happened in the parking lot at work."

"When did you first notice the damage?"

"It was on the morning of Tuesday, August 19th."

"So, you didn't see any damage when you left work on Monday, the 18th?"

"No, but my SUV was facing away from the building, so I didn't need to go around it. I just approached it from behind and entered by the driver's door. It drove fine, so I had no reason to think there was anything wrong with it."

"What time was it when you left the office that Monday?"

"I don't remember, exactly. I think it was a little after nine."

"Do you always work that late?"

"Not always, but often. We're a little short handed right now and it's hard to keep up with the work load unless we put in extra hours."

"So, you left the office at about nine or so. Did you see anything unusual as you were leaving?

"You mean the accident? Yes, the police were there, but I couldn't get a good look at what was going on because the entire area was roped off."

"Where did you go when you left work?"

"I was tired so I drove straight home."

"By home, you mean your parents' house?"

"Yes, I'm staying with them until I can find an apartment."

"So, what time was it when you got to your parent's house?"

"It was probably just before 9:30. I'm not exactly sure, but it's only a fifteen or twenty minute drive when there's no traffic."

"And when you arrived at your parent's house what did you do?"

"I parked in the driveway, went into the house, grabbed a bite to eat and then went to bed. I was exhausted and wanted to get some sleep before starting another long day."

"Were your parents home at the time?"

"Yes. They were watching TV in the den."

"Did they leave the house at any time that evening, after you came home?"

"Not that I know of. I think they went to bed after the eleven o'clock news."

"Who was the first person out of the house on the morning of Tuesday, August 19th?"

"I was. I planned to get into the office early, so I left the house at about 6:45 a.m. That's when I first saw the damage to my SUV. I was devastated. It's only a few months old, you know."

"And what did you do then?"

"I ran back into the house to tell my parents. We called our insurance agent at his home, and he told us to call the police to file a report, which I did."

"And in your report you stated that you were not aware of how the damage occurred, and that you hadn't noticed it until that morning. You also said that you hadn't been involved in an accident. Is that correct?"

"Yes."

At this point Detective Nagle decided to move on to another topic. He didn't want to let her know just yet that forensics had matched the DNA on her bumper to Ron Hayward. For all she knew right now, they were buying her story, and she still might be able to get away with it.

"So tell me, Sylvie, how well did you know Ron Hayward?"

"I knew him from the office. We worked for the same company, but didn't socialize outside of work. He always seemed pleasant enough."

"What were your interactions with him at the office?"

"He was an account manager, and I was in Operations, so we saw each other quite regularly. I often had to input data into our computer system for his customers."

"How did you know what data to input?"

"I would receive a written request for change."

"Did you ever make changes to the file that weren't requested on a form?"

"No, of course not. I can only process changes that are authorized by an account manager or my supervisor."

"What kind of changes did your supervisor authorize?"

"She really didn't initiate any changes, but sometimes would sign the request sheet if she got an authorization from an account manager. But I never made changes without a signed request sheet."

It was almost as though she knew exactly where the line of questioning was going and felt completely comfortable that she'd covered her tracks well. Nagle turned toward the window behind which Jake Hammond and the assistant DA were standing, and gave them a slight nod. He was about to ask a key question and wanted to make sure they were observing her expression.

"So, Miss Anderson, how do you explain the fact that your auditors have uncovered proof that you made unauthorized changes to the company's files on Saturday morning, August 16th?"

A shocked look came across her face, but she immediately tried to hide her surprise. It was obvious that the question had caught her off guard but she bounced back quickly.

"I don't know what you're talking about. I've never made any unauthorized changes to our company files."

"Ah, but you have, Miss Anderson. And what's more, you tried to make it look like Ron Hayward had made those changes."

"That's ridiculous. How could I have done that?"

"I won't go into all the details right now, but it's obvious you could have, and you did. We know about your technical background, and we've traced your activities on the morning of the 16th. We know you did it. Why don't you tell us why you did it and who's in on this with you?"

"I don't know what you're talking about and I don't like how this interview is going. I think I need a lawyer, and I'm not answering any more questions without one."

It was obvious the interrogation was over so the assistant DA knocked on the door and asked Detective Nagle to step out for a moment. Nobody except Sylvie wanted the interrogation to end, but they had no choice once she lawyered up. They weren't going to take a chance that any information she provided would be excluded by a judge at trial.

"What do you think?" Tim asked the assistant DA.

"With the DNA results I think we've got enough to hold her. Let her contact an attorney, but keep her here until he arrives."

Tim turned to Jake and said "Sorry I didn't get to ask any of your questions. I was hoping she'd give me more information before deciding to ask for an attorney. What do you think about what you heard?"

"There's no question that everything points to her, so far. I think it's a slam-dunk, but we'll need to dot our "I"s and cross our "T"s before this goes to trial. The DNA evidence may be easy enough for a jury to understand, but most of them would probably have some difficulty following the computer evidence. I'm going to head back to our offices right now and start working on the documentation we'll need to prove our case. I don't want to leave any stone unturned, and we still don't know what happened to the premium payments, which would seem to be the only motive she had to do any of what we think she did."

"I was just about to raise that very issue" said the ADA. "We have enough evidence right now to hold her, but I'm not sure we could get an indictment by a grand jury, much less a conviction at trial, unless we can come up with a plausible motive. You need to find out what happened to the money."

"Agreed" said Tim. "I'll check her bank accounts and those of her family. Jake, you keep going with your investigation and let me know as soon as you have anything."

"Sure thing. We've already found that the premium payments were sent to Great Waters Insurance Group, and all payments were made by check. I've emailed copies of the canceled checks to Great Waters for them to follow up at their end. It's starting to look like Sylvie was working with someone at Great Waters on this."

Jake left the police headquarters a little before one o'clock and grabbed a quick bite to eat on his way back to the office. He'd give Fred Campbell a call as soon as he got in.

***

Deb Cutter was pacing back and forth in front of her huge desk. Things were not looking good on the economic front, and she was worried. The price of New Commerce stock dropped another two points since the Exchange opened this morning, making it a loss of ten points in the past two weeks. The sub-prime mortgage fiasco was taking its toll on all financial institutions, even those that weren't in the sub-prime lending business, making it harder and harder for New Commerce to raise capital. Some of the members of the Board of Directors were starting to ask hard questions.

When Jake Hammond told her this morning that the potential exposure resulting from the insurance issue could be as high as $10 Million, she nearly lost it. Everything was going wrong. All of her hard work over the past few years was beginning to unravel. Delinquencies were increasing in the new product lines, it was getting harder and harder to increase originations because she couldn't raise enough capital to make the new loans, the stock price was taking a hit, and now the insurance premium scam. And to top it off, customers were starting to threaten law suits.

She'd done her best, but she couldn't do it all alone, and the other damn members of the Executive Committee were useless pieces of crap. If it hadn't been for her leadership and business insight, the company would still be a small-time finance company rather than a real player in the commercial finance industry. It was the changes she initiated in the product lines and the new, more aggressive, approach to loan approvals that helped push the stock price up in the first place. Under her leadership the stock went from $38 a share to $79 a share, making a great deal of money for a lot of people, including her. But now everyone seemed to forget that in just a few years their stocks increased $41 a share. All they knew was that it had dropped ten points, to $69 recently, but ignored the fact that it was still worth $31 a share more than it was when she'd taken control.

She contemplated whether or not she should exercise some of her stock options now before the price dropped any lower. She had some options at $38 which she received when she took over as CEO. Had she exercised them at $79 she'd have made more than eight million in profit, before taxes, but now it'd be only six million, and the amount was falling by the hour.

She was startled by the knock on her door, which opened just ever so slightly. Her assistant stuck her head in and announced that Tom D'Angelo was outside and wanted to see her. Deb was in no mood to put up with her CFO right now, but she knew it had to be something important for him to interrupt her without an appointment. She'd never had any patience for people who didn't go through proper channels and schedule appointments in advance, and she'd made that clear to everyone. They all knew better than to try to see her without advance notice, unless it was so important that it couldn't wait. With the wave of her hand she signaled her assistant to have him come in.

"Sorry to interrupt, Deb, but I thought you'd want to know that things are taking a turn for the worse."

"What the hell do you mean by that?" she almost screamed at him. "You can't just come in here and make some stupid comment and expect me to know exactly what you're talking about. What do I pay you for, anyway?"

It was obvious to Tom that this wasn't a good time to approach her, but she needed to know, and he had already broached the subject, so he had to go on, in spite of her verbal abuse. It's not like it was the first time he'd put up with this kind of treatment.

"I'm sure you've noticed that our stock has taken another hit this morning" he continued. "But now we have another problem. We're going to have to slow down our originations because I can't raise enough capital to fund the deals. It's starting to look like we're going to miss plan for this quarter, and probably for the year as well."

"I've told you before, Tom, that's not an option. I will not let this company miss its plan. We've never missed our plan since I took over as CEO and we're not about to now. You'd better find the damned money you need to fund the deals the divisions are coming up with. That's your job, and I pay you damned well for doing it. If you can't do it, I'll find someone who can."

Tom knew it would be useless to continue the conversation so he thanked her for her time and left. He'd have to figure out how to handle this crisis on his own. Deb never did understand finance. He was now more convinced than ever that all CEO's should be required to have a finance background in addition to operational experience. Understanding the day to day operations of a business is one thing, but if you don't understand the financial aspects, or at least take the advice of your CFO, then it's difficult to be successful in today's business environment. Unfortunately, Deb Cutter had neither the financial background nor the inclination to listen to her CFO. It was a recipe for disaster.

Down on the tenth floor Norm Cassidy's phone rang, and the caller ID told him the call was coming in from Atlanta.

"Norm Cassidy" he said into the receiver.

"Norm. It's Jake. The police just interrogated Sylvie Anderson, and they believe they have enough evidence to hold her for the hit-and-run of Ron Hayward, and it looks like they're going to go for an indictment. The problem is we still don't have anything that we can call motive. I'm working with Jim Seversen over at Great

Waters Insurance on that part of it, but in the meantime, I want to make sure we've got all of our ducks in order. If this thing goes to trial we'll be asked to testify about the insurance premium scam, and I don't want any surprises."

"I couldn't agree more, Jake. What can I do from this end?"

"We need to be absolutely positive that Sylvie was the one who downloaded the program to Ron's PC. I've got to tell you, she looked genuinely surprised when Tim Nagle confronted her on that issue. My gut tells me I need to look into this further. I don't suppose you looked at Sylvie's PC to see if there are any rogue programs on it?"

"No, I'm afraid not. Once the police found that Sylvie's SUV was involved in the hit and run, we thought there was no doubt it was her, so we didn't think of checking her PC for that kind of software."

"I'd like you to take a look at that right away and get back to me as soon as you can."

"I'll give Nick Hurley a call and ask him if he can pick it up and check it out. Hopefully, he can take it to his police lab and get back to us within a few hours."

Meanwhile, an attorney hired by Jeff Anderson to represent his daughter had shown up at the Marietta police headquarters and was in the interrogation room with Sylvie. The intercom had been turned off, at his request, so he could have a private conversation with his client. Tim couldn't hear what they were saying, but he was observing them through the one way glass and could see Sylvie gesturing broadly with her arms and hands, while her new attorney listened attentively. Every so often she'd stop, during what appeared to be a question from him. This went on for about a half hour before the attorney came to the door and knocked, indicating that he was ready to speak with the detective.

As soon as Tim opened the door, the attorney began. "My client denies all allegations. Unless you are charging her with something right now, we're leaving."

"As a matter of fact, counselor, we *are* charging her. For starters, we're charging her with leaving the scene of an accident. We may follow that up later with vehicular homicide, and possibly a few other things. Your client has been a very busy lady." Tim then turned to a uniformed officer standing by the door and asked him to take her away and book her.

***

In Milwaukee, Jim Seversen was looking at the email and attachments he'd received from Norm Cassidy, and saw that each had a notation indicating the policy number for which the premium was being paid. Norm had also sent an 'accounts payable' report which showed the policy number as well as the customer's name and address for each payment. From what he'd seen, it certainly looked like New Commerce had indeed sent premium payments for the policies in question. He'd have to have his staff track this down ASAP, paying particular attention to the endorsements on the back of the checks. He had to know who cashed them, and when and where they were cashed. He called in his senior person and assigned him that task.

Chapter 27

Tuesday, August 26, 2008

At the Marietta police headquarters, Nick Hurley had just finished his analysis of Sylvie Anderson's hard drive. He'd picked it up as soon as Norm Cassidy called him yesterday afternoon and began his review first thing this morning. What he found was interesting, but not what he expected. Not only did he not find any evidence of an unauthorized program that might have been downloaded, there was nothing at all on the hard drive. Someone had permanently erased everything. There wasn't even anything to retrieve as there usually is after the files are erased. Whoever did this wanted to make very sure that no one could read what had been on the hard drive. Although he couldn't determine when this had been done, Sylvie hadn't been in the office since Friday and hadn't had access to the PC since then. She must've done it before the weekend, but he couldn't figure out why she'd need to. What could've been on her hard drive that she didn't want anyone to see? He called Norm Cassidy to tell him what he'd found and then brought Tim Nagle up to speed. Norm called Jake Hammond to give him the news.

"Sorry, Jake, but if anybody downloaded a program to Sylvie's PC, it's long gone. Someone's erased the hard drive, and they did it with a special program that wipes everything clean. We can't even reconstruct, as we normally could when someone just deletes the files."

"If Sylvie was the one who downloaded the spoofing program to Ron Hayward's PC, why would she erase everything on her own hard drive? It doesn't make sense at all. And when would she have done it? She wasn't in the office on the weekend, and if she'd done it last week she wouldn't have been able to process her own work because some of the software she needs for her day-to-day responsibilities had to be on her hard drive."

***

Jim Seversen was in his office with his senior auditor, who was filling him in on what he'd found so far. It wasn't looking good. The premium checks from New Commerce had come in and had been cashed, but none of the amounts were ever credited to any policies. From the endorsements on the back of the checks they were able to determine they'd been deposited at a local bank, and additional research revealed it was a business account opened under the name of Great Waters Insurance Group. Unfortunately, it was not one of the company's authorized accounts, nor was it with the bank where all of their accounts were kept. There were now more questions than answers, like, who opened the bank account, who was endorsing the checks, and how much money had been diverted. And beyond that, the most basic question of all was how were these payments being intercepted at delivery?

He thought that the controls in place were effective in preventing such a thing from happening. This couldn't have been an easy thing to accomplish. He'd have to get more information from the bank where the checks were being deposited, and he couldn't do that without the help of the local police. As much as he hated to, it was time to get them involved, but first, he'd have to notify the proper management folks here at Great Waters. He picked up the phone and dialed Doug Armstrong's number.

Doug's assistant Jennifer answered the phone. "Mr. Armstrong's office. How may I help you?"

"Jennifer, this is Jim Seversen. Is Doug available to take my call?"

"One moment, please. I'll check."

A few seconds later Doug Armstrong picked up the phone. "Yes, Jim. What can I do for you today?"

"I was wondering if you'd have a few minutes to sit with me. We've uncovered something that I believe will require us to contact the local police, and I wanted to fill you in on what's going on as soon as possible. Can I come up there now?"

"Well, sure, I guess so. I'll have Jennifer cancel my next appointment. Come on up right now."

A half hour later Jim had brought Doug Armstrong up to speed and Doug agreed they'd have to get the local police involved, but first wanted to make a call to Fred Campbell, the Chief Credit Officer at New Commerce. He and Fred went back a long way, and he wanted to make sure Fred was on board with this. He asked Jennifer to place the call, and a couple minutes later his phone rang.

"Doug Armstrong" he answered.

"Doug. It's Fred Campbell. Good to hear from you. What's going on?"

"Fred, I'm sitting here with my Internal Auditor, and he tells me we may have a problem that involves New Commerce. Have you been in the loop on that?"

"If you're talking about what I think you're talking about, yes, I've been getting periodic updates. But I wasn't aware yet that you had an issue at your end too."

"Well, Fred, it seems we both have issues. From your side, I'm told someone's been tampering with your computer files and making premium payments by check rather than through the banking system. From our end, it looks like someone's been getting those checks and depositing them into a bank account that isn't an authorized Great Waters account, and not applying the premium payments to any policies. We're about to contact the local police to see if we can get more information on the bank account and determine who's using it, but I didn't want to do that until I spoke with you."

"Thanks, Doug. We're already working with the local police at this end. We've had quite an interesting time of it lately. Not only do we have customers who've suffered losses as a result of Fay and have no insurance coverage, but our files have been tampered with, and one of our account managers was killed in a hit-and-run accident that the police think was not an *accident* at all. I knew that our Chief Security and Compliance Officer, Jake Hammond, had been in touch with your guys, but I didn't yet know that you'd found anything suspicious at your end. Has Jake been told yet?"

"No, Jim came directly to me when he uncovered the evidence. I'll have him bring Jake up to speed before we contact the police."

"It's looking pretty much like there's been some collusion between someone here and someone at your place. Because we're in different states, I think the police will now want to get the FBI involved as well."

"I agree" said Doug. There's never a good time for fraud or embezzlement, but this has got to be the worst possible time of all. With the economy the way it is, and our new owners breathing down my neck, I don't even want to think about how this is going to end."

"We'll sort out liability issues later, Doug. First, we have to figure out exactly what's happened and who did what."

"Right! I'll ask Jim to work closely with Jake and have them both keep us posted. Hopefully, we can clear this thing up quickly."

Chapter 28

Wednesday, August 27, 2008

It was just before 8 a.m. and Sergeant Ted Stabler, of the Milwaukee Police Department, was in Jim Seversen's office listening to the story of the unauthorized bank account and the premium checks that were deposited into it. It was beginning to look like the FBI would have to be called in, not only because bogus information and identification had been used to open a bank account, which constitutes bank fraud, but also because embezzled funds had crossed state lines. Whoever was involved in this little scheme probably hadn't counted on that.

"We can interview the bank employees without a problem but we're going to need a subpoena to look at the bank records" he told Jim. "I've got a contact at the Bureau and I'll give him a call as soon as I get back to the station. I'd rather have the subpoena in hand before we have any contact with the bank or its employees, just to make sure we can get our hands on everything we need before anything can be changed or altered. From what you're telling me, things related to this case have a tendency to disappear."

"Sounds good to me" said Jim. What do you want us to do at this end?"

"I think you should probably keep a low profile. Whoever's involved in this from your company may not yet know that you're onto him. We need to move quickly, and with as little attention as possible. I'll keep you posted as our investigation proceeds. In the meantime, if you can work behind the scenes to try to quantify the extent of the problem, like how many accounts or policies are involved and how much money's been diverted, that would be great. But again, I'd prefer it if you do this quietly, and without raising any suspicions, if possible."

"I think we can do that. I'll continue to work with the folks at New Commerce."

Stabler headed back to the station and Jim dialed Jake Hammond's number in Marietta. The receptionist who answered the phone put him right through to Ron Hayward's office, which Jake was now using as his office.

"Jake Hammond" he answered.

"Jake. It's Jim Seversen from Great Waters. How are things going?"

"Hey Jim. Things are moving pretty quickly down here. How are things going at your end? Any luck with tracking those checks?"

"As a matter of fact, that's why I'm calling. Do you have a few minutes to discuss it right now?"

"Absolutely."

"Well, it turns out that the checks in question were deposited into a bank account in the name of Great Waters Insurance Group. However, the account isn't an authorized account and is in a bank we don't do business with. Our CEO, Doug Armstrong, has been speaking with Fred Campbell at your headquarters. It seems they've known each other for some time. Anyway, they agreed we needed to get our local police involved so we can subpoena the bank records. I just met with Sergeant Stabler of the Milwaukee Police Department and gave him a complete run down of what we have so far. He's going to contact the local office of the FBI and get going on the bank records."

"I figured we'd need to get the FBI involved sooner or later. I'll alert our police contacts at this end because I'm sure the FBI will want to speak with them as well."

"No doubt" added Jim. "In the meantime, I think we need to try to quantify the extent of this issue. We're going to need to know exactly how many of your customers are impacted, and how many premium payments have been diverted. Do you have a complete list of those customers yet?"

"I'm not sure I'm a hundred percent confident that we've identified them all. One of the things we'll need to do is somehow compare our data files to yours. But since our current files have been altered, we'll have to figure out how far back we'll need to go to get an accurate picture. Once we've done that, I can figure out which ones had their premium payments diverted. It may take a day or so to get to that point."

"Once you get there, send me a list of policy numbers, and we'll go back into our records. For the policies that *did* exist at one time, we should be able to easily figure out when the premium payments stopped being applied. However, for the policies which never existed, I'm afraid you're going to have to figure it out at your end. Eventually, we may be able to piece it all together based on the bank records, but I'm not sure we can count on that."

"Not a problem. We'll get right on it. Anything else I should be aware of?"

"No, I don't think so. You know everything I know at this point. If anything else comes up, I'll let you know."

After they hung up, Jake called Norm Cassidy in Augusta.

"Norm, here's what I need you to do next. Go to the oldest backup file you have. We generally keep year end files for several years, so you should be able to go back at least three or four years, whatever is the oldest file. Using that file, pull out all inventory financing accounts that had insurance coverage arranged by us and create a new working file. Then compare the information on that file to the most current back up file, the one created just prior to the unauthorized changes. We need to figure out how long this scam has been going on. Once you've done that, produce a file with all accounts, both currently opened accounts as well as those that have been closed. Make sure your file shows policy numbers for each account. But for the time being, only include those accounts that were insured by Great Waters. That's the file I want to send to Jim Seversen. Right now there's no indication of a problem with any of the other insurance companies, but we can look into that next."

"I can do that" offered Norm. "Hopefully it won't take more than a few hours. Do you want me to send you an electronic version of the new file?"

"Actually, I'd rather have you send it directly to Jim Seversen. Once he gets it, he can start looking into the policies and trying to find out when the premium payments stopped. The problem is, for those policies that never existed, there won't be much he can do for us. At best, he'll probably be able to send back a file with those customer names so we can follow up from our end. I think all we'll be able to do on those is find out how long the insurance premiums have been collected, and we'll know how much money has been diverted from those accounts."

"Sounds logical to me. I'll get on it right away and get back to you as soon as I have something."

***

It was one of the newer buildings in Tallahassee, and very upscale. The offices of Stallwood and Stallwood were on the fifth floor. Tom Stallwood and his wife Rebecca (she liked to be called Becky) had been in practice together for about five years, ever since they were married. Before then, each had been a successful litigator with other law firms. They met during a civil trial when Tom's client was suing Becky's for breach of contract. The plaintiff was a homeowner who had paid for major renovations to his home, and the defendant was the contractor who failed to deliver the agreed upon work. Although Tom's client won the lawsuit, the monetary award wasn't as high as he'd hoped, primarily because of the outstanding defense presented by the opposing counsel, Rebecca Atwell.

In addition to having gained a healthy respect for each other's professional abilities, they were clearly attracted to each other. They dated for about eighteen months before getting engaged, and were married a year after that. All in all, it had been just about six and a half years since they'd faced each other in court for the first time. Now they were partners in their own law firm, with an outstanding record of wins. They'd built a solid reputation, not only for winning cases at trial, but also for getting huge out of court settlements for their clients.

Their assistant buzzed them on the intercom at 8:30 sharp and informed them that their new client was here for his appointment. Of course, they'd been expecting him, and they were ready. Tom asked her to send him right in.

As the office door opened, Tom got up to greet his new client. "Good morning, I'm Tom Stallwood, and this is my wife, Becky. We're glad to meet you Mr. Jones. Please come in and have a seat. Can we get you something, maybe some coffee?'

Randy Jones looked a little uneasy, but accepted their offer. "Yes, thank you. Coffee would be great." He took a seat in the large leather chair in front of the desk, and looked up at the surroundings. Clearly, Stallwood and Stallwood was a very successful law firm. The rent on this office must be costing them a small fortune. And the furniture was very expensive indeed. Hopefully, if they were that successful, they'd be able to help Walters Marine. After the assistant delivered the coffee, Tom opened the conversation.

"So tell us, Mr. Jones, how we can assist you."

"First of all, please call me Randy."

"OK Randy. How can we help you?"

"I'm here representing Walters Marine, a marine dealership here in the city. Mr. Walters died in a traffic accident recently, and I'm trying to take care of the business for Mrs. Walters. Since she's really the owner of the business now, she will be your client, but she asked me to make the initial contact. I hope that's OK."

"Of course it is" replied Tom. "Please go on."

"Walters Marine specializes in selling personal water crafts (PWCs) and small to medium sized boats. They've been financing their inventory through the Atlanta area office of a Maine commercial finance company called New Commerce Commercial Finance. As part of their agreement with Walters Marine, New Commerce arranged for inventory insurance on all equipment at the store, and also arranged for life insurance on Mr. Walters, as he was considered a key person to the success of the business. New Commerce made the premium payments to the insurance company, Great Waters Insurance Group in Milwaukee, and billed Walters Marine for the amount of those payments." Randy paused to take a sip of coffee and to collect his thoughts. He wanted to make this as clear as he could in the shortest time possible.

"I'm with you so far," said Becky. "Please continue."

"When tropical storm Fay hit Florida, the dealership was hit hard, and the inventory was damaged. When we tried to file a claim with Great Waters, we were told we didn't have coverage. We also found out there was no life insurance policy on Dan Walters. That was two weeks ago, and I've been in contact with both the finance company, New Commerce, and the insurance company, Great Waters, on several occasions since then, but to no avail. In the meantime, we can't get our inventory replaced by the supplier and we're losing money and customers every day. I don't know how much longer we'll be able to survive. I need some help getting these guys to move."

"And so, what, exactly, is it you would like us to do, Randy?" asked Tom.

"First, I'd like you to contact both the finance and insurance companies to see if we can get things moving. Maybe the dealership can survive if we get some inventory soon. At the very least, however, we'll need to recoup lost sales resulting from their lack of action, and at the worst, if the dealership goes out of business, we'll be looking for complete compensation."

"We'll be glad to help you, Randy. Hopefully, we can get you some inventory before the worst happens. But if we have to sue following bankruptcy, that case could take a very long time to settle. You realize that, don't you?"

"Yes, Mrs. Walters and I both understand that, but we have no choice."

"If we take this case, we'll need to meet Mrs. Walters before proceeding. Will that be a problem?"

"Not at all. I agreed to do the initial leg work for her, but she's perfectly willing to meet with you if you're interested in the case. Oh, and there's one more thing you should probably know."

"What's that?" asked Becky.

"From what I can gather, we're not the only New Commerce customer having these problems. From my discussions with people at both companies, I get the feeling quite a few of New Commerce's customers are in the same situation we're in. I think there's something going on at one or both of those companies that isn't on the up-and-up. I'm guessing that, if this goes to trial, it could turn into a class action lawsuit. That might be something you want to give some thought to."

"That's very interesting, Randy. We'll certainly keep that in mind. In the meantime, we'll discuss your case and get back to you by morning" said Tom. "But I'm confident we'll be able to help you. We'll set up an appointment to meet Mrs. Walters as soon as we've made our decision. In the meantime, is there anything else you want to add to what you've already told us?"

"No, I think that covers it. I certainly hope you decide to represent us, and I hope we can move forward quickly. Every day that passes puts us closer and closer to bankruptcy."

"We'll let you know after we talk it over. Thank you for coming in Randy." Tom and Becky both stood, signaling the end of the meeting, and escorted Randy to the door. Once he'd left, they recapped what they'd heard and discussed the pros and cons. Clearly, it wouldn't be a problem to contact New Commerce and Great Waters. That kind of saber rattling was always easy to do. The real question was whether or not they'd be willing to initiate and handle a lawsuit, if it came to that. They both agreed it could take years to resolve, and financial rewards were unpredictable. However, as they discussed the possibility of a class action lawsuit, they became more and more convinced that it might be worth their while to at least look into this further. They agreed to have their assistant call Randy later this afternoon to let him know they'd at least talk to the companies involved, and then decide where they'd go from there. They'd need to charge a small fee for the initial work, but if they decided to take legal action against the companies, then they'd do it without any up-front payments, settling instead for 30% of any settlement. They'd also need to speak with Mrs. Walters before moving forward, and they could do that first thing tomorrow morning.

***

Everyone at the headquarters in Augusta was on edge. The New Commerce stock price was plummeting, along with everyone else's. Investors were taking a beating and the Board wasn't happy, to put it mildly. New Commerce was now trading at $59 a share, down another ten points in the last two days, and twenty points below its high of just a couple of weeks ago. Everyone was talking about a major recession, but the government hadn't jumped on the band wagon yet. The President was still talking about "a slow down" of the economy, not a recession. The sub-prime mortgage fiasco was taking its toll across the board and no one seemed to know where it'd all end.

As Tom D'Angelo had tried to explain to Deb Cutter, New Commerce was having difficulty raising capital. Credit markets were tightening up, and analysts were taking a hard look at all company ratings, including those of New Commerce. The housing market was in disarray and foreclosures were rising. Unemployment was beginning to go up in most areas. And at New Commerce, the inability to raise capital wasn't their only problem. Delinquencies were rising because small businesses could no longer make payments, which in turn hurt New Commerce's credit ratings.

Members of the Executive Committee were meeting behind closed doors more often than ever, trying to figure out a way to survive the current economic crisis. Things hadn't looked this bad in recent memory. Certainly not in the past four years, under Deb's leadership. She was getting more and more difficult to deal with, always blaming the other members of the Committee for New Commerce's current problems. Morale in the company was at an all time low, as far as most employees could tell. There were rumors of layoffs and pay cuts coming soon.

Now, Deb was glad she'd decided to exercise some of her stock options at $69. There was no telling how low the stock price of New Commerce would go, especially if there were to be any lawsuits as a result of that insurance fiasco down in Atlanta. She'd taken enough of a hit already. There wasn't any need to wait until things got worse.

***

It was a sunny day, so Ted Stabler walked the half dozen or so blocks from his office in the District 1 police station on West State Street to the FBI headquarters on E. Kilbourn Avenue. These days he didn't get much opportunity to exercise, so the walk did him some good physically and also helped to clear his mind. It took him less than a half hour to get to the Plaza East Building. He entered by the south entrance and took the elevator to the sixth floor. When he got to Suite 600 he knocked on the door, walked in, identified himself to the receptionist and asked for Special Agent John Rich.

Ted and John had known each other most of their lives, having grown up together right there in Milwaukee. They attended most of the same schools, and started at the police academy at the same time. But John had moved on to the FBI a few years ago saying he wanted something more challenging. They occasionally worked together on special cases, but for the most part, only saw each other socially a few times a year. Nevertheless, they tried to keep in touch as much as possible.

John met him at the receptionist's desk and led him back to a small conference room so they could talk in private. Even though he was a special agent, John didn't have a private office, as only the supervising agent was allowed to have one. All the other agents worked out of cubicles and used one of several small conference rooms when they needed more privacy.

"So Ted, what brings you here today?"

"I'm working on a case and I think it's something the FBI should be involved with" replied Ted. "We've got a situation down at Great Waters Insurance Group and it looks like someone there has misappropriated some funds with the help of an accomplice in the Atlanta area, and then deposited those funds in a bank account that was opened fraudulently in the name of Great Waters."

"So we have some bank fraud as well as interstate movement of stolen funds, is that right?"

"That's what it looks like. We haven't been able to look at the bank records yet, because we'll need a subpoena for that, and we thought you guys would probably want to be involved" said Ted.

"That's a good call. We definitely want to be involved."

By the time Ted left the FBI Division Headquarters just before 4 p.m., they'd agreed on their next step. John would get the subpoena this afternoon, and they'd meet at the main office of the United Bank of Milwaukee just before 9 a.m. tomorrow.

Chapter 29

Thursday, August 28, 2008

The United Bank of Milwaukee, one of the oldest banks in the State of Wisconsin, was established in 1879 as a mutual savings bank, and was converted to a commercial bank in 1965. More than ninety percent of its customer base is made up of individual depositors and borrowers. The main offices are located in the original five-story red brick building it first occupied in 1879, with the branch on the first floor and administrative offices taking up the remaining four floors.

Today, when the main branch opened at 9 a.m. sharp, as it had on every work day since 1879, there were several people standing outside the door or waiting in their cars, which wasn't at all unusual. Most of the early morning customers were people from the neighborhood who stopped in regularly, but this morning there were two strangers in dark suits among them. They looked like businessmen who probably should have been at work by now. When Ken Long, the branch manager, unlocked the doors, the two men were the first ones to come in.

Ken didn't recognize the two men, which struck him as odd since he knew most of the branch's customers by name. He'd always made a point of remembering names, knowing that it gave him a competitive edge over the larger, less personal banks he had to compete with, because people appreciate being recognized and treated like a friend. He studied the men for a moment trying to figure out what they might have in mind. For a second he thought maybe they were planning a bank robbery. But, once inside, one of the men flashed some credentials and identified himself as Special Agent Rich with the FBI.

Ken had been the branch manager for almost five years and was used to dealing with almost any problem that came up, but this was something he'd never encountered before. He wondered what the FBI could want with him, or his branch. He nervously led the two men to his office so they could talk in private. They showed him the subpoena they'd brought with them and gave him the details of the account they were interested in looking at. After taking a closer look at their identification, he decided to call the bank's in-house attorney for guidance, and after a brief discussion, told the agents he'd give them his full cooperation.

John Rich had been assigned the lead role in the investigation, and the Milwaukee Police Department volunteered Ted Stabler to represent them on the team. Together they had to figure out who had opened the account in question, find any related accounts opened by the same individual, interview all bank employees with any knowledge of the account or its owner, and review all transactions posted to the account. And they had to do it all without tipping their hand or alerting the owner that they were onto him, which meant they had to work fast. Ken showed them around the branch, making sure they knew where all the facilities were, then set them up in the small conference room next to his office.

The first thing they asked for after getting settled in was the signature card for the account in question, which he was able to retrieve for them in about two minutes. A quick review gave them a lot of the information they needed, including the date the account was opened, the name of the platform person who opened it, and the name of the business for which the account was opened. But there was no indication of a company authorization or Board of Directors' approval, as is customary when business accounts are opened. Without such documents there was no way for the bank to verify that the account was a legitimate business account, and it was highly unusual, at the very least, for any bank employee to open the account without them. The first thing they'd be doing today was to interview the employee who opened the account.

The account had been opened as a business account for Great Waters Insurance Group, the authorized signor was someone by the name of Annabel King, and the bank employee who opened the account was Justine Smart. They asked Ken to have Justine come into the conference room for an interview and a few minutes later she was seated in front of them, looking very uncomfortable.

"Miss Smart, I'm Special Agent Rich, with the FBI, and this is Sergeant Stabler, with the Milwaukee Police. We'd like to ask you a few questions about a business account you opened a couple of years ago."

"Well, of course" replied Justine. "I'm not sure I'll remember a lot about an account that was opened years ago, but I'll try."

"Thank you, Miss Smart" replied John. "Please, take a look at this signature card if you would, and tell me if you can remember anything about the person who opened it." He handed the card to Sergeant Stabler on his right, who passed it along to Miss Smart. She took a look at it and her expression changed ever so slightly. It was as if she'd been expecting this, but had hoped it would never really happen. Her mind was racing, trying to figure out what to say or do. But before she could respond, she heard Sergeant Stabler's voice.

"Miss Smart. Is everything OK? You look a little pale. Can I get you anything, maybe some water?"

"Oh, no, thank you. I'll be fine. It's just a little warm in here, that's all."

"Miss Smart" continued Agent Rich, "Can you please tell us what you remember about Annabel King, the person who opened this account?"

She thought about it for a moment, and decided there was no sense in lying about it because it was sure to all come out now that the FBI was involved. She decided she'd be better off telling them the entire story now and hope for the best.   She still didn't think she'd done anything illegal. Over the next half hour Justine Smart told Agent Rich and Sergeant Stabler everything.   In all her years as a bank employee she'd always done things strictly by the book, and always with the highest level of integrity. Annabel had been a close friend of hers for many years, and Justine trusted her completely. So when Annabel first approached her, the fact that she didn't yet have the corporate resolution had seemed like a minor detail. She'd known she was breaking bank rules by opening a business account without the proper corporate resolution, and that had bothered her for a long time. But she didn't think she was doing anything illegal, and certainly nothing that would require FBI involvement. Annabel had told her she needed to get this new account set up right away, and promised to bring in the corporate resolution authorizing it, right after the next Board of Directors meeting.

But once the account was opened, Annabel never got around to bringing in the resolution. Justine had asked for it many times, but there was always a reason why it wasn't ready. The one thing she'd let herself be talked into doing that she really wasn't comfortable doing, was now coming back to haunt her.

"Can I ask why the FBI is interested in this account?" Justine asked.

"I'm sorry, but we can't give you that information. Can you tell us where we can find Annabel King?"

"Yes. She works at Great Waters Insurance Group, which is why I thought it would be OK to open the business account for them. I also have her home address." Justine wrote Annabel's address on a paper and handed it to Sergeant Stabler. "I hope I haven't done anything to get her in trouble" she added.

"Thank you for your time, Miss Smart. You can go back to work now. And please remember, everything we've discussed here this morning is strictly confidential. You are not to repeat any of it to anyone, and you cannot have any contact with Annabel King. If you do, you can be charged with conspiracy and obstruction of justice. Is that clear?"

"Yes, very clear."

After she left the conference room, Stabler asked Ken Long to step in for a moment.

"Mr. Long" Agent Rich began, "We're going to need a complete list of all transactions that have been posted to this account. How long will it take you to get that for us?"

"I'm not sure" he said honestly. "I'll contact our Information Technology Department and find out. I know we have history files, but I'm not sure how far back they go. I'll give them a call and get back to you in a few minutes, if that's OK."

"Sure. And we'll also need copies of any checks that were deposited into the account. I'd imagine you probably have those on microfiche or something like that? And we also need to know if there are any other accounts at this bank that were opened by Annabel King."

One by one the other bank employees were interviewed to see if any of them had any additional information to offer. It was clear by the end of the morning that Justine had been the only bank employee to deal with Annabel King. No one else knew her, or had ever heard of her.

The first trip to United Bank of Milwaukee had wrapped up more quickly then they could've hoped for. Ken Long told them they'd have their requested reports by end of business today and that Justine Smart would probably be suspended, or even fired. They decided to head back to headquarters to plan their next step. On the way, Sergeant Stabler called Jim Seversen and told him he needed to meet with him, and they agreed to meet in Jim's office at 2 p.m. That'd give them enough time to discuss their approach over lunch, and complete their notes from the Justine Smart interview.

At 2 p.m., Tom Rich and Ted Stabler were sitting in Jim Seversen's office. They gave him a quick update on the information they'd gotten at the bank and asked about Annabel King.

"What, exactly, is her job here at Great Waters?" Rich asked.

"She's a clerical person with a number of minor responsibilities, one of which is to sort the mail when it's delivered by the post office. However, unless something was addressed to her personally, she wouldn't be able to open it without someone else present. It's part of our system of controls to help ensure everything's properly accounted for and no money is diverted."

"So you're saying that you always require that two people accept the mail delivery?" asked Stabler.

"That's right."

"Well, what happens if there aren't two employees in the mail room when the mail comes in? I'm sure that situation must come up once in a while."

"It's not supposed to" replied Seversen. "Our employees are told there must always be two people in the mail room at all times. If, for whatever reason, someone happens to be alone when the mail delivery is made, they are supposed to refuse delivery. The post office knows this as well."

"That doesn't sound very practical to me" added Rich. "You might miss receiving something that's time sensitive, wouldn't you?"

"It generally doesn't happen, but if it did happen, we'd send two people to the post office to pick up the items not delivered. I can't remember the last time that occurred."

"So I guess what you're saying, if I understand everything I've just heard, is that the only way Annabel could have diverted the mail was if it was addressed to her personally. Is that correct?"

"Yes. You've got to understand that we can't open an employee's personal mail. We discourage them from using our business address, but nevertheless, sometimes they do. In that case, they're given the mail and they can open it whenever they wish."

"Actually" added Agent Rich, "this may fall under the same rules as reading an employee's email. Anything they received on company equipment or premises is subject to company review, so long as you have a policy which states that, and the employees are told of the policy."

"I didn't know that" responded Seversen. "I'll have to run that one by our company attorneys."

"So, let me recap" said Stabler. "You have an employee, Annabel King, who works in the mail room, who opened a business account at United Bank of Milwaukee under the name of Great Waters Insurance Group, and who apparently is diverting premium payments received from New Commerce which most probably are addressed to her, personally. Does that about sum it up?"

"Sounds like it to me" replied Seversen. "So, where do we go from here?"

"We're going to need to talk with Annabel King, and I'd prefer to do it at FBI headquarters. Can you call her in here? We'll *invite* her to come along with us of her own free will, but can force her, if need be. Once we leave here, you should probably call Jake Hammond at New Commerce to fill him in on what's happened so far today."

Jim felt that a phone call to Annabel might not be appropriate, so he decided to take a walk down to the mail room himself. He was back, with Annabel right behind him, within ten minutes.

"Annabel, this is Special Agent Rich with the FBI, and Sergeant Stabler, with the Milwaukee Police. They're going to need to ask you a few questions."

The look of shock, mixed with a great deal of fear, crossed her face. She hadn't been comfortable when the

Internal Auditor asked to see her in his office, but they could tell she was darn right terrified, now.

"Miss King, we're going to need you to come with us to headquarters to answer some questions" Rich said.

"What's this about?" she asked.

"We'll get into more details at headquarters, but for now all you need to know is that we're looking into some missing funds, and we believe you have some information that can help us in our investigation."

"Am I under arrest?" she asked.

"No, you're not. As I said, we just need to ask you some questions, for now."

"Do I need an attorney?"

"As I said, Miss King, we just want to ask you some questions. It would be much better for you if you just came along with us right now to see if we can clarify some things. You are not under arrest."

That seemed to appease her somewhat, and she decided to go along with them. By 2:30 they were in an interrogation room at FBI Division Headquarters on the sixth floor of the Plaza East Building on E. Kilbourn Ave. The ride over was uneventful and quiet, with Annabel in the back seat looking very uncomfortable. They offered her coffee or a soft drink, both of which she turned down.

"Let me begin by telling you, Miss King, that we're looking into some premium payments that appear to have been diverted. These payments were for inventory insurance for customers of New Commerce Commercial Finance in Marietta, Georgia. The payments were made by check, but never applied to the policies at Great Waters. We've been looking into the bank account the payments were deposited to at United Bank of Milwaukee."

She was looking more pale than ever, and began fidgeting in her chair.

"Are you familiar with the United Bank of Milwaukee, Miss King?"

She thought of saying no, but realized they probably already knew she'd opened an account there. Why else would they be here right now? She decided to test them to see exactly how much they knew, and began giving them little pieces at a time. No need to spill her guts right up front and maybe find out later they didn't know as much as she thought they did.

"Of course I know of that bank, I have a friend who works there."

"What would that friend's name be?" asked Stabler.

"Her name is Justine Smart. She's been with the bank for many years, and I've known her for most of my life."

"Have you ever done business with United Bank of Milwaukee, Miss King?"

"As a matter of fact, I did have some money deposited there some time back."

Since they hadn't yet received the computer reports from the bank, Rich and Stabler had no way of knowing if Annabel had any personal accounts there, either currently or in the past. They'd know soon enough, but for now, they'd have to play this one by ear.

"When you say you *had* some money deposited there, does that mean you no longer have any money there?"

"I started banking at the local branch of Bank of America a while back because it's closer to the office here, and much more convenient."

"But you didn't answer my question. Do you currently have any money on deposit at United Bank of Milwaukee?"

"As I tried to tell you, Agent Rich, I now do all my personal banking at Bank of America."

"I'd like to move on to another question, Miss King, but I need to clarify this issue first. Let me ask the question in another way. Do you now have any accounts, personal or otherwise, at United Bank of Milwaukee?

"No" she replied.

She knew it was probably not a good idea to lie to a federal agent, but she couldn't think of anything else to say. If they knew there was a business account with her name connected to it, they'd have to prove that she was the person who opened it. At that point Rich decided to play his ace, and use the copy of the bank signature card he'd taken with him when he left the bank.

"Miss King, I'm going to ask you to do something right now." He put a blank piece of paper in front of her and pushed a pen toward her. "Please sign your name on this paper for me."

When she had done so, he looked at it for a moment, and then pulled out the copy of the signature card and compared the two. They were identical. Now he showed her the signature card.

"Miss King, please take a look at this signature card from the United Bank of Milwaukee. Do you recognize that signature?"

She stared at the card for a few moments before responding. "I have no idea what's going on here. That *does* look like my signature, but I never signed that card. As I said, I previously had an account at United Bank of Milwaukee, but closed it some time ago. This card is for a business account, and I never had a business account there."

"Really?" replied Rich. "Then how do you explain this signature card?"

"I can't explain it, nor do I have to. I'm telling you that I never signed that card, and anyone who says otherwise is lying."

"So, you're saying that you never opened this particular bank account at United Bank?"

"That's correct."

"It might interest you to know that we've been at the bank examining their records and we've interviewed all of their employees, including your friend, Justine Smart. Justine told us that you did, indeed, open this account, and promised to get her the appropriate corporate resolutions as soon as the Board of Directors meeting was held. You don't recall that?"

"I don't know why Justine would have said such a thing. We've been friends for a long time, and I've always trusted her, but if she said that, then she's lying. She's had plenty of opportunities over the years to get a copy of my signature. Maybe she's the one who forged my signature on that card you have there."

"We'll, it'll be easy enough to have a handwriting expert take a look at this and determine if it's a forgery or not. In any event, we have a few more questions to ask you. Like, do you have any friends or acquaintances who work at New Commerce Finance in the Atlanta area?"

"I've never been to Atlanta and I don't know anyone there" she replied. And I don't like the way this interview is going. I think I'd rather not answer any more questions without an attorney."

Unfortunately, they didn't yet have enough information to hold her. They needed to track the transactions against the business account at United Bank and also wanted to look at her bank records at Bank of America, so they decided to let her leave for the time being.

"That'll be all for now, Miss King. Thank you for your cooperation so far. I'd advise you to speak with an attorney and arrange to have him present the next time we speak with you. In the meantime, please do not leave the city without letting us know. We'll be in touch."

***

As Special Agent Rich had suggested, Jim Seversen put in a call to Jake Hammond at New Commerce as soon as Rich and Stabler left with Annabel King. He spent a few minutes bringing Jake up to speed on the latest development in Milwaukee, and then inquired as to what was happening in Marietta.

"We've made quite a bit of progress at this end too" said Jake. "The police have one of our employees in custody right now, but it would be helpful if we could establish a link between your Miss King and our employee. Do you have any ideas?"

"Nothing right now, but maybe after I hear from Special Agent Rich I'll know better how to proceed. I expect to hear from him as soon as his interview with Miss King is over. Maybe he can work with the Marietta police in figuring out where to go from here. Surely, there has to be a way we can find a connection between Miss King and someone at your location."

"You're right. It's probably something the police will have to figure out. Give me a call as soon as you hear from Rich."

"I'll do that."

***

Just before five o'clock, an employee from the United Bank of Milwaukee showed up at the FBI Divisional Headquarters with a stack of computer printouts. He identified himself to the receptionist, asked to see Special Agent Rich and then took a seat in one of the well upholstered chairs to wait. Within five minutes Rich came out to greet him.

"Good afternoon. I'm Special Agent Rich."

"Hello. I'm from United Bank of Milwaukee, and I have some printouts for you. Mr. Long wanted these hand delivered to you as soon as possible. He said to tell you that everything you asked for is in here, but if you need anything further to just let him know."

"Thanks. Please tell Mr. Long that I appreciate his fast response to our request."

John hadn't expected the reports this soon, and had been getting ready to leave for the day, but now his plans changed. He'd need to go through these reports as soon as possible, and decided that now was as good a time as any. He was anxious to get to the bottom of this case. He grabbed the pile of reports and headed back to his desk.

A few hours later he had found what he'd been looking for. Annabel King did, indeed, have a personal account at United Bank some time back, and had closed it about a year ago. There were no other accounts under her name, except of course, the business account for Great Waters. But more importantly, he had a complete list of all the transactions processed to the Great Waters business account since it was opened two years earlier. He picked up the phone, dialed the Milwaukee police headquarters for District 1, and asked for Sergeant Stabler.

Chapter 30

Friday, August 29, 2008

It was 9 a.m. when the phone on her desk in the reception area rang. As always, she answered it with "New Commerce Commercial Finance, how may I direct your call?" The voice at the other end was polite and to the point. "I'd like to speak with Fred Campbell please" he said. "This is Tom Stallwood of the law firm Stallwood and Stallwood in Tallahassee, Florida."

"Please hold while I try to contact Mr. Campbell for you" she said. She put the caller on hold and dialed Fred's number.

"Fred Campbell."

"Mr. Campbell, I have a call for you from a Mr. Tom Stallwood. He says he's an attorney with the law firm of Stallwood and Stallwood in Tallahassee, Florida. He didn't say what the call was about, though. Should I put him through?"

"Yes, thanks Sue. I'll take it."

As soon as he'd hung up the phone, Sue put through the call.

"Hello, this is Fred Campbell."

"Mr. Campbell, this is Tom Stallwood from Tallahassee. I'm representing Walters Marine, one of your customers. Since you've been in contact with Randy Jones, one of the Walters Marine employees, I thought I'd give you a call first before dealing with your company's Chief Counsel. I hope that's alright with you."

"Well, I guess that depends on what you want to discuss, Mr. Stallwood. I really should have someone from our legal staff present for any discussion of legal issues. Why don't you tell me briefly what it is you'd like to discuss and then we can decide how to proceed."

"Fair enough Mr. Campbell. As I said, my firm is representing Walters Marine in Tallahassee, Florida. They've recently suffered some damage to their building and inventory as a result of tropical storm Fay. I believe Mr. Jones has been in touch with you about that damage, and the need to replace their inventory as soon as possible. Is that correct?"

"Yes, that's true."

"The thing is Mr. Campbell, Walters Marine has been closed now since the 13th, sixteen calendar days, because they haven't been able to obtain replacement inventory, primarily because New Commerce hasn't paid the insurance premiums on their policy, and hasn't yet contacted the supplier to arrange for replacement inventory. As a result, the dealership has lost a significant amount of income, and has lost customers to their competition. At this point it is uncertain whether they will be able to survive, and even if they do, the financial damage to their business is significant."

"Mr. Stallwood, I've already informed Randy Jones that New Commerce will arrange for replacement inventory, at our expense. I apologize for the delay, but there have been a number of problems we've had to deal with as a result of Fay. I will get to this shortly, I assure you."

"Well, Mr. Campbell, I'm afraid that's not good enough at this point. What Walters Marine needs is not only to obtain replacement inventory, but to be made whole regarding their lost income over the past sixteen days, and also to somehow offset their loss of future income due to lost customers. Oh, and let's not forget about the life insurance policy for Mr. Walters, which apparently also doesn't exist. I believe that was in the amount of one million dollars. This is a courtesy call to give you an opportunity to resolve these issues before legal action is taken."

"Of course I'll have to speak with our Chief Counsel about this, and I'll ask her to get back to you. Can you give me a ball-park figure of how much we're talking about?"

"I'd say that if we're limiting this discussion to just the Walters Marine case, they'd need at least three million in addition to the replacement inventory."

"What did you mean when you said if we're limiting the discussion to just the Walters Marine case?" asked Fred.

"Frankly, Mr. Campbell, from what I understand, you have some issues that probably affected a significant number of your customers. I wouldn't be surprised if a class action lawsuit resulted from those issues. But for now, I'm primarily concerned with your corrective actions regarding Walters Marine."

"I see" replied Fred. "Obviously, I will immediately contact our Chief Counsel to discuss this. I'm sure she'll get back to you very soon."

"I certainly hope so, Mr. Campbell. I look forward to hearing from her no later than early next week."

Fred hung up the phone and headed to Barbara Cullen's office to fill her in on his conversation with Tom Stallwood. He hoped they could resolve this issue without going to court but, based on what Stallwood said about a possible class action lawsuit, it wasn't looking too promising. This is all they needed right now, in the middle of a significant financial crisis that was killing their stock price. He wondered what else could go wrong.

That's exactly what Deb Cutter was asking herself as she watched the price of New Commerce stock go down again. The market had just opened a few minutes ago, with the price of New Commerce stock at an all time low, and it already dropped another five points since then. It was now trading at $30 a share, down from $79 a share at the beginning of the month, a 62% drop. It was a fiasco that no one could've predicted. Certainly, Deb had done everything right, at least in her mind. But the Board of Directors wasn't buying it.

That's when she got the call from Barbara Cullen, telling her that she and Fred Campbell needed to speak with her as soon as possible. Now what? It seemed like Fred brought nothing but bad news lately, and it made her think that maybe she should have gotten rid of him along with Hank Talbot.

At 9:30 Deb's assistant told her that Fred, Barbara and Tom D'Angelo were waiting outside her office. The last thing she needed right now was to have those three gang up on her, but she really didn't have much choice. "Show them in" she told her assistant without fanfare.

As they filed into her office, Barbara was the first to speak. "Thanks for seeing us on such short notice, Deb. We have another problem surfacing that we need to bring you up to speed on."

"No problem" Deb replied, without sounding very convincing. They all knew how she hated to be surprised and always insisted on ample notice before scheduling a meeting. Anyone who knew her had to know that she hated this with a passion.

Barbara continued. "The situation in Florida is getting worse. We've just heard from a law firm in Tallahassee which is representing one of our customers. They gave us a courtesy call, but made it clear they're ready to proceed with a lawsuit. They also hinted at the possibility of a class action suit. That would be really bad news for us."

Over the next half hour the three of them filled Deb in as much as possible, and they agreed on a course of action. Barbara would contact the law firm of Stallwood and Stallwood and try to negotiate a settlement. She'd start low, say around a million and a half, and see what happened. Their own insurance would cover most of that, minus a relatively small initial out-of-pocket amount. If that didn't work, she'd go as high as 2.5 million, but no higher. She'd also make sure that the supplier was able to replace the inventory that Walters Marine lost during the storm. With any luck, this whole messy business might end there. Otherwise, they'd be in for a hell of a ride, especially if anyone got the notion to go forward with a class action lawsuit. In addition to the potential legal costs and jury award, the negative publicity would kill them.

After they'd left her office, Deb checked the price of the stock one more time. It was now at $28.50. She decided to sell more of her shares before any news of a potential class action lawsuit hit the wires.

***

Things were getting pretty hectic in Milwaukee. Jim Seversen got Norm Cassidy's email with attachments that showed all premium checks that New Commerce sent to Great Waters over the past two years. There were thousands of them, and the total dollar amount exceeded $500,000, and represented payments from more than one hundred New Commerce customers, and there was no telling how many of those customers had suffered losses during tropical storm Fay. The company's potential liability was staggering, and could have a major impact on its future. Ping Industries would need to be contacted soon to bring them up to speed, but first, Jim wanted to get more details as to who was involved in the embezzlement and fraud so that he could have a clearer picture of how the liability would be shared between New Commerce and Great Waters.

He was about the pick up the phone to call Doug Armstrong when an incoming call came through. He noticed from caller ID that it was the FBI Headquarters, and picked it up immediately. "Jim Seversen" he answered.

"Hello Jim, Special Agent Rich here. How are you?"

"I've been better, John. What can I do for you?"

"I'm calling because I got the bank reports yesterday afternoon showing the activity to the business account at

United Bank of Milwaukee. I stayed late to go over them, and I'm ready to fill you in on what I found, and then turn the reports over to you for further research. Can I meet with you sometime this morning?"

"Sure John. Can you come over right now? I've got some additional information I can share with you, too."

"I'll be there in fifteen minutes or so."

"OK, I'll see you then."

After his conversation with John Rich, Jim decided to hold off on his call to Doug. It'd be better to have as much information as possible when he *did* make that call, which would have to be fairly soon. Knowing the kind of pressure Doug was getting from Ping Industries about financial results, he knew the new problems wouldn't be easy for Doug to disclose.

By ten o'clock John Rich and Ted Stabler were in Jim Seversen's office showing him the reports from United Bank of Milwaukee. There were thousands of transactions to the account, both deposits and withdrawals. It looked like the money was put in on a regular basis, and once the checks had cleared, the money was withdrawn. Clearly, it was a pass-through account, but the FBI didn't know yet who had made the deposits and withdrawals. When the account was set up, Annabel King had been listed as the person authorized to do so, and John had no reason to believe anyone else had made the deposits or withdrawals, but he didn't have proof of that yet. That would be his next step. In the meantime, Jim could compare the transactions to the bank account with the data he received from New Commerce.

As soon as they left Jim's office, Agent Rich and Sergeant Stabler headed straight for the main branch of United Bank of Milwaukee. He needed to take a look at the actual deposit and withdrawal slips to see the name and signature on those documents. Ken Long had assured him that he'd be able to retrieve those from microfiche, and hopefully he'd be able to have copies of many of those by mid-day. He only needed to see a handful to move forward with the warrant for Annabel's arrest. The remainder would be needed for the trial, but he'd have the bank personnel work to retrieve those once he had enough of them to proceed with the warrant.

***

In Marietta, Sylvie Anderson was meeting with her attorney in the visitor's section of the local jail. The evidence against her was substantial, especially the DNA from her black SUV, which proved it was the vehicle that killed Ron Hayward. Coupled with the information New Commerce had discovered regarding the data file alterations made with her log on ID, it was looking pretty grim for her. Her attorney was talking about a deal she might be able to make with the DA.

"Listen to me, Sylvie" he said. If this goes to trial, you don't stand much of a chance. Your SUV is the one that killed Ron Hayward. And the evidence showing that you made the file changes seems pretty much iron-clad. You were in the office when the changes were made and you were the one who authorized the premium payments to be made by check rather than ACH."

"I told you that my supervisor is the one who authorized that payment method. She asked me to process the requests, but it was her decision."

"Can you prove that? Do you have a written request from her, or a recording of her asking you to do that?"

"No, of course not. I'm not in the habit of asking my supervisor to put every request in writing, and I'm certainly not going to record all of our conversations. She's my boss and I'm expected to follow her directions."

"I thought you said you never processed a change without a written request form. Isn't that what you told us?"

"That's true for all data file changes. But this wasn't a data file change, only a change in the premium payment method. That didn't require a written request."

"Well Sylvie, there is your problem. It'll be your word against hers, and considering the DNA evidence, who do you think the jury will believe?"

"I don't care about the stupid DNA evidence. I'm telling you I didn't run down Ron Hayward, and I didn't alter the company's data files. I can't explain how all the evidence points to me, except that someone is obviously trying to set me up. I'm not guilty, and I won't say that I am, just so I can take a deal from the DA. I'd rather take my chances in court. And I think you should be trying to prove my innocence rather than convince me to plead guilty. If you don't believe me, maybe I need a new lawyer."

"Alright, alright, I believe you. But it was my duty to explain the options to you. If you want to go forward with a trial, I'll be there for you. In the meantime, I'll work with the police to see if we can come up with any other suspects. If you didn't do it, and I believe that you didn't, than someone else obviously did, and there's got to be a way to figure out who."

"I think you should speak with Jake Hammond over at New Commerce. He's got a reputation for fairness and for getting to the bottom of things, and his people have access to all the computer information. If anyone can figure out who really did this, I believe he can."

"I'll give him a call and see if I can meet with him. In the meantime, keep thinking about who else might have been able to change the data files. Anything you can think of would be helpful. I'll be back to see you tomorrow."

"Thanks, Mr. Carter."

"I told you, call me Al."

"OK. Thanks, Al. I don't know what I'd do without your help."

The guard motioned that time was up, and Sylvie was taken back to her cell. Al Carter headed back to his office to make the call to Jake Hammond.

***

At the Marietta offices of New Commerce things were starting to get back to normal; at least as normal as things can be in the middle of an investigation of fraud, embezzlement and homicide, and in light of the economic crisis the entire country was beginning to experience. The day-to-day activities were continuing, but at a much slower pace. Credit was drying up and with it, customer demand, which in turn impacted the dealers who were New Commerce's customers. They didn't have to worry as much about raising capital anymore, because there weren't many deals to finance anyway.

A temporary replacement for Jeff Anderson had been brought in from the west coast, and Jake had sent Joe Nash home, as most of the leg work in the investigation was done. He, himself, hadn't seen his family in ten days, and he missed the kids and his wife Amie. But this wasn't the first time he'd been away for an extended period of time, and he was sure it wouldn't be the last. Talking to them every evening on the phone had helped a little, but he was itching to get back to Augusta.

Jake had moved out of the conference room and into Ron Hayward's office, which provided him with a little more privacy and also freed up the conference room for other activities. The phone on Ron's desk, now temporarily his, rang a few minutes before 4 p.m. "Jake Hammond" he answered."

"Mr. Hammond, I have a call for you from a Mr. Carter. He says he's Sylvie Anderson's attorney and he'd like to speak with you."

"OK. Put him through please."

He hung up and the receptionist put the call through.

"This is Jake Hammond" he answered. "How may I help you?"

"Mr. Hammond, this is Al Carter, Miss Anderson's attorney. I've just spoken with her at the local jail and she asked me to give you a call. I was wondering if I could meet with you sometime tomorrow to discuss a few things."

"That seems a bit unusual, Mr. Carter. What, exactly, did you have in mind?"

"Sylvie has convinced me of her innocence, and I need to understand a little more about the evidence against her before we proceed."

"Shouldn't you be speaking with the ADA?" I understand that they need to share their evidence with you before trial."

"True, but I'd rather get to the bottom of this sooner, rather than later. And Sylvie seems to think you're our best bet when it comes to proving her innocent."

"I'll tell you what, counselor, I need to check with Detective Nagle and the ADA before committing to a meeting with you. I just want to make sure they're OK with it."

"That's fine with me, Mr. Hammond. In fact, they're more than welcome to join us if they wish."

"Give me a number where you can be reached, and I'll call you back first thing Monday morning."

After they hung up, Jake put in a call to Tim Nagle, who indicated it'd be OK for Jake to meet with Al Carter, and then he decided to call it a day. He packed up and headed out to his hotel room, a room which had become like a second home. It was wearing thin, and he couldn't wait to get back to Maine. All he wanted now was a drink, or maybe two, to help him relax.

Chapter 31

Monday, September 1, 2008

By nine o'clock Jake had already spoken with Jim Seversen who'd filled him in on the latest developments in Milwaukee and asked if he could find out *exactly* how the premium payments checks were addressed when they were mailed. Jim explained how their controls don't allow any one individual to receive or open mail, unless an item is addressed to a specific individual, in which case it's considered personal mail. If the premium payments were sent to the attention of Annabel King or any other individual at Great Waters, it could be an important break in the case. Jake agreed and had already asked Norm Cassidy to look into it.

***

Special Agent Rich had reviewed the bank's microfiche records on Friday, and was convinced that the signature on all of the withdrawal slips he looked at were those of Annabel King. This morning he was headed out to the bank to pick up the printed copies of the deposit and withdrawal slips for hundreds of transactions, which the bank printed for him over the weekend. Once he had the hard copies, he'd be able to have his handwriting expert take a look at them and compare the signatures to the one he'd obtained from Annabel during her initial interrogation. If they matched, he had enough for a warrant, and he'd be able to pick her up immediately.

Ken Long greeted him as soon as he came into the branch, and led him to his office, where stacks of papers were mounted on the corner of his desk. "Good to see you again, Agent Rich. I've got all the printouts ready for you, right here" he added, as he pointed to the stack of papers on his desk.

"Thanks, Ken. I appreciate the fact that you had your folks work over the weekend to get these for me. I know it must've taken a while to find and print all of these. And please, call me John."

"Not a problem, John. We knew you were anxious to get these, and the weekend was the only opportunity we had to do this, now that we're down one person. In case you didn't know, Justine Smart has been suspended, pending further review. It's likely she'll be terminated for breaking bank rules regarding the opening of business accounts."

"I know you had to do that, but I'm still sorry to hear it. The way I see it, she was taken in by her so called *friend*, Annabel King. After all of her years as a trusted and loyal employee, she had one lapse in judgment that cost her everything."

"Unfortunately, that's the way it has to be. The bank cannot have employees who break the rules."

"I know. Well, thanks for this information. It may be one of the key things that help us solve this case."

"If you need anything else from us, please just give me a call."

John Rich was back at his office before ten o'clock, and dropped off the printed copies of the deposit and withdrawal slips, along with the signature of Annabel King he'd gotten previously, to his handwriting expert. He asked him to give this a priority, as a special favor to him. With any luck, he'd have an opinion by end of day.

***

The reception area of the offices of Stallwood and Stallwood was a tastefully decorated room with comfortable chairs, upholstered in expensive materials and accompanied by solid wood end tables. It could easily accommodate eight clients while they awaited their opportunity to speak with one of the firm's principals. There was a coffee pot on one of the corner tables, with freshly brewed coffee in it, along with all the necessary accessories; china cups and saucers, silverware, and also cream, sugar and other sweeteners. Tom and Becky wanted to make sure their current and prospective clients were comfortable while waiting for their appointments, although they tried their best not to keep anyone waiting too long. There were seldom more than two people in that room at any one time.

This morning there was only one person in the reception area. Tom was running a little late, and was just about to ask his assistant to show his client in when she told him that someone by the name of Barbara Cullen was calling from New Commerce Commercial Finance. He decided to take the call, and asked her to apologize to the client, and assure him that he'd be with him shortly.

"Good morning, this is Tom Stallwood" he answered when his assistant put the call through.

"Good morning Mr. Stallwood. This is Barbara Cullen from New Commerce Commercial Finance. I'm the Chief Counsel here at New Commerce and I'd like to speak with you about a customer of ours, Walters Marine, who is apparently now one of your clients."

"Certainly, Ms. Cullen. How may I assist you this morning?"

"As you know, we've assured Mr. Jones that we would contact his supplier to make certain Walters Marine would receive replacement inventory. We've now done that, and I'm told they will be in touch with Mr. Jones shortly to make arrangements for delivery of the new inventory and the removal of the old."

"I'm glad to hear that, and I'll be even happier when they actually *do* deliver the new inventory. However, as I explained to Mr. Campbell, Walters Marine has suffered significant financial losses as a result of their inability to obtain timely replacement of the damaged inventory. Furthermore, their owner, Mr. Walters, was killed in a traffic accident, and his family is expecting to collect on the insurance policy that was *supposed* to be in effect for him."

"I understand that, Mr. Stallwood. I've met with the other members of our Executive Committee, and I'm authorized to offer your client financial assistance to help them through their current difficulties. Of course, we'll need approval from our Board of Directors before we can finalize any agreement, but I'm confident that they'll approve any reasonable settlement. And that's what I'd like to discuss with you this morning."

"Go on" replied Tom.

"Although we do not yet know why it happened or who is responsible, we understand that, for whatever reason, the life and inventory insurance policies that should have been in place for Mr. Walters and Walters Marine, actually weren't. We will, of course, get to the bottom of what happened and determine who is liable for any damages. But, in the meantime, for the benefit or our customer, your client, we're willing to provide compensation."

"That's very good to hear Ms. Cullen. What did you have in mind?"

"Obviously, it will be to everyone's benefit to arrive at a settlement that'll be fair to all parties and will avoid the need for any extended legal actions. In light of the amount of the life insurance policy and the number of lost business days, New Commerce Commercial Finance is willing to settle any and all potential future claims against it for a one-time payment of one million five hundred thousand dollars."

"Ms. Cullen, I thought I'd made it very clear when I spoke with Fred Campbell that Walters Marine would need at least three million to settle, and possibly more if the replacement inventory didn't arrive soon. Maybe Mr. Campbell didn't understand me. If not, let me make it clear for you. Walters Marine will not consider any settlement of less than three million dollars. The longer it takes for the replacement inventory to arrive, the higher that amount will be."

"You understand, Mr. Stallwood, supporting your claim for lost income for that amount would be very difficult. For the benefit of our customer, we were not disputing the amount of life insurance that might be due to the family, assuming they have proof that the coverage was, in fact, obtained and they paid the premiums for that coverage. The issue, however, is the amount of financial loss suffered as a result of the damaged inventory. You would need to prove that any delay in replacing that inventory is what contributed to the loss, and not just the time the dealership was closed because of the storm. Acts of God are not our responsibility, after all. The dealerships have to provide for their own insurance for such things."

It was obvious to Tom from what he'd just heard that New Commerce would be playing hard ball. They didn't actually admit any wrongdoing for the missing insurance, and clearly weren't going to pay a penny more than was absolutely necessary to settle this case.

"I understand that, Ms. Cullen. Unfortunately, I'm not certain you understand the seriousness of my client's situation. A million and a half simply isn't acceptable, period."

"New Commerce has always had the best interest of its customers at heart. For that reason, I'd really like to assist Walters Marine to get back on their feet and return to profitability. We understand that our customers' success is good for our business as well. For that reason, I'm willing to go out on a limb here and say we might be able to go as high as two and a half million. Of course, I'd have to discuss this with the other members of our Executive Committee, and any final settlement would still need Board of Directors approval. I think this is a very good offer, Mr. Stallwood, and I think you should present it to your client."

"If that is your best offer, Ms. Cullen, I will, of course, discuss it with my client. I must tell you right now, however, my client is not likely to accept it. I'll try to meet with Mrs. Walters in the next day or so, and I'll get back to you once I've spoken with her. In the meantime, let's hope that the supplier comes through with the replacement inventory."

"I appreciate your cooperation in this matter, Mr. Stallwood, and I look forward to hearing from you in the next few days."

After they'd hung up, Tom asked his assistant to bring in the prospective client, Mr. Burke. His call with Barbara Cullen had only lasted ten minutes, so he wasn't too far behind schedule.

As she led the new client into the office his assistant made the introductions. Mr. Stallwood, this is Mr. Melvin Burke.

Tom walked around to the front of his desk to meet this new client. Extending his hand, he said "Good morning, Mr. Burke. I'm glad to meet you." He shook his hand firmly and, guiding him to one of the plush chairs behind an Oak coffee table, added, "Please take a seat. Now, how may I be of assistance to you, Mr. Burke?"

"Well, Mr. Stallwood, I think I may need to take legal action against someone, though I'm not yet sure exactly who. You see, I own an RV dealership, and my inventory was damaged during Tropical Storm Fay. My finance company had arranged for inventory insurance and paid the premiums themselves. They then billed me for those amounts, and I've paid them regularly. It now seems, however, that the insurance policy doesn't exist, and I don't know if the blame rests with the finance company or the insurance company. All I know is that I've lost my inventory and can't get it replaced."

***

By three o'clock the handwriting expert had completed his task and dialed John Rich's number. It'd been a fairly easy job since all documents contained the exact same signature.

"Special Agent Rich" he answered.

"John. It's Mike. I've completed my evaluation of the documents you gave me."

"That's great, Mike. What do you have for me?"

"There is no question in my mind that all the documents, the deposit and withdrawal slips as well as the slip of paper you gave me were signed by the same individual. If the paper you gave me was signed by Annabel King, then she's the person who signed all of the bank documents as well."

"And, you'd be able to testify to that in court?" asked John.

"Absolutely."

"Thanks for your help Mike. I really appreciate the quick turnaround too. This is all I needed to go forward with the arrest."

John called Sergeant Stabler to give him the news and to invite him along for the arrest. At 4:35 p.m. they arrived at the headquarters of Great Waters Insurance Group and proceeded to Jim Seversen's office. Jim accompanied them to the mail room on the first floor, only to find that Annabel King had not come to work today. They had her home address, which Justine Smart had given them, so Agent Rich and Sergeant Stabler headed out to see if she was at home.

***

Jake Hammond had gotten back to Al Carter earlier in the day to say he could meet this afternoon, if Al had an opening. He arrived at 4:50 p.m., a few minutes before the appointed time of five o'clock. Jake felt it would be better to meet at the end of the day, when fewer employees would be around to see what was going on. The receptionist asked Al to take a seat for a moment while she checked with Mr. Hammond, and then dialed Jake's number. As soon as she'd hung up from that call, she informed Al Carter that she could show him right in.

"I apologize for the delay, Mr. Carter, but Mr. Hammond will see you now. Please follow me." She led him to Jake's office, previously known as Ron Hayward's office.

As soon as he saw them approaching, Jake stood and moved toward the door to greet him. "Mr. Carter, please come in and have a seat."

"Thank you for seeing me, Mr. Hammond. I really appreciate it. Did you want to have Detective Nagle present during our discussion?"

"As a matter of fact, he should be along momentarily. In the meantime, would you like anything, coffee, a soft drink, or water?"

"Thanks, but no. I'm fine."

Before they could go any further with their conversation there was a knock at the door, and Detective Nagle came in and greeted them both. Once they'd all made themselves comfortable, Jake was the first to speak.

"Well, Mr. Carter, you asked for this meeting, so why don't you start by telling us what you had in mind for our discussion today."

"As I said on the phone, Mr. Hammond, my client convinced me of her innocence. Now, I can't honestly say that I always believe my clients to be innocent, but in this case, I really do. Ms. Anderson asked me to speak with you personally because she feels confident in your ability to get to the bottom of this thing." He looked over at Tim Nagle and realized he needed to say something to ensure he wouldn't be offended by the comment. "It's not that she doesn't have faith in our law enforcement officers, mind you. But she believes that Mr. Hammond has both a remarkable technical background and a complete understanding of the operations of New Commerce and, therefore, he is best qualified to resolve the outstanding issues in this case."

"I appreciate her confidence in me, Mr. Carter, but I'm still not sure what you would like of me."

"Let's say, for the sake of our discussion this afternoon, Ms. Anderson is innocent. If that's the case, then clearly, someone else is guilty. What I'd like to do is to see if we can develop a scenario that might shed light on who the guilty party might be."

"And how do you propose to do that?" asked Detective Nagle.

"I've spent a considerable amount of time with Ms. Anderson, and she's given me a great deal of information about the work environment, her co-workers, and the events of that fateful evening when Ron Hayward was killed. She's also come up with some scenarios that could explain how the data files changes appeared to have been made by her, even though they weren't. As you know, she has some technical expertise, and after spending some time thinking about it, she has a few theories."

"Tell us about her theories" replied Jake, "I'm sure Detective Nagle is as interested in hearing about them as I am."

Over the next half hour Al Carter described a number of scenarios, both about the hit-and-run accident and about the data files changes. Sylvie Anderson had obviously given this a lot of thought, and she believed someone had taken her car keys on the evening of the 16th while she was in the copy room and used her SUV to run down Ron Hayward. She also believed that same individual had changed the data files using her ID and IP address. Her conclusion was that it had to be another New Commerce employee with a sufficient technical background to make the system changes and who also had access to her vehicle on the evening of the accident.   She only knew of one individual who qualified.

Jake and Tim gave each other a surprised look and then Tim spoke.

"That's very interesting information, Mr. Carter. Who might that individual be?"

***

After Al Carter left the office, Jake and Tim spent a few minutes going over the information they'd received from him and they had to admit, it had some merit.

"What do you want to do next" asked Jake.

"I think I should get the forensic folks to take a closer look at the SUV. If someone else used it to run down Ron Hayward we might get lucky and find some prints that don't belong there."

"Good idea, Tim. In the meantime, I'll follow up on my end by digging deeper into the technical aspects of Sylvie's theories."

"Thanks, Jake. You and your folks have been a great help, and I want you to know that I'm glad you're on the case. In fact, if you ever want to leave the business world and do some *real* good, law enforcement could always use someone with your background."

"Gee, thanks, Tim. But I'm not sure how my family would feel about going back to living in poverty. We've been there and done that."

They both had a good laugh, and then Nagle headed back to his office at Police Headquarters while Jake started to pack up to leave. But before he could get out, the phone on his desk rang. The caller ID told him it was Augusta. "Jake Hammond" he answered.

"Jake, it's Norm Cassidy. I'm glad I caught you. I've got that information you asked me for this morning."

"The mailing addresses used for the premium payments?" Jake asked.

"Yes. I've looked at a couple of dozen so far, and have a lot more to go, but I thought you'd want to know. All of them were addressed to the Great Waters headquarters, but they all also had a notation that read "Attn: Annabel King.""

"That pretty much seals it" said Jake. "It looks like Annabel was able to convince them that it was personal mail, which meant she was allowed to open the envelopes without another employee present. What I don't understand yet, though, is why they kept allowing her to get "personal" mail at her business location. I'm sure Jim Seversen will want to look into that as well." He picked up the telephone receiver and dialed Jim's number.

Chapter 32

They arrived at the address Justine Smart had given them just before 5:30 p.m. It was an older two story building on the south side of the city, in a neighborhood that had seen better days. They checked the mailboxes in the entryway and noticed there were four apartments in the building. Annabel King was listed as apartment 2B.

As Rich and Stabler slowly climbed the old stairway each step creaked under their weight, and they had to assume that anyone in the apartments could hear them coming. They were thankful they weren't here to arrest a violent criminal, because they probably could no longer count on the element of surprise. When they reached the top they saw a long hallway stretching from left to right, with a door at each end. Each door had old metal numerals about four inches high on it. The door on the right was 2A and the one on the left was 2B, the one they were looking for.

They headed for the left door, but before they got there it slowly opened and a woman backed out, a suitcase in her left hand and a key in her right. She apparently hadn't heard them coming up the stairs, and at first she didn't notice them in the hallway as she bent over to lock the door behind her. Finally, as they approached, she heard their footsteps and turned toward them, a surprised look on her face.

Agent Rich had interviewed her on Thursday, and immediately recognized her, in spite of the poor lighting in the hall. "Good afternoon, Ms. King" he said. "Are you going somewhere?"

She jumped back a little when she saw them, and was now trying to compose herself. "Agent Rich" she said. "You surprised me. What are you doing here?"

"I see you have a suitcase there, Ms. King. Where are you off to on a Monday afternoon?"

"I, um, […] I'm just going to visit my sister for a while. She hasn't been feeling at all well lately and I thought I'd give her a hand."

"So you're taking a little vacation time?" asked Sergeant Stabler.

"That's right."

"That's strange, because we were just at your office, and no one there seemed to know anything about your vacation plans. In fact, they were surprised that you didn't show up for work today, and said you hadn't called in sick either."

She looked at him for a few seconds without saying anything at all. He could tell she was trying to figure out what she could say to make him believe her.

"This came up suddenly. I didn't have a chance to call the office, but was going to do that tomorrow morning from my sister's house. I have plenty of vacation time coming, so I knew it wouldn't be a problem."

He thought the small talk had gone on long enough, so at this point Agent Rich stepped in. "I'm sorry, Ms. King, but you're going to have to postpone your trip. You need to come with us."

"What do you mean? Am I under arrest?"

"As a matter of fact, yes you are."

As Rich read Annabel her rights, Stabler did his part by taking her suitcase from her and placing handcuffs around her wrists. Then they led her down the creaking stairs and out of the building. Within a half hour they were in an interrogation room at FBI Divisional Headquarters.

Agent Rich started the questioning. "Ms. King, you're here because we know you opened the business account at United Bank of Milwaukee, and that you've been depositing and withdrawing money from that account on a regular basis. We've had a handwriting expert verify that you're the person who signed the deposit and withdrawal slips, and we know that you're the person who opened the account. Additionally, we now know that you've had insurance premium payments sent to you, personally, by someone at New Commerce Commercial Finance."

"I've told you before that I never opened that account. Whoever forged my signature on the original signature card must have also forged it on the deposit and withdrawal slips. I hate to say it, but I can't imagine who else it could be but Justine Smart."

"Nice try, Ms. King, but it's not going to work. As I said, we have a handwriting expert who will testify that you're the one who signed all those documents. And the police in Marietta have confirmed for us that the premium payments were mailed to you personally. And beyond that, the amounts and dates of the deposits to the business account you opened match exactly to the premium payments you received from New Commerce. You might as well give it up, Ms. King. The only thing left for you to do is tell us who was in on this with you. If you cooperate with us things will go easier on you."

"I think I would like a lawyer" she said. "I'm not answering any more questions until I get one."

***

In Marietta, the police weren't having much luck identifying the remaining fingerprints from Sylvie Anderson's SUV. They'd already eliminated those of Sylvie and her father, and whoever the remaining ones belonged to apparently didn't have any criminal record, had never served in the armed forces, and had never had any other reason to be fingerprinted. Without something more to go on, they'd have to hope that Annabel King would give up her accomplice. In the meantime, they decided to re-interview the employee Anderson had pointed to as a possible suspect. What the hell, they had nothing to lose and maybe they'd get lucky.

Tim Nagle called Jake Hammond to tell him of his plan, and asked if he wanted to observe the interview, which, of course, he did. Jake told him he knew she was still at the office, because he'd just seen her a few minutes ago. Tim agreed to go to the New Commerce building to pick her up. If she was gone before he got there, he'd go on to her house and pick her up there. Either way, she'd be taken back to police headquarters, and Jake could meet them there. Once again, he'd have to observe through the one way glass, but that was better than nothing.

Detective Nagle arrived at New Commerce at 6:30 and proceeded to the third floor where he was met by Jake Hammond, who informed him Kathy was still at work. They went to the Operations area together and found her at her desk, working on her PC. She looked up as they approached, and Jake thought he detected a slight frown on her face.

"Ms. Brown" said Detective Nagle. "I have a few questions that I need to ask you. Would you be so kind as to accompany me to my office at police headquarters?"

"Am I under arrest?" she asked. - Lately, it seemed like that was the first question anybody ever asked. People watch too much television, Tim thought.

"No, you are not. But we do need to ask you some questions, and would appreciate your cooperation."

"Well, OK, I guess. Just let me log off my computer and get my things."

Within a couple of minutes Kathy Brown was accompanying Detective Nagle to his car, with Jake Hammond following right behind them. When they got to the parking lot, the detective opened the back door of his car and helped Kathy in, while Jake went to his own car, a rental that he'd been driving for way too long. Nagle pulled out, with Jake right behind him, and in less than fifteen minutes they were at police headquarters. Kathy and Detective Nagle went directly to one of the small interrogation rooms while Jake took up a position just outside the room, where he could observe the interrogation.

"I understand, Ms. Brown, you were at the office working the evening Ron Hayward was run down. Would you mind telling me what you were doing, and what time you left?"

"Well, let me think. It's been a while now, but if I remember correctly, I left the office sometime between nine and nine thirty. I know it was after the accident, because the area was already roped off, and the police were everywhere. I had to walk around the accident scene to get to my car."

"And why were you working late that evening, and what were you working on?"

"It's not unusual for me to work late; I do it a lot. We've been understaffed in the Operations area for some time now, even though the company's been trying to increase volumes. They added staff in the underwriting and related areas so they could bring in new business, but we, in Operations, have had to do more with the same staff, and so we all put in extra hours on a regular basis. If I recall properly, on that particular evening I was trying to catch up on documentation reviews."

"And who else was in the office that evening?"

This line of questioning went on for some time, until Detective Nagle innocently said, "I'm sorry, Ms. Brown. Where are my manners? Can I offer you something to drink? Coffee or a soft drink, maybe?"

"No, thank you" she replied.

"How about a glass of water" he added.

"Well, OK, I'll take some water, please."

Yes! Now I have her. He excused himself and returned with a glass of water seconds later. A half hour later they were finished with the interrogation, and he asked a uniformed police officer to give Ms. Brown a ride back to her car. As soon as she'd left the room, he took out his handkerchief and wrapped the glass in it. He finally had a sample of her fingerprints.

Chapter 33

Tuesday, September 2, 2008

Joyce Walters was sitting in one of the plush armchairs in the private office of Tom Stallwood. Tom and his wife Becky were both there, as was Randy Jones. Tom had set up this meeting to discuss the offer he'd received from Barbara Cullen at New Commerce.

"Thank you for coming in this morning Mrs. Walters. As I said over the phone, I've been in contact with the Chief Counsel over at New Commerce Finance and she made a settlement offer which I promised to pass along to you. Even though they are not admitting any fault at this time, they realize that the life insurance policy on Mr. Walters, and the inventory insurance policy, somehow have both disappeared, and you need to be compensated."

"We still haven't received any replacement inventory, Mr. Stallwood. Randy tells me we've lost many of our long time customers to competitors. How do they plan to compensate us for long term damage to our dealership?"

"That's the problem, Mrs. Walters. They know they don't stand a chance to contest the life insurance issue. The policy was for one million, and they will pay that amount. However, lost income from the lack of inventory, and long term damage to the dealership from lost customers, are not as easy to pin down. They're hoping we won't want to gamble on trying to prove a dollar figure in court so they've offered a million and a half for that, for a total of $2.5 million."

"Of course, it's up to you, Joyce," said Randy, "but I don't think that's enough. There's still a chance the dealership won't survive, and you will need more than that to compensate for the loss of your livelihood."

"I tend to agree with Mr. Jones" added Tom Stallwood. I think we could win our case in court and get a much larger settlement. Also, some additional information has recently come to my attention regarding New Commerce customers."

"I bet we aren't alone, are we, Mr. Stallwood?" asked Randy.

"No, you're not. Another client came to me with the exact same scenario Walters Marine has had. In my opinion, there may be cause for a class action lawsuit against New Commerce. If we should go that route, anyone who was financially hurt by their actions could be eligible to share in the final settlement, which could be very substantial."

"So what are you suggesting, Mr. Stallwood?" asked Joyce. "Do you want us to join a class action lawsuit?"

"That would be entirely up to you, Mrs. Walters. You have several options open to you. The first, of course, would be to accept the New Commerce offer of two and half million. That would be a final settlement, and you would not be entitled to any additional compensation, under any circumstances. The second option available to you would be to pursue legal action on your own and the last option would be to join a class action suit against New Commerce. There are pros and cons to each approach."

"Please continue, Mr. Stallwood. I'd like to know more about the pros and cons."

"OK, let's take them one at a time. First, the current settlement offer. If you accept, you should have the money in a relatively short time, probably a matter of weeks. That will allow you to get back on your feet sooner, and minimize any additional long term harm to your business. It will also let you avoid a potentially long court battle. However, once you accept the settlement, you cannot change your mind and decide to sue them at a later time, either individually or as part of a class action suit."

"I understand. Please continue."

"The second option is to take legal action against New Commerce on your own. Obviously, the outcome of any trial is in doubt until the final judgment is made. In my opinion, you are likely to receive a much larger settlement in court than what New Commerce is currently offering, but there are no guarantees. The down side is that it will take some time for us to get this to trial. It could be a year, at least, and then even if you win, New Commerce could appeal."

Randy asked "If Mrs. Walters says she's going forward with a lawsuit, isn't New Commerce likely to come back with another, higher offer?"

"That's very possible, and in fact, likely. However, keep in mind that they will only offer you the minimum amount they can to avoid a trial. It's not likely that they will ever offer as much as you might be awarded by a jury. But as I said, there are no guarantees when you go to trial."

"What about the third option?"

"In the third option, you'd join a class action lawsuit brought by all the customers of New Commerce who have suffered as a result of their wrongful actions. Often, when a class action suit is brought, a company is more likely to settle for a larger amount, knowing that if it goes to trial, the final award, including damages, could be far greater. However, they may not offer any settlement, and the case could take many years to come to trial, and many more years could be spent on appeals."

"I see" she said. "What is your recommendation, Mr. Stallwood?"

"To be honest, Mrs. Walters, I'm not yet certain there would be a sufficient number of plaintiffs to warrant a class action suit. I will need to look into that, because, at this time, I'm only aware of Walters Marine and one other New Commerce client, though there are likely to be many more. Furthermore, we aren't certain a judge would allow a class action suit, even if there were more plaintiffs. There are many factors to consider in that decision. My recommendation, for the time being, is that you turn down the New Commerce offer and begin legal action of your own. You can always join a class action at a later date, should one develop."

"Just one more question, Mr. Stallwood. If we do proceed on our own, what settlement do you think we'd be looking to get?"

"One of the challenges is to figure out the worst case scenario regarding lost income. If we assume that Walters Marine will go out of business, we can extrapolate, using earnings over the past few years to estimate lifetime earnings. Based on the preliminary information Mr. Jones has given us, I'd say that we'd be asking for at least ten million, and we could possibly get more, if the jury decides to award damages for New Commerce's reckless or criminal behavior."

"If we decide to go forward with this lawsuit, will we still be able to push for replacement inventory?" asked Joyce. "Rather than close up shop completely, I'd prefer to get that inventory and try to minimize our losses, if possible."

"That may be a problem, Mrs. Walters. I was told by Ms. Cullen, New Commerce's Chief Counsel, that they'd already contacted your supplier and arranged for replacement inventory to be shipped. If it's already been shipped, you may be in good shape. If it hasn't been shipped, New Commerce may back out of that deal once they hear of our intention to sue them."

"Can they do that?" asked Randy. "Aren't they legally obligated to arrange for replacement inventory?"

"They can, and might try to, at first. They could figure they've got nothing to lose, and playing hard ball might get you to change your mind about the lawsuit."

"Can we wait to see if we get the replacement inventory before we move forward?"

"Yes, we can.   However, even if you have the inventory at the dealership, the supplier could very well come back to get it if New Commerce doesn't pay for it."

"What if they've already paid for it by the time we file our suit?"

"It would make it a little more difficult for them, but they'd still be able to back out if they have a solid relationship with the supplier, which I assume they do. The only thing going for you at that point would be the fear that they'd have of taking a bigger hit at trial for being so heartless as to strip you of your ability to make a living. All in all, I'd say your best bet right now is to wait until the inventory is delivered and paid for, and then file suit. We can stall New Commerce for a while regarding their offer."

"So, just to make sure I understand clearly, let me reiterate. Our plan is to stall New Commerce on our answer regarding their settlement offer until we receive the replacement inventory and have confirmation that it's been paid for. Then, we will reject their offer, and file a lawsuit."

"That's correct."

"But one last question, if I may. If we go that route, our suit will not involve the cost of inventory, since we'll already have the replacements, but only the lost life insurance payout and loss of business. Is that it?"

Randy stepped in at this point.   "The thing to remember, Joyce, is that we never paid for the inventory in the first place. New Commerce paid the supplier directly, and we only paid New Commerce when the items were actually sold. In the interim, we only paid interest on the loan."

"Oh, that's right" replied Joyce. "So we really can't claim the cost of the inventory, since we never paid for it in the first place."

"The best we can hope for" added Tom Stallwood, is that New Commerce decides it's in their best interest to let the inventory replacement go forward. I'm pretty certain they'd understand how a jury would react to their actions if they refused to let you get back into business."

"OK then. Let's wait for the replacements to arrive, and then notify New Commerce that we're moving forward with legal action. As you said, Mr. Stallwood, we can worry about whether or not we want to join a class action lawsuit later, should one develop."

***

The economic crisis was worsening each day. No one could have imagined, just a few short weeks ago, that things could get bad so quickly. The price of New Commerce stock was now $25.04, another drop of almost three and a half points since Friday, and a total of almost fifty four points in the past few weeks. And business was going in the same direction, with volumes down and delinquencies up. The inventory finance business was being hit the hardest, because folks just couldn't afford the luxury items most of the dealers carried. When you're struggling to put food on the table or pay your mortgage, you can't buy a new boat, RV, or other things that New Commerce customers sold. And if the dealers couldn't sell their inventory, they couldn't pay New Commerce. It was a vicious circle.

Deb Cutter hadn't heard yet if there were any actual lawsuits initiated as a result of that insurance fiasco in Marietta, but she decided she'd better sell more of her stock, just in case. At this point it looked like things were going to get far worse before they got better.

***

Annabel King's attorney was now with her in the interrogation room. Also present were Special Agent Rich, and the Assistant US Attorney for the Eastern Wisconsin District, Michelle Solomon.

Special Agent Rich opened the discussion. "Ms. King, let me introduce you to Michelle Solomon, Assistant U.S. Attorney for Eastern Wisconsin. I've asked Ms. Solomon to join us this morning, because I'd like to wrap this case up, and with your help, I think I can do that rather quickly. Ms. Solomon is in a position to be able to decide how much credit you could get for your cooperation. Now, as your attorney has probably told you, the evidence we have against you already is enough for a conviction, and we expect to get even more evidence. So, I strongly suggest that you cooperate."

"What kind of *credit* did you have in mind, Ms. Solomon?" asked the attorney.

"If Ms. King tells us who her accomplice at New Commerce is, and testifies against him or her in court, we will ask the judge to give her the minimum sentence required by law, and recommend that she be sent to a minimum security facility of her choice. Otherwise, we will request, and probably get, the maximum sentence. It could mean a difference of several years."

Annabel and her lawyer looked at each other, then she whispered something in his ear, to which he nodded assent.

"Ms. King will cooperate in exchange for your recommendation" he told them.

Her lawyer nodded to her again, and Annabel spoke up. "First, let me say that none of this was my idea. There isn't any way I could've thought this up. Hell, I'm just a mailroom clerk. What do I know about insurance premiums, computer systems and embezzlement? I'm just trying to make a living, making ends meet one day at a time."

"Go on" said Agent Rich.

"Well, one day I got a call from a relative in the Atlanta area who asked if I want to make some easy money. "What's the deal, I asked? What do I have to do to get the money?" She tells me how easy it'll be. Just take the checks she sends me and deposit them into a special bank account, and once they've cleared, take the money out and send her half. Nothing to it, she said.

"Did she tell you where the money was coming from?" asked Rich.

"Yeah, she said they were insurance premium payments from some New Commerce customers."

"And what did you think would happen when those payments weren't applied to their accounts? You didn't realize that you'd get caught sooner or later?"

"I asked her about that. She said no one would ever know, unless a claim was filed, and that almost never happened, and if it did, she'd take care of it."

"Do you know what she meant when she said she'd take care of it?"

"No. But I know she's a computer whiz, so I figured she knew what she was doing. And it worked for a long time, too."

"OK. So now tell us, Ms. King, who is this relative of yours who's been sending you these premium payment checks?"

***

The forensic folks in Marietta checked the unidentified fingerprint taken from Sylvie Anderson's SUV to the one on the glass Detective Nagle gave them. There was no question that they were a positive match. Based upon those results, Nagle obtained a search warrant for Brown's apartment, where he found a white blouse with a button missing. They'd found a button in Sylvie's SUV and the ones on this blouse were a perfect match for that one. He now had enough to make an arrest for the hit and run death of Ron Hayward, and he knew it was just a matter of time before he had enough to charge her with embezzlement as well.

As he was preparing to head out to make the arrest, his phone rang. "Detective Nagle" he answered.

"Nagle, this is John Rich in Milwaukee. How are you?"

"Good, John. And you?"

"I'm doing much better now" he answered. "We've just gotten a major break in the case. Annabel King has given up her accomplice there at New Commerce."

"Fantastic. You going to share that name with me, or what?" he joked.

"Someone by the name of Kathy Brown" was the answer.

"Well, imagine that. I was just on my way out to arrest her for the hit and run death of Ron Hayward. Now I can add an embezzlement charge as well. "

Chapter 34

Monday, September 15, 2008

A month is a short period of time in the lives of most people, yet, in the month since Tropical Storm Fay hit Florida, many lives were changed forever. Although the storm itself caused relatively few deaths and only a limited amount of property damage, it's timing couldn't have been worse. It hit just as a worldwide economic crisis was about to unfold, and it abruptly revealed a business situation that, under normal conditions, would have been discovered and corrected with little or no public attention and with minimal impact on the victims of the fraud. Instead, the scheme perpetrated by Kathy Brown and Annabel King had a devastating impact on many peoples' lives.

Ron Hayward, a young and promising manager at New Commerce, had been framed for an embezzlement he knew nothing about, and then brutally run down and killed to hide the identity of the true criminal. Sylvie Anderson was also a casualty of the unbridled greed and corruption of Kathy Brown, and would never fully recover from her ordeal. She'd been released from prison when Kathy was arrested, but her life would never be the same again. Justine Smart lost her position at the United Bank of Milwaukee because she allowed her long time friendship with Annabel King to cloud her judgment, and she'd never be able to work in another bank. Her career was effectively over.

The cases against Kathy Brown and Annabel King looked promising, and prosecutors were confident that they could get convictions at trial, if the defendants didn't agree to a deal. Annabel was charged with bank fraud and embezzlement, and agreed to a plea bargain that would keep her behind bars for five to ten years. Kathy Brown was charged with first degree murder and embezzlement. She was still proclaiming her innocence, and it was beginning to look like a lengthy trial might be in her future.

Jake Hammond had spent weeks in Georgia, away from his wife and kids, and returned to Augusta to find things somewhat changed, both at home and at the company. Amie was getting more fed up with their lifestyle, and was pressuring him to spend more time with the family. And at New Commerce things were getting even more interesting, with the slide in the stock price, pending litigation resulting from the embezzlement, and sagging loan originations. Although he hadn't thought it possible, as each day passed Deb Cutter was getting even more difficult to deal with. Under her watch, the stock plummeted from $79 a share to its current low of $12.40. Investors had lost fortunes, the Board was on a rampage, and Deb, sometimes affectionately called the "Teflon Lady" made sure to pass along the pain to her subordinates.

Walters Marine got their replacement inventory, paid for by New Commerce, but was moving forward with its lawsuit against New Commerce, having served notice of intent just last week. The law firm of Stallwood and Stallwood was now preparing to file another such notice for their new client, Melvin Burke, owner of Burke's RV and Trailer Sales in Tallahassee. Tom Stallwood was also continuing his research into other New Commerce customers who may have suffered losses as a result of missing or non-existent insurance policies. He still considered a class action lawsuit a real possibility.

Hurricane Gustav, which began as a tropical storm on August 25th and had made landfall as a Category 2 hurricane on September 1st, now had fifteen deaths attributed to it, and damage in the U. S. alone totaled $15 billion. While most of the damage was along the Louisiana coast, some Great Waters customers had been impacted, and claims were pouring in. Ping Industries sent someone from their corporate headquarters in Tokyo to *consult* with Doug Armstrong about the proper way to run Great Waters Insurance Group. They were not happy with the earnings hit they'd taken because of Fay, and the negative publicity surrounding the embezzlement only made things more difficult for everyone. Now, Gustav had arrived, and claims had jumped again. Doug Armstrong had a feeling it was only a matter of time before he'd be asked to *retire.*

***

In his office on the twenty-third floor of 33 Arch Street, in Boston, the Regional Director of the Securities and Exchange Commission was reviewing a report given to him just moments ago. The pending lawsuits against New Commerce Commercial Finance had made headlines throughout New England, and he'd asked his assistant to look into the trading patterns of New Commerce over the past month or so. He'd seen a number of cases of insider trading during his years with the Commission and knew the telltale signs. When executives had news that something was about to happen that would negatively impact the company's stock price, they sometimes tried to dump large blocks of their stock before the price went down, in violation of securities laws.

It only took him a few minutes to zero in on the information he was looking for. As he suspected, trading of New Commerce stock had been brisk for several weeks, and the biggest trades were done by none other than Deb Cutter, the CEO of New Commerce. In the past month she'd sold stock on three separate occasions, dumping a total of more than a million shares. In some cases, she had exercised stock options, but in others, she sold shares that she owned outright. Early on, when the price started to drop slowly, she probably turned a profit, especially if her options were a few years old, but after that, all she could hope for was to minimize her losses.

He picked up the receiver of his desk phone and dialed a number. When the call was answered, he simply said into the receiver "I want you to begin a review of possible insider trading at New Commerce Commercial Finance Company, headquartered in Augusta, Maine, and pay particular attention to the CEO, Deb Cutter." He hung up the receiver without any additional directions. His staff knew exactly what to do.

***

Jake, Joe Nash and Norm Cassidy were in Jake's office discussing the Kathy Brown embezzlement. They'd tied down most of the loose ends, and Kathy was now enjoying the hospitality of the Georgia Department of Corrections while awaiting a trial date. But they still had two unresolved items, and it was driving Jake nuts. They knew how Kathy had taken Sylvie Anderson's car keys, slipped out of the office, and then used her SUV to run down Ron Hayward; and they also knew when and how she'd initiated contact with Annabel King over at Great Waters Insurance Group. But they still couldn't prove she was the one who'd made the data file changes under Ron's ID, using Sylvie's PC to hide her tracks, and they hadn't yet been able to prove that she was the one who authorized the premium payments to be made by check. The paper trail for that issue still pointed to Sylvie Anderson, even though they were convinced she was telling the truth when she said Kathy had instructed her to process the changes.

The police believed they had Brown cold on the hit and run, and were confident they had enough circumstantial evidence to also convict her of the embezzlement, but having solid evidence of how she did it would be the final nail in her coffin, and Jake intended to get that evidence.

After they'd discovered that Sylvie Anderson's hard drive had been wiped clean, they'd gotten tied up in other aspects of the case, and were just now getting back to the question of how they could prove there'd been a bogus program installed on it. Once things started to point to Kathy Brown as Annabel King's accomplice, they'd asked Nick Hurley to take a look at her hard drive, but he hadn't found anything unusual. If any evidence had existed there, it was long gone by the time he took a look. Now, they'd have to do it the hard way, trying to pinpoint the date and time of the download to Sylvie's computer and then look through the activity logs to see if they could come up with anything helpful. It promised to be a difficult and very time consuming process, but it was one that Jake felt they needed to do to put this thing to bed.

Throughout the investigation, Norm had been working closely with Steve O'Brien, from the Tech Support Department, and they'd produced a staggering amount of data regarding the inventory insurance issue. They now knew precisely when the premium payments were first paid by check, how much money was diverted, and how many policies were involved. Based upon the information they'd obtained, New Commerce had been able to work with Great Waters to ensure that canceled policies were reinstated, and missing policies were issued. Now they were ready to tackle the last technical issue.

"The way I see it, boss" said Norm, "Kathy had no reason to download the spoofing program to Sylvie's hard drive until she realized that things were starting to unravel. We know that the data file changes weren't made until the morning of August 16th, so I think we can safely assume that the download was done shortly before that time, probably within a few hours or a day before then. I'm betting on Friday the 15th, or Thursday the 14th. There wouldn't have been any reason for her to do it before then. That's when things started to come apart."

"It sounds logical" replied Jake. "You can start looking at those dates, but if you don't find anything, we'll have to consider widening the search. Let's hope we don't have to do that, because the scheme's been going on for almost two years, and we'd never be able to look at all the activity that took place in that time frame. Do we even have the activity logs for that far back?"

"I don't know" replied Norm. "I know we *do* have them for last month, so our initial plan is definitely doable. I guess we'll have to cross the other bridge when, and if, we get there."

Joe Nash excused himself and headed back to his own office to get started on his next project, and Norm headed out to begin his review of activity logs. The rest of the staff had continued with their normal schedules while the special investigation was underway, and Jake hadn't managed to stay on top of the audit reports, so he began reviewing the first of the fifteen reports sitting on the corner of his desk.

It was only nine o'clock, but Jake was already on his fourth cup of coffee of the day. He knew he should cut back, but the caffeine helped him keep up his grueling pace. Much to Amie's chagrin, he hadn't gotten much sleep over the weekend because he was busy trying to clean up work papers and review notes. They'd had another argument about his work schedule and lack of attention to the family, and it hadn't ended well. But he had a job to do, and he was going to do it no matter what.

***

Everyone at Great Waters Insurance was tense. The word had spread quickly about the visitor from Tokyo, and even though there hadn't been any public statement, they all knew that the executives at Ping Industries weren't happy with the recent earnings reports. Claims had skyrocketed during Tropical Storm Fay, and now they were being hit again because of Hurricane Gustav. Those events, coupled with the now famous embezzlement by Annabel King, made the future look grim. There was even talk about the possibility that Ping Industries would try to sell Great Waters, or maybe even close them completely.

Harry Strong, Supervising Claims Adjuster, was in his boss's office being berated and belittled again. Even though he was only 5'5" and weighed a mere 125 pounds, Al Goff could be an intimidating person. He liked to let his staff know who was boss, and he never hesitated to shout obscenities and pound his fist on his desk if he thought it'd help make a point. And he was making a point now.

"What the hell do you think you're doing, Harry?" he shouted. "Can't you control your own staff? I thought, when we spoke a few weeks ago, you understood that Ping Industries would not put up with an increase in approved claims. Did I not make myself clear?"

Even though he'd closed the door to his office, people in the surrounding areas could clearly hear the tongue lashing Harry was getting, and they sympathized with him. Many of them had been in a similar spot before, and no one particularly liked Al Goff, at least no one on his staff.

"Al, I told you I'm doing my best. I don't know what you want from me. We can't deny all claims out of hand, and get away with it. We're using every possible loophole to deny or delay paying claims, and we've already denied more than eighty percent of the claims from Fay and Gustav."

"Do I have to spell it out for you, Harry? If that's the case, maybe I need a Supervising Claims Adjuster who can do the job he's getting paid to do."

"What is it you want me to do, Al?"

"It's very simple, really. From now on, every claim is initially denied, period. No exceptions. I don't care what excuse you use to deny the claims, just do it."

"You can't be serious. That'll result in some expensive litigation, and will be a huge liability for the company. We've already stretched things to the limit with the denials we've issued so far."

"Listen to me. After they've complained a few times, most customers will just give up and go away. Those who have the tenacity to hire an attorney will be dealt with when the time is right. We can drag this out for years and years. By then, who knows where we'll all be. At the very least, we'll have a temporary reprieve from the Ping chopping block."

"I don't like it, Al."

"Damn it! Stop arguing with me Harry. If you can't do this, say so now, and hand in your resignation. I'll find someone who can show more loyalty to the company."

As Harry Strong was leaving the office, a well dressed gentleman of Asian descent was standing outside the doorway. He had a slight smile on his face and nodded politely to Harry as they passed each other. He must have heard the entire *conversation* Harry thought. I wonder why he's smiling.

Chapter 35

Tuesday, September 16, 2008

Even though he was only forty five, he'd been contemplating what *retirement* might be like. Not that he *wanted* to retire, but he didn't think he'd have a choice. The fact that he might be forced to retire would never have entered his mind a few years ago, "BP" as he liked to call it; Before Ping. He knew that because of his contract, he'd get a decent severance package if they got rid of him, but there weren't many positions available in the area, and he didn't cherish the idea of moving his family. And he didn't particularly look forward to being retired, either, because he was much too young for that. Maybe he was worrying too much, he thought. They couldn't really hold him responsible for things beyond his control, could they? What a naïve thought, he told himself. *Of course* they could hold him responsible, and they certainly would.

Jennifer knocked on the door and opened it slightly, sticking her head in just enough to be able to speak with him. "Mr. Armstrong, Mr. Hitachi is here to see you. Shall I show him in?"

Oh great, he thought. Just what I need when I have a migraine, [. . .] a real pain in the ass. But he didn't vocalize his thoughts, and instead replied "Yes, please, Jennifer, show him in."

"Mr. Armstrong" Hitachi said as he bowed his head before extending his hand. The Japanese are always very polite, Doug thought, even when they're getting ready to chop your head off.

"Mr. Hitachi" Doug replied as he also bowed. He shook the outstretched hand and added, "Won't you please come in and have a seat." He pointed to the comfortable, over-stuffed leather chairs behind the coffee table. He once loved those chairs and everything else in this office, but now they didn't seem to matter much anymore. The furniture his wife had helped him pick out, the spacious office, the CEO title, all meant very little to him at this point. Now that he was a puppet for Ping Industries, he took pride in practically nothing at all. Even his community service efforts had been curtailed, at Ping's insistence, of course.

Although his head was pounding mercilessly, he somehow managed to get the words out. "How may I help you this morning, Mr. Hitachi?"

"As you know, Mr. Armstrong, Ping Industries is concerned with the recent drop in earnings here at Great Waters. You will obviously miss your business plan for this quarter and for the year, even if no additional losses are incurred. We realize that you've had more claims than expected from this year's hurricane season, but we believe better planning could have minimized the impact on your plans. Also, that matter of the embezzlement has our Board of Directors very concerned. They feel that your internal controls should have prevented it, or at least detected it sooner, before we suffered the embarrassment of having another company call it to our attention.

"I understand their concern, Mr. Hitachi. As you know, there isn't any way of predicting how many hurricanes we'll have in any given season, or how many claims we'll receive as a result. And, of course, you are aware that our plan was pretty much dictated by Ping Industries." He couldn't resist putting that little ding in there, because, after all, it was true. If it hadn't been for the pressure Ping put on them, their plan would have been far more realistic. "I do, however, share their concern over the recent embezzlement, and assure you we are taking the necessary steps to prevent any similar occurrence in the future."

"Yes, Mr. Armstrong, I understand. I am certain you have taken steps to improve your controls, and that you are comfortable providing your assurance that nothing like this will happen again. Unfortunately, not everyone in Tokyo is as understanding as I am, Mr. Armstrong, and our Board of Directors believes that Great Waters needs a new direction, and new leadership, if it is going to survive these difficult times. They have sent me here to make certain their wishes are carried out."

"And what, exactly, are their wishes, Mr. Hitachi?"

***

Deb Cutter had called a special meeting of the Executive Committee to discuss a number of pressing issues. The price of the stock was dropping like a lead balloon, new loan originations were down, and they were now facing at least two lawsuits as a result of the embezzlement and insurance fiasco in Marietta. Everyone had known it was going to be a tough year, but they'd figured they could get through it without too much trouble because they'd just had two record years in a row, and the stock was at its highest level ever. But in a few short weeks, all that had changed. The economy took a nose dive because of the sub-prime mortgage crisis, which was impacting their ability to raise capital, and consumer credit was drying up as well. Then the insurance fiasco hit, and all hell broke loose. It wasn't just turning into a tough year, but a downright disastrous one. They had to come up with a plan of attack fast, before it was too late.

"Ladies and gentlemen" Deb said. "Please settle down so we can get started. We have much to attend to today." Everyone quieted down and took their seats, giving her their full attention.

"We have a number of items on our agenda today" she began, "and some important decisions to make. As you know, the price of our stock has taken a nose dive, along with just about everyone else's. Additionally, originations are down and it's looking more and more like we're going to miss plan for the year. On top of that, we're facing some legal actions as a result of the insurance fiasco in Marietta. By the time we leave here today, I intend to have a detailed plan to address these issues and get us back on track."

They all looked around the table at each other, many with an expression of disbelief on their faces. They knew it would take a great deal of work to come up with that kind of plan, and no one really expected to have the details worked out today, but when Deb had her mind made up, there wasn't much any of them could do to change it. It was going to be a very long meeting.

"First" she said, "We need to talk about the pending lawsuits. Barbara Cullen will fill us in on what's happening there." They all turned their attention to Barbara, who was sitting at the opposite end of the table, across from Deb.

"The law firm of Stallwood and Stallwood, in Tallahassee, Florida, has informed us of their intent to bring two separate legal actions against New Commerce. Both of the cases involve clients of ours whose dealerships have lost business because their inventories were damaged during Tropical Storm Fay and their insurance policies were not in effect. In both situations, they have proof that New Commerce billed them for insurance premiums, which they paid timely. They've also indicated that there may be more lawsuits to follow, and that a class action lawsuit is still a possibility."

"Do we have any idea yet what the damages might come to if we lose these suits?" asked Tom D'Angelo.

"If this turns into a class action suit, it could be hundreds of millions of dollars. If we're lucky enough to dodge the bullet on that one and only have to settle the two existing ones, it might be as little as twenty million."

At that figure, there were a lot or murmurs. Clearly, they were all taken by surprise, but Deb was the first to speak up.

"Are you kidding me?" she said. "How can you say something like, as little as twenty million, and keep a straight face?"

"Trust me, this isn't a joke, and yes, if we get away with twenty million we'll be lucky."

"This isn't acceptable" said Deb. "You've got to do something to head this off."

"What would you have me do?" replied Barbara. New Commerce is clearly responsible. In my opinion, we don't stand much of a chance in court. The only possible option is to offer settlements to the two current plaintiffs. However, that will not lessen the possibility that a class action suit might still be filed."

Tom D'Angelo stepped into the conversation once again. "What if we play hard ball with the two current plaintiffs until we can figure out the odds that a class action lawsuit might be filed? In the meantime, we should figure out how many customers might have been impacted."

"How do you propose to do that?" asked Deb.

"We've already arranged with Great Waters to have all inventory policies reinstated, so we no longer have any customers without coverage. All we have to do is find out which ones tried to file a claim and were denied, and contact them directly, before Stallwood gets to them. It may cost us some money, but probably a lot less than any settlement from a lawsuit would cost."

"OK. Let's go that route" replied Deb. "Barbara, you take whatever actions you need to take to ensure that the lawsuits are delayed. Jake, since you've been working extensively with the people at Great Waters, you contact them to see if they can give you a list of any claims filed by our customers that have been denied. Tom, what are we going to have to do, if anything, regarding our financial statements?"

"If we haven't settled the existing lawsuits by the end of the quarter, we'll have to provide a footnote telling investors that litigation is in process, and provide an opinion about the potential impact that they'll have on our bottom line. It'll scare some folks away, I'm sure."

"Alright, let's hope we don't have to do that" replied Deb. Now, let's get on with the meeting. The next thing I'd like to discuss is the drop in loan originations."

The meeting went on for several hours and, as most in attendance suspected, there were no easy solutions to the problems facing New Commerce. The consensus was that they'd have to stop originations completely in some business lines, and probably even sell off the portfolios, if the remaining businesses were going to survive. Much to her chagrin, Deb had to agree that the inventory finance business, one of the new lines she'd introduced a few years ago, was in trouble and would have to go. Now all they had to do was find someone to buy the portfolio. They all hoped that this would decrease their delinquencies and non-performing assets which, in turn, would help their stock price. At least, that's how it should work, in theory. Only time would tell.

***

In his office on the twenty-third floor, Bob McKenzie was reviewing the information his staff had put together on the recent stock trades of New Commerce Commercial Finance. As Regional Director of the Security and Exchange Commission, it was his job to identify violations of the securities laws, and he was very good at his job. Since taking over as Regional Director three years ago, he'd already initiated ten investigations, three of which resulted in criminal prosecutions. It was beginning to look like he'd have another feather in his cap with this one. There was no doubt in his mind that Deb Cutter had dumped a huge block of stock based upon insider information. His staff would be knocking on her door very soon.

Chapter 36

Wednesday, September 17, 2008

Norm Cassidy and Steve O'Brien had been reviewing the computer activity for the period surrounding the unauthorized data file changes in an effort to figure out if a bogus program had been downloaded to Sylvie Anderson's PC. It had taken longer than they'd anticipated, but they finally found what they were looking for. Norm gave Jake a call.

"Well, Jake, we finally found it" Norm said. "We now know that someone downloaded a program from Kathy Brown's IP address to Sylvie Anderson's IP address on the morning of August 16th, the day the unauthorized file changes were made. Immediately after that transmission, there was another download, this time from Sylvie Anderson's PC to Ron Hayward's. Of course, we can't prove exactly what was downloaded, because both hard drives were cleaned, but the fact is, the transmissions actually did take place. That much is irrefutable. Also, the time it took to complete each download is exactly the same, strongly suggesting that the same information was transmitted in each download. Coupled with all the other evidence in the case, my guess is that a jury will find the evidence sufficient to convict Kathy Brown of the embezzlement."

"Great job, Norm. I knew you could do it."

"Sorry it took us so long, Jake. Steve and I worked full time on this since you asked about it. But, there were tens of thousands of transmissions that took place in a relatively short period of time, and we had to examine each and every one to find what we were looking for."

"Not a problem. I'll give Detective Nagle a call to fill him in. In the meantime, you'll need to document everything you've done, and then prepare a recap that will summarize it in a way a jury can understand. There's no question but that you and I will be testifying in court on this one."

"I'll get right on it" replied Norm.

One more thing out of the way, thought Jake. Now, if only we could prove that Kathy Brown was the one who authorized the premium payments to be made by check rather than ACH, we'd be in great shape. After that, the only thing left to do would be to nail down the proof of where the money went after Kathy and Annabel got their hands on it. Annabel had given them the leads, but they still needed the hard evidence they could use in court. Then, they'd be able to turn their attention to defending New Commerce against the lawsuits that seemed to be springing up everywhere.

Annabel King was now in the minimum security section of the Metropolitan Correctional Center (MCC) in Chicago, and administrative facility designed to house Federal prisoners of all security levels, and the only facility in the area to house female as well as male offenders. She had pleaded guilty to charges of bank fraud and embezzlement, and was given the minimum sentence in exchange for her cooperation, which included a detailed accounting of where the money went. It seemed Kathy Brown had helped her open an off-shore account in the Cayman Islands, and each month Annabel would withdraw all of the previous month's deposits from the United Bank of Milwaukee and put them into her Bank of America account. Then she'd periodically wire money from that account to the bank in the Caymans. Most of the money she'd gotten from the premium payments was now in the Cayman's account, but she'd invested a little into stocks. Kathy also put the bulk of her money in a Cayman account, but she used a bigger portion of hers to buy stocks. In a cruel twist of fate, Kathy had invested heavily in New Commerce stock.

They knew it'd be difficult to get any information from the bank in the Caymans, since the Cayman Islands do not have any legal requirements for customer identification and record keeping, and supervisory authorities could not access any such records, even if they did exist. But they could subpoena the records of Bank of America and determine, from the wire transfers, the account numbers the money went to. With that information, they could paint a very graphic picture for the jury of exactly how much money was taken, and where it went.

***

Deb's assistant knew all too well that she didn't like to be disturbed when she was going over the latest operating results, and in light of the recent drop in earnings, she knew this would be a particularly bad time to do so. But she had no choice. The person in the reception area was very insistent, and based on the title he'd provided to the receptionist, she didn't think it was a good idea to keep him waiting too long. So she hesitatingly knocked on the door and opened it ever so slightly, just enough to stick her head part way in.

"Excuse me, Ms. Cutter."

"What?" she yelled from behind her desk. "I told you not to bother me when I'm going over the financial results. What is it now?"

"I'm sorry, Ms. Cutter, but there's a gentleman in the reception area who's very insistent that he speak with you right away. He says he's from the Securities and Exchange Commission."

Chapter 37

"Hold on a minute" said Deb, "I'm not talking to anyone from the SEC without Barbara Cullen here. Give her a call and tell her to come to my office immediately."

"Yes ma'am." The assistant left to place the call and five minutes later Barbara Cullen was in Deb's office.

"What's this about, Deb?" she asked.

"I have no idea, Barbara. Your guess is as good as mine. But when the SEC shows up on my doorstep, there's no way I'm going to meet with them without someone from the Legal Department present."

"That's always a good idea. But tell me, is there anything that any of the Executive Committee members have done lately that I should know about? Has anyone dumped large blocks of stock?"

With that question Deb turned a little pale and Barbara noticed it. Not a good sign.

"What?" Barbara asked. "You obviously know something, so you're better off telling me now, before we meet with this guy."

"I don't know if this has anything to do with his visit, but I *did* sell quite a bit of stock in the past few weeks."

"Tell me you're not serious" said Barbara. "You can't be serious. That was a stupid thing to do. Why didn't you consult with me first?"

"I didn't see anything wrong with what I was doing. Why wouldn't I want to sell before the price dropped even more?"

"Because you're not just any stockholder, you're the CEO of the company and have access to information that people on the street don't, like the pending lawsuits for example."

"You think that's what he wants to see me about?"

"Yes, more than likely it is. Is there anything else you should be telling me before we ask him in?"

"No, nothing I can think of."

"OK. Have your assistant bring him in."

Deb opened her office door and told her assistant to go to the reception area to get the SEC person and show him in. Then she and Barbara each took a seat around the large coffee table to wait for him. Less than a minute later there was a knock on the door and the assistant opened it without waiting for an invitation. She walked in, and following directly behind her was a fairly short man, about 5'7", dressed in a dark business suit, looking very somber. Deb and Barbara stood as he approached.

"Good morning" he said as he extended his hand to Deb. "My name is Eric Peterson, and I'm with the Division of Enforcement of the Securities and Exchange Commission." He shook Deb's hand and then turned to Barbara, who in turn extended her hand to take his.

"I'm Deb Cutter, and this is our Chief Counsel, Barbara Cullen" Deb said as she motioned toward Barbara. "Please have a seat, Mr. Peterson, and tell us how we can help you this morning."

"Thank you" he said as he took a seat next to Deb. "The reason I'm here today is to ask you, Ms. Cutter, a few questions about some recent stock trades you executed."

Deb and Barbara exchanged glances, and Barbara nodded slightly toward Deb, as if to say, here it comes.

"Please continue" said Deb.

"According to our research, on three separate occasions over the past few weeks, you sold a large number of New Commerce stock. In fact, if I'm not mistaken, the exact number is slightly more than a million shares. Does that figure sound right to you, Ms. Cutter?"

"Well, I can't really say for sure. I'd have to consult my broker."

"Can you say, at least, if it's in the ballpark?" he asked.

"It probably is" she responded. But I'm sure you already know the exact figure, don't you, Mr. Peterson?"

He ignored her question and pressed on. "Please tell me, Ms. Cutter, what prompted those sales?"

"I frequently buy and sell stock, including New Commerce's. I can't recall the reasoning behind each and every decision I make" she replied.

"Ah, but how often do you sell more than a million shares within a few weeks? I would think that the reason for selling that number of shares would stick out in your memory."

"Not particularly, Mr. Peterson. As CEO I am a very busy person, and make many very important decisions on a daily basis. And as I've said, I often buy and sell stock. My guess is that a decline in the market prompted me to dispose of some of my holdings."

"Do you recall what other stocks you sold recently, Ms. Cutter?"

"Not off the top of my head. I'd have to consult with my broker."

"Let me refresh your memory. During the period when you disposed of approximately a million shares of New Commerce stock, the number of shares of other companies that you sold was, let me see now" [. . .] he riffled through some of the papers in the folder he was holding. "Oh yes, here it is. The number of shares of other companies that you sold during the past few weeks was exactly zero." He looked directly at her to gauge her reaction.

Barbara's head slumped slightly at the news but she tried to hide her surprise. Things weren't looking good for Deb Cutter right now, and it was her own damn fault. Her huge ego and belief that she was exempt from the rules that mere mortals had to follow finally caught up with her. She deserved whatever she'd get, but Barbara hoped she wouldn't take New Commerce down with her.

"Does that help refresh your memory, Ms. Cutter?"

Barbara spoke up. "As Chief Counsel for New Commerce, I need to ask where you're going with this line of questioning, Mr. Peterson. Are you suggesting anything improper in Ms. Cutter's actions? If so, I will have to advise her not to answer any more of your questions at this time."

"I'm not implying anything, Ms. Cullen. All I'm doing is trying to get a better picture of the recent trades executed by Ms. Cutter. If I understand her response correctly, she sold the stock because of declining market conditions. Is that a fair statement, Ms. Cutter?"

"Yes, that's what I've said."

"And there was no other reason for selling those shares?" he asked.

"She's made her statement" interjected Barbara. "Is there anything else we can help you with today, Mr. Peterson? If not, I'm sure we all have a very busy schedule and would like to get on with our previously planned activities." It was a not too subtle jab at him for showing up without an appointment. But she knew that the SEC seldom bothered to make appointments, because they preferred to catch people off guard, with little or no time to prepare responses to their questions.

"I think that will be all for today" he answered, with special emphasis on the *today* part of his comment, as if to send a clear message that this wasn't the end of it. Barbara felt a slight chill go up her spine, knowing that SEC actions against the company or its CEO were the last thing they needed right now.

They all stood, and Barbara immediately motioned toward the door, almost taking him by the arm and leading him to it.

"Thank you for your time this morning, ladies" he said. "We'll be in touch if we need anything further."

It had felt like the longest fifteen minutes of her life, and Deb Cutter wasn't in the mood for a lecture, but one look at Barbara told her she was about to get one.

"What the hell were you thinking?" Barbara practically yelled out at her. "I know that you know better than to sell stock based upon information that hasn't yet been made public. The pending lawsuits could have a serious negative impact on our stock price, and you knew that, and that's why you dumped so many shares, isn't it? Do you think the people at the SEC are stupid? Don't you think they already know exactly why you sold those shares?"

"Enough" said Deb. "I don't need you to lecture me. I did what I thought was best for me, and it's done. There's nothing I can do about it now, so lighten up."

"That's what it's always about, isn't it? You always do what you think is right for you, regardless of who it hurts. Well let me tell you something, Deb, this time you really screwed up. You don't seem to understand the seriousness of what you've done. In case you haven't yet figured it out, it is very possible that you will end up in prison."

At the sound of those words, Deb's jaw dropped, and she lost a little color in her face.

"No" she said. "You're just trying to make a point here, aren't you? No one's going to send me to jail for selling some of my stock."

"You don't really believe that, do you?" asked Barbara.

Deb looked frightened when she replied. "So what should I do?"

As she glanced at her watch, Barbara said "I'm already late for a meeting with Jake Hammond to discuss a number of pending legal issues. But I'll set up a follow up meeting through your assistant for later in the week. In the meantime you might want to give some thought to retaining your own personal legal counsel. As Chief Counsel of New Commerce my primary responsibility is to the company and its stockholders. If, at any time, it appears that there may be a conflict between your best interests and those of the company, I will no longer be able to represent you. As such, it might be beneficial for you to have your own representation right from the start." With that said, Barbara left to go to her next meeting, and Deb went back to the reports she'd been reviewing before the interruption. But she could longer concentrate, so she decided to go out for an early lunch today.

***

On the tenth floor, while waiting for Barbara to show up, Jake Hammond was reviewing the first of many audit reports that would require his attention today. Since returning from Georgia it'd been a constant game of catch up for him, and he'd put in even more hours than before the insurance fiasco came to light, with fewer and fewer of those hours spent at home. Even though he'd often worked from home so he could at least see the kids before their bedtime, there'd been a lot of friction between Amie and him lately, and it just seemed easier to stay in the office to do work. It was going to be another long day today, and even though it was barely noon, he already knew that he wouldn't be leaving before ten or eleven tonight.

Barbara knocked on his door and let herself in. "Sorry I'm late, Jake, but something came up that I needed to attend to right away. Hope I didn't screw up the rest of your day."

"Don't worry about it, Barbara. I was able to find something to keep me busy while I waited for you" he said with a smile.

"Great. Let's get right down to it. We have two general types of legal actions we need to prepare for. The first will be the criminal prosecution of Kathy Brown, and the second will be the lawsuits against New Commerce being brought by customers who've lost income because of the missing insurance policies. I expect that you'll be asked to testify in all of these cases, so we need to start preparing you for that right away."

"Lucky me" Jake said with a smile. "I just can't wait."

She ignored his attempt at humor and plowed ahead.

"Let's begin with the criminal prosecution of Kathy Brown. It's my understanding that the district attorney has charged her with murder and embezzlement. Unless I'm missing something, I don't think there's much that you'll be able to add to the evidence the police have on the murder charge. Do you agree?"

"Basically, I think you're correct. However, in speaking with Tim Nagle, the detective involved in the case, it appears that they're expecting to have one trial for both charges, and our evidence will probably be instrumental in convincing the jury of her guilt on the murder charge, as it will show motive for running down Ron Hayward. So, I don't know how we can really separate the issues."

"Good point. So I guess we'll need to ensure that you're ready to respond to questions related to both charges."

"If I may offer a suggestion" Jake said, "I think I understand why you're differentiating between the two types of legal actions. Clearly, they're totally different in nature, and I'm sure the legal strategy will differ as well. But, from my perspective, the testimony I'm likely to have to give in each case should be basically the same. I can only testify as to the systems of control that exist here at New Commerce, and the actions my staff and I took in investigating the insurance issue. So, in my mind, my preparation for either of the two types of cases is probably the same; that is, I need to be ready to present the facts, supported by clearly documented evidence. Do you agree?"

"I guess you're right, Jake. Sounds like you've had some experience in these matters."

"I've testified in a few cases in the past, and if there's one thing I've learned, it's that there's never too much supporting evidence, which is why I'm so insistent that all our audit work and results are clearly documented. I can tell you first hand that it's almost impossible for anyone, including me, to remember all the facts and details of an audit a year or more after the review. Unless the work papers can stand on their own and help everyone who might read them understand what was done and why, they're basically useless."

"I see you don't need any coaching from me at this point. So, if you agree, this is how I think we should proceed. You put the finishing touches on your work papers, and organize all supporting documentation. I'll put together a list of questions you're likely to be asked, as well as the evidence you're likely to need, in each of the cases. Regarding the civil actions against New Commerce, it'll be important for us to show that we have an adequate system of controls in place, proving that we were not negligent in the administration of our policies and procedures. When each of us has completed our tasks, we can get together again to make sure we've got all our bases covered."

"That sounds like a reasonable plan to me. How long do you think we have before these cases go to trial?"

"It's hard to say for sure. The criminal case against Kathy is likely to proceed more quickly and a trial could begin in a matter of months, or maybe even sooner. The civil cases against New Commerce could take a lot longer, especially if they turn into a class action lawsuit."

"Well, I can assure you that I'll be ready, even if I need to find extra hours in a day to get it done."

Chapter 38

Monday, January 5, 2009

Deb Cutter had made it through the holidays, but she hadn't felt joyful. The SEC had been pursuing her relentlessly since mid-September and she was worn out. Why the hell couldn't they just leave her alone? She hadn't done anything more than what hundreds of other executives had done for decades, and most of them had never heard from the SEC. Why the hell where they persecuting her?

Even though it was early afternoon, she was still in her nightgown and slippers. Ever since the Board had relieved her of her duties she'd had no energy to do anything. The days were long and the nights even longer. She didn't socialize with anyone and seldom took phone calls, because in recent months most had been from reporters and others interested in digging up dirt. What few friends she'd once had, kept their distance, probably for fear of being dragged into the insider trading mess. She couldn't have imagined, just a few short months ago, how miserable life could be. It hadn't taken long to fall from the top of the world, with money, perks, power and friends, to the bottom of the heap with no more perks, no one to talk to and the threat of legal action hanging over her head.

She'd been given a hefty severance package when she was let go, but the life-style to which she'd grown accustomed required much more than that. Hell, just the monthly mortgage payment on this ten-room Tudor home was more than some people made in a year. And now that she no longer had the use of the limo and chauffer, she had to pick up the cost of a car and driver on her own. It was either that, or buy a car and drive it herself, which she certainly wasn't yet desperate enough to do. There was a limit, after all, to how low she'd sink.

She wandered aimlessly from room to room for a while and finally decided to go for a swim, thinking maybe that'd help cheer her up. She headed for the pool house, which was behind the main residence, and attached to it by an enclosed walkway. It was one of the features that had first attracted her to the property. She loved the fact that hers was the only house in the area with an indoor pool and she used it year round, even though she wasn't far from the ocean. She preferred the privacy and convenience the pool offered over the beaches that were crowded with common folks. She'd worked hard all her life and she deserved better than that.

Within minutes she was in the pool, and the water was perfect, as usual. She made sure the temperature was kept at exactly seventy degrees, which to some might seem warm, but to her was just right. She did a few laps and could feel herself relaxing. A short stint in the hot tub would certainly help finish off the therapy, she thought, and was about to head in that direction when the housekeeper interrupted her.

"I'm sorry to bother you, ma'am. But Mr. Jacobsen is here to see you."

Jacobsen, the other half of the law firm of Jacobsen and Peters, had agreed to represent Deb in the pending suit against her for insider trading and perjury. His partner, Jack Peters was representing New Commerce against the civil suits brought by Stallwood and Stallwood, but they felt there'd be no conflict if Dave represented Deb.

"I don't recall having an appointment with him" Deb said.

"He apologizes for coming without notice, but said it's very important that he see you" the housekeeper replied.

"Very well, have him wait in the study. I'll be there in a few minutes."

Deb got out of the pool and grabbed a towel from the rack near the steps to dry off with. She wasn't in a good mood, and had a feeling that things were only going to get worse when she heard what Dave had to say. He would never have stopped by without an appointment if it weren't important. This could only be bad news; probably that a trial date had been set. Fifteen minutes later she was in the study with Dave Jacobsen, who gave her the bad news she'd expected. Formal charges had been filed, and her trial was set to begin within a month. If convicted, she could face several years in prison, but he'd do his best to make sure that didn't happen. Nevertheless, she should start preparing for the worst, just in case.

***

She'd pleaded guilty to the embezzlement charge but not the murder charge, and while awaiting trial on that count, was enjoying the hospitality of the Georgia Department of Corrections. Each day was a challenge to survive, and the fact that she never had visitors, other than her own lawyer, didn't help matters. So when she was told she'd have an opportunity to give a deposition to some Florida lawyer who was suing New Commerce, she was glad to help out; she'd do anything to break up the boredom of prison life, and she certainly didn't mind screwing New Commerce over. There was no love lost between them. As long as there were no questions that could hurt her chances of getting off on the murder charges, which her lawyer would make certain of, it was no skin off her nose.

When she was brought into the small room by the prison guard, three people were already there waiting for her. Tom Stallwood and his locally hired stenographer had just arrived, and Kathy's attorney, Christopher Dodd had gotten there about fifteen minutes ago. Dodd was the only one to stand when she entered the room, and he immediately pointed to a chair and asked her to be seated. He introduced Tom Stallwood and the stenographer, and then turned it over to Tom.

"Ms. Brown" he began. "As you know, I'm here today representing a client in a civil action against New Commerce Commercial Finance. You will be sworn in by the court stenographer, and your statements will be made under oath, and recorded. Any false statements you make could result in a perjury charge against you, just as it would in a court of law. Do you understand this, and are you ready to proceed?"

"Yes" she replied.

The stenographer administered the oath, and the deposition began. Tom Stallwood had read the transcripts from Kathy Brown's trial, and he felt her testimony would go a long way in showing that New Commerce had, indeed, been negligent. He was especially interested in showing how, in spite of the additions to staff that took place in various areas of the company over the past few years to ensure increased origination volumes, no additions were made to the Operations staff responsible for processing the higher volume of transactions. That, he believed, was a direct factor in Kathy's ability to perpetrate the insurance fraud and embezzlement which led to his clients' losses.

Over the next three hours he asked and received answers to dozens of questions dealing with New Commerce's operations. He established what the normal work day for the Operations staff had been before Deb Cutter's entry into the new product lines, and then examined how the work day had changed after that period. It was clear from Kathy Brown's statements that everyone in Operations had been working a significant number of extra hours every day since the new product lines were introduced, and the number of processing errors had increased dramatically. She also testified that it would have been more difficult, if not impossible, for her to perpetrate the insurance fraud under conditions which existed prior to the addition of the new product lines. This was just too good to be true, and Tom knew he had to pursue this further.

"Ms. Brown, just to be certain that I understand what you've said, I'd like to ask a few follow up questions to clarify your last statement. Did I understand you to say that the staffing shortage in the Operations area of the Marietta Division of the New Commerce Commercial Finance Company had a direct impact on your ability to perpetrate your insurance fraud?"

"Yes, that's correct."

"Could you please elaborate for me, so that I may better understand exactly what you mean?"

"Certainly. Prior to the addition of the new product lines about three or four years ago, there was, in my opinion, adequate staffing in our Operations area to handle all transaction processing accurately and timely. Error rates were extremely low, and employees were seldom required to put in extra hours. Like everyone else at the division, we worked a normal thirty eight hour work week and things ran smoothly. Then, as volumes began to increase due to the new product offerings, it became more and more difficult to keep up. Our work days started to get longer and longer, and error rates skyrocketed. Eventually, people were so stressed that things really started to fall apart."

She paused to take a drink of water from the glass that had been placed before her.

"Before the increase in transaction volumes, we followed very strict procedures that required all transactions to be properly authorized and documented. We always had adequate segregation of duties, and no one individual could process a transaction from start to finish. There were always multiple people involved in every aspect of the processing cycle."

"Does that mean, Ms. Brown, that policies and procedures were changed when the new product lines were introduced?" Tom asked.

"No, the formal policies and procedures were not changed, but we simply didn't follow them as closely as before. We just couldn't, because there wasn't enough time."

"I see. But if the existing policies and procedures weren't being followed, why was it that no one put a stop to the violations?"

"Who was going to put a stop to it?" she asked rhetorically. "Everyone was trying to keep their heads above water and no one had the time to double check what anyone else was doing. Underwriters were busy booking new business; account managers were busy trying to manage the dealer inventory reviews and other record keeping things; and the legal folks were snowed under with UCC filings and other legal documentation issues. In Operations, we had to cut corners just to survive."

"Did you, or anyone else in Operations, ever discuss this situation with company management or ask for additional staff?"

"Yes. I discussed the situation with our division manager, Jeff Anderson, who said he discussed it with members of executive management at headquarters."

"And, to the best of your knowledge, what was the response Mr. Anderson received from headquarters?"

"He told me they said they couldn't consider more additions to staff, and that we'd have to make do with what we had."

"And do you know if he made the request just that one time?"

"In fact, he told me that on at least two other occasions he'd made the same request and received the same response."

Tom was getting pretty encouraged by what he was hearing. True, as a convicted felon, Kathy Brown might have a bit of a credibility problem in the eyes of a jury. Nevertheless, her comments would be damaging. And maybe, just maybe, he'd be able to corroborate them by speaking with other New Commerce employees. Things were really starting to look up for his clients. He'd be taking a lot more depositions from New Commerce employees in Georgia.

***

Mr. Hitachi was having some difficulty settling into his new office on the fifteenth floor of the Great Waters Insurance building. He wasn't accustomed to such opulence, and didn't particularly like the expensive oak and leather furniture that now surrounded him. In Japan, executives worked in much more modest environments, and in some cases, even the CEO's didn't have private offices. Here, everyone from a junior manager on up had a private office, and most were furnished expensively. No wonder the company was struggling. It was clear that things would have to change drastically, and soon.

There was a knock on the door before it opened ever so slightly, and his assistant poked her head in to announce his next appointment had arrived. "Please show him in," Hitachi said and stood to greet his visitor. "Mr. Goff" he said, "It's so nice to see you again. Please, won't you come in and have a seat?"

The visitor looked nervous as he followed Hitachi to the sitting area, and when he sat in the large, richly upholstered leather chair to which he'd been directed, he almost disappeared. A man of 5'5" who weighed barely 125 pounds was clearly not who this furniture had been designed for. Even Hitachi, at a heftier 160 pounds seemed lost in his own chair, probably another reason he so disliked the furniture in this office.

"May I offer you some refreshments?" asked Hitachi.

"No thank you, Mr. Hitachi. I'm OK."

"Very well, then. You may be wondering why I asked you here today."

"Yes, in fact I am. It isn't often that the Claims Director is asked to meet with the CEO. Frankly, it's a little intimidating."

"Please do not worry, Mr. Goff. I assure you, you are not in any kind of trouble. In fact it is quite the opposite. I asked you here because I am very impressed with how you have been managing your department."

"Thank you for saying so, Mr. Hitachi. I really appreciate that. I always try to do my best."

"Yes indeed. You, Mr. Goff, are exactly the type of manager that Ping Industries needs more of. Someone truly concerned with the financial welfare of the company. Someone who is a visionary, and can do what is best for the future, not just the present. Your cost cutting efforts in the claims adjusting area have not gone unnoticed. Thanks, in great part to you, our losses during this hurricane season were lower than they could have been. So I am going to offer you a better opportunity to help Great Waters Insurance Group continue on the road to recovery. In addition to continuing with your current responsibilities for overseeing all claims processing and adjusting activities, I would like you to set up a new department that will be responsible for improving operating efficiencies and cost cutting activities company-wide. With your additional responsibilities, you will receive additional recognition and compensation. You will be, if you decide to accept my offer, the new Vice President of Operations."

For the first time ever, Al Goff was speechless. This diminutive man with a loud voice and typically foul tongue who was known for abusing his subordinates was now the newest member of the executive team. Who could have imagined it? Certainly, it would never have been possible before Ping Industries, or BP as some liked to say.

"I don't know what to say, Mr. Hitachi, except thank you for your confidence and trust in me. I will certainly do my best to make sure you're not disappointed."

"I know you will, Mr. Goff. I'm counting on it."

The news of Al Goff's promotion spread like wild fire and, for the most part, was not well received. Those who didn't know him well couldn't quite figure out what qualified him for the new position, while those who *did* know him, were certain he *wasn't* qualified. And they all wondered what the future held in store for them, but none more so than those on the fifth floor, including Jane Donahue and Peter Wild, the claims managers.

Chapter 39

Thursday, January 8, 2009

In Tallahassee, Tom and Becky Stallwood were devoting most of their time on their new cases, having cleared their plates of most of their other clients. Becky was continuing to work on the class action lawsuit against Great Waters Insurance Group, and its parent company, Ping Industries, and things were beginning to look up now that she had more than two dozen clients lined up. Tom was still working on the suit against New Commerce, and was meeting with Joyce Walters and Randy Jones in preparation for Monday's depositions.

"As you know, Mrs. Walters, Monday's deposition may be just the first of several that New Commerce may request from you. Unfortunately, we need to make every reasonable effort to accommodate them, just as they've done for us. I know it can be a little nerve racking, but you'll be just fine. I'll be there with you if you need me, and once we've finished our prep work, you'll know exactly what to expect."

"I just want to get it over with and go on with my life. If only they'd been more reasonable with their settlement offer we could've avoided all of this."

"That's true, but they may still see the light before we go to trial. I can't imagine they actually believe they can win this case. The evidence points clearly to their negligence. I'm betting that they'll reconsider as the trial date approaches."

"I hope you're right, Mr. Stallwood" added Randy.

"Alright, now let's get started." Tom spent the next several hours grilling both Joyce Walters and Randy Jones with questions they should expect to be asked by Jack Peters. They also discussed the issue of lost income, a topic likely to be brought up during the depositions. They'd spent weeks putting together the financial information which they believed accurately depicted the amount of lost income to date, as well as the amount of potential loss they were likely to suffer in the future, based upon historical results prior to the storm, and projecting forward over the next decade. They wouldn't volunteer the information unless they were specifically asked about it, but needed to have it ready, just in case.

By five o'clock they decided to call it a day, and Tom walked them to the elevator and they agreed to meet again in the morning to finish up. He barely had time to get back to his office when Becky knocked on his door. She walked in before he had a chance to invite her in, something she rarely, if ever, did. Something big must've gotten her pretty excited, Tom thought to himself.

"You won't believe what I just stumbled across" she said. And before he could reply, she continued. "I've found an employee of Great Waters Insurance Group who's willing to testify, under oath, that it's been their practice, and in fact, a mandate to employees, to initially deny *all* claims outright. Their VP of Operations, to whom the claims adjusters report, believes that most customers will not hire an attorney to represent them but will, instead, simply go away quietly. If any *do* get an attorney involved, then the claim is re-examined and, if necessary, paid. Otherwise, no payment is ever made."

"Talk about a smoking gun" Tom said. "How did you find this guy or gal?"

"It's a guy. He's a claims adjuster, and his name is Harry Strong. Apparently he's been talking to some of the customers, and apologizing for the denied claims. One of them gave me his name, and I contacted him directly. He said that his boss, who's now the VP of Operations but was then the Claims Director, gave him specific instructions to deny all claims. His first such directive was made in mid-August, as claims began to come in during tropical storm Fay, and another was made on September 2nd, when he told Mr. Strong that if he couldn't follow instructions to deny all claims, he'd be replaced with someone who would."

"That's incredible" said Tom. "Based upon that testimony, you shouldn't have any difficulty getting access to their records. Is this guy still employed there?"

"Yes, he is. And he's concerned that, because he's been following instructions and denying all claims, he might, somehow be held liable. That's why he decided to come forward right now, before he gets a subpoena."

"You know that you need to get his deposition ASAP, right?"

"Of course. I'm flying out to Milwaukee in the morning."

Chapter 40

Monday, January 12, 2009

The call came in at 1:35 p.m. "911, what is your emergency?" the operator asked.

"I need an ambulance. Please send someone right away, I think she's dead."

"What is your name?"

"Please, send someone."

"Ma'am, I have the rescue and police on the way. Please try to stay calm. Tell me who this is, and what has happened."

"I'm the housekeeper. I just found Ms. Cutter on the floor, and I don't think she's breathing."

"Tell me what you see. Is she bleeding?"

"No, I don't think so."

"Have you checked her pulse or other vital signs?"

"No, I don't know how to do that."

"OK. Please stay calm. The rescue is on the way. They'll be there in about three minutes. Please stay on the line with me until they get there."

After a short pause, Mrs. Martinez was back on the line. "I can hear the sirens now. I think it's them."

"OK. Don't hang up the phone yet. Let them in, and then come back to let me know they've arrived."

"OK."

There was nothing the paramedics could do except wait for the medical examiner. Deb Cutter was already dead when they got there. A few minutes later, some uniformed police officers arrived, followed immediately by the medical examiner. Detectives had been called, and they were on their way. Everyone had heard about Deb Cutter recently, and whenever a high profile person was involved in an incident, there had to be a thorough investigation. Although they hadn't seen any evidence of a struggle and there was no reason to believe foul play, there also was no suicide note in sight, so they weren't going to take any chances. As they waited for the detectives, the officers on the scene began to speak with the housekeeper.

In her statement to them, Mrs. Martinez drew a pretty clear picture of how depressed Ms. Cutter had been recently. She often would just lie around the house in her nightgown until late afternoon, she told the officers, and often, even later than that. Sometimes she didn't get dressed or leave the house for days on end. She'd been drinking heavily lately, even more than normal, and Mrs. Martinez had been concerned. But she was only the housekeeper, and it wasn't her place to say anything. Surely, she'd have been fired if she had.

When the detectives arrived, they did their preliminary sweep of the area, and found nothing unusual. No furniture was misplaced or broken, nothing seemed to have been moved, and there was no blood. But even though there wasn't any obvious indication of a crime, they secured the area until the crime scene unit could get there.

Chapter 41

Wednesday, February 4, 2009

It'd taken Jake longer than normal to make it to the office this morning because of the snow, which had already accumulated to three inches. That wasn't all that much for Maine, especially in February, but his beloved roadster, for all of its wonderful features, really wasn't very good in the snow. He finally arrived at about 8:15 a.m., with a few minutes to spare before the Executive Committee meeting began.

At 8:30 sharp those in the Augusta headquarters convened in Tom D'Angelo's office on the twenty-fifth floor, and his secretary set up the video conference with the remaining Committee members who were in the field. Today's meeting had only one topic on the agenda. New Commerce was in serious financial trouble and needed to consider alternatives, like finding a buyout partner.

"The question is" said Tom, "where do we go from here? In my opinion, we need to move quickly to find a partner, and I have something in mind. I suggest we hire a firm that specializes in mergers and acquisitions to find a new partner for us." There were some murmurs from around the table and finally, someone on the video conference asked the question everyone seemed to have in mind.

"How do we go about doing something like that? I've never been involved with an M&A firm, and wouldn't even know how to start. How can we be sure we'd get the right company?"

Everyone turned to Tom and waited for a response.

"I've made some calls, and my contacts tell me that the best firm for us is one that's recently arranged some of the biggest and most notable mergers in history, the Grisswell Investment Group, located in the D.C. area. I'm told that, besides having arranged some pretty spectacular mergers, they're also known for their contacts on Capitol Hill and their extensive lobbying activities. They also have contacts in corporate boardrooms throughout the country. If anyone can find a buyer for us, surely they can, that is, if they'd be willing to work with a company as small as New Commerce."

"What about the cost?" someone asked.

"My understanding is that we can negotiate an arrangement. Under the right conditions, we might be able to have their costs covered by the buyer, or included in the overall buyout agreement. That's something we can discuss with them if they agree to meet with us. Remember, they're a big player in the business, and I'm not at all sure they'd be interested in helping us out. I think it really all depends on what they have in the pipeline; in other words, if they already have one or more clients who might be interested. I doubt if they'd spend a whole lot of time on us otherwise."

There was some animated discussion, and after a half hour or so, it was unanimously agreed that Tom should make the initial contact with Grisswell to see if there was any interest. The meeting broke a little after nine o'clock, and Tom immediately placed a call to Ken Grisswell, managing partner of Grisswell Investments.

When Jake got back to his office on the tenth floor there was a phone message waiting for him from Detective Nagle, in Marietta. *Now what? I might as well find out sooner, rather than later.* He picked up the phone and dialed Tim's number.

"Tim Nagle" the voice at the other end answered.

"Tim. It's Jake Hammond. How are you doing?"

"Hi Jake, thanks for returning my call so quickly."

"Well, to be honest, your call kind of got me curious. Tell me what's going on now?"

"It looks like we aren't finished with Kathy Brown just yet. We've just heard that her attorney is filing a motion to suppress some of the evidence in the murder case."

"I was expecting it, Tim. I knew it was just a matter of time. She gave a deposition to Tom Stallwood in his suit against New Commerce, and her attorney made it clear that she wouldn't say anything that'd hurt her chances of successfully fighting the murder charge."

"Well, I'm sorry to tell you this, Jake, but it's likely you'll have to testify again."

"Don't worry about it, Tim. I really don't mind. Besides, I like Atlanta. I'm even considering relocating there. You guys really made an impression on me" Jake said, smiling to himself.

"Are you kidding me?"

"Not at all, Tim. Things are not going well for New Commerce, and if we end up being acquired, there's a good chance most of us on the Executive Committee may be asked to move on. We're all anticipating it, and keeping our options open."

"You remember what I told you, Jake. There's a lot of demand down here for someone with your experience. I've got contacts, and I'm sure you'd be able to set yourself up in business, offering consulting services to the local and even the state law enforcement agencies. And beyond that, there's a huge need for security consultants in this area."

"I know, Tim. I've been looking into it, and it's very interesting."

"Well, just remember what I said. Give me a call anytime, and I can start putting you in contact with some folks. And if you do it soon enough, you may be down here already when Kathy goes to trial. That'll save you some travel."

"I'll keep that in mind, Tim. And thanks again for the offer of help with the contacts. I'll probably take you up on that."

"OK. I'll talk to you soon, then."

"Bye."

Chapter 42

Monday, April 20, 2009

It was only nine o'clock, but it was already obvious it was going to be a spectacular day, probably the best since late fall. Forecasters had said it might reach the mid sixties, or even higher, a rare thing for mid-April in Maine. Jake was looking out onto the courtyard below his tenth-floor office window, thinking about all that had transpired over the past few months. February and March had been challenging, with the Walters Marine trial against New Commerce taking up several weeks, and the due diligence review by the team from Worldwide Banking Group taking the better part of a month. But in spite of it all, he'd managed to spend more time at home than he'd done in years. Amie and the kids loved the fact that he no longer brought work home every night and most weekends. Things were winding down at the office, and the takeover was imminent.

Grisswell had done his job well. With his contacts on Capitol Hill, he'd managed to arrange for Worldwide to get a decent chunk of the $700 billion in bailout money, and then arranged to have them use some of that money to make some key acquisitions, including the New Commerce one. Even though that wasn't how the bailout money was *supposed* to be used, when you have contacts on the *Hill*, you can get away with a great deal. And so it was with the bailout money. The whole process had moved quickly, and the deal was scheduled to close later this month.

Things hadn't gone well at trial for Joyce Walters, and Tom Stallwood was concerned they might lose after all, so she finally agreed to a settlement before the case went to the jury. Ten million dollars was nothing to sneeze at, and it'd keep her and her kids living in relative comfort for some time, if it was invested wisely. The Burke lawsuit was still in progress, but Worldwide would be taking over responsibility for that one once the acquisition was finalized. Jake would probably still need to testify if it went to trial, but Worldwide was confident they'd be able to settle this case now that New Commerce had settled the Walters case.

Jake had been asked by Worldwide to stay on, as had Fred Campbell and Tom D'Angelo, but only Tom had made a decision to stay. Fred was taking an early retirement package, and Jake was still considering relocating to the Atlanta area, but hadn't made a final decision. Amie and the kids were very excited about the prospect, and for the first time in many years everything was alright on the home front. All in all, life was good.

He'd heard, though, that things weren't going so well at Great Waters. The class action lawsuit was in the discovery phase, and it was looking like Becky Stallwood had ample evidence of wrongful denial of claims. Several current and past employees had already stated in their depositions that Al Goff, with the knowledge and blessing of Mr. Hitachi, had required them to initially deny all claims, regardless of their merit. And based upon the number of people who'd joined the suit, any judgment against Great Waters Insurance could be in the ball park of a hundred million dollars, or maybe even more. Again, Ping Industries was not happy with what was going on in their US subsidiary. In their opinion, Americans just didn't seem to understand how business should be conducted.

It'd been a snowier winter than normal, so Jake decided to take advantage of the sun and take a few hours off, something he'd never done before, at least not in recent memory. The kids were in school, but Amie was home, so he decided to give her a call. He dialed his home number, and she picked up on the second ring.

"Amie. It's Jake. What are you doing this morning?" Before she could answer, he continued. "How'd you like to take a ride to the ocean? It's a nice sunny day, and we could walk along the beach. It won't be crowed this early in the season. What do you say?"

"Jake, is that really you?" is all she could bring herself to say. Taking time off on a Monday morning, without having planned it for weeks in advance, certainly didn't sound like something Jake would do; at least not the Jake she knew.

"Of course it's me. I can pick you up in a half hour. We'll ride with the top down and enjoy the sun and wind, and after we walk on the beach, we'll have lunch at one of our favorite restaurants, and then we can head back in time to be home when the kids get there."

"It's fine with me, but what about the office? Don't you have a lot of things to do today?"

"The staff can handle anything that comes up. I'm going to head out now. It'll only take me a few minutes to change when I get there, and then we can be off."

An hour later they were on Maine's route 17 going east toward Rockport, their favorite seaside town. Although it was only a thirty-nine mile drive, it'd take about an hour, but it would give them an opportunity to relax and enjoy the wind and sun. It'd been a very long time since they'd done that, and they were both looking forward to the peace and quiet of the beach and the ocean. They arrived a little after eleven o'clock, which was perfect. They'd have time to take a leisurely walk on the beach before enjoying lunch at Andre's Oceanside Café.

They parked the roadster and got out, and then Jake clicked his smart key remote to raise the top and lock the doors. He'd changed into light khakis, and a short sleeve shirt and Amie had on a pair of jeans and a tank top. They both brought light sweaters, just in case, but now realized they probably wouldn't need them. They tied the sweaters around their waists, took off their deck shoes, which they wore without socks, and headed for the beach.

"Why haven't we done this more often?" she asked.

"I'm sorry we haven't. I kind of lost track of what's important in life, I guess. I know you tried to tell me, but I just couldn't see it. It took the current economic crisis and the problems at New Commerce to help me realize that sometimes things just aren't worth the sacrifice."

"So, what happens now?" Amie asked, as they strolled on the beach, the tide gently caressing their feet.

"I think it's time for a change. You know I've been thinking about the offer from Worldwide to stay on after the takeover, but I don't think my work requirements will ever change, if I do stay. What I, [. . .] what *we* really need is something different, I think; a new start."

"So, you're serious about Atlanta?"

"Yes, very serious. Tim Nagle's put me in touch with some people in the area. I think there's a real need for computer security professionals down there, and there aren't enough of them to go around. I've talked with some people at a couple of the big corporations headquartered in Atlanta, and they've indicated a willingness to hire me as a consultant. Of course, there are no guarantees when you're in business for yourself, but I think there's enough corporate work for me to be able to make a go of it, and I'm also pretty sure I could get some work consulting for various law enforcement agencies, because Tim has already laid the groundwork for me there.   And we have enough of a nest egg to keep us going for a while, if the income isn't what I expect, at first. What do you think?"

"I know you, Jake. You always do your homework before you mention anything to me, so I'm confident that you can make this work, financially. But the important question here is this. What will you have to do to make this work? In other words, will this allow you to spend more time with me and the kids? That's really the issue. If you're not going to be able to spend more time with us, then you might as well stay put at New Commerce. But that's not what I want. What I really want is for you to spend more time with your family, regardless of what your income is. You know we can live on less."

"I know.   And even though starting my own consulting practice may require a lot of time, I think I can make sure it doesn't totally consume me. Let's put it this way, I *will* make sure it doesn't totally consume me."

She looked up at him with a huge smile on her face, wrapped her arms around his neck, and gave him a hug. It's what she'd been waiting to hear for several years, and almost couldn't believe her ears. "I love you" she said.

"I love you too" he replied.

They walked hand in hand like school kids, and headed toward Andre's for what Jake was sure would be the best lunch he'd had in years. He was happier than he could ever remember being.

Epilogue

Sandy Springs, GA – December, 2009

Relocated New Englanders almost always find the late fall and early winter weather of the Atlanta area to be a pleasant change from what they're accustomed to. And so it was with Jake. It was the first time in memory he was actually enjoying December weather, although he wasn't all that certain he'd like a Christmas without snow or really cold temperatures. But Amie and the kids loved everything about their new lives and didn't miss the cold weather a bit.

He leaned back in his swivel chair and looked out the window onto the large yard below, admiring the lawn that was still amazingly green. For the time being he was operating his consulting business out of his home office, using one of the five bedrooms for that purpose. He loved the view, and most of all he loved the fact that he was so close to the family whenever he wasn't at a client's location. But he felt he'd soon have to move into something more elaborate, and probably even take on some help, because things were going better than he could ever have imagined even in his wildest dreams. His computer security skills, investigative talent, and disciplined approach, all learned during his years as an internal auditor, were proving to be in great demand. Computer hacking, identity theft and other high tech crimes were on the rise.

But even though he had more consulting opportunities than he could handle right now, he was keeping the promise he'd made to Amie, seldom working more than fifty hours a week. To some of his new acquaintances in the South, that still seemed like a lot of hours, but to the Hammond family, it was just fine. He never worked after dinner, and seldom, if ever, worked on the weekends. The kids couldn't remember when they'd spent so much time with him. Now the challenge would be to make sure he didn't fall back into his old routine as a workaholic. He thought maybe it was time to seriously consider the new opportunity he'd just been given.

Jake had been approached recently by a private investigator who had heard of his fast growing reputation and was interested in discussing the possibility of a partnership. Normally Jake would never have given it a second thought, but some of his contacts in law enforcement told him Aaron Stillwater was on the up-and-up, and didn't let himself get dragged into the gutter by taking on messy divorce cases or disreputable clients. Most of his cases involved unsolved murders, disappearances, and other similar matters that police hadn't been able to resolve, and his clients were generally financially well to do. Now Jake was thinking that together they could build a practice that was even more lucrative, and take on additional resources, which in turn would allow him to spend even more time with his family.

As he contemplated the possibility of a partnership he realized things were looking better and better each day. The concerns he'd had about finances were proving to be baseless, and he didn't regret his decision to set up his own practice, leaving the New Commerce problems behind. In fact, he was almost beginning to forget about New Commerce. He hadn't had to testify in the Burke case against them because Melvin Burke gladly accepted the five million dollar settlement Worldwide had offered him. It was less than the Walters settlement, but then again, no one in the Burke family had died. And Kathy Brown's trial was still a long way off, so it looked like Jake's days of testifying in court were over, at least for the time being. He had no delusions, however, about the future. The type of work he was doing for his corporate clients virtually assured him of more time in the courtroom, and of course, the same was true of his law enforcement clients. And then again, there was still the unsolved death of Deb Cutter.

Deb Cutter's death had, at first, appeared to be a suicide, but the case hadn't yet been closed because the detectives were trying to tie up some loose ends. The lack of a suicide note bothered them somewhat, but apparently not as much as the coroner's report. At least that's what Jake had heard. Although he didn't have specifics about the report, he'd been told there was something in it the police considered suspicious, and they were continuing their investigation. If it turned out that Deb's death was anything but a suicide, there was a better than average chance Jake and other senior officers of New Commerce would be questioned about anything they knew, and they could very well end up testifying in court, if a trial should ever materialize. That didn't really bother Jake all that much, but he sure was intrigued at the possibility that Deb's death was anything other a suicide. He knew that very few people liked her, but he hadn't really given much thought to the fact that someone might dislike her enough to kill her. It would be interesting to watch things unfold.

He was ready to get back to work when Amie knocked gently on the door and came in. The kids were in school and they were home alone, as usual. And although Amie often stopped by to chat when he was in his office, this time was different. The sparkle in her eye and the negligee she was wearing told him she had something other than chatting on her mind.

Made in the USA
Charleston, SC
26 April 2010